# DARKSTONE

Noikos Fields
The River Rule
The Irian Range
Mildaresh
Felian Pass
Karlese
The Broken Coast
Caravel
Senna
Cricklebek
Lake's End
Gifford's Well
Marchland
West Haven
Evenstill
Idira
Sild
The Elgrave
The Boot
Isle of Baktah
Ciris
Noktum
Earl
The Singing Isles
Auri

Terrastial
Calkinon
The Cranok
Forest of Ustaar
The Grove
Zondra
Calibrae
Skarfell
Ford of Elan
Elan River
Jerra-bal
The Enigmata
Pendle Ring
Merrywinds
The Kenting
Farndale
Wiseman's Crook
Ferridale
Bixdale
Gravelton
The River Tella
Grey Shard
Scrimpton
Mistlands
The Bruinin Forest
T'al Agria

# STONES OF THE AZURI

Book 1: *Taelstone*

Book 2: *Heartstone*

Book 3: *Darkstone*

# DARKSTONE

STONES OF THE AZURI

BOOK 3

ROBYN PROKOP

First published in 2025

© Robyn Prokop, 2025

Toutouwai Publications



A catalogue record for this book is available from the National Library of Australia.

ISBN (Print): 978-1-7641873-0-5
ISBN (Ebook): 978-1-7641873-1-2

Cover design by Noknok Studios.

❀ Formatted with Vellum

*In memory of Ross (Ruby) Reid, who would have made a fine pirate.*
*8 July 1959 – 13 May 2022*

# CONTENTS

# 1

## SONG ON THE WIND

There were voices on the wind. Rising in broken snatches, they plucked at Ash's mind like fingers. A melody lifted high above the rest, and the ethereal beauty of the woman's voice tugged at his heart. He staggered, putting out a hand, as if that might help him brace against its power. *Don't listen. Just don't listen.* Giving in to the Song was the way of madness.

Ash drew a deep breath, closed his mind to the tantalising melodies and dragged his attention back to the path. The three friends had been walking since daybreak, zig-zagging ever more steeply, following the mountain track up through beech forests, towards the Lewin Pass. The trees had black trunks here, adding to the foreboding gloom of the morning.

It was supposed to be spring. But that hadn't stopped it from snowing overnight. Ash had decided that spring snow was the worst kind of all. Neither fluffy nor pretty, this stuff was just wet. The slopes above them sagged beneath the unexpected weight of a fresh blanket.

More treacherous than the patches of snow were the water courses. They ran across the path in cloudy ribbons, like the trails of some enormous snail. The higher the friends climbed, the trickier these icy hazards became. Ash clutched at saplings and pulled up handfuls of ferns as he tried to negotiate another of the slippery obstacles. Just when he thought he'd made it past, he misjudged the moss-covered rocks. His boot slid beneath him, wrenching an ankle. Over-compensating, he stuck out a hand and crashed to his knees.

Ash let out a soft moan as he nursed his wrist. For a moment he stayed there in the mud. Then he brushed moss from his hands. The joint wasn't injured, just protesting the harsh treatment. The blister on the inside of his right heel was much worse. It nagged at him, a raw, biting pain. The young man gritted his teeth. None of that mattered. Kep was in trouble, and he had to push on. Mastering his wobbling legs and ignoring the tearing sensation in his lungs, he hauled himself back to his feet. Taking a deep breath, he set his jaw and carried on climbing.

Ash wasn't naïve. He hadn't expected the journey to be easy — his prior experience in the wilderness fleeing with Kep from slave-hunters had taught him better than that. He *was* worried he would slow his friends down, though. Sarin and Ordelle, his two companions, had trained as warriors over the past few months. And Sarin was Aurum — his clan was used to walking all day.

Ash had spent his winter sequestered in a tower in the ancient city of T'al Jazure, reading books and staring into lore-stones, trying to fathom the mysteries of the Song. Hardly ideal groundwork for an impromptu trek into danger. Ash was becoming uncomfortably aware that the cosy beds and plush carpets of T'al Jazure had made him soft. Now he was all too keenly remembering the aches and pains that came from sleeping rough, not to mention the agony of blisters. But the physical challenges of the journey were the least of Ash's concerns. His greatest worry was the Song.

The ancient city had a strange power that dulled the Song's effects. Now, two days into the trek, Ash was vulnerable again. He should have known. The Song was his burden. It didn't matter that it had passed to him almost by accident — Ash was the *taelstaun* now, Keeper of the Song. If only he knew what that really meant.

Even so, Ash hadn't expected to encounter problems here in the mountains. Cities and ancient sites troubled him most; places steeped in the memories of humankind. The wilderness had different rhythms, the soothing sounds of Nature. But this place disturbed him. He furrowed his brow as he walked. People had made their homes here once, he felt sure of it. Their music was all around, haunting the canopy. He made out the sharp ring of axes, intermingled with the joyful beat of drums.

When a single thread rose above the others, he smiled in recognition. It was a song of making. *One craft! The joy of the people!* His heart lifted, unable to resist the power of the Song. They were singing to the forest! Giving thanks for its sacrifice.

*Children move through the trees, dancing. Some hold feathery branches overhead, forming an archway. They wave to him, inviting him ...*

No!

As Ash pulled back from the ghostly vision, panic made him stumble and trip over his own feet. The sensation of something hot gushing inside his sock matched his rush of anxiety. The blister had burst. Every step was agony now, no matter how much he tried to adjust his gait. Ash moaned through clenched teeth as leather rubbed at his raw flesh. He trudged on, thinking the day couldn't get any worse. And then it began to snow.

Within seconds of the snow beginning to fall, a black form materialised, leaping onto Ash's shoulder, and letting out a disgusted grumble near his ear, as it wrapped a damp tail around his throat. Tarlyn hated snow even more than Ash did. Taking care not to knock the creature from her perch, he reached behind her and raised his hood. She let out a burr of appreciation and snuggled closer into his neck.

Ash was still astounded at Tarlyn's ability to shrink; it seemed to defy the laws of nature. Nevertheless, he appreciated her companionship. She could have stayed in T'al Jazure, safe and warm. She *should* have. And perhaps the same was true of himself.

Hearing a cry from behind, he glanced back. Ordelle had closed the distance between them. She cupped her hands around her mouth and shouted again. 'Sarin! Stop!'

Ash halted, letting Ordelle catch up. Wet pieces of her usually impeccable fringe plastered her forehead. Like him, she was gasping for breath. And yet, despite the exertion, she still had a deathly calm about her. The dim forest light made her skin look paler, her hooked nose more prominent. Regret struck him, and not for the first time. Why had they agreed to Ordelle coming? The Cryer's daughter was an unlikely choice of companion on any day, and the very *last* person you'd want on a rescue mission. Ordelle's pale blue eyes interrogated him for a moment, but she didn't speak. She jerked her head, indicating that they should join Sarin.

By now Sarin had reappeared, some twenty paces up the track. He frowned, sweeping his long black hair into a tighter bind at the back of his neck as he waited. As they drew closer, Ash realised he had never seen his friend so drawn. The shadows beneath Sarin's eyes were darker, accentuating his strange golden irises. Sarin was usually lithe and alert; today he actually looked tired.

Ash frowned as he tried to catch his breath, his concern for Sarin driving out his own problems for a moment. Sarin had arrived back in T'al Jazure only two days ago, from a long journey north to see his clan. On discovering that Kep was gone, he had insisted on setting out to find her. The old Sarin — the self-sufficient woodsman who had rescued Kep and Ash from the clutches of Rufen Karendon — would have scoffed at such reckless behaviour. Ash remembered his friend's warning, because at the time he'd found it embarrassing: lovers are unpredictable, he'd claimed, and that makes them dangerous acquaintances. Sarin's earlier sentiments seemed forgotten now, and Ash wasn't about to remind him.

His friend folded his arms, scowling. 'What's wrong? We can't stop. We need to be through the pass before nightfall. Or risk camping in the snow.'

Ordelle blinked in that owl-like way of hers. 'It is more efficient to halt. Ash has blisters. His pace will suffer if they remain undressed.' She frowned at Ash. 'You are favouring your right foot.' Ash winced, but the accusation was accurate. 'We are coming to the edge of the tree-line. This might be our last refuge from the wind. Even if we make the pass before nightfall, it's a three-day walk from there to Farndale. He needs to attend to his foot.'

Ash grimaced. He doubted he could manage for another day, let alone three. In Farndale they planned to catch a river-boat south — but they had to get there first.

Sarin's scowl deepened. 'Ash?'

Arguing with Ordelle's logic was pointless; she had the annoying habit of being right. 'It *is* slowing me down a bit.' An understatement. Now that they'd stopped, Ash's whole foot was throbbing.

As the snow turned to sleet, Sarin held up a hand. 'Fine! We'll take a brief rest. But not here. There's a likely place further up. It will give us some cover.'

Sarin's 'likely place' was a clump of smooth rocks, dominated by an enormous tree. The giant roots held the boulders in position, like jealous claws protecting a clutch of eggs. Hollowed out beneath the nest of rocks was a shallow cave, shaped like an ear.

Ash perched on a root at the back of the depression, shielded from the wind, and eased off his boot. When he peeled the sock away, a flap of skin came with it. Sarin tossed him a small pouch containing the healing candrel leaves he'd gathered the day before. His tone was gruff. 'Need help?'

Ash shook his head, determined to make as little fuss as possible. He took a single leaf out of the bag and stared at it, unsure how to proceed. Beside him, Ordelle gave an exasperated sniff. 'You need to chew it and then bind it to the raw patch.' Producing a strip of cloth from one of the many pockets on her large, square pack, she passed it over. 'Use this.'

'Thanks.'

Ash was retying his bootlaces when he sensed a shiver. He lifted his head, listening. The sensation had nothing to do with the cold. It began as an awareness, the barest whisper of contact. Something seemed ... different. The rhythm of this place had shifted. He couldn't decide if something had started, or if something had stopped. With a sharp intake of breath, he focused his attention.

Sarin had already shouldered his pack and was staring up at the track, impatient to be gone. Ash's sudden gasp made him turn, his eyes narrowing. 'What is it now?'

The premonition hit Ash in a jolt — as if somebody had dashed water in his face. His voice cracked as he yelled out: 'Take cover!'

A split second later, they all heard it.

It started with a muffled rumble, similar to firecrackers exploding in a bag. Then it grew into a clattering din. Sarin dived into the hollow, collecting Ordelle in a tackle. The world shook and lurched as Ash backed further into the little cave. As rocks showered down, he threw up his arms to shield his head. Through squinting eyes, all he saw was a tumbling mass of white. The noise was terrible: a monstrous, roar. It sounded as if the mountainside was coming down around them. Perhaps it lasted for a minute or two before dying away. It felt much longer.

At last, everything was still.

Ash eased his eyes open to stare at the sight before him. They were trapped! Closed in by a wall of snow and debris! An enormous section of broken tree blocked the entrance to the small hollow. Packed with snow and splintered branches, it had saved them from being buried alive.

'An avalanche,' announced Ordelle. 'The snowfall was too wet.' Ash nodded, unable to find words.

Beyond the wreckage, the wind continued howling. Sarin closed his eyes and slumped against the back of the cavity. His despair was obvious.

Ash gulped, staring at the barrier of white. Had they not delayed to attend to his blisters, the avalanche would have swept them away. He heard Kep's voice in his mind. *The gods are with you.* Ash bit his lip, frowning. *Had* it been the gods? Or was something else at play here? He made the sign of the triangle anyway, bowing his head and whispering a prayer. There was air and light enough to see. And they were alive.

After checking that her bag was intact, Ordelle folded herself into a cross-legged position. She arranged her hands in her lap, placing one on top of the other. Then she turned her head to Sarin. 'What do we do now?'

Sarin's jaw was tight. 'What would you *like* to do?' The young woman blinked, trying to work out the question. Sarin took a breath, composing himself. 'Sorry. Don't answer that, Ordelle. We rest. Wait out the storm and let the snowpack settle. Then we dig ourselves out.' He sighed. 'We're alive and we're out of the wind. That will have to do.' When he closed his eyes, even Ordelle knew to keep her silence.

So they rested, huddled together like small animals in a burrow. They ate a little food and sipped icy water from pouches replenished with snow. Ash poked about in the leaf mulch with a stick, disturbing bugs for Tarlyn to pounce on. Then he buried his nose inside his cloak. It was drier in the shelter, but not much warmer. Freezing air blew through the gaps. Ash told himself he should be happy there *was* air. It just made him think about suffocating.

Cracking noises began to come from overhead, announcing the strong possibility that the tree could give way. Ash closed his eyes, shutting out thoughts of being crushed by snow and earth. He deepened his breath, following the patterns he had learned at T'al Jazure.

*Slow inhale. Hold. Longer exhale. Repeat.* It did little to calm his nerves, but at least it channelled some warmth down inside his cloak. After a few minutes, Sarin's voice broke his concentration.

'Ash? How did you know? That something was wrong?'

Ash lifted his head. He could feel Ordelle's curiosity as well, although she was pretending to watch Tarlyn's efforts to catch a centipede. He hugged his knees closer to his chest. 'Just a feeling, I guess.'

'A feeling?'

Ash hesitated, unable to put it into words. He groped for an answer. 'I can't explain it. Something changed. It was ...' He frowned. 'It was ... You know when cicadas stop singing, and that's when you notice them?' Sarin looked uncertain, but he nodded. 'It was like that. A bit.'

Ordelle turned her head to stare at him. 'A cicada is an insect.'

'I know that.'

'Can you hear cicadas now?'

'No!' He scowled at her. 'I'm not hearing things, Ordelle.' *Apart from the Song.*

'Good. Because cicadas can't live up here. It's too cold.'

Ash blew out his cheeks, regretting speaking at all. 'I know! It was just a comparison.'

Sarin moved them into more dangerous territory. 'Is it the Song?' The concern in his voice was obvious. He'd seen first-hand what happened when Ash got lost in the Song's visions.

Ash shrugged, trying to look unconcerned. 'Maybe. But don't worry. I've learned to shut the music out now.' *Liar.*

'Good.' Sarin ran a tongue over his lips thoughtfully. Ash knew he wasn't fooling him — he wasn't even fooling himself.

Of *course* it was the Song. Since that dreadful day in Credé's hut, everything revolved around the Song. But things were even more complicated now. T'al Jazure had changed the whole situation again. As he read the expressions on his friends' faces, Ash renewed the promise he'd made to himself earlier: to keep his thoughts about the Song to himself. Sarin and Ordelle didn't need to worry that he was losing his mind. What was he supposed to say? That a city haunted him, too?

Because it hadn't just been a change in the rhythms of the Song. Ash had recognised a presence. It was the Heartstone, the curious sphere at the centre of the Knowledge Stores. From the moment he'd touched it, Ash had felt a strange connection to the stone. If anything, the link seemed stronger now. He hadn't dreamed it would follow him beyond the city's rim. But he could point out the direction of T'al Jazure with certainty now, just as he could tell the position of the sun by feeling its warmth.

When he'd asked Nirias whether the Heartstone could think, Nirias had reassured him that it was merely a tool — a tool created by the Azuri to organise knowledge. The explanation had seemed reasonable. Nirias should know about such things. He was the last of the ancient Azuri. Ash had *trusted* Nirias then, putting aside the fact that he was one of the Malshorne, a shape-shifter and, worst of all, brother to Credé, the person who had passed the Song to Ash — and who'd tried to kill him. Now, Ash wondered whether he'd misplaced his trust.

Ordelle was watching Ash from the corner of her eye, in that analytical way of hers. He frowned and shifted the conversation. 'Why do you think Nirias lied to Kep?' Kep had placed full trust in the League's leader. She'd accompanied him and the warriors, believing the gods themselves had selected her for the mission to eliminate Kara-fell. But they had proof that the Malshorne had lied. Her token had never been in the sacred vessel. Sarin had swapped it with his own. Nirias had cheated. But why? Why would he lie?

Sarin answered darkly. 'Why does Nirias do anything?'

'Nirias is very attentive to Kep.' Ash and Sarin turned their heads to stare at her. 'It's true,' said Ordelle. 'He often puts a hand on her arm or shoulder. And he keeps it there longer than seems necessary.'

Ash searched his mind, trying to remember any interactions between the two. Was she right? Did Nirias have a special interest in his friend? Or was that just Ordelle's interpretation? She didn't like to be touched herself, and she was terrible at reading emotions. But she *was* highly observant. The thought made Ash very uncomfortable.

Sarin's scowl had deepened. 'Kep is blind in her loyalty to Nirias. She'd do anything for him.'

Ordelle nodded. 'She is devoted to the League. And she takes her oaths seriously.'

Sarin sighed. 'That's *precisely* what makes Rilka's vision so worrying. Kep doesn't exactly shy away from danger.'

An uneasy silence followed. Ash wanted to ask Ordelle whether she believed in Rilka's vision. He didn't dare. Sarin could be prickly about his sister. And besides, Ordelle's logic was simple. Nirias had knowingly put Kep in harm's way with his lie. That was enough for her. She'd left the safety of the city and her father behind. Kep was

Ordelle's only friend, he supposed — unless you counted Ash and Sarin. Ash blinked with a sudden realisation. Ordelle probably did.

Ash rubbed his hands over his face, pressing his fingertips over his eyelids. Thinking about Rilka and her visions always made him feel anxious. Rilka believed he was the saviour from her nightmares: a boy with grey hair and matching eyes. She called Ash the 'Grey Boy' and said he was 'paired' with the swirling evil that had plagued her dreams since childhood — the evil they now knew as the Melk. Whatever that meant, it did not sound good.

But Rilka dreamed about Kep now, too. Her visions depicted Kep locked in a cage. But that wasn't the worst thing. According to Rilka, their courageous friend wasn't herself. Sarin had leapt to the obvious conclusion — Kep was in imminent danger of becoming a thrall of the Melk, just a mindless slave with empty pits for eyes and no will of her own. That was a reasonable assumption, given the mission. Nirias and the others had gone to the Singing Isles to destroy Kara-fell, a nexus of the Melk.

Ash had accepted that Kep would face the Melk one day. She was a League warrior, sworn to its destruction. But now? With so little experience? His anxious mind circled back to the same problem. It wasn't the gods' plan. Nirias had sent Kep on the mission. But why? Why had the Malshorne lied?

Ash sighed, staring at the barrier of snow and debris and overcome by a deep sense of powerlessness. Their expedition had been purposeful — despite blisters or any other obstacle. He had believed they could get there in time to warn Kep. Now their dashing off unprepared, telling none of the League captains, seemed foolish. They could die here, and nobody would ever know. And if Kep was safe …

A small pebble hit Ash on the shoulder, and he turned to see Sarin frowning. 'Stop fretting, Ash. Sleep while you can.'

It made sense. So Ash curled himself into a ball, lumping his pack beneath his head and tucking his cloak around his feet. The position couldn't have been more uncomfortable. Something crawled at the nape of his neck, and he couldn't stretch his legs out without kicking

Ordelle. Sleep was impossible, even if Sarin did command it. After a short while, Ash pulled himself upright. He moved furtively, trying not to draw the others' attention. Fishing about in his pack, he found the object that had started all this.

The Taelstone grew warm in his cupped hands, like a flame coming to life. Nirias had warned against the dangers of handling the stone. Not only because Ash was untrained in using bonded lore-stones — Credé's memories tainted this one. And yet the orb had a calming magic. He knew it could soothe his nerves. And make him feel braver. He just needed to be careful.

Ash's anxiety diminished almost immediately. His mind calmed as he cradled the orb. He could still hear the storm, the slow creaking of the tree and the near-silent breath of snow settling. If anything, those sounds were crisper. But his other senses sharpened, too. He could feel the energy of the tree at his back, could sense its flowing sap. *It was all part of the Song.* When melodies rose in his mind, he held himself motionless, letting the music flow around him.

This place held countless stories. Some were origin tales, belonging to pilgrims who had come and stayed, building homes and raising children. They told of mountain journeys, hardships overcome and the simple pleasures of hearth and family. Other stories were lighter and full of enchantment. The legend of Forien featured a poor woodcutter's son, with a single possession to his name — his mother's magical axe.

Ash held himself apart, listening, aware of everything. Before long, the song of making returned to him.

*The people are red-faced, muscles straining. But they smile, singing as they work. Everyone heaves together, encouraged by the eager voices of drums. They drag at the ropes, hand-over-hand, hauling their burden. Up, up through the forest. Laughing and singing. The music climbs with them, then erupts in joy. It is done!*

*The mood shifts to one of elation. The craft is beautiful! Rejoice! Her gleaming hull is adorned with garlands of yellow flowers. The people sprinkle libations on her decks. Wine and honey. They tuck gifts into the bow, sweet cakes wrapped in woven packages. The homage is worthy. Worthy of the gods. The whole village cheers when the entrance swings open. The drum beats out the time. Behold. The wise ones come!*

Ash gasped, opening his eyes. 'It's warm,' he said. 'It's warm inside the mountain!'

## 2

## THE SLAVERS

The road to Skarfell changed as it went north, as if aware of the need to adjust its nature, bracing for the harsh realities of the sprawling slave port. In the south, it meandered quietly through the dappled woods of the lower Kenting, bending on a whim to take in the occasional inn or village. Now, drawing nearer to the coast, it became a true highway, broad and uncompromising. The woodland turned patchy, giving way to rolling hills and tussocky grasslands studded with grey-faced boulders. Prey scurried for cover here, evading the ever-circling hawks.

The wagon which trundled northwards under the late-afternoon sun was unexceptional for these parts. Drawn by two thickset horses, it was framed out with stout timber bars. A slavers' wagon. Somebody had thrown a dirty canvas tarpaulin over the top as an afterthought; roped down at the sides, it gave the eight occupants some measure of shelter.

An observant person might have sensed a peculiarity about these prisoners. Something in the way they held themselves, the glint of challenge in their eyes. Despite their rags, these men did not radiate the usual despair of slaves bound for market. There was no banter, but their jostling exchanges suggested they had a history together.

Theirs was a caged energy that had nothing to do with the bars — these individuals knew their strength and were waiting for an opportune moment.

To a curious eye, something was odd about the slavers, too. The outrider wore leathers and a battered hat. Three tattooed stars sat high on his cheek. He appeared a hard-mouthed slaver, if a little on the ancient side. The beast he rode was majestic, though, and she stepped proudly. Like her owner, she bore the scars of battle, suggesting they had once seen military service together.

The woman driving the wagon was small and wiry, with silvery hair. With an uncompromising glare, suited to one who traded in lives, she was of an age to be the man's wife. If that was true, she was most displeased with her situation.

The man sitting next to her was a complete anomaly. His hair was black, falling in extravagant curls to his shoulders. His dark moustache drooped, disheartened, at the corners. Puncture marks in his ears suggested he was accustomed to wearing many more earrings than he was. Several rings adorned his hands, but telltale bands of lighter skin revealed that others were missing. Occasionally, his cloak flapped open, revealing a black, embellished leather waistcoat over a bright red shirt. His black breeches were tucked into boots with deep cuffs and shining buckles. The man's fingers were constantly drumming, his knees jiggling in time to some beat of their own. Now and then he would catch an irritated glance from the woman at his side and stop fidgeting, only to start up again moments later.

Following the wagon, a second guard rode a chestnut mare, her face obscured by a wide-brimmed hat. An observant person might have caught a flash of blue when the rider lifted her gaze. Despite having tucked her hair beneath the hat, a thin black braid had escaped to dangle at her nape.

At the sight of two travellers approaching from the north, the young woman stifled a gasp. With a nudge of her knees, she urged her mount closer to the shaggy grey hitched to the back of the wagon. Sweeping her cloak around her, she tipped her hat even lower. The outrider growled words over his shoulder. 'Anyone so much as squeaks and I'll run them through.'

Thankfully, the advancing riders noticed none of these things — they were not observant men. All *they* saw was an opportunity. 'Hold, traders!' called the taller of the pair. 'This is fortuitous indeed! If your stock is healthy, we can save you the trip to Skarfell!'

The leathery guardsman didn't make eye-contact. 'Not selling,' he responded. The wagon rolled on.

Dressed like merchants, with debonaire plumes on their hats, the riders were undeterred. The man who had spoken wheeled his horse around, bringing it to trot alongside. His face broke into a knowing grin. 'Ha! You know your business well, sir. But come! Let us strike a bargain. This road is long and tiresome. Our coin is as good as any you'll get in Skarfell. Better! On account of you saving the auction-eer's fee.'

Both riders peered into the wagon, sizing up its occupants with interest. 'It's a mixed bunch you've got here, that's true enough. Look a bit on the wild side. But our own trip to Skarfell was ... let's say, disappointing. I daresay we can strike a fair price for the lot — even the skinny lad.'

The second rider looked as though he was intending to make his way around to the back of the wagon. Instantly, the outrider's horse surged ahead, hooves pounding, nostrils flaring in a snort. The travellers reined in their startled mounts as the slaver twitched his cloak aside. Nobody could miss the threat of a partially drawn sword. Not even a self-absorbed pair of country merchants. But it was the wagon driver who spoke, her words quiet but firm. 'Best if you men were on your way.' The two fellows exchanged glances. The unmistakable edge of warning in her voice, as much as the guardsman's steel, confirmed the suggestion's merit. Without so much as a farewell, they spurred their horses, resuming their journey south.

Kep blew out her breath. Ignoring the low chuckles and leery glances of the pirates, she reined Berry in and let the wagon pull ahead. The encounter had left her heart thumping. The road was busier now. Every passing stranger heightened the risk of discovery.

Calkinon offered a rich reward for news of the runaway slave from Mildaresh. The disgruntled riders would remember something if asked.

Kep's heartbeat had just returned to normal when the wagon slowed. Jen-Jay jumped down, released the shaggy grey and leapt into the saddle. The spirited stallion tossed his head, but his rider brought him swiftly under control. A sidelong glance told Kep that her captain was as weary as she was; the wrinkled creases of her face deepened by worry. 'Skarlon says there's a suitable place up ahead.' Jen-Jay's sour expression made it clear how little she thought of their companion's judgement. 'You and I will scout it out. Come.' Somewhat surprised, Kep pushed Berry to a canter. The tired horse responded eagerly — perhaps she, too, was happy to be leaving the wagon-full of pirates behind. *If only that were possible.*

As they pulled ahead, the young woman did her best to put the pirates out of her mind, appreciating the sweet breeze on her face. After a while, she ran her tongue over her lips. Salt! The air tasted of salt. As they topped a rise, she strained her eyes west, towards the horizon, yearning for her first sight of the ocean. Nothing. Kep still didn't quite believe that such a thing could exist. How could water stretch as far as the eye could see? As eager to see it as she was, she was dreading it in equal measure. The coast offered nothing but danger.

Skarlon said Split Apple Cove, where Grady's gang had taken Rodine and the other League members, was only a few days' travel away. Kep's tired thoughts scouted ahead, willing them to be alive, wishing she could send word that help was coming. Her friends faced a worse fate than slavery. They would die in the arena of Kara-fell, or, more horribly, become creatures of the Melk. Kep shook her head, brows creasing with thought. They *had* to get there in time. But it wouldn't be today. The horses were flagging, and the sun was going down; they would barely have time to set up camp before nightfall.

The women found the marker where Skarlon said it would be: five stones stacked to form a tower. They cleared a few fallen branches from the track, making it wide enough for the wagon to pass. The sound of gurgling water led them to a rough clearing, which swept up from the weedy stream to a small rise. Jen-Jay sniffed, giving a curt nod of approval. 'It'll do. Skarlon and Curly can sleep on the flat with the wagon. You and I will camp on that rise. If we need to take defensive action, there is sufficient cover and an adequate escape route. You'll take Berry, crossing the creek in the shallows.' Kep nodded, even though she had no intention of doing any such thing.

Jen-Jay narrowed her eyes, as if detecting the mutinous thought. 'I'll head back and tell the others.' She sighed. 'Enjoy the peace. While you can.' *The peace.* To halt its tremor, Kep clamped her lower lip between her teeth. Jen-Jay's expression softened to one of concern. 'The first is the hardest, Kep. The memories will lessen, I promise you that.' Moments later, she was gone.

Kep swung onto her belly and slipped from her mount. The mare's neck was dark with sweat. Squeezing her eyes against the sting of tears, she ran a hand over Berry's warm chestnut coat, taking comfort in the earthy smell of the damp horse. 'Good girl,' she murmured. 'Time for a rest now.' She led the horse to the stream for a long drink. Then she removed her saddle and rubbed her down, first with handfuls of dry grass plucked from the bank, then with the soft brush from her saddlebag.

For the first time since Bixdale, the clenched feeling in Kep's stomach eased. She would have liked to have drawn the task out, but Berry kept tossing her head, eyeing the lush grass. The sensible mare wouldn't wander far, so Kep set her free to make the most of it.

The little clearing was far from silent. Above the sound of Berry munching, Kep heard birdsong. The invisible creatures were calling messages to each other, a perky prelude to their nightly chorus. Insects buzzed sleepily, and spring blossom scented the air. It was deeply peaceful — a place she once would have enjoyed. She sighed. Tonight, there would be no peace. Just more whispered arguments. Time was running out. They had to decide about the pirates.

Kep swallowed the anxiety which rose in her chest. Her water pouch was almost empty, so she moved upstream to fill it. Her old self would have delighted in the dazzling dragonflies and laughed aloud at the frog which leapt into the bright stream on approach. Now, she stared at the current, feeling numb. Ever since Bixdale it felt as though her own shadow had replaced her.

No one had used the fire-pit for a long time; a few determined plants even grew among the blackened remains. Kep thought about gathering kindling. But she couldn't find the energy. She just stood there, frowning at her own shadow. The silhouette of a warrior, tall and dark. Her stance was alert; the outline of bow and quiver across her back; and the slant of a sword at her side. To become a warrior was all Kep had wanted. She'd trained hard throughout the long winter in T'al Jazure, striving for that very outcome. That was before Bixdale.

Bixdale had changed everything. The journey to the village was supposed to have been a quick detour, just to check out rumours — a chance for the novices to practise their skills. But a gang of pirates had seized the hamlet, their leader enthralled by the Melk.

Kep shivered as unwanted images flooded back. The empty holes where his eyes should have been. And that voice! Visions plagued her sleep, ambushing her by day. She kept reliving the awful moment of Grady's death, at her hands — by the blade of Jaibari's sword. Memory would crash over her like a wave, smelling of blood. What hurt most was that Jen-Jay had been right. *Sarin* had been right. Kep wasn't ready for this.

An eagle's cry interrupted the young woman's thoughts, and she looked up. She followed the bird's flight, letting her mind drift toward the northeast and the far-off mountains. Somewhere among those peaks was the hidden city of T'al Jazure. What would her friends think if they knew where she was? Ash would be worried sick, of course. And Sarin ... No. She wouldn't think about Sarin. Better to picture Ordelle, in the cosy room they had shared, laying her belong-ings out on her bed in that peculiar routine of hers.

Perhaps Ash was sitting with Aechon, picking out melodies on one of the Cryer's lutes? Or in the Lodges, helping cook the evening meal? Kep shook her head. She hadn't been prepared for how much she would miss her friend's serious smile and those thoughtful grey eyes. Poor Ash. He'd begged her not to leave the city's protection. But Kep had known better.

The eagle had become the smallest speck. Just a wish. Kep let out a sigh. Yearning for her friends was pointless. They were far, far away. And she was glad. In their place, she had a cranky pair of ancient warriors who couldn't agree on the colour of the sky; a stinking band of pirates with murder on their minds; and the oath of a man who'd proved himself traitorous.

A cracking branch sound made Kep turn her head. The wagon! Its trundling wheels were bringing the pirates. *Her* pirates. She wasn't just a warrior for the League; now she was Kep-Váli and, in the strangest twist of all, Simbab, the pirate leader. She closed her eyes and took a deep breath. The gods had willed it, she reminded herself. Nirias had drawn her token from the sacred vessel. *Hers*. This was her task. She only hoped the gods knew what they were doing.

3

___________

# CURLY

Kep was more than happy to follow her captain's orders and set herself apart. She sat on a log in the raised camping area overlooking proceedings. The wagon nestled beneath the draping fronds of a willow tree, still containing a full complement of pirates. The men hollered and banged on the bars. A futile protest. Horses came first in Skarlon's book.

Near the smoking fireplace, and deaf to the cries of their captives, Jen-Jay was skinning a rabbit. They had bagged several along the way, plus a brace of speckled grouse. After days of cold rations, there would be a hot meal. Kep might have foraged herbs for the stew, and root vegetables. But she had orders. And, besides, she didn't care what the food tasted like — only that it was warm.

The night air was chilly for spring. Morning snow on the mountains wouldn't come as a surprise. Not for the first time, Kep blessed her Azuran garments. Dark blue, the fabric resembled linen. But the weave had some magical quality that trapped the warmth of her body, keeping out the cold and wet.

The young woman looked down at the weapon she'd been polishing. A deadly yet beautiful blade, it bore Jaibari's house sigil: two serpents, intertwined, near the hilt. How many times had she seen the dark-eyed warrior sharpen it? Practising routines for hours upon end? What would Jaibari think when she learned Kep had used her ancestral blade to kill a man? *Blood. The smell of blood.* Kep took a breath. Swallowed. The weapon was spotless now. She had polished and sharpened it every evening since, keeping it in perfect condition for return to its owner. Letting out a heavy sigh, she turned her attention back to the pirates.

Under Skarlon's stern supervision, Curly had unlocked the back of the wagon and was letting the scoundrels out, two at a time. They stumbled under the threat of a sword, attending to their needs. Then, grumbling and cursing, they were bound again — slave-style, in a line.

Kep felt no pity. Although dressed like slaves, they remained pirates — nine of the most unscrupulous men imaginable, including Curly. She chewed at a thumbnail as she watched the man. How could anybody trust a pirate?

Perhaps Jen-Jay was right — they should rid themselves of the trouble and have Curly drive the rest on towards Skarfell. And perhaps that would be justice — they'd inflicted the same fate on the unwary travellers through Bixdale, after all. And selling people into slavery was the pirates' least heinous crime. Their treatment of the villagers deserved far worse punishment. Kep did not accept their excuse that they'd just followed their leader's orders. To her mind, that was no excuse at all.

During the past few days, the three League warriors had exhausted every possibility. And it *had* been exhausting. Jen-Jay and Skarlon kept changing their minds. The only thing they seemed to agree on was their determination to disagree with each other. They couldn't kill the pirates — that was against the League's code. Even if the men deserved it. But the pirates couldn't be trusted with freedom either — Calkinon was paying gold for information about the girl called Kep-Váli. That left two choices: send the pirates to Skarfell's slave markets with Curly, or keep them and continue to Split Apple Cove, a known den of dangerous smugglers.

Both plans demanded that they trust Curly, who could very well betray them, just as he had his former leader. But Curly could be the least of their problems. Any of the pirates could be a thrall of the Melk and linked to its evil nexus Kara-fell, just as their leader had been. *Find me. Fight ... me.* Kep would never forget that voice. It haunted her nightmares. Pirates were bad enough. Pirates possessed by evil? That was something else altogether.

Kep watched Skarlon limping across the clearing. When he began climbing up the rise towards her, Jen-Jay followed, after giving Curly some final instructions. She seemed to think Skarlon needed watching just as closely as Curly. Kep sighed. Steeling herself for another argument.

Skarlon cleared his throat as he lowered himself to sit on a flat stump next to Kep. His face was even more uncompromising in profile. Three tattooed stars punctuated his many scars. As was his habit, he addressed himself to the horizon, his voice rasping, dry as his leather armour. 'Sheath that sword, Kep. It's clean enough.' Kep frowned, but obeyed, slipping the blade into its sheath. *Breathe.* Skarlon cleared his throat a second time, his eyes on the trees. 'That was a null that you killed — not a man. Remember that.' Kep nodded, not trusting herself to speak.

Jen-Jay joined them a moment later, puffing a little from the climb. She gave no sign that she'd overheard the brief exchange and settled herself cross-legged on the ground. It no longer surprised Kep that a woman of Jen-Jay's age could be so supple. After all, this was Jen-Jay — Grey Wolf, the legendary League warrior, back from the dead and dangerous as ever. 'Curly is seeing to the immediate needs of our murderous friends,' the old warrior informed them with a sniff. 'I've told him if he so much as sneezes without permission Kep-Váli will stick an arrow in his gullet.'

Skarlon made a growling noise, deep in his throat. It was as close as he'd ever come to agreeing with Jen-Jay. Jen-Jay might be a wolf, but Skarlon was a stubborn old dog — hairy and a bit smelly. Kep knew little about the couple's history, but one thing was clear: the shadow between them was Nirias.

Skarlon's loyalty to the League's leader was unswerving, almost part of his own identity. If Nirias had given him orders, he would follow them to the letter. But Kep was still uncertain what Skarlon's orders were. To track their party, making sure Kep came to no harm? It seemed odd.

Jen-Jay swore she'd known nothing of it. And she agreed Skarlon was hiding something. Mind you, the little woman thought that about most people. Right now, she was scowling. 'You claim to know this road, Skarlon. How far is it to the coastal track?'

Skarlon scratched at his chin. 'Assuming we're heading to Split Apple Cove? And that Curly is telling the truth?'

'Yes. Let's assume that.' Jen-Jay glared down at the figure of Curly. 'For now.'

Skarlon's grimace made the tattooed stars jump. His answer was careful. 'We've made fair going. Reckon we're a day from the turnoff. Maybe two. Depending on the road. 'Course we'd go faster without the wagon.' As he spoke, a bird landed in the tree above them. He frowned. A hand went up to brush the stars on his face. Of the three gods, Skarlon was closest to Argess; he was far more at home with animals than he was people. Did he read some omen into the bird's arrival? Sensing Kep's eyes on him, the man rolled his shoulders. 'There's no use trying to make a decision on an empty stomach. Is that stew on its way?'

Jen-Jay answered with a harrumph. 'I've no idea. Why don't you drag your old bones down there and find out?'

Kep smothered a sigh as she watched Skarlon head back towards the campfire. How had she landed herself with such a crotchety pair? Skarlon was right, though: it would be easier to plan with a hot meal in the belly. Her stomach groaned in agreement. Turning her head, she noticed how Jen-Jay glared at the man's back. 'You don't trust him.'

'I never said that. But that man is League through and through.' Jen-Jay stabbed a bony finger in his direction. 'He'll follow the code no matter what ... and carry out whatever commands Nirias has seen fit to issue.' She sniffed. 'No matter how misguided.'

'Mmmm.' Kep couldn't fathom Jen-Jay's deep mistrust of Nirias, nor why the woman had stayed in exile for so long, assumed dead. She suspected Skarlon was still angry with Jen-Jay for abandoning the League all those years ago, but Nirias was the main bone of contention. Kep was sure of it.

Jen-Jay's scowl deepened. 'I'll tell you one thing. I trust Skarlon a darn sight more than I trust that one.' She cast a dark nod towards Curly, who had strolled over to join Skarlon at the fireplace. 'A cut-throat pirate and a traitor to boot. The worst possible combination.'

Kep didn't answer. She was trying to read what Curly was saying. He gesticulated for a while, then, ignored by Skarlon, seemed to give up. After a while, he looked up, scratched at his head and headed up towards them.

Curly still looked every bit a pirate. Despite the confiscation of much of his gold, he still wore strings of curious ornaments around his neck. With flowing curls, tanned, olive skin and a flashing smile, women might consider him handsome, in a dashing sort of way. His soft brown eyes and drooping moustache were quite endearing, even if they made him look a little mournful. Jen-Jay was right, though. Even without his wicked daggers, something about the man seemed crooked. The seasoned warrior reckoned he reeked of deception — but that could just be the strange-smelling gum that he favoured. Kep caught the bitter whiff of orange peel and cloves as he climbed towards them.

'Don't worry. I'll stay here,' said Jen-Jay, 'until the pirate's gone.'

'No!' Kep snapped, then winced. A League warrior shouldn't bark at her captain like that, even when exhausted. She softened her tone. 'Please, Jen-Jay. Let me speak with Curly, alone. He might let something slip.' *Without your constant disapproval.* 'I'll be perfectly safe.'

Jen-Jay scowled, but she relented with a nod. 'I'm going to wash. Shout if there's any trouble.' The glare she gave Curly as he stepped up could not have been clearer: she was watching him.

Curly wasted an elaborate bow on her departing back. Then he smiled, unperturbed. 'May I join you, Kep-Váli?'

Kep motioned at the stump that Skarlon had vacated. 'It's Kep. Just Kep.'

Curly lowered himself down. Then he shook his head. 'Forgive me. That is not wise. You are Kep-Váli. This is the name the pirates will swear to. You have earned it.' His voice was mellow, with a lilting quality. It went up in odd places. 'To cast such a title aside would be foolish, I think.'

Kep sighed. She understood. But it didn't mean she had to like it. 'And Simbab? Is that a name I have earned, Curly?' He hadn't used the title to address her, she noted.

The answer was swift. 'Yes.' The pirate's dark eyes seemed troubled. 'Of course.'

'You will be true to your bargain, then? The return of your ship for your help in rescuing our friends?' Kep made herself look directly into his eyes. 'Can I trust you, Curly?'

Curly seemed to flinch. He held her eyes, but only just, and he licked his lips before answering. 'For a pirate, a sworn bargain is as sacred as an oath.'

It wasn't what Kep had asked. She frowned, eyeing his fingers, which were tapping out a beat on his thigh. Was that a sign of deceit, or just one of his habits? 'And what of the others? Their choices at Bixdale hardly paint them as men who can be trusted to keep an oath.'

'Choices?' Curly gave a sad shake of his head. 'Men do not always have choices. To stand up to a man like Grady? That is not a wise decision. That is to choose pain.' Curly clasped his hands, bringing his thumbs tight against each other. 'Or death.' For a moment, he was still. 'Grady was not scared of mutiny. He enjoyed it.'

'But you defied him, Curly. You made the choice to free those people in the mine at Bixdale, instead of burying them alive. You betrayed Grady and your friends to do what was right.'

'My friends?' Curly looked taken aback. 'These men are not friends.' He gestured at the wagon. 'As for choice ...' His eyes were serious. 'It is Fate that rules our lives, Kep-Váli. Not choice.'

Curly reached a hand into his pocket and Kep heard the soft click of stones. Kep knew what they were, even before he drew them out. Runestones. Curly was never without them. She'd seen him cast the stones before, at Bixdale. Then he'd headed to the mine to release the villagers. What sort of man left decisions of life and death up to a pair of stones? Suppose they had landed otherwise?

Kep sighed. If she couldn't trust the man, she should at least try to understand him. 'But you *chose* to do the right thing,' she insisted. 'You stopped the death of those villagers, even when it meant danger to yourself.'

Curly cupped the runestones in his hands, elbows resting on his knees. 'It is true. I released the villagers. But not to fight. I told them to run. *That* was my plan. To run away.' Curly turned sad brown eyes on Kep. 'I'm no hero, Kep-Váli. I am not an honourable man. But I *will* help you find your friends ... for the *Lady Lee*. That ship is the love of my life. That is the deepest oath I can give.' His passion was undeniable, but could Kep trust Curly not to betray them at the first opportunity? The stones ground circles in his hand.

'Those runes. Can I see them?' Curly looked reluctant, but he handed them over.

The runestones lay warm and heavy in Kep's hand. The dark charcoal stone had eight faces, the pale grey stone, ten. Each face had symbols engraved on it. Kep had no idea what any of them meant. Curly seemed relieved when she handed the stones back. He offered her a smile. 'The runes ... they show me the way.'

*Ridiculous.* Kep raised her eyebrows. 'And if they said to double-cross your friends? Would you?'

'No!' Curly looked shocked, his dark brows jumping together. 'These are Fate runes ... they show the path of right.' He scratched at an ear. 'How is it you say? They are of the gods.'

Kep scowled. She couldn't see how chucking a couple of stones could help a person decide what was right. It seemed like superstitious nonsense. But the man appeared earnest. She came to a decision. 'Throw them now. Let us see what the gods say about our bargain. If it serves justice, then Narsis will guide your hand.' A curious expression crossed the pirate's face at the mention of Narsis, but he nodded his head in agreement.

Curly held his fist to his forehead in a moment of composed stillness. Then he cast. The stones tumbled to the ground, landing between his boots with a thud. They both leaned forward to look. 'Well?' demanded Kep. 'What do they say?'

Curly's lips parted, and he drew a breath. 'I do not know the words.' He glanced at the runes, then at her, then at the runes again. His eyes were bright with wonder. Then he dropped to one knee. 'I trust you, Kep-Váli. You have my oath. I swear! I will do all I can to help you free your friends.'

If he was acting, his performance was convincing. And Kep knew faith when she saw it. 'Very well. Remember, Narsis will hold you to your bargain.' She frowned at the grovelling man. 'Please. Get up now.'

When Curly had regathered himself, Kep repeated her earlier question. 'Tell me about the others. They might swear an oath to me, but will they keep it?'

Curly met her eyes now, more confident. 'You are Simbab, by the pirate code. You triumphed over Grady and claimed his place.' He gestured at the weapon at Kep's side. 'Grady was proud of that sword. It is right that you have claimed the plunder as your own.'

Kep felt anger leap inside her. *Plunder?* The sword was Jaibari's, passed down through her family, bound to her by honour and trial. Kep felt uncomfortable wearing it — she barely knew how to wield the thing. The pirates, of course, cared nothing for that. To them, the sword was a treasured prize, a sign of conquest. 'Grady was ruthless,' said Curly. 'But he also had a reputation as a thinker.'

Kep glowered. 'The man was a *snake*.'

'Yes. But he was outwitted by you, Kep-Váli.' The pirate spread his hands. 'Your story is not new to us. All in these parts have heard of T'al Kep.' Kep felt a shiver go down her spine. 'But now,' he pointed to his associates, 'they have witnessed the power behind your name.' He seemed oblivious to her scowl. 'The arrow you shot from the rooftop? They say it was impossible. Except by the help of the gods.' Kep swallowed. *Or the Azuri.* Curly nodded. 'The pirates will swear the oath. They will follow you, Kep-Váli, especially the younger ones.'

Kep sensed his hesitation. 'But?'

'You must show them you are leader ...' he hesitated, 'of *all*.'

Kep bit her lip. He meant Jen-Jay and Skarlon. She drew a long breath, knowing it wouldn't go down well. But Curly had more to say. 'These men are raiders, it is true. But they are proud. They do not like being slaves, Kep-Váli. Not even as a trick.' He tugged at his ear and frowned, as if rueing the loss of his gold earrings.

Kep gave him a hard stare. 'I'm quite sure they don't, Curly.' Rage welled inside her. 'Yet they were happy to sell others into slavery. Or send them to their deaths.'

Curly nodded. 'This is true. Men follow bad leaders as readily as good ones.' He paused. 'Nobody chooses the life of a slave. You understand this. But these men? Not all *chose* to be pirates. Most inherited little but poverty. Some were kidnapped in the slums.' He blinked several times. 'A person can wake up and find themself betrayed, and at sea.' The catch in his voice made Kep suspect he was talking about himself. 'The young ones,' Curly shook his head sadly, 'they have not seen choices.'

Kep was silent for a moment, considering his words. The sky beyond the trees was deepening to an apricot-pink. She breathed in the scent of smoke and the cool draught of evening. At last she nodded, turning to the man beside her. 'Then that is what must change.' She gave him a stern look. 'If I'm going to trust you, you need to tell me everything.'

The pirates watched the proceedings with furtive interest from seats on the ground. They saw meat go into a pot with onions and herbs. They observed the huddled conversations of their captors, noting the prickly stance of the older man and the way the grumpy woman threw up her hands.

A short while later, another scene unfolded — off to one side, yet just within view. The man in leathers fetched extra water from the stream and used it to fill a shallow vessel. He bowed to his young companion, and she thanked him with a nod of her head. With the sweet aroma of cooking drifting over them, the bemused pirates bore witness to Kep-Váli's ritual.

First, the girl washed her face and arms. Then she knelt, dipping her head to make the sign of the triangle. It was impossible to tell what offerings she sprinkled into the water, nor did her murmured prayers carry to the pirates' ears. Despite this, many were captivated by the moment's simplicity. In later years, some would report a deep sense of longing, and being struck by a desire for redemption. Nobody would believe them, of course — they were rascals after all.

The men exchanged glances as their captors placed logs around the fire-pit. The stew's hearty fragrance made them drool like a pack of starving hounds. Their eyes followed every movement. When the old woman lifted the lid on the pot and gave her companions a nod, every pirate licked his lips.

Kep-Váli walked up to the line of prisoners, as calm as you like. She stared at each one in turn, with those blue, blue eyes of hers. Eyes that could see into a man's soul. Then she drew her knife.

She cut the pirates' bonds herself, using a peculiar blade which glinted green in the firelight. None of them had seen the like. Then she bade each man wash and take his place at the fireplace. The fighter with the stars on his face doled the stew into bowls, with Kep-Váli supervising. 'Equal portions for all,' she commanded. And so it was.

The pirates ate in silence, some stealing glances along the line. The portions were generous, with meat falling away from the bone in luscious chunks. Some shovelled the food into their mouths, fearing it would disappear. Others chewed more thoughtfully. Aware of Skarlon prowling at their backs, they wondered whether the meal was their last.

At last, every bowl was licked clean. The pirates went back to watching. More logs were added to the fire. They watched the flames leap up. They watched each other. They watched their captors. And they waited.

At long last, Kep-Váli stood. The firelight painted her skin with gold, making the falcon on her arm flicker, almost as if its feathers were real. It was unnerving. For a long moment, the young woman stared at the ground, those dark curls cascading over her face. Her lips seemed to move. Perhaps in a prayer to her gods? Then she lifted her head, frowned, and began to address them.

# 4

## OATHS

Kep swallowed, running her eyes along the semi-circle of men. The pirates appeared more menacing by firelight. An assorted bunch, they were bound by a defining characteristic: they were cut-throats every one. The younger lads, Ratskin and Spike, seemed expectant, fidgeting from time to time. The expressions worn by the rest of the group ranged from sulky to angry to hostile contempt. Kep had to persuade all of them to her cause. By Telion, how had she landed herself in such a mess?

Kep knew nothing about how to address a group of pirates. Her knees seemed convinced that she wasn't up to the job and were threatening mutiny. Skarlon and Jen-Jay looked on edge, too, weapons at the ready. The veteran warriors radiated disapproval. But one thing was certain: Kep needed these men. The gods were with her, she reminded herself. She was *supposed* to be here.

Kep had watched Nirias give many speeches at T'al Jazure. The leader of the League could hold an audience in the palm of his hand, moving his listeners to loyalty with perfectly chosen words. But Kep was not Nirias. She was just an escaped slave. She took a steadying breath. That was it. That was where she would begin.

'Thank you ... for your patience over the past few days.' The pirates frowned. A couple looked up, fixing her with suspicious glares. 'Nobody wants to be a slave — not even a pretend one. I know this, because *I* was once a slave.' A few of the pirates nodded. Somebody cursed beneath his breath. Kep was fairly sure it was Greigo, the stocky man who sat at the end. The green-inked tattoos which covered his bald head flickered in the half-light. Skarlon's boot silenced the man, confirming Kep's guess. She forced herself to breathe.

Not for the first time, Kep wished she had thrown her knife at Greigo on that fateful day in Bixdale. This was after he'd set fire to the village hall, with women and children locked inside. Kep had knocked him out with a rock, her obedience to the League's code saving him. Now the decision haunted her. If the Melk possessed any pirate, it would be Greigo. She knew he harboured vengeance. But she couldn't dwell on that. Not now. She pushed on with her speech.

'The gods have set me on a different path now. I am the *enemy* of slavery. And injustice. So ... even though it's what most of you deserve, I won't sell you for slaves.' A collective shiver rippled through the group. Kep frowned. 'I'm fully aware of the poor people you loaded into wagons and sent down this road to slavery. But I will not condemn you to the same fate.' The pirates' relief was obvious, but their grins didn't last for long.

'Neither can I simply set you free. Your actions at Bixdale cannot be dismissed and they cannot be undone. So ... I'm giving you a choice. You can either enter *freely* into the life of a slave, or ...' a few scratched their heads at this, 'you can choose to follow me. I'll be honest ... the first option might be safer. The second could end with death. Because I *am* set on rescuing my friends.'

This announcement caused widespread muttering and obvious concern. Evading Jen-Jay's eyes, Kep pushed on. 'Curly has told me all about Grady's operation.' He'd done no such thing, but the pirates weren't to know that. 'He's also informed me about Grady's deal with the smuggler, Bahjak. If my friends are not already aboard the *Lady Lee,* they will be at Split Apple Cove — in Bahjak's keeping.'

The pirates looked very alarmed now. Kep put her hands on her hips, trying to pretend her stomach wasn't doing somersaults. The reaction to the mention of Bahjak convinced her that Curly had withheld information. Yes, he'd warned her that those frequenting Bahjak's cove were sworn to secrecy — on pain of death. But why did these hardened men look so afraid? Kep felt her palms begin to sweat. Her mouth was dry. But it was working. Stirring up the pirates was all part of the plan. She motioned to Curly, who waited in the shadows.

The small wooden chest drew every eye. Setting it on the ground at Kep's feet, Curly threw back the lid. The pirates' eyes gleamed, reflecting the glitter of all those golden coins and jewelled ornaments. 'Some of you are already aware of Grady's secret stash,' said Kep. The men straightened, frowning sideways at their companions — it was news to them.

At the end of the line, Greigo scowled. His glinting eyes narrowed to slits of displeasure. He, at least, had been in Grady's confidences, then. Kep was unsurprised.

Ignoring the rebellion in her stomach, she pointed at the treasure. 'This is just a small part of the plunder which Grady held back for himself — I believe there are several more chests stashed aboard the *Lady Lee*.'

Some pirates did a better job of hiding their reaction to this news than others. Harden, the short, fat-bellied one, stared bug-eyed at the riches. Despite his name, Harden was the least threatening. With his roly-poly figure, bald crown and wispy hair, he looked more like a baker than a pirate — a somewhat frightening baker with a squashed nose and gold in his teeth. The two younger lads joined Harden in his slack-jawed astonishment.

The toughest-looking man was Rawlins. The burn marks down one side of his face, a souvenir from Bixdale, added to the wicked lines of his countenance. Kep had dragged his unconscious body from the fire's advances. A mistake perhaps, because right now Rawlins stared into different flames as if he was contemplating murder. Kep feared it was hers.

The pirates simmered with hostility, trying to figure out which of their group had been privy to Grady's private dealings. *It was working.* 'Your previous Simbab was a greedy man. A hoarder of wealth. I am not like that. Plunder doesn't interest me at all. I wish only to release my friends — and any other slaves who have been taken.' Kep hesitated. Then, her eyes avoiding Jen-Jay, she went on: 'If you've heard of my legend, then you know already that Narsis is with me. They call me Kep-Váli, because I fight for those who cannot fight for themselves. But ... I don't expect *you* to fight for justice alone.' A few of the men licked their lips. The man called Creely stroked his beard and smiled. *Crafty Creely.* That was how Kep remembered his name. His gaze had not left the treasure chest. But Creely was not alone in that.

Kep took a breath. 'As soon as the *Lady Lee* is secure and my friends are set free, this plunder, and the treasures aboard the ship, will be distributed among you, in *equal* shares. You will have your reward. And ... you will have your freedom. What you do with those is up to you. Curly might take you on as crew, or you can find your own ways, as free men.' She paused. 'As *wealthy* men.'

Ratskin stared with his mouth wide open. A misshapen lump of a lad, he wore clothes that resembled the skins of rats stitched together. His sharp-looking friend nudged him in the ribs, and he nodded. Kep wasn't worried about Ratskin and Spike. According to Curly, tales about T'al Kep had been their favourites. The expression dawning on Spike's face, though, made her heart sink: the boy looked as if he expected her to perform a miracle right there and then. She just hoped that freedom and money of his own would be miracle enough.

The cool breeze shifted, sending smoke into Kep's face and making her eyes smart. She made herself stand tall, despite her burning throat. 'I'm offering you a simple choice. Will you take your chances at the slave markets, or will you swear an oath to fight for my cause?'

A horrible silence fell. Then Skarlon stepped into the semi-circle. Lit by firelight, he made a menacing figure as he issued the ultimatum. 'Your decision must be unanimous. Either you all swear to Kep-Váli or no man does.' He growled, baring his teeth. 'And make no mistake. You will be held to your oaths. If one man slips, all will pay the penalty.'

Kep gave a grim nod. 'That is my promise. If a single one of you breaks your oath, the plunder will be cast into the sea.' The threat was real. Kep would do it. In fact, she'd prefer it that way. The thought of rewarding these awful creatures made her sick in the stomach. 'So now you must decide — as one. Take your chances as slaves, or choose to follow me.'

'Yulia won't be happy you killed her man.' The observation came from a man with a thick shock of white hair and thoughtful eyes.

Kep felt a shiver at the base of her neck. *Who is Yulia?* From out of the corner of her eye, she saw Curly duck his head to inspect his boots. Greigo's face slid into a leer, and he chuckled, scratching his crotch. Others shook their heads. 'Orrick's right. And what about Bahjak?' The speaker was small, with mottled skin. Kep had forgotten his name. His nervous energy reminded her of a rodent, as did his squeaky voice. But this question, she had expected.

Drawing a knife from the sheath on her belt, Kep swept it through the air, showing off its filigreed design. It was the weapon that Grady had kept inside his boot. She hated even touching the thing, but the pirates understood what it meant for her to carry that blade. 'Bahjak will acknowledge me as Simbab. I mean to strike a bargain — to buy back my friends. But if the smuggler chooses to fight,' she scowled to mask her fear, 'then we fight. You've seen what my friends can do.' The men who had fought Jen-Jay and Skarlon at Bixdale nodded. They bore the scars as proof.

The fire added drama to the moment, giving a loud crack, sending sparks into the sky. The younger lads exchanged wide-eyed glances. 'No more questions! Your choice is simple,' barked Skarlon. 'Swear to Kep-Váli or carry on as you were — down that road to slavery.' His finger stabbed towards the track. 'What say you?'

With the promise of plunder on one hand and the miserable life of a slave on the other, the outcome was not surprising. One by one, the pirates knelt, bowing their heads to swear the oath. Greigo was the last to sink to one knee, and he made a show of it. Kep smothered her feelings of revulsion as she stared at his patterned head. The tattoos looked like evil curses. She detected a smile in the man's voice as he muttered his oath: 'I swear to follow Kep-Váli, the new Simbab, and mistress of the *Lady Lee*.' Greigo was unlikely to remain faithful, but Kep accepted his oath anyway. As soon as Rodine and the others gained their freedom, she'd be rid of the man — and all his stinking mates.

'It is done,' said Skarlon. 'Your lives belong to Kep-Váli now. And you serve at her command.' He wrinkled his nose. 'First thing in the morning you will bathe. Your own clothes will be returned to you

Creely smiled. 'And our weapons?' His expression was all innocence. 'If you want us to fight Bahjak, we'll need weapons.'

Skarlon snarled. '*When* we reach the cove and not before. And on the way, you'll tell us *everything* you know about Bahjak and his operation. Be helpful and who knows? You might not end up dead.'

A knowing smile crossed Greigo's face. Kep wished she knew what it meant.

The appearance of a small barrel of rum proved a welcome distraction. The pirates were encouraged to believe it was part of Grady's stash, whereas in fact the rum had been a gift from the innkeeper at Bixdale. The poor man had relinquished it gladly, so grateful was he to be rid of the scoundrels. Kep's unwanted associates accepted their change of fortune with varying degrees of suspicion. Only the youngsters beamed from ear to ear. According to Curly, Grady had been a merciless bully, especially towards them. There were sour faces, too, but the wearers didn't refuse their share of the rum.

Slipping away to the shadows of the trees, Kep had time for only three slow breaths before Jen-Jay joined her. 'That was quite the performance.'

Kep bristled, trying not to sound defensive. 'If I have to pretend to be Kep-Váli to save our friends then I will. There are worse things.'

'Yes. There are worse things.' The words fell softly into the night. After a pause filled only by the sound of grazing horses, Jen-Jay let out a sigh. 'Well, what's done is done. Rest now, Kep.'

Kep's eyebrows went up. 'We're not training?'

The little warrior shook her head. 'You'll train at dawn now, with Skarlon.' Catching Kep's startled expression, she sniffed. 'If you *must* wear that sword, then you'd best learn to wield it. And there's none better to teach you than a blade-master.' Kep's eyes shot to Skarlon, who was prowling around at the perimeter of their camp. *Skarlon? A blade-master?* But Jen-Jay was in no mood to elaborate. Perhaps she noticed how Kep trembled with fatigue and nervous exhaustion. 'Get to your blankets, girl. Skarlon has the first watch and I'll take the second. He'll wake you early.'

Kep was more than willing to obey. She didn't bother with a lantern — the moons were bright and her bedroll laid out ready. She rolled herself up in her cloak, still wearing her boots. Telion's stars poured across the sky in rivers of light. She closed her eyes to their beauty, too exhausted to care.

**5**

---

# A DOOR

Ash shivered. And not just because he was freezing — the scene of destruction was enough to make anyone tremble. The sheer miracle of their survival was rammed home as they contemplated the ravaged tumble of snow and debris. Somewhere, beneath all that chaos, lay the path.

Sarin's expression was grim. 'Well. We're not going that way. Not until that lot melts.'

Ash clenched his jaw to stop his teeth from chattering. The wind had already stolen any warmth generated by the exertion of digging their way out of the hollow.

Sarin squinted, his hair whipping around his face. 'Are you sure about this, Ash?'

Ash nodded. He could still hear the half-singing chant of worship. 'I'm sure.' *As sure as he could be.* 'There's a door in the mountain. And ... it's warm.' He faltered, unwilling to say more.

Ordelle pulled her cloak more tightly around her. 'One thing's certain. We'll die of exposure if we stay out in this.' Her lips were pale, and tinged with blue.

Sarin's eyes were tight with worry, but he nodded. 'Ash, lead the way.'

Wading through knee-deep snow, they negotiated the slip and regained the path. Downhill. Retracing every hard-won step. Ash gritted his teeth. His boots had discovered fresh places to rub, but his feet were so numb he could scarcely feel the damage.

They were once again in deep woodland when Ash paused. Tilting his head to listen, he pointed. 'That way. We need to go that way.' He understood the looks of bewilderment on his friends' faces. Nothing marked the place as special — just trees and tangled undergrowth as far as the eye could see. 'I think there's a path. Through the trees.' It seemed highly unlikely.

Sarin ignored Ordelle's raised eyebrows. 'It's worth a look. If we can't find anything, we can build a shelter and rest for the night.' His weary sigh betrayed a lack of hope. 'And I can hunt for game.'

'It's dange—'

Sarin cut Ordelle off, more snappish than Ash had ever known him to be. 'Yes, Ordelle. It's dangerous to leave the path.' Earlier, she'd given them a lecture with unnecessary detail: the mountains were limestone, and riddled with the chimney-shaped pits formed by ancient trees. 'We'll be careful,' Sarin added more gently. Ordelle's frown cleared. She gave a nod of approval, and they followed Ash off the path, into the tangled undergrowth.

Somehow, the lack of a track proved helpful. It would only have been a distraction, making it harder to follow the music. For just when Ash wanted it to be clearer, the Song eluded him, coming in faint wafts of harmony. The terrain was difficult, thick with ferns and blocked by fallen branches studded with tiny pink mushrooms. It was a relief when the forest opened out, once more ruled by beech trees with their grim black trunks. They couldn't see any trace of a path, nor signs of any ancient dwellings. Ash was beginning to think he'd dreamed the whole thing when he caught a movement in the corner of his eyes — ghostly figures walked in procession through the trees. His heart pounded as he followed their zig-zagging progress. The melody faded, and they vanished. He turned to the others. 'They climbed up that way.' He closed his eyes, grasping after the Song. It was like trying to get a hold of smoke.

When he opened his eyes, he saw Ordelle and Sarin staring back at him, hot-faced and covered in mossy grime. 'Who?' they asked in unison.

Ash faltered. 'The people ... of the forest.' The place was deserted. Just trees and silence.

Sarin raised an eyebrow, his frown silencing a protest from Ordelle. 'Good. Lead on then, Grey Boy.' Ash scowled as he turned away. One day, he promised himself, he would tell Sarin how uncomfortable the name made him feel. He let it go for now, making allowances for his friend's frustration, and continued climbing.

The incline grew steeper as they dragged themselves upwards. Often they fell onto hands and knees, slipping and scrabbling over drifts of wet leaf mulch. By now Ash's foot was a raw lump of burning pain. But the chanting was clearer now. The melody urged him on. *Heave. Heave on. We all pull together. Heave on! Heave away together!*

At last, they found themselves on a small plateau, bounded by a deep gully. A dead end. A sheer cliff rose before them. Birds squawked at the intruders from high nests in the escarpment, fearing for the safety of their chicks. Ash looked around him. 'This is it. This is where they came.'

Sarin and Ordelle's faces were a match for the grim rock face. But Ash found himself smiling. This was the place! He was certain. It wasn't just the Song and the allure of that strange chanting. The scene felt oddly familiar. *The waiting craft has wings of white.* He blinked, jarred by the displaced memory, but he couldn't dwell on that now. Exposed to the elements, this place was bitterly cold. The wind tugged at his cloak, intent on claiming it for its own. Pushing the bracken aside and trampling down heather, he reached out his hands.

Even before his fingertips touched the rock face, Ash knew what would happen. The doorway materialised, as if summoned to the surface. He gasped at the design. Identical to the one in the mountains near Mildaresh, it featured a deep blue archway, inset with pearly leaves. This was wider, though, with a more intricate frame.

Ignoring his astonished companions, Ash half-closed his eyes, seeking the right notes. The melody came in a surge, rocking him on his feet. It flowed from his fingertips, sinking into the rock and sending golden veins spiralling across the surface. A sharp tingle traversed his skin. Then, in a cascade of shining notes, the stone dissolved. The breath of the mountain billowed out at them, steamy and warm, smelling of rotten eggs.

Ordelle recovered from her shock in rapid time. She wrinkled her nose, testing the air. 'Sulphur. And possibly more toxic gases as well.'

'Maybe,' said Sarin. 'I vote we take our chances.'

Ash led them in, holding up his dymiril lamp to light their way. The passage was impressive, and wide enough for three people to walk abreast. The marble-smooth floor, inset with decorative tiles, swept away at a gentle gradient. Almost immediately, a doorway opened to the right. Without hesitation, Ash stepped through it, leading them down a smaller tunnel. The air grew steamier as they walked, diffusing the light of the lamp and making it harder to see. The sound of trickling water grew louder. Ash had to control his thoughts to stop them from wandering off to pursue its tinkling melodies.

The passageway ended, leaving them unsure of their destination. Billowing clouds of steam made it impossible to see more than a few paces ahead. Through the haze, they caught tantalising glimpses of carved stone. All around was the echoing music of water.

Before anyone could speak, Tarlyn made the chittering noise she used to get Ash's attention. He followed her through the vapours with one hand outstretched, fearing he would collide with something. A shape materialised and Tarlyn let out a chirrup. She jumped up onto a shallow dish set on a stone pedestal. Etched with symmetrical markings, it reminded Ash of a sun-dial — except he couldn't think of a more peculiar place to put one.

Ordelle darted to his side. 'What's that?' She pointed to a star-shaped aperture at the centre of the object. Her tone implied that Ash should know. He didn't have a clue. He counted seven symbols around the perimeter. They gleamed bright silver. Each had a ring set into its middle. Sarin studied them and raised an eyebrow at Ash. 'Keys of some sort?'

Ash frowned. 'Maybe.'

Sarin shrugged, hooked his finger through the nearest ring and pulled. The hexagon-shaped rod lifted from its housing with a gentle grate of stone against stone. 'It's heavy,' said Sarin. They all peered at the curious object.

'It looks as though it could fit in that central aperture,' said Ordelle.

Sarin nodded. 'My thoughts exactly. Let's see what happens.' Ash held his breath, bracing himself for some new shock, as Sarin reached out and slotted the silvery rod into the centre of the dial. It settled into place with a muted clunk.

The effect was immediate. All around them, lanterns burst into life. The three companions gasped, dazzled not just by the light but by the sheer scale of the place. The cavern was enormous, lit by hundreds of lanterns. Some dangled like miniature moons from the craggy canopy. Others threw light upwards from stone lampposts. Tiny ones twinkled like constellations of stars.

The cavern's walls were pearly pink and white, its roof dripping with crystalline cones. Steaming and glistening, the terraced pools overflowed in cascades of water and sculpted rock. The effect was much like a display of cakes in a baker's window — a drunken baker who'd got rather carried away with the sugar frosting.

Steam obscured some pools, while others glowed in shades of blue and impossible greens. Mysterious grottos beckoned from beyond stone staircases, hanging walkways and carved bridges. The stone-craft was exquisite. Gorgeous creatures emerged from the rock, part-human, part-animal.

The trio crossed a bridge and followed a winding stair to one of the higher terraces. There they found a deep turquoise-coloured pool, filled to overflowing by water that spouted from the jaws of a crouching beast. The creature's enormous claws gripped at the sides of the pool. Its bright silver wings were half-open, as if it was poised to take flight. Sarin smoothed his fingers over the graven scales on its neck. 'Is this work Azuran, do you think?'

Ordelle put her head to one side. 'It does not make sense to think of Azuran art as a school. The Azuri were never a single people. Thus the art at T'al Jazure is eclectic, reflecting the cultures of many.' Sarin shot her a look, and she blinked. 'But, yes, there are similar elements. And the engineering is equally sophisticated.'

Before Ordelle could launch into a treatise on plumbing, Sarin clapped his hands. 'Well, I think one thing is certain. This is a bath house. And we could all do with a bath.'

Ash sank deeper into the pool, letting hot water lap around his ears. It sent a delicious shiver all over him. The warmth was blissful, even though it made his blisters sting. Ordelle had advised that the minerals in the water would help with healing, but he didn't much care. Right now, he was enjoying a break from her company. Earlier, she'd informed the young men that she didn't mind if they stripped off. It was nothing to her — she'd seen plenty of naked bodies. Sarin had burst out laughing, telling Ordelle he had no intention of letting her measure him for a shroud, and suggesting she find her own pool. To Ash's considerable relief, she had discovered one at the 'optimum temperature' a couple of terraces down.

Sarin and Ash's pool resembled a lagoon. Some spots were much hotter than others, with jets directing hot water. Ash kept to the edges as he investigated the various nooks. He envied Sarin's ability to swim to the other side, but, with their clothes laid to dry on the hottest rocks, it just felt good to soak, letting the water ease his aches.

Soon there would be a hot meal, thanks to Sarin's clever idea of setting a pot of gruel in one of the hottest pools to cook, which they'd located before going for their bath. Its water near to boiling, the natural cauldron contained the bodies of several unfortunate frogs who'd leapt to unexpected deaths. Ash had found the sight of their poached-pink bodies disturbing, but they had fascinated

Ordelle. He'd half-expected her to fish one out as a gruesome souvenir.

Now rubbing his wrinkled fingertips, and still reflecting on the young woman's oddities, Ash heard a soft splash. Across the pool, Sarin had disappeared beneath the water, ignoring Ordelle's dire warnings about diseases that could swell your brain. Holding his own breath, Ash watched the water. He had to take a second breath long before Sarin surfaced next to him, his hair a slick wave of black. Hooking his arms over the warm stone edge, Sarin rested his chin on his hands. Ash rolled over to copy him, bringing them elbow-to-elbow.

For a while the only sound was the eerie music of the caves — a constant watery murmur, on the verge of becoming melody. Ash shut his mind to it. After a few moments, he looked sideways at his companion. 'I'm sorry.' He cleared his throat. 'About the pass I mean.'

Sarin smoothed a hand over his head, squeezing water from his hair. 'It wasn't your fault. If it wasn't for your blisters we'd all be dead.' Ash nodded. It was a sobering thought. But the fact remained: they'd failed at the first obstacle. It would be hard to slip away from T'al Jazure a second time. Ash doubted the remaining captains would allow it. Nor were they likely to believe that Nirias had acted against Kep's interests. They'd probably suspect one of Sarin's tricks.

Sarin half-turned his head. 'So ... Is this what you saw? In your vision?'

Ash swallowed. Sarin had every right to ask. He should at least *try* to explain. 'No.' He sighed. 'The Song only gives me fragments. The memories are all broken up. I think ... maybe they even come from different times.' He stared up at a statue of a young man with wings. 'I think you were right, though. What you said before ... This place does feel Azuran.'

Sarin nodded. 'And ... the Song? Can you hear it now?'

'I'm doing my best to block it out.'

Sarin frowned. He was silent for a long moment. Then he half-turned his head, making a fist to rest his chin. 'Tell me. What *did* you see?'

Ash took a breath. 'I saw the doorway. That's where the people were going. But ... they couldn't have built this place. They seemed like simple forest folk. Their song was rustic, with a simple melody. A working song.' He frowned, trying to capture the feeling. 'About community.'

Sarin smiled. 'I know the kind.'

'But ... it didn't make sense. They were building a boat. I saw it. And they dragged it all the way up here, through the forest.'

'Are you sure it was a real boat? Could it have been symbolic? Like in Rilka's visions?'

Ash shook his head. 'No. It really was a boat.'

Sarin's laugh was gentle. 'That sounds like a lot of effort. And what for? This is a gigantic pool, kin. But a boat? Seriously?' Ash knew he wasn't mocking him, not really. And it did sound ridiculous.

He wished he could recall more detail. Catching hold of the images was like trying to grasp a fish with his bare hands. 'It wasn't *just* a making song. It was a song of worship.' His frown cleared with a sudden realisation. 'The boat was a gift! And they mentioned the wise ones.' He blinked. 'That's why they dragged it up here.'

'The wise ones?' Sarin raised his head. 'The Azuri?'

Ash considered it. 'Maybe. The Azuri were healers and teachers. It makes sense.' Except it made no sense at all. He understood why Sarin was frowning.

A moment later, Sarin cleared his throat. 'Right. The gruel should be done by now. Let's eat, and explore. Who knows? We might even find this boat of yours.'

They didn't find a single boat. They found a whole flotilla.

After their simple meal, they'd followed the stream of colder water, as suggested by Ordelle. Having crossed a series of stone bridges, the path took them through a low tunnel, lit with eerie green light. Skirting a terrace of steaming waterfalls, they reached a second cavern, even bigger than the first. There they found an underground lake, green and sultry beneath the mists. Stalactites dripped in massive clusters like crystalline fingers.

Sarin let out a whistle. 'It's like an underground river market.' It was an apt description. The stone piers jutted far out over the water, crowded on both sides by a clutter of ghostly boats. They shone with a pearly luminescence.

Many of the boats remained afloat, after a fashion. Venturing out along one pier, they realised that many more vessels had sunk beneath the turquoise waters, succumbing to the slow passage of time. Objects crammed the boats: assorted pottery vessels tucked around other indistinguishable shapes.

Working their way back and around the shoreline, they discovered a stone ramp leading to the water's edge. More of the boats waited there, lined up ducklings. How long had they queued here in the eerie underworld? Centuries upon centuries, Ash guessed. But what crafts! Shaped like fat seed-pods, they had closed-in bows and sharp sterns rising to a tail. Shining scales covered them, like those of a fish. Sarin marvelled as he ran his hands over one of the iridescent hulls. 'I've never seen anything like this.' Ash put his hand out to touch the nearest boat, proving to himself that it wasn't a dream. Because *he had*. He'd seen a vessel just like these, in Credé's memory!

Credé's miniature gift for Leynore differed only in its colour. It had been white. *The waiting craft has wings of white, with shining prow and raindrop bright.* The words of Credé's poem ran through Ash's mind, intermingled with snatches of the Song. He held his head, trying to think.

Ordelle was carrying out her own inspection. 'A hardening agent has been applied to the hulls. Resin, perhaps?' She frowned, using the point of her knife as a chisel. 'I can't make a mark. It's almost as if it's been fired in a kiln. They are very resilient.' Clambering up, she stepped into the front boat. She handled the objects with respect, returning each to its place when she was done. 'Offerings.'

Sarin nodded. 'That fits with the worship theory. But ... There are a *lot* of boats here. I mean, why go to all this trouble? Why make such beautiful crafts to just float here in the darkness until they sank. It's bizarre.'

'The boats *were* used.' Ash cleared his throat. 'I think the Azuri used them.'

Ordelle paused halfway out of the vessel. She cast doubtful eyes over the ghostly flotilla. 'What for? Some sort of ritual?'

'No. To float down the river.' His friends were frowning in disbelief, and he knew it sounded crazy, but he pushed on. 'Do you remember me telling you about Credé's poem? The one he wrote for Leynore, mocking her tutor?'

'I remember,' said Sarin. 'It was the first memory.'

Ash nodded. For a long time, the intimate tryst had been the *only* memory he'd managed to retrieve from the Taelstone, making its importance to Credé obvious. The scene made Ash blush, even now. 'It's just ... The words of the poem keep coming back to me, as if they're somehow connected to this place. And these boats ... They're *exactly* like the model that Credé made for Leynore. Exactly. Down to the shimmering scales.'

'Recite the poem for us,' demanded Ordelle.

Ash took a breath. ' "The waiting craft has wings of white, with shining prow and raindrop bright, we'll draw it from its plashy dell and float along the Elanelle." '

Sarin looked around. 'It's hardly a "plashy dell", but ... Credé was writing a parody of an existing poem. We should allow for that.' Once again, Ash was shocked by Sarin's ability to remember tiny details. 'But "wings of white"? These boats don't exactly have wings. Poetic licence?' He rubbed his chin. 'Could refer to a sail, I suppose?'

Ordelle looked thoughtful. 'Some scholars claim that Elanelle is the ancient name for the Tella. It is a geographical possibility that one of its tributaries begins here.'

Sarin frowned as he considered it. 'Maybe. But why are there so many boats?'

'Perhaps the ritual continued, long after T'al Jazure was hidden. It may have been passed down, even though the wise ones were gone.'

Ash had been holding his breath as he listened to his friends argue. He *hated* boats. And he hated what he was about to suggest even more. 'So … ?' he asked miserably. 'Do you think we should try?'

Sarin's face split into a disbelieving grin. 'What? Launch a thousand-year-old boat and ride the currents of a mythical underground waterway?' He let out a hoot, making Ash blush. 'You really *are* full of surprises, Grey Boy.'

'We are going to die,' pronounced Ordelle with grim satisfaction.

**6**

———

## CAVE JOURNEY

By the time Ash had finished eating the bread and cheese which counted as breakfast, he was regretting what now seemed a ludicrous plan. A sound night's sleep on a bed of warm sand had done nothing to convince him otherwise. Even if Credé's fancy was based on truth, more than a thousand years had gone by since that memory. The river's course had probably altered. Ash couldn't stop his imagination conjuring up several frightening scenarios: getting lost underground, being dashed on rocks, or the boats sinking, leaving them to drown here, in the dark . . .

Ash's sense of trepidation only grew as Sarin and Ordelle prepared to launch the first of two chosen boats. The only task entrusted to Ash was to select a paddle from the rack on the wall, and he was even struggling with that. Like large leaves, the paddles were all individual. The beautiful carvings made them look more like art than functional tools. At last, conceding that he knew nothing about paddles, he simply grabbed one at random and stood there clutching it.

As the first boat splashed into the water, Ash held his breath, waiting for it to sink. He half-wished it would. But the boat showed no sign of sinking. It bobbed proudly on the water, as if eager for an adventure. Within minutes, a second craft joined it. Sarin and Ordelle paddled around in graceful circles for a while before declaring that the crafts were watertight. 'They handle superbly,' called Ordelle. Ash's heart fell. Of course Ordelle could handle a boat — she was from Calkinon. Everyone in the lake city could, according to her. It was the most efficient way of getting around. They could swim, too.

As he climbed into the front of the vessel they would share, Ash knew what Ordelle was thinking. How could anybody make such a mess of getting into a boat? He felt sure she'd moved 'capsizing' up her list of probable ways to die. Before he could organise his legs, they were underway.

Ash expected them to follow the shore, but Sarin's confidence in the curious vessels was so great that he headed straight out into the middle of the lake. Ash shivered as he peered into the deeper water, which was now inky in colour. Eerie light from lamps on the boat's prows illuminated the water's surface. It made it seem as if they were suspended. *Suspended in a world of dreams.* Ash pushed the melody away. *Don't listen.*

Glancing back, he realised they were already a long way from the jetty. The boat seemed to be gliding forward of its own accord, pulled by some unseen force. 'Are you paddling, Ordelle?'

'No. The current is taking us.'

Just then, Sarin called out. 'Look! See where the water is bubbling up? That's the spring. It'll be the source of this entire system.'

Ash gazed at the roiling mass until it passed out of the lamplight. It was disturbing to think of all that water, eternally flowing, never stopping. But soon something else caught his attention, giving him something new to worry about. The cavern's far end was looming unexpectedly fast.

At the same time the current grew swifter, and for a horrible moment Ash thought they might smash straight into the rock wall. But then he saw it — a gaping mouth. And the current was sucking them towards it.

Sarin let out a cry. 'Duck!' Folding himself into his boat, Sarin disappeared from view as the maw under the overhang swallowed him.

Ash threw himself sideways as their boat shot through the gap, too. Before he had time to sit up again, his stomach flipped, caught out by a sudden drop. The prow plunged as the little boat surged forward at an alarming angle. He stifled a scream. Then the boat levelled out. Their journey into the underworld had begun.

It was difficult to calculate how long it took to navigate the labyrinth. Sometimes it felt as though they were stationary — as though the boats were somehow suspended in time and the cave walls simply flowed past them. The paddles were superfluous, since the boats moved of their own accord, following a predestined route. In some ways, it was a relief. There were no choices to be made here. At the mercy of the current, they could only drift and marvel.

At times some of the formations on the cave walls looked almost like sculptures that humans could have carved. Ash made out giant harps strung with stone spurs, cities with spires and impossible stairways, and what looked like crowds of people waiting on the shore. Other spaces, though, were utterly alien. Organic, crystalline wombs, shining with an unworldly light.

Every grotto had its own distinct music, too. Some tinkled with the dripping melodies of flutes and harps, others projected majestic choirs of sound. The companions scarcely uttered a sound during that time. Even Ordelle was speechless. When Sarin let out a shout, it came as a shock. 'Put out your lamp!'

Ash obeyed, then gasped at what the sudden darkness revealed. Stars surrounded them. As though they were floating through the galaxy itself. 'Glow-worms,' breathed Ordelle. There were billions of the minuscule creatures, each a pinprick of light. Ash leant back, gazing upwards until his neck ached. He'd never seen anything so magical. Not even in T'al Jazure. Gradually, the lights grew fewer until there was just darkness.

Ash was beginning to wonder whether they would be travelling underground forever when he detected a peculiar smell. He took a sip of water, wrinkling his nose. The scent caught at the back of his throat, intensifying. The walls were closing in, too, narrowing to a worm-hole shaped tunnel. 'It's like an anus,' Ordelle stated matter-of-factly.

Sarin chuckled grimly. 'Smells like one, too.'

He was right. The stench was feral. And powerful. But what creature could produce such a foul odour? Ash gagged from fear as much as from the stink itself. 'If you're going to be sick, do it over the side,' said Ordelle.

Ash nodded, his eyes watering. Then he lifted his head higher, training his ears. 'What's that sound?'

It began as a scratching twitter, far ahead of them, then grew suddenly much louder.

Ash would have blocked his ears, except he was already holding his nose to keep from vomiting. Looking up, he saw a chimney-shaped structure, alive with tiny fur-clad bodies. Seconds later, everything was in motion. The boats were under attack! A cloud of whirling bats overwhelmed them.

Transfixed by the horrible flapping cacophony, Ash didn't register the growing light. He was busy shielding his head with his arms. Through all the chaos, though, he became faintly aware that the boats were picking up speed. Then Sarin was shouting another warning. 'Hold on!'

They burst into a world of light, funnelled by a squall of bats. Ash let out a scream of terror! Struck blind by the sudden glare, he clutched at the rails. The boat surged, tipping almost vertical and plunging them forward. Expelled from the mountain, they were swept into a chasm of pounding water.

7

----

# RIVER SONG

The little boats charged on, at the mercy of Narsis. All was blinding fear and white turmoil. The river humped and bucked, oblivious to the tiny crafts which rode its back. Ash had already lost his paddle. He clung to the sides in desperation — praying that they wouldn't smash into the rocks or get tipped upside down. There was no sight of Sarin in the roiling rapids. Ordelle had been right after all: they were going to die.

It felt like hours until the current finally slowed. Then rounding a bend, Ash let out a cry. He'd spotted the flash of a paddle! Then Sarin's boat dropped back out of view again. But it was enough. Ash whooped, yelling over his shoulder. 'He's all right, Ordelle! Sarin's all right!'

'Of course he is,' said Ordelle. 'There would have been wreckage.' She corrected their own course with a deft turn of her paddle. For the first time that day, Ash allowed himself a measure of hope. That they'd got this far was all down to Ordelle's expert handling of the boat. Only her split-second reactions had prevented them from being smashed to pieces in the rapids.

Ordelle gestured at the tin mug which she'd tied to Ash's seat. 'Bail. We have taken water.' Once again, her assessment proved correct. The little boat was riding lower and icy water was soon sloshing around Ash's feet. He bailed for all he was worth, trying to take in their surroundings at the same time.

Rock walls loomed on either side of them now, grey and impassable. Swivelling his head, Ash caught a last glimpse of snowy peaks before the river turned away. The mountains seemed so distant now. Had they really come so far?

They journeyed on, slaves to the whims of the river and its endless, hurtling charge. Ordelle was silent and grim-faced, all of her attention focused on the river. Her sudden exclamation made Ash start. 'That is not good.'

Ash tensed, jerking his head around. 'What's not good?'

'We're on the wrong side of Grey Shard!' Ash turned his eyes upwards, following her gaze. To their right, a jagged clump of rock thrust skywards. It looked like a giant's fortress. 'This can't possibly be the Tella!' Ash's stomach dropped. This time, it had nothing to do with the movement of the boat. The river was sweeping them in the wrong direction! Further from Kep.

A sense of desperation swept over Ash as thundering announced another patch of churning water ahead. Ordelle shouted a warning over the din. 'Hold on!' Ash gripped the rails and clenched his teeth. White knuckles showed through his skin. His muscles cramped, every sinew quivering. The little boat bucked, swept down into another sickening drop.

As the afternoon drew to a close, the river subsided and the boats finally came together. Sarin flicked wet hair from his eyes. Like them, he was soaked to the skin. 'That was fun.' Ordelle raised her eyebrows, detecting his sarcasm with no trouble this time. Sarin glanced over at Ash, who was shaking uncontrollably, his limbs numb from cold and exhaustion. He made a swift decision: 'We can't ride this monster in the dark. We need to get warm and dry, and we need to rest. Keep an eye out for a suitable spot to camp. We'll stop as soon as we see one.'

As it turned out, the spot Sarin chose seemed decidedly *unsuitable* to Ash. It was just a ledge. And the current was still frighteningly swift. He feared they might shoot past, but at the last moment Ordelle dug her paddle deep into the water, swirling them into a tight circle. Ash did his best to help. He lunged for a half-submerged tree. It proved ill-advised; the boat almost capsized. Ordelle yelled at him to sit still.

Sarin stepped from his own boat to the shore with well-timed grace. There was nothing remotely dignified about the way Ash half-rolled, half-crawled onto the rock shelf. His only saving grace was that he didn't fall into the water.

Forming a natural wharf, the stone ledge was small, and crowded with ferns and tree roots. There was little space for a make-shift camp. But Ash didn't care a bit; he was just relieved to be on semi-dry land. They worked quickly to set up camp, exercising joints that had stiffened from cold and cramp as they did so. Tarlyn eventually nosed her way out of Ash's bag. She gave herself an indignant shake that spoke volumes about her own distaste for boats. Then, after washing her paws, she slunk away to hunt among the ample foliage that clung to the face of the gorge.

Sarin began making a fire, having checked that the boats were secure. In no time, he had produced a smoky blaze, using an abandoned bird's nest for kindling. Determined to do something useful, Ash wrestled with the branches of a dead tree. After a couple of unsuccessful attempts, he cracked one off and dragged it over. Then he gazed about, while he tried to rub some feeling back into his hands.

Although the gorge had widened from the narrow chasms of earlier, its walls still rose steeply. The sun had abandoned them to shadows. A person felt insignificant there. The rocky cliffs looked prehistoric and ravaged, as if some gigantic creature had raked at them with terrible claws. Ancient trees grew from the crevices, draped with dangling vines.

The branches had developed sinuous lumps, evoking naked human bodies. Grotesque faces appeared to stare out from the rock formations, their mouths seeming to scream, either in anguish or at some demonic joke. A trick of the light made them look alive — they made Ash shiver.

It wasn't just the strange figures that made the place otherworldly; it was the water. The endless flowing water. The Song sounded a distant thrum here — as if it ran beneath the river itself. Perhaps that was why Ash felt drawn to its green-tinged depths. He turned to the others, avoiding the allure of watery music. 'Where are we?'

Sarin didn't look up. The fire seemed to be resisting his efforts. 'Who knows?' A burning brand shifted, and he cursed, pulling his hand back. He sucked at his wrist, leaning back on his haunches. Then he glanced up at Ash. 'I think we can safely say this isn't the Tella River, though.'

Ordelle nodded. 'We are on the wrong side of Grey Shard.'

The breeze lifted as she spoke, sending harsh smoke straight towards Ash. He circled the fire, eyes streaming. Everything had gone wrong, and it was his fault. He sighed. 'Sorry.'

Sarin manoeuvred a billy of water onto the fire with the aid of a long stick. 'No need for sorry.' He stood back, brushing off his hands. 'Contrary to Ordelle's dire predictions we didn't die on the mountain. And we haven't drowned in the rapids. Not yet anyway.' Sarin flourished the stick and laughed. 'We live to die another day! Don't look so glum, Ash. We have our lives, we have food and, it has to be said, we have a pair of *exceptional* boats. As to where we are ...' Sarin's eyes slid over the fantastical setting. 'I rather think we've found the river Alph.'

Ash frowned. 'The Alph?' He couldn't remember any such name on the maps.

Sarin gave a sly smile. 'Ordelle. Why don't you tell Ash about the river Alph?' He perched on a rock, still brandishing the stick. 'Neither of you touch that fire. It's playing hard to get.'

Ordelle had been folding her cloak into a square. Arranging it on the ground, she settled down, hands clasped around her knees. For a moment she tilted her head, as if pondering the most accurate response to Sarin's request. As was often the case, Ash had the feeling she was reciting from a book, rather than giving voice to her own thoughts. 'The Alph is a mythological waterway of uncertain origin. Most scholars agree that the river is merely a fable, with no actuality in the real world. In folklore the Alph resonates as a metaphor for death, the gateway to the netherworld. In poetry the Alph might symbolise a descent into madness. To sleep on the banks of the Alph is to lose one's mind, or suffer visions. Some tales claim that just to trail one's fingers in the Alph is to be cursed forever.' Ordelle blinked at Ash, whose mouth had dropped open. 'The evidence of the latter is inconclusive.'

Sarin chuckled. 'That's a relief, isn't it, Ash?'

Ash frowned. 'So you're saying the mythology shifts ... just like a river?'

Ordelle shrugged. 'Yes. That is apt. The Alph is an uncertain topic. It is common practice when happening across an uncharted river to claim it as the Alph. I believe it is an established joke with cartographers. Cartographers seem fond of jokes.' She frowned. 'It is very odd.' The fire spat, and she flinched. Then she turned to Sarin. 'What of the Aurum, Sarin? Does the Alph appear on their maps?'

Ash glanced sideways at Sarin, who typically evaded Ordelle's attempts to winkle information out of him about his people. This time, though, he favoured her with an answer. 'Rivers are sources of life for all the Haelrum clans. We certainly don't associate rivers with death and madness.' Sarin paused, looking around. 'But, if there ever was a river Alph, this would be the perfect setting. Since passing Grey Shard, we've been heading roughly southwest, and that brings us closer to the Mistlands. The place of your ancestors, Ash.' Catching Ash's expression, Sarin pulled a face of mock despair. 'That's right, Grey Boy. We'll have to be extra careful now. The mists are full of ghouls and tormented spirits that prey on lost souls.'

Ash knew Sarin was teasing. He shivered, nonetheless. Even in far-off Mildaresh, children savoured tales of mist ghouls for their delicious creepiness. However, such stories were more readily dismissed under sunny skies, with warm dust between your toes. Sarin went on: 'Of the five clans, only the Dain ventures into the

Bruinin Forest, and never so far as to risk the mists. The forest is pretty impenetrable on its own, without the added risk of getting lost in the Veil.'

'The Veil?'

'It's a swathe of mist. It varies with the seasons, but the southern parts of the Singing Isles are covered in perpetual fog.'

Ash half-listened as Sarin and Ordelle argued about the vagaries of mists. His eyes returned to the point where the river vanished into the darkening gloom. Once more, the water pulled at him, drawing his thoughts. He imagined he could still feel the boat's motion. If he closed his eyes, he saw the tumult of ceaseless water. Now a singsong voice intruded on his thoughts. *By wind and wood the river runs; down to the vale of Linden. Where rushes sing and white gulls keen; there in the vale of Linden.*

Ash opened his eyes as the sound of the verse faded. 'What's a gull? Is it a bird?' He blushed, aware of his friends' sudden curiosity. He hadn't meant to speak out loud.

Ordelle looked perplexed, but Sarin just laughed. 'Yes. It's a seabird. My bet is you'll see one soon enough. Because one thing is certain: all rivers run to the sea in this part of the world — even the mystical ones.' He drew the billy off the fire, pouring the water into the three waiting mugs as Ordelle passed around shares of salted venison and flatbread.

The bread had stiffened to the consistency of cracked leather. It took effort to rip it into pieces. Ash was grateful for the tea, which helped wash it down. The small beads Sarin had dropped into each mug unfurled in the golden liquid, revealing themselves as dried flowers. Sarin grinned at Ash's surprise. 'Peach pearls. Courtesy of Nalina. She sends you greetings by the way.' Ash had never eaten a peach, but they smelled exactly like the tea — he'd peeled enough to know. Poached peaches were Marlashetta Feyindi's favourite. His past mistress considered them beneficial for her digestion.

Ash frowned as he took another sip of the honeyed-coloured brew. Sarin's grandmother didn't strike Ash as the kind of woman who sent greetings, nor tea for that matter. His memories of the

Aurum's chieftain were daunting to say the least. He stole a sideways glance at his friend, wondering again whether Sarin had questioned Nalina about Nirias. That had been his intention, the night he'd dashed off, without even saying goodbye to Kep: he would make Nalina tell him everything she knew about the mysterious leader of the League and the time he'd spent with the Aurum. Now that Ash thought about it, Sarin had been conspicuously silent on the matter. He swallowed a mouthful of tea and broached the subject. 'So ... um ... you spoke with Nalina, then?'

'Yes. We spoke about many things.'

Sarin then promptly changed the subject, asking Ordelle if she'd spotted a certain type of speckled watercress. Oblivious to the undercurrent of emotion, Ordelle reported seeing several species. She seized her notebook, demanding a more detailed description of the particular plant and its properties.

Sarin could be evasive, especially when matters touched on the Aurum. He was, by nature, secretive. Ash found it hurtful at times.

It wasn't just Nalina. Sarin had discovered a letter on the body of Kep's tracker. He should have given it to Kep straight away — he'd confessed as much to Ash. Instead, he'd kept it secret, hiding his suspicions that Braig, the boy whom Kep had risked her life for, might still be alive. Sarin claimed he'd been worried that Kep might do something stupid. That there wasn't any real evidence; just the word of a slave hunter. It made sense. But Braig had been Ash's friend, too. Why hadn't he told Ash?

Ash swallowed the last gulp of lukewarm tea, contemplating the impossible. How *could* Braig be alive? Ash had watched the life drain from his friend. Had witnessed his lifeless body. Hadn't he? The scene was vivid in his memory. Blood soaking through Braig's tunic. The hilt of the knife. The stranger, and the musky scent of her perfume. And her warning: *Run, fool!* Ash had obeyed her command to flee. Now, doubt gnawed at him. Should he have stayed?

The question wouldn't leave Ash alone as he tried to get to sleep. Finally, he succumbed to exhaustion after a long struggle. Even then, the night passed in a series of fitful dozes, connected by the strange music of the river. Other visions and dreams about Braig mingled in his sleep. Armoured warriors fighting on wings of silver. A woman shouting orders from a longboat's prow. She wore red, and her fingers were long and claw-like. The sky was heavy with battle cries and the terrible storm of war.

Tarlyn woke Ash at dawn by poking his cheek with a wet nose. A rescue — of sorts. But Ash wasn't awake. Not fully. The Song's power was stronger now. He sensed it beneath the birdsong, intertwined with the music of the river. It called to him. He could join it. All he had to do was let go.

They journeyed down the river of uncertain name for several days, the river slowing and broadening as they went. Soon there were no more rushing rapids, just the gentle meandering of water and time.

With the quieter waters came new songs: birds, crickets and the throbbing chorus of frogs. The sheer cliffs shrank back, allowing more sunlight in, too. Sarin had given Ash the spare paddle from his boat. However, since Ordelle rarely trusted him to use it, there was little to do other than sit and worry, letting the river take them where it would.

They drifted. Paddling by day, making camp wherever the river allowed. Until one pale morning, they awoke to a curtain of fog. Their campsite was damp and inhospitable, so, after a tense discussion, they took to the boats. It felt preferable to loitering in the clammy gloom.

The going was slow as they eased their way forward, avoiding the pull of the current and back-paddling to avoid obstacles. They could see the stretch of water ahead, but little else. The shores were grey and mysterious. Then the mists receded — as if Telion had lifted a veil — and they found themselves in a drowned forest, shrouded in mist.

Immense trees wallowed in the water, sending uncertain reflections into the depths. Many wore frilled garments of speckled lichen.

Most of the giants were long dead, but they still sported wild mops and straggling beards of vegetation. 'Epiphytes.' Ash was used to Ordelle's single-word declarations. She didn't expect an answer. Labelling things out loud was just her way, like pressing specimens, lining things up, or making detailed sketches in her notebook.

Out in front, Sarin craned his neck as he paddled, studying the mighty canopies and the huge white birds that cawed at them from twiggy nests.

As they drifted through that strange world of mist and fractured reflections, Ash found himself tapping an unconscious rhythm on his paddle shaft. The Song here felt ancient, its melodies interwoven with the papery rhythm of drums. The trees seemed to whisper, joining an earthy chorus.

*Twist the ropes, weave the cloth. Build the bowers strong. The Mukel folk are weaving cradles. Every bower is strung with charms. The clay faces tinkle from strings, laughing with the breeze. The gods of the Mukel are small, like them, with round bellies and laughing mouths. Fertile, benevolent gods. But the wind is rising now. The Song shifts on its wings. The pottery faces chink and spin, singing out a warning.*

Ash gasped in dismay, pulling back from the vision. Ignoring Ordelle's curious gaze, he leaned over the side and dashed his face with cold water. She was right to look concerned. This watery world increased his vulnerability to the Song. He needed to be on his guard.

The images of the little folk continued to haunt him as they travelled on, the memory lingering like mist. But the Mukel people were lost. Lost to time. Long before this valley was drowned, their weavings had unravelled, taking their smiles and dances with them. Now their song was both lullaby and lament, a sweet song that a mother murmurs long after her babes have passed.

Ash turned his face to the sun. Flat, like a beaten coin, it seemed to hum, as if pleased at its own pale halo. A fresh voice blossomed, like sunshine breaking through clouds. He felt his heart lift in response. *Yellow lilies of the morning.* Ash smiled, realising that he'd been singing — softly beneath his breath. It should have worried him. But how could it? After all, one did not refuse the river maiden!

Her music took him in a rush, joyous and wilful like the river itself. *Her reedy garments bore him down; his eyes shone clear and bright; the river maiden drew him on, her laughter clear and light.* Resistance was in vain. No man could withstand the lure of the river maiden. The Song swept him from himself: the poet king, enraptured, caught in her amorous embrace.

8

———

# THE DROWNED CITY

'Ash!' Ordelle scowled, plunging her paddle deep into the water to correct their course. They'd missed smashing into one of the dark trunks by a whisker. A quick glance over her shoulder confirmed her suspicion: Ash was drifting off, caught up in another of his trances. Earlier Sarin, sensing Ash's preoccupation, had suggested a spell in the stern might help their friend stay focused. Ordelle should never have agreed. Even the lazy current presented danger. She was about to call out when Sarin looked back over his shoulder. His ability to read Ash's mood was uncanny.

Turning his boat broadside, Sarin allowed them to bump alongside and gripped their gunwale. Ordelle latched on, too, locking the boats together. Sarin took a quick look at Ash's dazed expression and shook his head. Ordelle caught his eye and nodded. Ash was worse. Working together and with the help of the current, they back-paddled, nursing the boats into a deep raft of reeds before coming to an uncertain halt.

As Sarin tried to recall Ash to the present, Ordelle let her eyes rove over the drowned trees to the wooded shore. At first she dismissed the stone edges, so reminiscent of a stairway. As she knew very well, the human mind had a fondness for discovering meaning in natural forms. Then her eyes discovered the tower. With broken windows, it peeped shyly from behind a veil of ivy. Something moved and Ordelle drew a sharp intake of breath. For a brief second, she thought she saw a figure. She scanned the bushes for movement until Sarin spoke again. 'We need to switch places. But not mid-river.'

Ordelle nodded her agreement. Ash seemed unable to grasp the basics of what made boats tip. 'That is sensible.' After a pause she added, 'Sarin ... there are ruins.'

Sarin gave a stiff nod. 'Yes. And submerged hazards, no doubt.'

Ordelle tilted her head, calculating consequences. A stone's edge could rip through the hulls. Drowning aside, that would mean continuing on foot. There could be poisonous insects, spiders ... and large carnivores, like wolves. She maintained her silence. Sarin knew these things already.

They made the switch as soon as they reached the shallows, with Sarin in the stern. Ordelle took the lead now, pulling into the current. Managing her own boat meant she could keep one eye on the shore. The next few bends of the river revealed more stone ruins, suggesting that they were drifting through the remains of a sizable city. Water had inundated the entire place. Every staircase that rose above the surface had a submerged counterpart. The stonework hinted at a grand civilisation with superbly talented craftspeople.

On either shore, fluted rounds of stone were strewn about like the pieces of an abandoned child's game. Ordelle let her mind play at reconstructing one of the tall pillars, calculating the angle of fall and the drag of the river, stacking one round upon another. A low whistle from Sarin put paid to the endeavour.

The statue that rose from the waters was huge, commanding her full attention. Submerged almost to its waist, it forced the water into reluctant eddies around it. A warrior queen standing sentry over her realm. Her crown was moss-ridden and crumbled, her eyes were like mouse-holes. The queen extended one hand towards them, the weathering of time making the gesture ambiguous. A warning? Or a greeting? Her other arm was missing. As they passed, Ordelle peered into the submerged depths, catching glimpses of greening robes and a silted-over plinth.

Wondering at the woman's identity, Ordelle turned to speak, letting her boat slow. Ash's peculiar expression drove the thought from her mind. His grey eyes shone. She could hear him humming beneath his breath as their boat overtook hers, trailing mist in its wake.

Nothing like the vapours in Calkinon, these mists seemed to cling to their boats. The long, wispy tendrils made it seem that fingers were questing towards them, from somewhere beyond the curtain of this reality. Ordelle shook her head. *Impossible.* She wondered if Sarin had noticed the phenomenon, too. 'This mist is very peculiar,' she ventured.

Sarin's voice sounded muffled. Unnatural. As grey as the sky. 'Yes, I've never seen anything like it.'

Ash was looking about, half-dazed. 'I have,' he murmured. 'There were marmon.' Ordelle raised her brows at Sarin. *Seriously? Marmon?* She was about to point out how rare marmon were when Ash gave her the most peculiar smile. 'Don't worry, Ordelle. The river maiden is here. She will guide and protect us.' Ordelle let out a loud snort. She very much doubted that! Songs about river maidens all ended the same — with a drowned hero. Aechon's favourite featured a vain young prince, lured to his death by the watery nymph. River maidens, if they existed, were not to be trusted.

Ordelle was about to alert Ash to that fact when she noticed something even more alarming. The mist was crowding in, getting closer and thicker. Seeing required effort now. Everything was oppressive, grey. She grabbed the other boat, holding fast.

Sarin had become a shadowy form. Ordelle reached out her hand. It was a comfort to feel solid flesh beneath the weave of Sarin's sleeve. He jumped at her touch, but his voice was firm. 'We can't travel blind like this. Let's lash the boats together. We'll make for the shore ... just as soon as we can see one.' A coil of rope landed in Ordelle's lap, its tail whipping across her face. 'Tie that off. Wherever you can.'

Working blind, Ordelle lashed the rope around invisible cleats and clinched it tight. Trailing a hand in the water revealed nothing about their speed or position, only that they were drifting broadside. 'I think you should keep singing, kin,' muttered Sarin. Ordelle considered it unwise, but Ash nodded. The glimmer in his eyes was most unsettling.

The mist responded as soon as Ash resumed, swirling around him like a cloak. The song had a strange magic. Rising and falling, it was full of vowels and slides, light and ethereal. Ordelle had encountered nothing similar; Aechon would have been captivated.

With the mist playing about the boat, caressing them with ghostly fingers, Ordelle thought her mind was playing tricks on her. She was not a person given to wild fancies, not by any means. But she swore the vapours took on colours and the shape of creatures. Beasts with wings and fins, and luminescent dolphin-like creatures seemed to swim round them in rippling crests of sound.

Ordelle shook her head. Just figments wrought by her own imagination. And the radiance that played about the boat? That could be phosphorescence. Perhaps some tiny organism was giving off that turquoise glow. Ordelle cast her mind about for examples, but found none. Perhaps she was dreaming? Or hallucinating? Had they inadvertently eaten something strange? She was worrying about the wood mushrooms they had gathered the previous day when a shadow loomed without warning.

A shuddering jolt announced that the hull of her boat had met with the inevitable — a tree trunk.

Sarin cursed as both boats swung about, shunted into a spin. 'Telion, give us light! Ordelle! Are you taking water?'

'Yes.' She could hear it gushing, somewhere near the bow.

'Bear left, but gently! We'll make for the western shore.' The hesitation in Sarin's voice told her he was guessing.

Ordelle murmured her assent. It was a sound enough idea. Except that hitting something else seemed unavoidable. In no time, a second collision proved her correct. Not the bash of wood on wood this time — but the tearing of stone teeth scraping right along the hull.

Timbers splintered as Sarin swore, more loudly this time. The hull was breached.

The little boat filled faster than Ordelle expected. Abandoning the paddle, she probed the depths with her quarterstaff. Still too deep to stand. But her boat was sinking. Fast. Water sloshed about her boots. She preferred swimming to being dragged under by the wreckage — notwithstanding the wiles of the river maiden. 'I'm going to swim for it,' she shouted, her fingers working to release the ropes. Losing two boats served no purpose.

'Wait!' Sarin's voice was urgent over the confusion of splashing and bumping wood. 'Look! There's a light!'

It was true! There was a halo of light. Too low for the sun, it had to be on the shore. 'Paddle!' commanded Sarin. 'Paddle, Ordelle!' In a hectic panic, they paddled for the shore. Stone pylons appeared first, followed by the sharp edge of a dock, as the hazy light revealed its realm.

Ordelle wasted no time. Springing onto the nose of her sinking boat, she half-slipped and half-leapt from the wreckage. Rough stone claimed the skin of one knee as she tripped and fell. She banged her elbow and grazed the heel of her hand.

The others joined her moments later, having disembarked in a more controlled fashion. Sarin cleared his throat, probably to make some joke about them not being dead. He never got the words out. Two cloaked figures sprang from the haze. Tall, with high helms, and dressed all in grey. 'Halt, spies! In the name of the Temple!' The tip of a shining spear swung around to rest at Ordelle's throat. She frowned at its owner. What temple?

**9**

---

# HARDEN'S FOLLY

The coastal road was prettier than the main highway to Skarfell. It wandered through bushland, splashed with morning sunlight and the colours of spring. The honeyed fragrance of flowers and birdsong should have lifted Kep's mood as she travelled. They did nothing of the sort. She still had pirates to contend with. The return of their colourful clothes had only worsened the scoundrels' behaviour. Raucous and smelly, her unwanted associates were full of curses and rude remarks.

When they weren't belching or farting, the wretches spent their time boasting about all of the revolting things they'd done or — even worse to Kep's mind — planned to do, now that they were to be rich men. She detested hearing about the wenches they would tumble and the revenge they would exact for real or imagined slights.

The pirates weren't the only source of her irritation. There was Skarlon, too, and his pointless pre-dawn training sessions. Kep might have welcomed the gruelling hours of practice if he'd only let her handle a sword. Instead, he drilled her in the same sequences of the Dance of Blades, over and over until she met his exacting standards. Whatever they were!

For nothing Kep did was ever good enough for Skarlon. Not her breath, nor her stance. Nothing! Half the time she had no idea how to improve; he'd just bark at her to stop and do it again. Jen-Jay was a hard tutor, but Skarlon was a tyrant. Something about the man caused Kep to make mistake after mistake, messing up the simplest of moves. It didn't help that Jen-Jay insisted on rising early and would stand there watching, arms folded. She could never tell whether her captain's scowl of displeasure was down to her own poor performance or a critique of Skarlon's methods.

The early-morning training sessions had given the pirates something new to scoff at. The ball of anger in Kep's stomach burned more hotly as she recalled Greigo's clowning imitation of her swordplay. But perhaps his mockery was justified. She couldn't be Simbab if she couldn't handle a sword, could she? If it came to a fight with Bahjak's people, what part could Kep play in rescuing Jaibari and the others?

Caught up in her thoughts, Kep didn't notice that Berry was trotting faster, picking up on her rider's emotions. A snort from the mare finally pulled her back to the present. At once her anger dissolved, swept away by panic. She reined Berry in, her heart banging with fright. Riders! On the road ahead.

As the travellers came closer, Kep saw their steeds were large and powerful, with shaggy hooves. She sat straighter, remembering her training. *Take a breath and assess the threat. Details are everything.* Kep counted seven tall spears, one for each rider. Their shields were round, painted in green and red. Fighters, but not from Calkinon — that at least was a consolation.

Berry danced, whinnying and tossing her head. Her behaviour added to Kep's apprehension. Glancing over her shoulder, she saw an empty road stretching far behind. She could only blame herself. Adjusting her cloak, she made Jaibari's sword more visible. Not that she was planning to draw it. Not on horseback. She'd just injure herself or — even worse — Berry. Cursing her stupidity, she slowed the horse, wondering whether to circle back. The riders had reduced their pace to a walk, regrouping into a block.

They were all dressed in similar garb. They had no helmets, but wore leather armour and patches on their arms, green and red, with the same insignia as their shields. The private guard of a local lord, perhaps? The leaders were now close enough for Kep to read the expressions on their faces. Arrogance. And amusement to discover a young woman riding alone. 'Ho there!' one called out.

Kep's throat constricted as the riders now fanned out, blocking her way. Their smiles were wide and hungry. She swallowed, casting another look behind. The sight of the wagon crawling around the bend made her want to cry in relief. Within seconds, Skarlon and Twinkle came thundering towards them. The strangers' smiles faded.

Kep found her voice, once more able to breathe. 'Greetings. I hope you travel well?'

The man who seemed to be their leader had long grey hair, a hard muscular frame and an even harder mouth. His eyes raked over her in a frank assessment. 'A good day to you, young lady.' The flash of his teeth made her shiver. 'Do you travel to Merrywinds?' He seemed rather too interested in the answer for Kep's liking. Thankfully, at that moment Skarlon arrived in a cloud of dust, saving her from the need to reply.

The stranger's stallion snorted and reeled as his master jerked his head around. There was nothing remotely nice about the niceties that followed. The riders eyed the wagon and its colourful passengers with a hostile curiosity, made worse by obscene gestures on the part of the pirates. It was a relief when the group moved on. The leader trailed last, his narrowed gaze still fixed on Kep.

Skarlon joined Kep to ride side-by-side in the lead, and they resumed their journey. The old man's silent rebuke was worse than a verbal reprimand. Because he was right. Kep had been foolish to ride so far ahead, drawing the attention of those strangers. *Reckless*. That's what Sarin would have said. Kep frowned, adding another reason to be annoyed at herself. *Stop it. Stop thinking about Sarin.* But as much as she tried, she couldn't help it. Perhaps the saying was true — the heart yearns for what it cannot have.

By now Sarin would have collected his sister, Rilka, from the Aurum. Perhaps he had already returned to T'al Jazure? Kep didn't want to think about the hidden city either — it made her long for a soft bed and a hot bath. Stretching in her saddle to ease stiff muscles, she determined to stop tormenting herself with thoughts of things she couldn't have. That was the problem with horseback riding. It left *far* too much time for thinking.

Kep expected they would stop soon, before the horses grew too tired. Nothing could hurry a trundling wagon. The break would give them another chance to question the pirates about Split Apple Cove and Bahjak's smuggling operation. Thus far, they had scant information. Sulky and unco-operative, the pirates remained tight-lipped. At first Kep had blamed Skarlon for treating the conversations as interrogations. Now she wondered if the men were hiding something.

They had interviewed Creely first. With his blue frock coat, crimson waistcoat and purple tricorne hat, the man dressed more like an eccentric nobleman than a pirate — a somewhat grubby nobleman. He wore his beard in three braids, interspersed with silver beads. Empty holes pierced his ears; his gold confiscated in Bixdale, as compensation.

Creely had served eight years on the *Lady Lee*. Nevertheless, he shrugged elaborately at all questions about the ship and its location. He'd never been to the cove and knew nothing of Bahjak. 'It's not for me to say' was his favourite response. Kep felt sure he was concealing something. But what?

Now, as Kep shifted again in her saddle, Skarlon broke his silence. 'We'll be stopping soon. Curly claims there's a waterhole not far from here.' He threw her a sideways glance before clearing his throat. 'Which pirate do you want to question next?'

Kep blinked, surprised he was giving her the choice. She thought for a moment before deciding. 'I want to have another go at Ratskin.'

Skarlon frowned. 'Reckon that lad's an idiot.'

The enormous lump of a boy reminded Kep of a large potato — that someone had cleaned by rubbing it on their shirt. Ratskin never spoke, and his friend Spike never shut up. 'I know, but ... I'd like to speak to the boys again. Together this time. And ... on my own. They might let something slip.' She glanced at her companion, unsure how he'd take it.

Skarlon's growl suggested he was about to refuse. Then the side of his face twitched, making the stars jump. He gave a curt nod. 'I suppose it's worth a try.'

Ratskin and Spike were as unlikely a pair as you could ever hope to meet. Kep estimated Spike was a year or so younger than she was. He reminded her of Ash, perhaps because his body was so thin beneath his shirt. The resemblance ended there. It wasn't just his nose that was sharp. He had the eyes of a street urchin, missing nothing, on the lookout for danger or a quick opportunity.

Where the rest of the pirates wore bright colours, Ratskin and Spike were dowdy, as if it suited them better to be overlooked. Curly said the boys had met on the streets of Mandish, becoming inseparable. Both lads were awestruck by the legend of T'al Kep — again, according to Curly. Kep didn't know whether that would help or hinder her cause. Ratskin had shrunk into the layers of his curious garments, his head low, hands trapped between his knees. His eyes were intent on the ground between his feet.

Kep decided to begin with easy questions about the ship. 'How did you boys end up on the *Lady Lee*?'

'Cribben game.' Spike tugged at his ear, then scratched at his head. 'I mean: It was a Cribben game, Kep-Váli.'

'Is that cards?'

'That's right. Me an' Ratskin was won. By Curly.'

'What?' Kep sat up straighter, arching her brows.

Misreading the reason for her surprise, Spike tried to put her straight. 'That was back when he was captain of the *Lady Lee*. Captain Laggart, he was all out of gold, you see. He thought he held the cards. 'Cept he only had a cup and two crowns.'

'You were the wager in a card game?' Kep felt weak with shock.

Spike's grin split his face, revealing a couple of missing teeth. 'Yep. Three gold cups! That was a right good hand that Curly held. Wasn't it, Rats?' Ratskin bobbed his head in confirmation. 'A fine day for us lads, too. The *Lady Lee* is a pearler of a ship, Kep-Váli. An' Curly treated us better than ol' Laggart ever did.' Spike looked wistful as he scratched at the side of his nose with a fingernail. He tilted his head to look at her. 'Is it true, Kep-Váli? Is Curly gonna get his ship back?'

Kep blew out her cheeks and rubbed at the back of her neck, disturbed to discover she'd struck a bargain with a man who accepted the lives of boys to settle a card game. 'Do you want that?'

'Reckon so. *Curly's* a fair captain.' Spike looked over at Ratskin, and the larger boy nodded, his eyes quick and brown. More like a mouse than a rat.

Despite the promising start, Kep gleaned very little information from the pair. Ratskin said nothing — he just fidgeted, tapping the side of his knee with his fingers. Spike wouldn't discuss the other pirates. He seemed to be following some code of loyalty. When she asked about Yulia, he gave a secretive smile, shrugged and wriggled his fingers. The mention of Bahjak was worse. The lad froze and wouldn't say another word. And that, it seemed, was that.

That afternoon, they camped near the trail. Discouraged by her lack of progress with Spike and Ratskin, Kep let Skarlon resume the inquisition on his own. The woodland looked promising for hunting, so she picked up her bow, leaving Jen-Jay to supervise Creely building a fire. As she walked away, she heard Jen-Jay explaining, for the third time, which materials made the best kindling. It would be more efficient if she just did it herself, a fact Creely was no doubt playing on. Kep rolled her eyes at his pathetic performance. A toddler would pick it up more quickly.

Skarlon was overseeing Tibbs and Rawlins as they rubbed down the horses — the largest pirate paired with the smallest. Kep could tell the horses didn't trust Tibbs, and nor did she. His nervous energy made her uncomfortable, that and the way he stared at her. With red hair and a beard to match, the man had wild blue eyes below a red bandana. Quick with a taunt, Tibbs considered himself the joker of the group. Kep didn't think he was funny at all; a view that others clearly shared. Earlier, one of his remarks had earned him a cuff from Rawlins that was hard enough to knock him sideways.

With distance between herself and the campsite, Kep unwrapped her bow. She smoothed her fingers over its shapely form, appreciating the carvings. Falcons. Matching the tattoo on her arm. How many hours had Sarin spent making it for her? He'd kept the bow a secret, then, taking off without so much as a word, he'd left Ash to deliver the gift. Could there be a more peculiar person? Kep couldn't hunt without being reminded of him, which she found irritating and comforting all at once. Her feelings were so complicated where Sarin was concerned.

Loud shouting from the direction of the campsite made Kep sigh. Pirates! The ruckus would frighten any game away. As if to illustrate the point, several birds flew off, wings clacking. She shook her head. Somebody must have found a snake. Or a lizard that looked like a snake. The pirates' distress in the wilderness never failed to surprise her. For tough men, they were pathetic when faced by woodland creatures.

Spiders caused the loudest fuss of all. The previous evening, one had crawled out from beneath Rawlin's cloak. Kep had never heard such squealing and seen such flapping. The spider was quite large and hairy, and it had set them all dancing. Kep had to prevent them stomping the poor thing to death. They had watched in wide-eyed disbelief when she intervened and rescued the creature, placing it on a nearby tree.

The pirates hadn't an inkling of how to move stealthily, either. Somebody was crashing about now, off to Kep's left. Grinding her teeth, she prowled deeper into the bush. Any creature with sense would now have gone to ground. But she refused to give in. This was *her* time, a precious escape from the pressure of being Simbab.

Kep loathed the whole charade — especially when it involved the gods. Curly and the others had convinced her to conduct her rites of worship in view of the pirates. *Kep-Váli communing with her gods.* It shouldn't have bothered her. Worship honoured the gods, whether public or private. But it felt ... *dishonourable.* And it didn't fool Greigo for a minute. He still saw the slave girl.

Coming across a fern-fringed creek, she slowed. Creatures would gather here to drink. Searching for a suitable hiding place, she discovered some tracks, pushed deep into the clay. Shaped like two pears kissing, the hoof marks were large — very large. With wide eyes, Kep scanned the area for further signs. When she spotted a tree rubbed clean of its bark, her heart pounded a little faster. Somewhere along the creek, the creature would have a wallow. It was far too dangerous to linger.

Kep moved as quickly as she dared. Stumbling across the den of a cave hog would invite the hand of Argess. She needed to return and alert the others. Nobody should wander from the camp tonight. As she retraced her steps, she heard a curious noise. Subhuman, it rose in pitch, becoming a warble of terror. Kep rounded, pinpointing its origin. Running low to the ground, she peered through the trees.

Harden was impossible to miss — ridiculously out of place, with his garish shirt, bright blue breeches and wispy hair. The man was standing stock-still, frozen in mid-step. The idiot had blundered towards the mouth of the cave hog's den, oblivious to the warning signs.

Kep winced as the creature stepped out of the shadows. The warty boar sported four wicked tusks. Cave hogs didn't have wonderful eyesight, but this one stared straight at the pirate with mean, beady eyes. Taking a step forward, it snuffed at the air. Then it snorted through flared nostrils, stamping at the ground. An obvious threat. To Kep's horror, Harden just stood there, paralysed.

What was he playing at? The creature was about to attack! As the hog dipped its head, Kep let out a shout. 'Climb! Climb, you idiot!' She was already scrambling up the nearest tree. Just a sapling, it swayed beneath her weight, but the branches held. Thanking Argess, she climbed higher, to avoid being skewered when the creature charged — which it would at any moment.

Bracing feet and shoulders in a fork of branches, Kep reached back for an arrow, then changed her mind. A single arrow wouldn't stop a hog of that size. Harden still hadn't moved! She shouted down to him. 'Get up the tree, Harden! Hurry!'

It was excruciating to watch. Round of belly and far from athletic, the pirate simply wasn't built for climbing trees. He leapt for a branch, missed, and slipped over in the mud. Squealing with fear, he tried to shimmy up the trunk. That proved equally hopeless. His belly got in the way as his boots scrabbled for purchase. At last, with a quivering moan, he gave up. He just cowered there, behind the trunk, hands interlaced over the top of his balding head. What was he thinking? You couldn't hide from an angry cave hog!

The hog snorted in earnest now, infuriated by the peculiar antics of the strange creature that dared to invade its territory. It danced sideways, tearing up the ground with its hooves. 'Hey! Hey!' shouted Kep. Trying to distract the creature, she ripped a branch from the sapling and tossed it to the ground. The boar ignored it.

Now fear panicked Harden into action. Realising that the tree was no defence, he ran. The portly pirate was all flapping arms and bouncing belly. He hurdled fallen branches, wailing and screaming as he went. It would have been hilarious, except that he was bound to die.

Cave hogs have two curved tusks for goring and two short, stabbing ones. Kep had seen the remains of creatures savaged by such tusks. Soft pirate flesh wouldn't fare well. She needed to act. In a flash, she drew her knife. The young warrior yelled as she swung down from the tree. 'Leave him!' Three strides took her into the path of the enraged animal. The strange blade that Ash had taken from Credé's hut glowed green in her hand. Kep felt the weapon's eagerness to obey. It left her hand with a surge of energy, guided by the strength of her will. She sensed its flight, like a sizzling bolt in her mind. And felt its impact.

The knife hit the hog right between its eyes, plunging through the skull and deep into the creature's brain. The boar squealed. For a horrible moment, it kept coming, carried forward by momentum. Then it skidded to a stop, landing scarily close, legs splayed beneath its hairy bulk.

Fumbling to draw her sword, Kep charged, intending to drive the blade into the creature's heart. No need. The hog's body was already twitching, convulsing in its death throes. Its fearsome mouth stretched wide in a grimace of death. Kep drew the blade across the animal's neck instead, letting the blood flow. Dropping to her knees, she bowed her head, bringing her thumbs to the sides of her face to form the sign of the triangle. *All thanks to Argess.*

By the time Harden had gathered his wits, Kep had made a long incision. The knife sliced through the tough hide as if it were silk. She removed the steaming liver, her arms already painted with blood. Pausing her inspection of the organ, she looked up at the astonished pirate.

Harden was gaping at her, the skin on his forehead forming perplexed folds. Kep saw a mixture of horror and something akin to awe dawning on his face. 'It'll make the body lighter,' she explained, easing her hands around the warm guts and spilling them onto the ground. 'The meat's clean but we're losing the light.' Harden's eyes went wider, his jaw sagging. She frowned. Had he lost his wits? 'We'll need the others to help carry it.' She wrinkled her nose, an itch tormenting her. She rubbed her nose against her biceps. 'Harden? Can you find your way back to the camp?'

The pirate didn't answer. To her complete surprise, he let out a cry and dropped to one knee. He grasped her bloodied hand, lifted it to his lips, and kissed it. Kep was so shocked she nearly pulled her hand away. Harden tried to speak, but words had forsaken the man. He sobbed, his eyes swimming with tears. At last, still not releasing her hand, he blurted a single word. 'Simbab!'

# 10

## TALES AT THE FIRESIDE

'And there I was. Minding my own business. Just about to *do* my business, if you get my meaning.'

Kep rolled her eyes as the words drifted over to her ears. Harden's embellishments were getting wilder with every repetition. The pirates' guffaws went up into the night sky like sparks from the campfire. Kep recognised their individual laughs now. Curly's was a childlike hoot. Tibbs had a high-pitched giggle, while Creely hissed and spluttered between his teeth. Rawlins didn't laugh at all. At least Kep had ever heard him. Harden affected an indignant tone as he addressed his audience. 'Just looking for a quiet place to have a shit. That's all a man asks in life!'

Kep shook her head. The back steps of the wagon were broad and surprisingly comfortable. Her belly was taut, stuffed full of roasted boar — a little too full, to be honest. She made a mental note to keep an eye out for mint as they travelled. If they were going to eat pork at every meal, peppermint tea would be just the thing.

Stretching her shoulders and ignoring the sounds of more hilarity from the fireside, Kep sensed movements in the canopy. Caught in the light of the lanterns, a pair of bats flitted into sight. They performed an acrobatic dance as they snatched at bugs, and then were gone again, like figments of her imagination.

When Jen-Jay approached, bearing two mugs, Kep shifted over to make room. She was relieved and a little apprehensive when the older woman settled herself down — they hadn't spoken since dawn. Jen-Jay was yet to comment on Kep's sulky manners that morning, and her reckless behaviour on the road.

Kep wrapped her fingers around the hot mug, inhaling its steamy breath. 'I think this is the fourth telling.'

Jen-Jay shook her head. 'Fifth at least. Damn fool is lucky to be alive to tell it, that's certain. Tough pirates they might be, but they're as innocent as babes in the woods. What sort of idiot walks into a boar's den?'

Kep grinned. 'I think the boar was as surprised as Harden was. Maybe that's why it took so long to charge. I'm guessing it had never seen a pirate.'

Jen-Jay sniffed, a smile lurking in the corner of her grimace. 'Certainly not one wearing blue britches and a stripy orange shirt.'

Harden's voice rose again, this time high and with an imperious ring. '*Leave him! This man is under my protection!*'

Jen-Jay raised an eyebrow and cocked her head. 'Really? You said *that?*'

Kep scowled. 'Of course not!'

'Well, you can add another admirer to your list, that's clear enough. I can't see Harden crossing you now. And the others seem quite impressed, too. A bellyful of pork goes a long way.'

Kep shrugged, taking a sip of tea. As the silence between them deepened, she noticed Jen-Jay eyeing her falcon, the tattoo on her left forearm. Sarin had designed it especially to hide her slave marks. She sighed. *Sarin.* In her thoughts again. Whenever Jen-Jay looked at her tattoo, a wistful look would come over her. Kep frowned, wondering at the root of her sadness. Jen-Jay's whole body seemed to speak of it. The woman caught her eye, and the impression was gone — her shields back up.

Jen-Jay finished her tea and set the mug on the lower step with a firm bang. 'The gods certainly throw danger in your way, girl.' She sniffed. 'That knife of yours. I supposed it's Azuran-made?' The knife had been Credé's. Brought to T'al Agria from a different dimension, according to Ash. Whatever *that* meant. Credé and his brother had experimented with a forbidden craft, a method of creating objects that obeyed the mind. The misdemeanour had caused the brothers' exile from T'al Jazure. At least that was the theory. But the memories Ash drew from the Taelstone always seemed to result in more mysteries than answers. Kep felt a swift stab of worry for her friend. She'd rather face a charging cave hog than delve into the Malshorne's memories.

Jen-Jay was still waiting for an answer. 'Yes. The knife is Azuran, or … something like that.' Jen-Jay nodded thoughtfully. Kep was glad that she didn't push for further information. The less said about the secrets she and her friends had uncovered in T'al Jazure, the better.

The two women sat in silence for a while, listening to night sounds. From the direction of where the horses were tethered came the velvet stamp of a hoof and the slow rhythm of munching. Now and then, one of the shadowy beasts would lift its head, hold them in slow regard, then return to its grazing.

Jen-Jay breathed out a sigh, heavy with resignation. 'It's my turn to tell a story.' Kep blinked, taken aback. Not once, in all their time together, had Jen-Jay told her a story. 'You must promise to listen carefully, and pay heed.' Kep nodded solemnly. So, as the stars above grew brighter, Jen-Jay began her tale.

There once was a girl. Perhaps at one time she had been small and sweet. At the point when this story starts, that was no longer the case. For the girl was a slave, and slaves cannot afford to be sweet. Nobody knows who captured her, nor what happened to her people. Her home could have been one of many places — the shores of Skavia are only the most recent of Calkinon's conquests. Whatever the case, the little girl arrived on our shores in chains and, in the slave markets of Idira, was sold.

The unfortunate child's new master, as the story goes, was none other than Oster Val-Breiken. A terrible man by every account, Val-Breiken had a particular fondness for slaves. He owned over five thousand, employing them at his seat in the West Haven downs and on his many estates across the Marchlands. The man's great wealth was eclipsed only by the tales of his cruelty.

None of Val-Breiken's slaves could hope to live long. But the little girl had deft fingers and an even quicker mind. Obedient and silent, she became the favourite of the cellar master. Despairing that little girls must eventually turn into young women, he sheared her hair close to her head, dressed her in long aprons and concealed her dainty features with deep-hooded bonnets. There, among the aging barrels, she remained. Until, one terrible day, the inevitable happened.

It came to pass that Oster Val-Breiken had caught a powerful thirst while crossing his estates. He ordered his carriage to turn down into his vineyards, through the golden vines, so he might indulge in his favourite wines. Barrels were tapped, bottles were uncorked and wine was duly poured. The girl in our story was as sensible as she was pretty. She kept to the shadows as the cellar master brought out bottle after dusty bottle, praying that the high lord might drink himself into a stupor — as was his wont. Alas, all was in vain. At last, with a sly look, Val-Breiken plonked his tasting goblet on the table. 'I desire more.'

The cellar master gave a nervous laugh. "But, Sire ... you have sampled everything. There is only the fresh vintage left. It is too young to be palatable, Sire."

Oster Val-Breiken just laughed, waggling a knowing finger. "And yet ... I desire more." Beckoning the man closer, he whispered terrible words in his servant's ear.

'The little cellar maid was ushered forward. How she must have trembled beneath her master's hungry gaze. 'What is your name, pretty one?'

A sob escaped the wretched cellar man. 'She is mute, Sire! If she has a name, she has never uttered it.'

Oster Val-Breiken licked his lips. 'A woman without words. What a delight!' He clapped his hands. 'I will take her. And give thought to a suitable name. A pretty young thing must have a name to match. Don't just stand there, man. Have the slave taken to my carriage. And pour me more wine!'

The young girl must have been frightened. The dark thoughts beneath her master's throaty chuckle were all too easy to discern. Had she been able to speak, this was her moment to beg. But she kept her silence. The cellar man bowed his head. 'As you command, my lord. Gather your things, child.'

Perhaps Oster Val-Breiken should have read the danger signs. For which slave has things to gather? But wine and desire had fuddled his wits. He staggered to his waiting carriage, where the slave girl awaited him. In his diminished state he was unaware that silence could be as sharp as a knife. And although the little maid sat opposite him in the hurrying carriage, he missed the flash of hatred in her eyes. Nor did he note how her apron pocket bulged. He was too drunk, too greedy and too blind. Oblivious, he leered and then nodded off, lulled by the swaying of the carriage.

On awakening with a start and then entering his gilded villa, the lord sent his attendants away, all the better to enjoy the fresh novelty of his mute little guest. Imagine his surprise when, instead of welcoming his caresses, she pounced! A barrel-tapping spike has no preference for the colour of the wine, nor the vintage — it is just as happy to tap a rich man's jugular. The lord's blood gushed out of him like a fountain, dousing the floor.

The servants paid no heed to the commotion at first. It took several moments to recognise the shrieks coming from their master's chambers as belonging to Val-Breiken himself. Afterwards they would tell of bursting into the chamber to see a dark mass swirling about the pair. That, and the fell light which shone in the little slave's eyes.

The young girl, however, was unafraid of the shadowy forms that issued from her master's throat, writhing like eels. For she didn't fear the darkness — she embraced it as her own. As Lord Val-Breiken gasped his final breath, she looked into his eyes. 'I *have* a name,' she told him. 'My mother called me Kara.'

The girl spread her arms as the cloud of darkness whirled around her. Her voice grew louder and more terrible. 'But that child is dead. I am forged anew. My name is Vengeance. My name is Death. Tell that to the bullies. The oppressors. The tormentors of the innocent. Tell them! And let them tremble. For I am Kara-fell!'

Kep ran her tongue around her gums. Her mouth tasted stale. During the telling of the story, her muscles had tensed, her toes recoiling inside her boots. The night sounds were more ominous now that Jen-Jay had fallen silent. The gentle chorus of croaking frogs seemed to warn of danger. Marki, the smallest moon, hung like a bright scythe in the sky. Silver-edged, it looked too beautiful to be real. But clouds gathered in the west — before long, they would swallow the moonlight.

Kep broke the silence between them. 'She was a slave then.'

'Yes. A slave. By most accounts, Kara was just twelve years old when she spilt the blood of her master. That was some twenty years ago.' *Twelve winters!* Kep closed her eyes, trying to comprehend the horror.

'The story always ends at the point of Val-Breiken's death. Little is known about events thereafter. Many believe the servants protected little Kara; that, overjoyed by their cruel master's death, they enabled her escape. Nobody could have foreseen the consequences of such an action.'

'And the darkness? The swirling mass at the end of the story? It was ... ?' Kep faltered, dreading the answer.

Jen-Jay nodded. 'The Melk. The League had been alerted to the cruelty of Oster Val-Breiken and had him under watch. But our warriors came too late. The Melk had exchanged its host for another

— a nexus of far greater potential, it has to be said. Kara-fell was born from a hatred that knows no bounds. She didn't just kill in anger, she dedicated her life, her whole being, to vengeance. And she has exacted it. Slaving ships, wealthy merchants, captains of Calkinon. All have fallen to her dread hand. At first her victims were indeed the bullies and the tormentors of the weak. But evil breeds evil, Kep. Power breeds corruption, and the Melk has a dark energy of its own.'

Kep was motionless. Eventually she spoke, her voice small. 'Are you telling me this because *I* was a slave?'

Jen-Jay frowned, but the shake of her head lacked conviction. 'The story is a warning to every one of us. We must never forget that Kara-fell began as a young slave girl, torn from her family, ripped away from her lands. That is what makes the League's work so terrible. Evil people are not born, Kep. They are forged through misery, pain and fear.'

Kep gave a slow nod of her head. She understood. But the story still seemed aimed at her. She knew her mentor was worried about the growing legend of Kep-Váli. She frowned. Did Jen-Jay really think that Kep could become as evil as Kara-fell? It was laughable.

Battling with complex emotions, Kep took a deep breath. She needed to talk about something else. *Anything* else. Her fingertips found the bird tattooed on her arm, stroking its feathers. 'What does it remind you of? My falcon?' Avoiding eye contact, she addressed the trees. They were as likely to answer as the woman at her side. 'I see how you look at it, Jen-Jay. Why does it make you sad?' Her words tripped on her tongue. 'Is it ... Do you think a falcon is wrong for me?'

Jen-Jay looked up. The set of her jaw convinced Kep that her guess was right. The woman *was* upset about her choice. A surge of annoyance swept over her. It was *her* skin. And *her* tattoo. Wearing a bird on your arm was far preferable to the brand that marked you as somebody's property! Falcons were fierce hunters, but, above all, they were free. Jen-Jay would never understand that. How could she? She had never been enslaved. 'Tell me. What's so wrong with my tattoo?' Her anger made the question more intense than she intended.

Jen-Jay's eyes fluttered closed. The muscles in her neck were taut, her mouth a thin line. 'It's not wrong.' Opening her eyes, the old warrior turned her head to meet the eyes of her young companion. 'I don't think that. It was a good choice. In some ways it was the perfect choice.' Her words sounded both bitter and sad at the same time.

Kep scowled, not in the mood for riddles. 'What is it, then?'

Jen-Jay narrowed her eyes at the tone. Then she relented. 'As soon as I saw that tattoo, I knew. Against my wishes, against my very *judgement*, I knew I had to train you. The falcon was a sign from the gods that couldn't be ignored.' Kep's eyes widened as Jen-Jay blinked rapidly and looked away. 'I couldn't let it happen. Not again.'

Kep was more confused than ever. Let *what* happen? If she didn't know better, she could have sworn there were tears in Jen-Jay's eyes. 'What does the falcon remind you of?'

'Him.' Jen-Jay sighed. 'It reminds me of him. My son.' Kep's heart caught. She felt sick, regretting the question that couldn't be unspoken. 'You remind me of my son, Kep. There. It is said. You've always reminded me of him. From the moment I laid eyes on you. It's your passion. Your sense of justice. And your energy. If I seem upset when I look at that design, it is because you remind me so much of Davy.'

Kep didn't dare speak, for fear Jen-Jay would clam up again. And besides, she couldn't find the words. It was too strange to think of Jen-Jay being a *mother*. Kep couldn't imagine her being anything other than Grey Wolf, the legendary warrior. At last, she found her voice. 'Davy? Was that his name? Your ... son?'

Jen-Jay pursed her lips in pain. 'Yes. A farmer's name. And that was what he was, at heart. What we all were. Before the Melk. Before the League.'

Kep reeled as her mind caught up. 'Your son was a League warrior?'

Jen-Jay nodded. 'A falcon. He wore the symbol on his upper arm.'

The falcon jinn no longer existed. But nobody had told Kep why. 'What happened?' She felt cruel asking, but compelled to learn the truth.

'Davy died. A long time ago.'

Kep pressed a hand to her lips, wishing she had known. Jen-Jay tilted her face to study the sky, as if seeking stars among the gathering clouds. 'He was killed. Two blue-shafted arrows. Straight through his heart.' Kep drew a sharp breath. Jen-Jay nodded at her wide-eyed shock. 'Yes. Identical to the one in your quiver.'

Daska! Kep struggled to speak. 'Did Daska kill … ?'

Jen-Jay shook her head. 'No. The arrows belong to Daska now. That is true.' Her expression was curiously impassive. 'But it was Nirias. Nirias killed my son.'

Kep gulped. Things she'd been unable to understand now became horribly clear. *This* was the shadow that lay between Nirias and Grey Wolf!

Jen-Jay scowled, watching Kep put the pieces together. 'Very well. Since you've dragged it into the light. I will tell you the story. Once, and *not* in its entirety. And you must promise never to ask me again.' Kep nodded, swallowing. She had no wish to inflict such pain.

So, for the second time that evening, Jen-Jay began her tale. 'The story is not unique. My family were farmers, in the province of Fingel. An unremarkable place — barely meriting a footnote in the histories of the south. Our village had its problems, as all places do, but there was no real strife; that is, not until the coming of the Melk. I won't speak of the destruction that was wreaked … nor the blood that was shed.' Jen-Jay's profile hardened with her voice. 'All you need to know is that the conflict brought Nirias into our lives. He and his warriors swept in like avenging birds. And afterwards, when it was done, we followed him. What other choice was there? We had lost our homes and the people we loved. The League gave us purpose — a way to forget.

'Davy adored Nirias, right from the beginning.' Jen-Jay let out a tiny grunt of annoyance. 'Like you, the boy did nothing by halves. He trained and he fought, and he loved. Physically, he became a man. But he was broken inside, and full of anger. The code didn't sit well with my impulsive son. He couldn't see why the League should not fight injustice *wherever* they found it. He was too young. And too passionate.' Kep caught the meaning of the pointed look the old warrior shot her. *Just like you.* 'Nirias sent him out on missions anyway. Because that's what Nirias does.'

Jen-Jay sighed, as if wanting the tale over. 'It was after the siege of Lamont.' Kep caught her breath. The name of Lamont was synonymous with horror. The Calkinon masters brought the rebel city to account. They demanded retribution, in the form of children's eyeballs. Kep swallowed, her chest constricting. The Melk's darkness had fuelled those evil events.

'It happened on a day of terror and confusion. Without a senseer, the League couldn't identify the nexus — not for certain. Davy had been undercover for months, with several others of his jinn. That was a grave mistake, because unbeknown to anyone the boy had fallen in love.' Jen-Jay shook her head. 'I never knew the details. It was complicated. But things ended in the worst possible way. Davy burst from his lover's house, drenched in blood, twirling his swords and screaming vengeance. And Nirias ...' Jen-Jay's fists were a knotted ball in her lap. 'Nirias didn't hesitate. Believing my son was consumed by the Melk, he let his arrows fly.' Kep clamped a hand over her mouth, too horrified for words.

'Many years later, Daska sought me out. He was worried. About Nirias. He told me about the dark years after Davy's death, the period when Nirias disappeared. You know already that Sarin's people took him in. That the Aurum nursed him back to health.

'At first, I wouldn't listen to Daska's pleading. The death of my son had broken my heart. What I didn't realise was that it broke something in Nirias, too. Daska begged me to return to the League. For years I refused — the gods know I had little wish to fight again. In the end he convinced me of the danger. T'al Jazure had been found and neither of us knew what that meant for Nirias or the League.' Jen-Jay grimaced. 'Who better to watch over Nirias than Grey Wolf, the woman who understood the risks more deeply than any?'

Jen-Jay fixed Kep with a hard look. 'So, now you know. We will not speak of this again.' At that moment, loud exclamations erupted from the fireplace. Both women turned their attention towards the commotion.

With the story of Harden's hog squeezed dry, the pirates had moved on to a farting competition. A thunderous bark caused more jeering and hooting. In spite of everything, Kep felt a surge of laughter welling inside her.

Jen-Jay rolled her eyes. 'Pirates!' She hauled herself to her feet and picked up her quarterstaff. 'The fools will set fire to their breeches at this rate!'

Kep hid a grin, relieved that her gruff little mentor was back. Turning her face to the west, she took a deep sniff of the air. 'Smells like rain. We should get things under cover.'

Jen-Jay's chuckle was dry and wicked. 'Go on then, Kep-Váli. Give the orders. Be sure to tell them the message came directly from Argess.'

Kep pulled a face. 'That's not funny.'

11
______

# CREDE'S OATH

Ash rubbed at his thumbnails, struggling to reconcile the austere prison cell with the water-coloured beauty of the river maiden's song. Tucking his hands under his armpits, he hugged his legs closer to his chest, trying to get warm. He wore every garment he owned and still he shivered.

The cave-like cell was small and window-less. Corrosion and salty residue encrusted its ancient bars. The iron gleamed with a greenish hue under the sickly light. Everything was clammy here, including the single wooden bench Ash was sharing with Ordelle. The chamber was empty, aside from the bench and a couple of buckets.

Their captors had marched them here at spear-point, the captives staggering blindly over the moss-covered stone. Any stumbles had earned a prod from the butt of a weapon. Even Sarin had finally given up asking questions now, along with his exhortations that they were not spies. The only form of communication had been the thrust of the guards' spears. And now, this. A cage.

The two sentries watching from beyond the bars might as well have been statues. Despite Sarin's various attempts at negotiation — from arguments to pleading to angry taunts — they remained silent and impeccably still. They wore identical grey outfits, and long silvery cloaks. Their helmets were silver, too, with sharp-beaked nose-guards. Bird wings over each brow lent the wearers a stern countenance. Their shining breastplates depicted a bird in flight, encircled by stars. Ash suspected they were female, but he couldn't be certain.

The Keeper of the Song sank his face into his hands. They were supposed to be rescuing Kep from a cage, not putting themselves in one. Then his ears caught an eerie mewling, and he opened his eyes, lifting his head. The sound rose and fell, like the whimpering of an abandoned puppy. It called to him, stirring up complicated emotions. 'What's that?' His voice came out in a throaty rasp. 'What's that noise?'

Sarin sat on the ground nearby, his shoulders wedged against the hard curve of the cell wall. Only Sarin could have made it look comfortable. He angled his head to listen. 'It's gulls. They'll have nests on the cliffs.' He smiled. 'Unless you're referring to the background surge. That, my friend, is the song of the sea.'

Ordelle hadn't taken her attention off the guards. Now she turned. 'It is a reason to be hopeful. If we are close to the sea, we are closer to finding Kep.'

Sarin nodded. 'Exactly.' Dropping his voice to a murmur, he leaned forward. 'My guess is we're in a holding cell. At some point, somebody more important will come to investigate the so-called "spies". That will be our chance to plead our case.' His mouth quirked. 'Or escape and steal a boat.' He looked over at the guards. 'If only I could get at my bow.' Their captors had confiscated every weapon they carried, including the knife hidden in Sarin's boot.

Keeping their voices low, Sarin and Ordelle speculated about where the boats were kept, with Ordelle pointing out the perils of navigating in the Mistlands. Ash had nothing to contribute. The matter was hypothetical. Without knowing where they were, it seemed pretty hopeless. He frowned at himself and sighed. He missed Kep. But he knew what his friend would say: sinking into despair was the last thing anybody needed.

But this place disturbed him. It was the gulls, even more than the bars and the guards. Their melancholy cries recalled haunting melodies with slow, surging rhythms. Desperate to distract himself, Ash removed his boots and squeezed the water from his socks. His toes looked like soggy grey prunes. He rubbed them for a while, before wrestling his wet socks back on and lacing up his boots.

They'd agreed they needed to keep up their strength, so he nibbled at a chunk of hard bread. When Tarlyn pushed onto his lap, he offered her a sliver of dried venison. She didn't even bother to sniff it, so he popped it into his own mouth instead. He should have known better than to offer her anything dead. He stroked her head as he chewed, comforted by the warmth of her presence.

After a moment, Tarlyn resumed prowling around the cell. Ash frowned and stopped chewing to watch her. She usually assumed an air of bored watchfulness. Her manner today was very different. She slunk along the walls, her ears flat against her head. Did Tarlyn find the sound of the gulls unsettling, too?

Their cries called again. *Hear, oh hear, my tale of woe, a man who loved too...* The sensation of falling brought Ash back to himself with a jolt. Stabs of prickling panic assaulted him. *Not here. It couldn't happen here.* Jumping up from the bench, he stretched out his arms, pretending to ease his cramped muscles. The others ignored him. They were too busy tracing an imaginary map on the ground and running through escape plans. A surge of helplessness swept over him. *It's useless. No,* corrected a voice inside his head. *You're the one who's useless.* It was true. He should have been able to help. He was the Keeper of the Song, after all.

Ash had realised a long time ago that the Song worked like a map. That its stories and songs were intrinsically connected to places in the world. A trained taelstaun could have determined their whereabouts by connecting to the Song. But Ash didn't dare to try. Just thinking about it made his anxiety worse. He licked his lips, feeling the rock walls close in around him. His heart pattered wildly. *Pull yourself together.*

Taking a deep breath, he held it for six counts. Ignoring the pulsing in his ears, he let it out for eight. He was halfway through a second breath when a thought jumped into his head. *Credé*. Before he could finish the full sequence of breaths, he knew he would try. It was worth the risk.

Settling in the shadows against the back of the cell, Ash reached into his cloak. He cradled the orb in his hands, inhaling deeply. Credé might have travelled here during his long life. The Taelstone could hold some memory of this place. What was the worst that could happen? Ash shivered, not wanting to contemplate the answer.

The Taelstone sprang to life, welcoming his touch. The cell offered little in the way of triggers, apart from the distant sound of gulls, and he didn't dare dwell on that. Then a thought struck him. Perhaps his captors held a clue. He stared at the guards' helmets and the insignia on their breastplates, trying to imprint details on his mind. With a quiver of dread, he closed his eyes. Letting his focus slip, he reached out for the Malshorne's memories ...

The stench hit Ash first. Odious, laced with salt and stagnant water. The smell of despair. The walls sweated with a cold sheen under the light of torches strapped against stone. Water ran in gutters on either side, accompanied by the occasional rat.

Credé was moving with urgency through a labyrinth of tunnels. His feet splashed, disturbing the lurking puddles. Ash shivered. Something felt off about this memory. The boots seemed heavy and too coarsely made. The motion was peculiar, too. He lumbered along, his breath coming in loud, wheezing gasps. The shadow he cast was huge and wide-shouldered. In short, everything about the Malshorne felt wrong.

When he reached a recessed gate, Credé stopped to raise his torch, peering into a crudely hewn cell. Nothing. Just empty shackles chained to the wall and a couple of rats gnawing at bones. Ash shuddered, his own horror intermingling with the Malshorne's. What *was* this place?

A chained gate barred the end of the stone passage. Credé

propped his torch against the bars, and grappled with the set of keys attached to his belt. With a sense of shock, Ash noticed his wrists were thick and hairy; nothing at all like Credé's. Not only that, but one stubby finger was missing. After a short struggle, the gate clanged open, and the journey continued.

Ash sensed a wave of desperation as the Malshorne hurried toward a door at the very end of the passage. He flipped the door's wooden shutter and peered through the peephole. Then, bellowing like an animal, he attacked the door, flinging it wide.

The lantern's pale light revealed high cheekbones and gleaming, silver-blonde hair. Next to the body lay a battered plate, and a mug fallen on its side. All of the rats were dead here, twisted corpses strewn about the floor. The woman lifted her head from where it had been resting on the stone. She squinted into the light. 'Ah, Krugel. So soon?'

The Malshorne let out a cry. 'Leynore! It's me, Leynore!' He made as if to dash forward, then halted in his tracks. The sensation that followed was unlike anything Ash had experienced. A fierce tingling, it started at the crown of Credé's head. Ripping and burning, it coursed through his body, setting every atom alight. His skin rippled with a painful, tearing heat.

Mercifully, the seizure subsided. Credé dashed to Leynore's side. Sinking to his knees, he grasped her hand. His fingers looked familiar now, long and smooth. With a sudden shock, Ash knew what had happened. The Malshorne had transformed!

Leynore's skin felt icy. Her brows knitted in confusion. 'Is it you, my prince? Is it true?' A ghost of a smile wavered on her lips. Then her gaze drifted. 'Ah. Just another dream.'

'No, it *is* me! Leynore, I am here.' Credé tried to gather her into his arms, but she cried out at his touch. A feeble protest. Little more than a whimper. Ash took in the broken angles of her body. Somebody had hurt her. Badly. His heart constricted, matching Credé's own. The Malshorne had arrived too late.

For an awful moment, Credé's rage paralysed him. *The Wimsari will pay. Every single one of them!* He would make them pay! Then, sweeping off his cloak, he wrapped the garment around the woman he adored. Every bruise, every rip in her bloodstained gown was a knife in his heart. His voice cracked as he tucked the fur beneath her chin.

'My Leynore. You're cold ... So cold ...'

'No. Not anymore. You're here now.' Her breath rattled. 'And Tarlyn, of course. My valiant protector.'

Ash's heart leapt in sudden recognition as Tarlyn crept out from the darkness. Of course! That's why the rats were dead! 'Take her with you, Credé. Promise me you will.' Leynore's breath came in shallow rasps, as if drawing air was a struggle.

'Of course. We'll all go together.'

Her fingers were weak as she tried to clutch his arm. 'Listen to me. Please. T'al Jazure is locked. It *must* stay that way. Promise me. Never go back.' She coughed, a pitiful sound. 'Whole worlds are at stake. Promise!'

'I promise.' Credé wiped away the bright blood now dribbling from the corner of her mouth.

Leynore relaxed, the wild urgency fading from her eyes. 'Take my lore-stone, Credé.'

Credé smoothed her hair from her brow. 'I can't, my love.'

Even as her strength waned, this was a woman used to command. 'Take it. You'll understand. Artus ... your brother. It had to be done.' Broken as she was, she found him a smile. 'We should have run away, my prince.'

'It's not too late.' He held her hand, murmuring entreaties. 'Please ... dear one. My Leynore. Don't leave me. Not now.'

Her response was just a murmur. 'And as the waves of evening sigh ... we'll sail unto that spangled sky.' Ash recognised the last line of Credé's poem. The Malshorne groaned. He grasped her shoulders in desperation, as if holding her might prevent her from leaving. But Leynore had already slipped away.

The howl that Credé unleashed in that moment was terrifying. It slammed against the prison walls, shattering in splinters of grief. It was the sound of anguish, of unendurable pain tempered by a monstrous anger. A sound fit to break the world.

For a long time, all Ash could do was weep. Unable to speak, he was grateful for the pressure of Sarin's hand on his shoulder. 'Tell us, kin. When you're able.'

He gulped, extricating words from the tangled knot of emotion. 'I know why Credé hated me! It was the Wimsari. They killed Leynore and ... she was ... she was tort...' He couldn't bring himself to say it.

'Take your time, Ash. Breathe.' Sarin's eyes glimmered with an amber warmth. 'Remember, it was *Credé's* memory, not yours.' Ash took a shuddering breath. He knew that to be true, but he still felt as though someone had cut out his heart.

'You are shaking.' Ordelle blinked, looked at Sarin, then back at Ash, as if unsure of the protocol to follow. 'Take this,' she said after a pause.

Ash couldn't have been more surprised had Ordelle presented him with a flower. The handkerchief was clean and pressed, folded into a perfect square. It smelled of lavender and had embroidery in the corner. Three initials in purple thread. How had Ordelle kept a handkerchief in such perfect condition, after all they'd been through? Sarin caught Ash's eye and grinned. Appreciating the moment of distraction, Ash blew his nose. Ordelle told him to keep the handkerchief. She had a second.

He breathed deeply, trying to pull himself together.

Credé's anger remained with him, intermixed with a terrible, helpless grief. Emotion sabotaged his efforts to explain. 'They tried to break her.'

Sarin frowned. 'It makes sense. The Wimsari would have been eager to discover the whereabouts of T'al Jazure.' They all knew the history. Competing factions had persecuted the Azuri, hunting them down to learn the location of the fabled city. How many others had met a similar fate in those dungeons?

But there was more. Ash pushed on; his words now coming in a rush, interspersed with hiccoughs. 'The Taelstone belonged to Leynore. She told Credé to take it. Then she died in his arms. Tarlyn was there!' He stared now at the little creature, bewildered by a flood of emotion. Tarlyn gazed back at him with huge eyes, her ears flat to her head, as if she shared his distress. 'He kept her with him. Because of a promise.'

Ash felt that if he could just spill everything out, it might ease the pain. He could still hear Credé's howls inside his head. Sarin gripped his shoulders. 'Ash. Look at me. The Taelstone is *yours* now. You are its master. Tell us slowly. One thought at a time.'

Ash blinked. His throat was numb, but he swallowed and nodded. 'Credé told me about his oath. In his hut, just before he died. Tarlyn kept repeating that the taelstaun must go to T'al Jazure, but that just made Credé angry.' The Malshorne's rages made perfect sense now. 'He must have longed to return to his home, but he couldn't because of the oath!' Struck by grief, Ash could barely continue. 'He was bound to keep his word by his love for Leynore.'

Ordelle exchanged a worried glance with Sarin. 'Leynore. The Head of the Azuran Council. You're saying that she made Credé swear an oath? That he would never return to T'al Jazure?'

'Leynore begged him. She said it was perilous to unlock the city. That "whole worlds" were at stake. Those were her words.' His friends' faces reflected his horror back at him as he whimpered. 'What have I done?'

There was a deathly silence. Then Sarin raised his eyebrows. 'Well ... Possibly nothing. It was a long time ago, kin.'

'Nearly a thousand years,' said Ordelle.

Sarin shrugged. 'Things change. Whole worlds? That could mean anything. And, whatever the case, it's done. We should focus on the immediate problem.'

Ordelle nodded. 'Finding Kep.'

Sarin smiled. 'Yes. But first comes sleep. Even for me. I doubt we'll get a visitor this late. Rest while you can.' Casting a glance at the guards, he dropped his voice. 'Tomorrow we're getting out of here.'

Ash let Ordelle have the bench. She lay down on her back, her arms crossed on her chest, and was asleep within minutes. Sarin reckoned she looked like something from a crypt. The analogy was even more disconcerting in this place. Settling himself on the softest ground he could find, Ash turned his head away. The last thing he needed to think about was dying.

But when he closed his eyes, all he could see was Leynore's prison. And the corpses of rats. The sound of Credé's weeping haunted him. Was that to be their fate? To die in a cell, like Leynore? Ash knew he couldn't sleep. After the day's portentous events, he feared he'd never sleep again. He thought he'd done something important in unlocking the ancient city. That he'd given the League the edge it needed to destroy the Melk. Now he feared he'd done the opposite.

12
_______

# THE CHANGING OF THE GUARD

Judging by the pains in his body, Ash had slept for several hours. His neck ached, protesting the brutal hospitality. One leg was numb. He staggered to his feet, blinking and rubbing sleep from his eyes.

Since Ordelle remained stretched out like a corpse, he seized the opportunity to relieve himself in the bucket. A second bucket contained water for washing. That struck him as curious. A bucket to keep themselves clean, but no food?

Sarin had his back to the cell wall, knees drawn up to his chin, arms folded around them.

Ash settled down beside him and shuffled about, trying to get comfortable. He gestured at the guards. 'Still no movement?'

'The one on the right replenished the lamp and the other one scratched her nose. Other than that ... ? Sarin's expression soured. 'Nothing.'

Ash's stomach let out a loud growl. 'Do you think they mean to starve us?'

Sarin shook his head. 'They wouldn't have set a guard. The fact they haven't brought us any food is a good sign. It means we won't be here long.' Ash gave an uncertain nod, wary of the logic. 'Stop worrying, Ash. Somebody will come. I'm sure of it.'

Ash couldn't tell whether Sarin believed his own assurances. He swallowed, trying not to think about Leynore's dying moments. 'Do you think it's dawn yet?'

Sarin shrugged. 'Maybe.'

They sat in silence, contemplating their feet. Then a sudden movement made them start. Thumping their spears against their chests, the guards stamped their feet several times on the spot, rotating ninety degrees. Sarin was on his feet in a flash. 'So you *are* human!' Running forward, he shook at the bars, making the door jangle on its hinges. 'Hey! What's happening? Tell us!' The guards made no answer. In perfect synchronisation, they marched off. 'Stop! Hey!'

Ordelle sat bolt upright, rubbing her eyes. 'What is it? What's happening?'

Nothing. Nothing was happening. The guards seemed to have deserted them.

Before long, marching footsteps heralded the second watch. The new pair was indistinguishable from the last. Moving in perfect unison, they snapped into position, eyes forward with that same impassive stare.

'Brilliant!' said Sarin. 'At last some decent company. Are you sisters? You look like sisters.'

Ordelle moved forward to peer through the bars. 'They are not sisters. This one is young with fresh skin and bright eyes. The other is a wrinkled crone.' Her blunt assessment was accurate. The taller woman had puffy bags under her eyes and deep creases around her mouth. The skin of her neck hung in folds. Her partner was fresh-skinned. Ordelle was right; her grey eyes were very bright. Ash doubted Sarin could cajole either into speaking, but his companion unleashed a fresh tirade of questions and demands anyway. The guards didn't even blink.

Sarin threw up his hands. 'I get it. You've all taken a vow. Well, just so you know, that first guard spoke. "Halt, spies!" That's what she said.' Ash couldn't help but smile. Sarin's imitation was pitch-perfect. For a fleeting moment, Ash thought he saw a flicker of amusement in the younger guard's expression, but it vanished too quickly for him to be certain.

Sarin hadn't noticed. He launched into a full performance, probably to entertain himself as much as anything. He paced back and forth. 'She should be punished for letting down the ...' He turned on a heel. 'What *is* this exactly? Some sort of guild? A secret cult?'

No response.

'Slap her in a cell, I say.' Sarin folded his arms, considering the matter. 'I'll tell you what. She can share this one. We don't mind. Do we, Ordelle?' Ordelle raised her eyebrows and blinked, as if she was genuinely considering an answer.

It came as a complete shock when the younger guard spoke. 'The guards do not have your words.' Only her lips had moved. The older guard stiffened, her eyes darting a glare at her companion.

Sarin rounded on the speaker, throwing his hands wide. 'Right! So *that's* why they didn't laugh at my jokes. But you're different.' His hands closed around the bars. 'You speak the Common Tongue.' No response. It was as if the young woman hadn't spoken. Her grey eyes stared through Sarin, into the mid-distance.

Ordelle's nose was almost touching the bars. She might have been studying some sort of exotic animal. 'By her manner and accent, she is from the Singing Isles.'

Sarin nodded. 'I agree.' He bowed in the manner of his people. 'Greetings, singer of Zari. I am Sarin of Aurum and these are Ordelle Farbright and Ash Greyspoke.' Ash blinked, trying to look as if he belonged to the name. He hated it when Sarin improvised. 'We are not spies, merely travellers on urgent business. We mean no harm and apologise if we have caused offence. Please ask your superiors to release us, or, if it is in your power, do so yourselves.' His bow was courtly enough for royalty.

Neither woman responded. It was hard to be sure they were even breathing. Sarin let out a sigh, and threw up his hands. 'That's it! You leave me no choice. I'm going to have to whistle.' No reaction. Not so much as a flicker of confusion. Ordelle and Ash exchanged a look. *Whistle?* Sarin shrugged. 'Very well ... Don't say I didn't warn you.' Bringing the fingers of one hand to his lips, he blew.

The whistle was so piercing that Ash had to cover his ears. Sarin grinned, cocking his head in admiration. 'Outstanding acoustics.' He raised a finger. 'Nothing like a dungeon for whistling.' Their captors hadn't moved, but the muscles in their jaws confirmed that both were gritting their teeth. Sarin went on. 'I'm willing to bet you two are supposed to just stand there. I wonder if you're allowed to cover your ears?' Sarin gave a wicked chuckle. 'Let's find out. Ash, Ordelle. Find something to shove in your ears. That was a taster. You'd be surprised how loud I can whistle when I really try. And I can keep it up for *hours.*'

Ash and Ordelle obeyed, plugging their ears with their fingers. Sarin let out another blast. The shrieking whistle was louder this time, rising higher in pitch. Even with his fingers in his ears, Ash found it uncomfortable. To their credit, neither of the guards moved. Their faces were tight masks. But their eyes flickered in dismay.

When Sarin stopped to draw breath, the older woman turned to her companion. Ash caught his breath as she sang a series of notes. The utterance was melodic, more akin to a birdcall than any human language. The young guard nodded. She held up a hand, gesturing that Sarin should cease. After a moment's thought, she spoke. 'It is forbidden to pass into the realm of mists. The Watcher will receive you and pass judgment. You must not hope, for there is none. Your audience with the Watcher is merely a ...' she frowned as if trying to remember the word, 'formality. Your lives are forfeit.'

The guard's voice had a musical cadence, as if she was telling a story rather than pronouncing their deaths. Her partner made a motion as if to cut her off and she spoke more quickly. 'If you wish for a last meal, take it now. If you have prayers, sing them. This place is far more gentle than the Shelf. There—' The older guard put a hand on her shoulder and the speaker shook her head. 'I can say no more.'

Sarin made her a deep bow. 'Thank you for your courtesy.'

After a moment's hesitation, the young guard brought a fist to her heart. To Ash's surprise, she turned to look at him. Her expression was very intent. 'The Watcher sings as the Watcher sees.' With that, she returned to her vigil, as if transformed once more into stone.

Since further information seemed unlikely, the three friends retreated to the back of the cell. They sat in a huddle, heads close, speaking as quietly as they could. 'I do not like the sound of this shelf,' said Ordelle, her expression grim. 'If it is less gentle than a cell, it must be a hard place indeed.'

Sarin puffed out a sigh. 'True. But the guard was mistaken, on one count at least. There *is* hope. Because we've got you, Ordelle.'

Ordelle held him in slow regard. 'It is a play on my name.' Her eyes turned to Ash. 'Is it funny?'

'Not really.'

Sarin made a face and shrugged. 'A last meal, then? I'm only guessing, but the Shelf sounds cold and possibly wet.'

Ash nodded, frowning. His eyes returned to the young guard. He was still wondering about the meaning of her last words.

If this *was* to be their last meal, it was a pretty dismal one — all they had left were a few lumps of seed-loaf, a handful of withered hazelnuts and some wilted sorrel. Ash focused on chewing, pushing worries from his mind.

'So,' said Sarin, keeping his voice low. 'What have we learned?' When nobody spoke, he answered his own question. 'Let's start with the good news. We know we'll be taken from here to see this Watcher. And that means an opportunity to escape.'

'Or be released.'

Sarin smiled, rewarding Ordelle's obvious effort to be more hopeful. 'Yes, but you and I must be ready to fight.' Ash didn't know whether to feel relieved or insulted at being left out.

'This Watcher ...' Sarin's amber eyes were thoughtful. 'Ring any bells, Ordelle?' When Ordelle shook her head, he seemed surprised. 'My people tell stories of a sorceress with ancient powers who was said to dwell in the mists. In most tales she's a witch or a wise old crone, with a talent for reading omens. People seek her out, hoping for glimpses of their fate.'

'Humph,' said Ordelle. She pulled a face. 'Oracles are notorious for speaking in riddles.'

Sarin grinned. 'Of course. Riddles are the ultimate escape clause.' He turned his eyes on Ash. 'The stories hark back to before the fall of the three empires, long before Calkinon was formed.'

Ash caught his drift. 'During the time of the Wimsari.'

Sarin nodded. 'Exactly. These were Wimsari lands. Their empire stretched to the Kenting and beyond.'

'The Temple of Spires!' Ordelle's outburst caused Sarin to put a finger to his lips. They all looked over at guards. If either had heard, they showed no sign of it.

Ordelle continued in a lower voice, but with an uncharacteristic air of excitement. 'I've remembered something. My architecture tutor told me about a temple, so curious in design as to be mythical. If it existed — and she was far from convinced that it did — it lay in the heart of the Mistlands.'

Ash blinked. *Ordelle had a tutor in architecture?* She spoke matter-of-factly, as if every child had one. It reminded him again of the enormous gulf between them: the kitchen slave and the girl who'd grown up in Calkinon itself. Not for the first time, he wondered how much he really knew about the Cryer's daughter. 'The professor was primarily interested in ancient engineering. But she also spoke of an eye.' Ash felt a shiver down his spine. *An eye?* 'The ancient sources are confusing, leading to conjecture as to whether the eye was part of the structure itself or an actual person.'

Sarin raised his eyebrows. ' "The Watcher sings as the Watcher sees." '

Ash frowned, worried about the way the guard had seemed to single him out. 'So ... it could be the same Watcher?'

Sarin's mouth quirked. 'That would make her pretty old, kin.' Ash scowled at him, not in the mood for teasing. After a moment's thought, Sarin shrugged. 'Temple of Spires, or not, the Watcher will see us. Maybe she'll tell us something useful. Like where Kep is for instance.'

Ordelle snorted. 'I doubt that *very* much.'

Ash was silent. *An oracle.* Despite Ordelle's scorn, he couldn't help feel a flicker of excitement, intermixed with trepidation. If the Watcher *was* an oracle? Maybe she could shed light on his own destiny. Perhaps she could explain Rilka's belief that his fate was bound to the Melk. It was a foolish hope, but even a riddle would be better than nothing.

With the food gone and nothing to talk about that wasn't pure speculation, the conversation petered out.

Ash hunched at one end of the bench, biting at a thumbnail, still trying to decipher the guard's statement. Turning the words over in his head made them increasingly meaningless — until they didn't feel like words at all.

Ordelle fidgeted, repacking her things. Ash couldn't help feeling a surge of annoyance as he watched her fussing with the buckles on her bag. How could such a minor habit be so infuriating? He knew it shouldn't bother him — and the fact that it did made him even more irritated. Ordelle didn't even notice.

Claiming the centre of the cell, she settled herself in a cross-legged position, her hands forming the warriors' triangle. Ash watched from the corner of his eye as Ordelle practised the Breath. She seemed much better at finding stillness than he was. After a while, she rose, making a seamless transition from the Breath into the flowing patterns of the Dance of Blades.

Ash's eyebrows went up in surprise. Kep had told him about their first day of training, when Ordelle had complained that it should be called the Dance *without* Blades. Everyone had laughed at the Cryer's daughter back then, even though she had a point. Now, watching her move from one gesture to the next, Ash found himself impressed.

The Dance transformed Ordelle; all of her awkwardness gone as one sequence flowed into the next. Ash realised she must have trained hard to master so many moves in such a short time. To his untrained eye, the routines looked faultless. That didn't surprise him — Ordelle was nothing if not disciplined. But the Dance of Blades exposed a different facet of her personality. It was like watching a stranger.

Sarin watched, too, arms folded. He caught Ash's eye and grinned. Then he joined in, picking his moment, like somebody jumping into a skipping game. Sarin moved with casual grace, matching his movements to Ordelle's, adjusting for the limited space. A smile hovered at the edges of his mouth. Ash knew what it meant: 'I *can* do this, but don't either of you think for one moment that I'm taking this warrior business seriously.'

The Dance revealed things about Sarin, too. A lithe muscularity, strength balanced with ease. He had the restrained energy of a young animal, acutely aware of his own body. Ash blushed and looked away, aware that he'd been staring. Why did Sarin have to be so good at *everything*?

To cover his embarrassment, Ash turned to look at the guards, wondering what they would make of the Dance. Did they recognise the fighting sequences for what they were?

That was when he saw it. The curve of a smile on the younger guard's face. She caught him watching, and their eyes met. In a moment of human connection, Ash held his breath. Then the sound of marching footsteps drove everything from his mind.

13

## THE TEMPLE OF SPIRES

The three newcomers wore paler shades of grey than the other guards. They wore long swords at their hips. Ash guessed that the broader woman was in charge, by the silver embroidery on her collar and the way she held herself. She ran a dismissive gaze over the prisoners before uttering a sharp command. One of her companions jumped to obey, producing several lengths of silky grey rope. Sarin's eyes narrowed, but he shot a look at Ash and Ordelle. *We bide our time.* Ash nodded. His heart raced at the thought of being bound. But what choice did they have? They couldn't take on five armed guards.

The young guard who'd spoken earlier unlocked their cell. She headed straight to Ash. 'Your hands must be tied. Put them behind your back.' Ash obeyed, turning his back to her, wrists crossed. As she secured the ropes, he had the strangest feeling she might whisper something in his ear. He held his breath. Nothing. The guard's hands were firm as she tied the knots. When she stood back, her eyes were expressionless. Whatever connection Ash had imagined earlier appeared to have been just that — imagination.

As they passed into the outside world, Ash gulped in fresh air, savouring its taste. After the cell's confinement, it felt wonderful to be outside. The sun was veiled; just a promise. Its position insisted on it being early morning, but it felt more like dusk. While the thick fogs of the previous day had dissipated, lingering mists made the place feel creepy. Ash shivered. He had the strangest feeling that time was irrelevant here. They walked in single file, urged onwards by their captors into the gloom. Ash found it almost impossible to gather any clues as to their whereabouts — the mists shifted constantly, and he had to watch his footing in case he tripped over a rock. Snatched glances told him nothing: he saw only ferns and craggy-looking rocks.

He could hear the gulls, though. They wailed and cried overhead. Did gulls always sound so mournful? Looking up, he glimpsed wings — white blades against a thunder-grey sky. He could smell salt fish, rotting wood, and a plant reminiscent of sage. The mist had an earthy, rain-barrel scent of its own. He frowned. Can mist have a smell?

Ash was still puzzling over the qualities of mist and trying to work out what made these vapours so curious when they began a steep climb and more urgent concerns replaced his musings. Without the use of his arms for balance, he feared falling on his face and knocking out his teeth. Several times the guard behind grabbed him by the shoulders to correct his balance. So it was a relief when, after several flights of uneven steps, the steep path gave way to a wooden boardwalk. Now Ash could risk taking a proper look around.

Ash strained his eyes as he tramped on, trying to penetrate the mists. Below him, on the right, was water. It rippled like the surface of slate, disappearing behind a thick curtain of fog. If there were islands out there, they evaded his eyes.

Sporadic glimpses revealed the coastline, which was unlike anything Ash had seen or could even have imagined. The water moved in surges, charging up to suck at the rocks, then retreating, only to dash in again, urgent and foamy.

It was true! They had made it to the sea. A bubble of exhilaration swelled beneath his ribs. A thousand songs beckoned, inviting him into the arms of the Song.

Ash stopped dead in his tracks, overwhelmed by a wave of emotion. The guard behind let out a grunt of surprise as she crashed into him. She shoved him between the shoulder blades and he stumbled forward, tripping over his own feet and going down on one knee. His kneecap flared with pain. The guard lost no time in hauling him to his feet. Ash tasted fear in his mouth, sharp and sour. He was under no illusions: had he tumbled down the rocks and into the water, she wouldn't have troubled to fish him out. He stumbled onwards, legs shaking.

A short time later, they rounded the bluff. Ash gasped. Appearing from out of the mists, like an apparition, was the Temple of Spires.

The temple had gleaming, pearlescent walls with spires stretching skyward like tapering fingers. It sat on its own tiny island, connected to the shore by a bridge. As straight as a carpenter's rule, the bridge's span was very narrow — barely wider than a large man's shoulders. But that wasn't the worst thing: as they grew closer, Ash couldn't see any hand-rails. The bridge was a thin ribbon of shining grey, apparently made of glass. He gulped, trying to master his nerves.

The wheeling gulls called out a warning as Ash took his first step onto the miraculous bridge. He was far too terrified to pay them heed, though. He glanced down once, but didn't repeat the error. The sea below was a slavering mouth, all foamy, with black, broken teeth. Knees trembling, Ash willed his body forward, his eyes fixed on the striding figure of Ordelle ahead of him. The Cryer's daughter seemed to think nothing of being suspended, half-blinded by mists, above a foaming chasm of water.

Ash rarely prayed to the gods. His former mistress, Marlashetta Feyindi, had discouraged the habit — religion was the business of priests, she purported, not lowly slaves. In that moment, almost paralysed with fear, Ash sent entreaties to all three: to Telion that the bridge was as clever a construction as it seemed; to Narsis, ruler of troubled waters; and Argess, protector of life. He arrived at the other side, pale and trembling. Unsure whether he was about to faint or vomit, he folded himself in two, thanking the gods and promising to make an offering as soon as he was able.

The rush of blood to his head, and solid rock beneath his feet, went some way to restoring Ash. He stood upright, drawing in breaths of air as he stared around him. The Temple of Spires took up most of the island. Pinkish-grey and glassy wet, it seemed to be fashioned from molten shells. The central turret wore a spiky crown, the pink hue deepening to a rosy coral at its tips. Four elegant towers, each rising to a spire, surrounded the central structure. The Temple's foundations looked translucent, making it seem to hover above its saucer-like platform.

Ash goggled in disbelief, then drew his attention to the statues. Life-sized and uncomfortably realistic, they stretched all the way around the temple: a ring of women carved from pale-grey stone. With each boasting individual characteristics, Ash had the distinct feeling that these were likenesses of actual people. Perhaps they had once been priestesses, or even the Watchers themselves.

The ghostly forms were beautiful but disquieting. They looked naked and vulnerable, despite their flowing garments, and their long tresses were loose and wild, as if abandoned to the wind. They grasped chains at their sides: a ring of statues, each linked to the next. They gazed towards the temple's crown, straining against their chains, desperate and yearning. Ash shivered, unable to decide whether the women were in agony or in the throes of ecstasy. He tried to catch Ordelle's eye, but she ignored him, absorbed in her own analysis.

Sarin stepped off the bridge, took one look at the statues and lifted an eyebrow. 'This should be fun.' Before he'd finished speaking, the guards from their cell saluted, fists thumping against breastplates. The sudden movement made Ash jump.

They chanted in unison: 'The Watcher sings as the Watcher sees.' Turning on their heels, they started back over the bridge. The three remaining guards swept out their swords. For a heart-pounding moment, Ash thought they were to be executed on the spot. But the leader pointed her blade toward the tower entrance.

Crafted from pale grey stone, the portico was austere in its simplicity. It did nothing to prepare them for the splendour of the interior. They found themselves in a hexagonal room, taking up the entire central tower. Six mighty pillars supported the ceiling. Embossed with gold, they wore deep collars of coloured mosaics in shining tiles of crimson and cobalt blue. High overhead was a pressed-metal ceiling: embossed gold and copper, with motifs picked out in blue paint. It was impossible not to be impressed. Even Ordelle's jaw dropped in awe.

Given the general opulence, Ash expected plush carpets. Instead, white sand covered the floor. Pure and crystalline, the sand formed intricate patterns that radiated outwards from the centre of the room. Hexagons within hexagons, with curious symbols traced in the sand. Golden censers wafted fragrant incense, making it seem that the mists had made their way inside. The scent was heavy and aromatic. Had he been capable of thinking straight, Ash would have guessed at cloves and sandalwood. But the object at the centre of the room commanded his complete attention.

It was a cage. A very large and beautiful cage, with an exquisite domed roof, but a cage nonetheless. A cable suspended the creation inside a shaft that disappeared through a circular aperture in the high ceiling. The shaft looked fragile, as if woven by spiders. Golden light infused it from above. Gilded vines softened the sturdy metal-work of the cage itself, with leaves and flowers of mesh. Its ornate door was wide open — an invitation.

Behind them, a guard shuffled her feet. Her superior shot her a scowl and cleared her throat. Then she gestured at the path before them. The only part of the floor that was clear of sand, it led to the cage. 'The Watcher waits.' She looked at the prisoners, expectant, one hand on the hilt of her sword. Ash swallowed. Her meaning was clear. In order to see the Watcher, they had to enter the cage.

Ordelle and Sarin exchanged a look, and Ash sensed a moment's hesitation in his friends. He knew what they were thinking. Had they missed their only opportunity to resist? Ash swallowed. But what if he was *meant* to be here? Perhaps the Watcher could help him. Overruling his misgivings, he took a breath and began walking towards the cage.

As he followed the path, Ash had the distinct feeling that everything there was calculated. All part of a carefully constructed ritual, even the scented herbs on the path. As he crushed them underfoot, Ash recognised juniper berry, blue sage and candrel leaves.

With equal measures of dread and anticipation, he stepped into the cage. It accommodated the three of them, rotating gently as it took their weight. There was an inner rail for passengers to grip onto — assuming their hands weren't bound behind their backs. Ash planted his feet and wedged his hip against the rail. The smell of incense had grown stronger. Or was that just his imagination? He blinked. Yes, the haze was denser; its sickly sweet odour made him feel light-headed.

The guards tossed the trio's possessions in after them, as if even touching them was distasteful. When the door clanged shut, Ash fought a wave of panic. Ordelle stared upwards, her face bathed in golden light. The grating click of a key in the lock made them jerk their heads around. The guard didn't meet their eyes — never a good sign. Ash studied her grim expression as she turned away and his mouth ran dry. Sarin leaned towards Ordelle and murmured under his breath: 'As soon as we get a chance, we take it.' But Ash had a horrible conviction: it was too late.

A gong sounded from above, and the cage began to rise. The mechanism was quiet, its gentle whirring drowned out by the sound of chanting. The incantations were throaty and disembodied, as if they were coming from the walls themselves, growing louder as the cage ascended. Rising swiftly, it brought them up into an entirely different space.

The temple was unlike anything Ash could have imagined, even after the many miracles of T'al Jazure. Its walls were a deep midnight blue, sparkling with a thousand pinpricks of light. If you could craft a room from the very fabric of the night sky, this would be the result. Against the inky background the six golden pillars, overlaid with inscriptions and mysterious runes, were gorgeous. Huge, patterned urns stood at the foot of each pillar; flickering with fire, they sent up spirals of scented smoke. Overhead, six massive wedges of black crystal came together, forming an apex.

But nothing was as impressive as the enormous eye. Ash caught his breath. What magic could slice through solid stone to create such lines? And such a perfectly circular aperture? The design was breathtaking in its simplicity. Open to the mists and swirling with myriad shades of grey, the gigantic iris would never be still. All of the vagaries of the world were here. Captured. In a frame of stone. Ash's heart skipped to see that a figure stood there, on a raised plinth at the eye's centre. With her back to them, she was motionless, her attention absorbed by the mists. The Watcher!

A trick of perspective made it seem that the Watcher was the very pupil of the eye. Her gown shimmered like pewter, matching the statues below. Long, pale hair fell down her back. Her shoulders were bare, her body thin. Bony thin. Her arms dangled at her sides. Ash shivered. His gut warned him that something was wrong. He feared that the wailing in his head had nothing to do with the gulls.

Positioned around the Watcher's dais were three hooded figures. Acolytes. Their blood-red robes reminded Ash of those worn by the Seers in Mildaresh, except the fabric looked stiffer, like starched silk. The acolytes stood with their arms raised towards the Watcher, forearms perpendicular to the floor, their palms very flat. As if they were pressing against an invisible wall. They chanted in sonorous tones, the sound echoing against the walls, earthy and unsettling. It was a relief when they suddenly fell silent.

The acolytes to the left and right of the Watcher's dais bowed their heads, folding their arms, shelf-like, one on top of the other. The central figure turned and walked towards the visitors, taking slow and deliberate paces.

Everything about this priestess said she was important. Her girdle was a cord of twisted gold, finished with rich tassels. She wore golden bracelets around her wrists. Her hood was large and angular. Beneath its shadows, a netted veil, silvery grey, covered her face. It distorted her features, but Ash didn't need to see the woman's face to know that she was dangerous. He felt her keen scrutiny through the veil.

'Seriously?' Sarin cleared his throat in disgust, pulling a face. 'Is all this incense really necessary?' The priestess turned her head to regard him, her veil glinting. Silence. After a lengthy pause, Sarin sighed. 'This is getting tiresome. Are you going to tell us how it works? Or should we guess? Is it one question each? Or three, like in the stories?'

The veil shimmered as the priestess laughed. An unnatural sound, with a sour edge. '*Had* you been pilgrims, then yes: there *would* be questions.' Her emphasis on certain words made Ash shiver. All of his slave's intuition told him that this was a person to avoid. 'But *you* are not pilgrims. *You* ... are spies. Your presence befouls the sanctity of this place.'

Sarin scowled. 'Except we're *not* spies. We simply followed the wrong river. If your guards hadn't accosted us, we'd be far from here by now. We have no interest in your rituals.' Raising his voice, he inclined his head towards the dais. 'If your Watcher really is indeed an oracle, she knows that I speak the truth. Why not ask her?'

The priestess held up a hand, making her veil dance. 'Your words are of no consequence. The Watcher sings as the Watcher sees,' she intoned. Ash had the sense she was mocking them. 'The trespass cannot be undone. Your lives are forfeit.'

'Absolutely not!' Ordelle pushed forward, as far as the bars allowed. She seemed to grow taller as she spoke. 'I am Ordelle Farbright ...' For a moment she hesitated, as if she might have added more. 'High Citizen of the Calkinon Empire. Under the peace you are bound to release both myself and my companions, else negotiate terms with the Jade Bench.' Ordelle's tone of command startled Ash. Her visage was regal: the sort of profile you might find stamped on ancient coins. He blinked. Why had he never noticed that before?

The priestess drew herself up. Ordelle's evocation of Calkinon power seemed to take her aback. In the long pause that followed, Ash's heart flared with hope. Then came the reply, calm and melodic. 'Calkinon has no influence here.'

Turning her back on them, the priestess clapped her hands. The flames in the urns leapt up, turning a deep purple. Ash took a step back, but Ordelle raised a sardonic eyebrow. 'Salt fire. *Phft!*' Incense poured from unseen censers in earnest now, wreathing everything in a cloying blue-grey scent.

The acolytes resumed their chants, feverish now, and at a higher pitch. The priestess raised her arms. At her signal, the other two stepped up to the edge of the Watcher's dais, taking hold of large rings set into the stone. Still, the Watcher had not moved. What did she see in the mists that caused her to ignore all else?

The acolytes took up the strain, dragging at the metal rings. The dais turned, adding a new voice to the incantations — the sound of stone grinding against stone. Ash was finding it hard to breathe. The suffocating haze made him faint-headed. He also felt sick with anticipation. What strange portents might the oracle share?

The chanting continued as the platform turned, a single phrase repeating. Then, mercifully, both things ceased. Their work done, the acolytes bowed and disappeared into the depths of their hoods, leaving the visitors face-to-face with the oracle.

Curiosity, anticipation and hope all died. The Watcher wasn't the wise crone of Sarin's tales. She was *young*. Ash guessed the girl had fewer winters than he did, and they must have been dire ones. He'd never seen such an emaciated person — the stick puppets of Mildaren feast days had more substance. Her skin, stretched taut across her frame, glistened with a waxy pallor. It reminded him of the sheep's skull that Kep had found when they were children. The thing had given him nightmares for months.

Worst of all were the eyes! Those sunken, unearthly eyes! Ash had seen eyes like this before, rolling back to show the whites. And slack-jawed mouths like hers, too. They belonged to Blues — the drug-addled slaves who worked the noikos fields in Mildaresh. Blues were the lowest of the low. Inhuman. Expendable.

Ash's belief in the oracle had been frail to start with — now it vanished, as swiftly and completely as mist in sunlight. Their guard had spoken the truth. There was no hope here. Revulsion turned to pity. He doubted this poor girl could speak her own name, let alone read omens. Silver cords ran from cuffs around her wrists, tethering her to the platform. She couldn't have turned, even had she wanted to. The Watcher was a prisoner, bound to the eye and its ever-flowing mists.

Ordelle grimaced. 'She is an actor.' She glared at the priestess. 'And you are nothing more than a pedlar of shoddy tricks.' Was it true? Was all this merely a sham? Ash glanced at Sarin. He was watching the Watcher through narrowed eyes. Inscrutable. Ordelle began again: 'When my father hears—' An unseen gong drowned her words with a resounding boom. Ash reeled. The reverberating voice of the gong seemed to reach inside him, knocking against his soul.

The Watcher's reaction was instant. She dragged at her bonds, moaning and thrashing, like someone trying to awaken from the clutches of a bad dream. Her eyeballs were wildly darting about. Her hair whipped her face and neck.

Ash recoiled in horror. If she *was* an actor, she was very convincing. The gong sounded a second time, sending shivers through his body. The Watcher's gyrations slowed. She came to stillness, slumped forward, her head resting on her chest. The strange ecstasy appeared to be over. Ordelle snorted, more quietly this time.

Ash understood his friend's scepticism. Every ritual had led them to this point: the statues, the incense, the path and the chanting. It all climaxed at this moment; when the pilgrims were seen. Knowing that didn't lessen the thrill of expectation when the Watcher lifted her head, aware of them at last. As she did, the great eye came to life behind her. Mist poured through the aperture, reaching into the temple like fingers searching. The Watcher's eyes flew wide in shock. She didn't sing. Shying away from the probing tendrils, she opened her mouth and let out a high-pitched wail of terror. Then she collapsed, her legs buckling beneath her like snapping twigs.

The acolytes shrieked. This clearly wasn't part of the ritual. Robes flapping, they stumbled out of the reach of the freakish curls of mist. A harsh cry from their superior froze them in place. 'Halt!'

The priestess raised her arms, squawking like a crow defending its territory. 'The Watcher sings as the Watcher sees!' Gone was that languid tone of self-satisfaction. She whirled, pointing at the cage.

'They are spies! The mists confirm it! The temple must be cleansed. Consign them to the Shelf!'

Ash had a strange sense of detachment as the mist reached towards him. His mind captured the experience as a static scene. It made for a bizarre tableau: the wailing bundle of the oracle, her forehead pressed to the stone dais; the priestess, crimson with fury, with arms outstretched; the paralysed acolytes, in mid-flight, and the eye, that colossal eye, all-seeing, never blinking.

Perhaps the Watcher had indeed glimpsed a mystery in the mists. Some strange portent that could change his fate. Ash would never know, because the audience was over. An unseen lever set the cage in motion with a jolt. They dropped through the floor, and the temple disappeared from view.

## 14

## KNOTS AND WAGONS

The party woke to a sodden dawn — those who'd slept. Kep had made the mistake of spending the night curled in the hollow of a tree. Although the tree's canopy was dense, its overburdened leaves had periodically tipped water onto her head, the dousing splashes seeming to coincide with every time she was just beginning to nod off. It felt like the tree was doing it on purpose. What with that and Jen-Jay's earlier revelations, sleep had been near impossible. The birds began a raucous chorus just as the rain stopped, adding insult to injury.

All of which meant that Kep stumbled into the day, tired, cold and far from dry. As miraculous as her Azuran cloak was, she'd now discovered its limits. The pirates had fared somewhat better, having spent the night in the wagon. Although they grumbled over their breakfast, Kep knew for a fact that several had slept right through the storm, their snores as loud as the thunder. Curly, Ratskin and Spike had opted to sleep beneath the wagon. They had leaves and twigs tangled in their hair and clothes, but they looked dry, if somewhat bedraggled. Spike was as irrepressible as ever. Whistling as he went about his chores, he mimicked the birdcalls — until Rawlins shut him up with a well-aimed cuff to the head.

Breakfast, at least, was hot, courtesy of Orrick's ingenious oven. The night before he had buried an enormous lump of the leftover pork in the earth along with hot coals from the fire, cooking it to perfection overnight. The steaming pink meat fell apart in Kep's fingers as she ate, sweet and sticky with gobs of fat. Off to one side, she caught snatches of Skarlon's worried conversation with Curly about the soggy ground. She understood their concern. It was very muddy. Kep's boots made squelching noises as she packed up the gear.

Harden's presence behind the wagon came as a surprise. Typically the last to rise, he grappled with the cave hog's head, knife in hand. As Kep approached, he yanked the largest tusk free of the gory mess and gave her a toothy grin. After a moment's consideration, he offered her the bloodied trophy. He seemed relieved by her polite refusal. Kep watched bemused as he wrapped and stowed it away. Who knows what he intended to do with the thing? Perhaps he thought it would enhance the story of his heroic brush with death. Kep sighed, dreading the thought.

Orrick's arrival thwarted Harden's attempt to sneak away; he commandeered the man to help secure the remainder of the carcass to the wagon's sidebar. Kep shook her head as she watched. Skarlon would have his work cut out harnessing the horses that morning — no beast liked the smell of blood. She approved of the principle, though; meat should never go to waste.

The pair did a masterful job with the ropes, making quick work of hoisting the heavy carcass into place. Orrick's knots were intricate, almost decorative. The white-haired man looked up as he tugged the last line tight, sensing Kep's interest. She smiled at him. 'You certainly know your knots, Orrick.' A flash of pride warmed his sea-green eyes. 'I've never seen this one.'

The corners of his mouth drew up, just a hint of a smile. 'It's a sailor's secret. Pull this here.'

Kep pulled at the end, and the knot unravelled, almost like magic. She watched in fascination as the man recreated the configuration, his fingers moving so rapidly she couldn't hope to follow the steps. Shaking her head in admiration, she asked if the knot had a name.

Dimples appeared in Orrick's cheeks, making him look almost boyish. 'A witch's hitch.' He seemed about to say more, then his expression clouded. He dropped his head as if to check on something else.

At that same moment Kep detected a foulness in the air, identifying the person behind her without the need to turn. Greigo. She raised her voice. 'Thank you for showing me, Orrick. You truly are a master.' Orrick muttered an inaudible reply and kept his head ducked. The hairs on her neck prickled at Greigo's presence, but she forced herself to smile, making her tone light. 'I hope you'll have time to teach me that knot one day.' Putting her shoulders back, she left Greigo to glower as much as he wished, and strode off to saddle up Berry.

The draft horses snorted through flared nostrils, no doubt spooked by the scent of blood. But Skarlon had them hitched in double-quick time. He had a firmer hand with the creatures than Kep would have liked, but she understood his reasons. Given the state of the road after a night of heavy rain, they would be hard-pushed to make Merrywinds by nightfall and nobody fancied another night at the mercy of the weather.

It proved a day of two halves. With a gentle downhill gradient the going was fairly easy until midday. They picked their way through the rain-speckled woodlands, getting bogged down only a few times and never for long. However, after a lunch break, featuring the inevitable cold pork, the road climbed, turning to clay. Now they had to contend with ruts made by previous wagon wheels, which had become scoured out by rivulets of water. They stopped several times, improvising repairs to the road with stones and branches. The terrain was changing now, with grasses and tussocky hills dominating the landscape, so they took a few sturdier branches with them.

This was the realm of goat farmers: the grass not lush, but with feed enough for hardy stock. Small homesteads, surrounded by thin patchwork paddocks, dotted the landscape. A sturdy species of thyme covered many of the slopes, giving a herbal scent to the air.

Kep spotted animals grazing on the sides of the distant hills and wondered at the breed. She doubted her little flock of bug-eyes would have liked the place. The richer lands were in the east. Kep had heard talk of the fine horse breeds that originated in the Kenting and the lush downs around the Elan river. Somewhere down there, far beyond her sight, was Pendle Ring, the ancient meeting place of the Haelrum clans.

Kep and Ash had travelled towards Pendle Ring once, under the protection of the Aurum. Now the clans would have dispersed, following their travel lines, planting food forests as they went. It was comforting to think of Sarin's people travelling these lands, with proud Nalina at their head. She smiled, thinking how wonderful it would be to round the corner and see their colourful tents. But the thought was foolish. The Aurum would consider Kep an 'Outling' now and no longer welcome. Sarin sprang into her thoughts as she remembered her efforts to master the steps of that silly dance. She blushed at the memory of their first kiss. That unexpected, *inconceivable* kiss.

Sounds of alarm pulled Kep from her reflections. Flustered, she realised the wagon had lurched to a complete stop. Ratskin jumped down to chock the wheel not gaining traction with a large stone. After shoving it into place, he grimaced and hobbled off to one side. A split second later, Curly appeared. He scratched his head mournfully, surveying the mud. 'This will be trouble, I think.'

It was. The problem was an over-exuberant creek which had deviated from its usual course, taking half of the road with it. The washout cost them — in time, energy and tempers. This was the steepest section of road and, even without its passengers, the sturdy wagon was very heavy. It kept sliding backwards in the waterlogged clay. The powerful horses, flanks glistening with sweat, seemed unable to make headway. In the end it took the combined efforts of all the big men, and a few of the smaller ones, to heave the wagon up and over the gouged-out ruts and bumps.

Kep wanted to push as well, but a glare from Skarlon put paid to that idea. She knew he was right. She couldn't be Simbab *and* wrestle in the mud. Ratskin looked fit to burst a vein. His face was bright pink, muscles bulging with the strain as he shoved at one corner of the wagon. Spike was right there beside him, shoulder to the timbers and grunting encouragement. Kep doubted Spike's efforts helped much; his boots kept slipping in the mud, as if he was running on the spot. Greigo, of course, did nothing whatsoever. He stood with arms folded, sneering and making disparaging comments.

Fearful they'd lose the wagon down the bank, horses and all, Kep could only watch and pray. By the time the wagon was clear, men and beasts alike were steaming and panting. The poor horses looked spent. Kep was relieved when Skarlon announced the beasts couldn't continue with passengers. The pirates would just have to walk.

Since Jen-Jay was the lightest and also the most proficient driver, she took hold of the reins. Skarlon and Twinkle alternated between scouting ahead and falling back to turn circles and scowl. Kep's position at the rear gave her a perfect view of their now very muddy party.

The pirates looked quite different from above. Creely's tricorne hat had a patch on the crown. Rawlins had half an ear missing, and Tibbs walked on a lean, his left shoulder hunched, making his arm dangle oddly. Each man responded to the climb in his own way. Rawlins kept to himself, lolloping along, his long strides keeping up with the wagon. Harden took the opportunity to tell Creely and Curly about his plans to open a pie shop in Idira. Its signature dish would be individual pork pies. Harden's Hogglets, he would call them. Although Curly nodded encouragement, Kep doubted Creely was even listening — he was far too concerned with the mud on his velvet cuffs. Tibbs and Greigo walked together, their heads close. Their mutterings looked rather too furtive for Kep's liking. Now and then, Tibbs sniggered, rubbing his hands.

Their pace was dreadfully slow, trying Kep's patience. She couldn't stop thinking about the wagon that had passed this way a few days earlier, carrying Rodine, Ozu, Polkin and Jaibari to their fate. Like her, every one of them had set out on a mission to defeat Kara-fell. She hated to imagine the fearless warriors trussed up like animals for market. Kep gritted her teeth. The negotiations with Bahjak had to go well. She just prayed they had enough gold to appease the man.

Missing the sound of Spike's chattering, Kep looked back over her shoulder. She frowned. He and Ratskin had fallen a long way behind. The larger boy shuffled along, making hard work of the rise. Kep knew a lame creature when she saw one. Turning Berry, she made her way back down to them. 'Spike? Is there a problem?'

The boys shrank from the horse, their eyes not leaving her hooves. Their reaction only made Berry more nervous. To avoid further alarm, Kep slid from the saddle, regretting how her boots sank into the clay. 'Ratskin? Do you have a stone in your boot?' She didn't expect Ratskin to answer for himself. But it felt rude to address herself to Spike as if his friend wasn't there.

She noticed how Spike pulled his hand out of his pocket — the one closest to Ratskin. He answered cheerfully, explaining that their boots weren't all that good for climbing. As he spoke, his fingers fluttered at his side. Kep caught her breath. She nodded, listening to Spike, but paying careful attention to the boys' hands. Ratskin grimaced and said nothing. But, sure enough, his hand made a quick gesture: a fist opening and closing several times. Kep made a guess at the signal. *Pain.* The lad was in pain. Spike's eyes were worried, betraying his cheerful tone. 'I think he's hurt his foot.'

Berry was far more interested in a large clump of grass than a boy with a sore foot, so Kep risked letting go of her reins. The sweet mare would come when called. 'Right then. Off with that boot.' Ratskin's eyes flew wide, as if Kep had suggested he strip naked. She spoke gently, keeping her tone calm. 'We need to have a quick look at your foot, Ratskin. It's probably just a stone that you've picked up. I'll find a dressing, in case we need it.'

Kep made a show of looking in her saddlebags, watching from the corner of her eye. Sure enough, Spike's fingers made a series of twitches, then formed an inverted cup shape. At the same time, he spoke. 'What ya reckon, Ratskin? Take that boot off for a bit?' Kep rummaged some more, noticing how Ratskin's eyes darted to her and away again. Then his fingers moved, too. A flicker of motion and easy to miss. The curious conversation was over. Ratskin actually looked her in the eye as he nodded his consent. Kep rewarded him with a smile.

It proved quite a struggle to remove the boot. Ratskin's foot was puffy and swollen. A raised mound, just above the arch, was ringed with yellow. It had a cloudy grey centre. 'Aha!' Kep made her voice cheerful. 'That's a nasty bite. Did you see the spider?' As the boys stared at the foot in horror, she realised her mistake. They were trying to imagine the hairy beast that would leave such a mark.

Spike pointed, his words choking on fear. 'That ... that dark stuff? It's not ... baby spiders, is it?' Ratskin went a shade paler. Somebody had clearly fed them tales.

'No! Of course not. That's just in stories. Bites often puff up like that.'

It wasn't exactly true. This *was* a nasty bite. And Kep feared it wasn't a spider bite at all. Perhaps a rock scorpion? Given where the lads had slept, it could have been a Leaf Brown. If so, the poison would spread, eating into the flesh and blackening the whole limb. She kept her thoughts to herself.

'It's easy enough to fix. We'll just give it a bit of a jab to let the poison out.' Kep rummaged in her healing kit, giving the lads plenty of time to exchange hand signals. 'That all right with you, Ratskin?'

Ratskin was the ideal patient. He watched Kep lance his foot in staunch silence. Kep washed and bandaged the injury, with a candrel leaf poultice to draw the poison. They couldn't get his boot back on, though, and Ratskin could hardly limp barefoot the rest of the way.

Trusting Spike to convince his friend that the only option was for him to ride, Kep went about catching Berry. It was a struggle to get Ratskin settled in the saddle. Finally, using a helpful tussock and the uphill slope, they accomplished it. The chestnut mare was none-too-keen at the change of rider. Swivelling her ears at the additional weight, she rolled her eyes at Kep. Who ever heard of a pirate riding a horse?

Ratskin clung to the pommel of the saddle, white-faced, as if he was being led to his execution. But he eventually relaxed. Kep caught him looking about with a dazed expression on his face and smiled to herself. She remembered her first ride on a horse and the joy of finding herself so high above the ground. This was a day Ratskin would never forget, despite his pain.

Spike was quieter than usual, possibly overwhelmed by his friend's unexpected elevation and the fact that Kep-Váli had given up her mount for a lowly pirate. As they walked, Kep told the boys about her old life in Mildaresh. She was halfway through the story of the gang of piglets who broke into the Aranti dairy, and her attempts to catch the buttery porkers, when Skarlon came riding back.

Ratskin almost slid off the horse in his panic, convinced he was about to be punished. Spike stood his ground, defiant beneath the old warrior's accusing glare. Kep gave Skarlon a meaningful look. 'Thank you for checking on us, Skarlon. But we won't need an escort. It's just a few more miles. Spike and I can handle any trouble.' Beside her, Spike puffed out his puny chest. 'Or we can send Ratskin to ride ahead.' Skarlon must have seen how unlikely that was — the lad looked as if he might fall sideways at any moment. But Kep saw he'd got the message. The other pirates were far more dangerous — especially if they reached Merrywinds unsupervised.

Spike scowled as Skarlon rode away. 'He's a right grumpy old fart, isn't he?'

'He takes my safety very seriously.' Kep grinned. 'But yes, he's a right grumpy old fart.'

After that, with the road to themselves, Spike chattered freely. Kep learned that the pirates had been none-too-pleased at having to abandon their life at sea. They missed the wide horizons and the excitement of far-flung ports. But most of all they missed the adventure. Bullying country folk held none of the thrill of chasing down a prize ship. She nodded and listened, careful not to ask questions or interrupt, letting the lad babble on.

Kep gathered a considerable amount of gossip about the pirates as they walked, most of it irrelevant. Harden had three wives, all in different ports. One woman spoke Lyptic, a language he didn't have a word of, and she wasn't even pretty. Rawlins had been a soldier in the infamous Silver Battalion, but left under a cloud. Nobody knew the details, just that he'd murdered someone important. Creely's claim to nobility was genuine. The youngest of eight brothers, he'd been disinherited, thanks to gambling debts that would make your eyes water, and to a fondness for other men's wives.

As Spike chattered on, the sun began to sink, brushing golden light over the tawny grasses. Looking up, Kep noticed several white birds wheeling above them in circles. Their wings caught the light as they turned. Spike told her they were gulls. Astonished that she had never seen such a thing, he took it upon himself to identify the different types. The sharp scent of salt on the air was unmistakable now. At last, the road gave a final twist and took them over a crest. Spike let out a hoot of delight. Kep stood there in astonishment, hands on hips, gasping.

Nothing could have prepared Kep for that first sight of the ocean. Stretching toward them, as if Telion had rolled out a carpet, was a golden path of shimmering water. The sun was a ball of gold sinking into a molten horizon. The shadowy peaks of what she guessed was the Elgrave peninsula rose in layers of pink, made insubstantial by distance. Kep smiled at the small island closer to shore. It really did look like an apple, split right down the middle.

Nothing was still here. Wave upon wave swept in, white crested in fringed rows, like the lace on a noblewoman's petticoats. But the noise! The sea spoke with a booming voice, surging and crashing onto the rocks below. Kep found it difficult to tear her eyes from the foaming water. It was gorgeous! And terrible! When she touched her cheek, the skin felt fresh and salty. Both boys had grins on their faces, Ratskin's a wide, lopsided version. 'It's beautiful!'

'You ain't never seen the sea before, Kep-Váli? Truly?' Spike thought it was the craziest thing he'd ever heard. The way his eyes caught the golden light reminded her of Sarin for a brief second. She turned her face back to that glorious horizon and couldn't help laughing for joy. Lifting her arms, she felt the wind push against her body. Here, at the edge of the cliff, it seemed possible to take flight.

Beside her, Spike fell silent. Pulling her eyes away from the ocean, Kep noticed he looked quite crestfallen. Something told her he'd been communicating with Ratskin. He lifted an arm and pointed. 'That's it. That's Merrywinds.'

Perched on the edge of the cliff, Merrywinds might have looked precarious. Yet nothing was further from the truth. The building seemed defiant, as if it had discovered the secret of holding back the relentless surge of time and tides. Built from solid blocks of grey stone, the inn was double-storeyed, with pitched roofs and several squat chimneys. Kep's sigh was heavy with yearning. *A bath. Let there be a bath.* And food that wasn't pork.

'Kep-Váli?' Spike was frowning as he stared toward the inn. He tugged at his ear and blinked. 'Um ... Me an' Ratskin ... we think ... It's just ... you wanna be careful. He's dangerous. Bahjak.'

Kep felt a chill down her spine. She tried to smile. 'I know, Spike. He's a smuggler. It's his job to be dangerous.'

But Spike was in earnest. 'It's not just that. I mean ... Bahjak ... There's stories.' He glanced at Ratskin, whose face was equally glum. 'Simbabs who go to make deals ... they don't always come back.'

Kep nodded her head, trying her best to look calm — as if she'd heard the stories and knew *all* about dealing with smugglers. 'Thank you for the warning, Spike. And you, too, Ratskin.' Ratskin blinked as if startled by the inclusion. 'I'll be careful, I promise.'

When Kep turned her eyes back to the inn, its windows winked back, reflecting the dying light of the sunset. The place seemed more sinister than merry now.

## 15

# GRADY'S LEGACY

Merrywinds Lodge was far more than a wayside inn. Its windows were clear and bright, set in deep wooden casements. Everything spoke of craftsmanship, from the cobbled yards to the inn's smooth stone walls and the burnish of its thick red beams. This was a building financed by gold — by pirates' gold, to be exact.

Several groups of travellers had arrived already, seeking beds for the night. At the front entrance, servants scurried back and forth, toting bags and shouting orders. Several dogs had joined in the excitement, wagging their tails and adding their voices to the clamour as weary guests dismounted from horses and carriages.

Kep skirted the mayhem, leading her mare towards the stables. Getting Ratskin to the ground would be easier without an audience, and she hated the thought of Berry waiting in line for a feed and rubbing-down. Although Spike said nothing, his face was worried. His thoughts were obvious: the new Simbab should sweep in with a flourish, demanding attention, not sneak around the back like a servant. Kep gave him a rueful frown. He had a point. If she wanted Bahjak's respect, she was going about it the wrong way.

The stables were well-organised and clean, housing many more stalls than Kep had expected, most of them full. She sniffed in deeply, appreciating the rich scent of horses and the sense of industry as people went about the quiet work of caring for animals. Next to a large water trough, on their right, was a grey horse, saddled and expectant. The creature's ears pricked towards them, hopeful of apples. Kep was leading Berry to the water when a horse and rider came clattering in at full pelt.

As the newcomers whirled to a halt, Spike panicked, squawking in dismay. Stumbling over himself, he fell backwards into a pile of hay. The alarming display sent Berry into a skittering dance. Kep had to grab for the reins, and poor Ratskin was clutching at the saddle for all he was worth.

The glossy black stallion was silvered with streaks of lather. Steam came off him as he pulled in air through dilated nostrils. His rider threw a leg over the saddle and leapt. Even as her feet hit the ground, she tossed a pouch to the stable boy, who appeared like magic, just in time to catch it. The rider accepted a bottle of water and a pastry, downed the water in several gulps, gobbled up half the pastry, and then, shoving the rest between her teeth, seized the reins of the waiting grey. Seconds later, rider and horse were gone. The stable boy didn't so much as glance sideways at Kep — the exhausted horse came first. Patting and clucking, he led the stallion away, and they found themselves alone.

They restored Ratskin to the ground, where he wobbled about, testing out legs unaccustomed to riding. The adventure seemed to have taken his mind off his foot, though. Kep scanned her surroundings. There was no sign of Skarlon, but she recognised a huge black horse's rump several stalls down. Twinkle looked up from her manger, eyes rolling. 'You took your time,' she seemed to say.

Fresh hay and a bucket of water were waiting in the neighbouring stall. Kep was lifting Berry's saddle free when she heard a shout. 'Hey! Those stalls are taken!' Looking over her shoulder, she saw a scrawny lad, puffed up like a cat and just as indignant. Kep grinned, recognising his type: a young boy doing a grown man's job and very proud of himself.

'Hello,' she said, pushing curls out of her face. 'I'm Kep. What's your name?'

'Dalkin.' He frowned. 'But you can't—' Kep watched his brain catch up. When it did, his eyes nearly popped out of his head. 'K-Kep ... ?'

A smooth voice spoke behind him. 'Kep-Váli, I believe. The new mistress of the *Lady Lee.*'

Kep blinked. The young woman appeared from nowhere, as if conjured into existence. She had a snub nose, a sprinkle of freckles and tight reddish-brown curls, coiled like springs. Her apron was sensible, her dusky pink skirts caught up on one side to keep out of the mud.

'We've been watching for your arrival,' she said, eyes twinkling. Her meaning was obvious: nobody in their right minds would think to look in the stables. 'My name is Molly. I can take you to your quarters if you wish.' Detecting Kep's reluctance, she added, 'Don't worry. Dalkin's a good boy. He'll take excellent care of your horse.'

Kep licked her lips and swallowed. Time to pull herself together and start playing the part. She gave the boy a nod. 'Her name's Berry. She's had a hard journey, so please make sure she has the best of everything. Oh. Here ...' Rummaging in a pocket, she pulled out several of the coins from Grady's hoard. She handed him a thin silver one, with a hole punched through its middle. 'Here's something for your trouble.'

The lad stared at the coin in utter shock. You'd have thought she'd handed him a wasp. Molly clicked her tongue and patted his shoulder. 'It's all fine, Dalkin. Just be sure to put that somewhere safe. Not in that pocket with the hole. You heard Kep-Váli,' her eyes danced, as if she was trying not to laugh, 'the best of everything.'

Molly turned her attention to Spike and Ratskin. 'Windy's just tapped a fresh cask of beer. Off you go, now.' The boys' eyes lit up. They obeyed her without so much as a backwards glance. Kep frowned to herself. For a serving girl, Molly seemed rather used to getting her own way.

Refusing offers of help, Kep shouldered her only bag. A second later, she turned back. The hat! Grady's stupid hat. Shoving it into a saddlebag had ruined it — the red felt was crushed, its feather broken. Kep gave it a cursory bash, brushing off dust and trying to restore its shape. She hated the thing, especially that ridiculous feather. Skarlon and Jen-Jay had insisted that she keep it, with Curly offering the ludicrous suggestion that she should wear it. Everyone knew Grady's hat. It would signal that Kep had replaced him. Kep had refused such nonsense then, and she wasn't about to change her mind. If the pirates were going to break their oath, the stupid hat would change nothing. She frowned as she followed the girl's swaying skirts. Molly's smile seemed a little too knowing for comfort.

They passed through the back door of the stables and out through a courtyard, heading towards the main building. Judging by the delicious aromas of bread, roast vegetables and onions, the kitchens were on their left. Kep's stomach groaned, her mouth watering at the wonderful smells. A couple of dogs stood vigil at the door, tongues lolling, hopeful of scraps. Two heads turned, two tails wagging a greeting. Suddenly, the animals tensed, raising their hackles. The dogs rushed towards her, barking and snarling.

Kep froze, standing her ground. She wasn't afraid of dogs, but they'd never run at her like this. These dogs snarled with wrinkled snouts, black gums pulling back to reveal snapping fangs. The kitchen door slammed open, and a woman stuck her head out. Her body followed soon after. 'Chance! Puck!' The cook's face was hot and angry as she strode toward them, wiping hands on her apron. 'Silly mutts! Get here!' The dogs paid her no heed — all of their focus was on Kep. They kept growling and snarling, until the cook marched up and grabbed the largest by its collar, shoving the other dog aside with her foot. 'It's that 'at,' she scolded as she smacked at a snout. Looking up at Kep, she flinched. 'Dogs don' like 'ats like that one. That's all I'm sayin'.'

Kep's heartbeat hammered in her throat. But she swallowed, gathering her wits. 'Neither do I.' Moving deliberately, she dropped the hat on the ground, lifted her boot and stomped on its crown. It felt so satisfying! She kicked the hat away, and the dogs took their cue. They pounced on the hat with glee, tearing and tussling, ripping the hated thing to pieces. The cook shot a startled look at Molly, stared back at Kep, opened her mouth and shut it again. Then, remembering her pots, she hurried back inside.

Molly had remained calm throughout. She watched with eyebrows raised as the dogs exacted revenge on the hat. Kep couldn't decipher the meaning behind her smile.

The quarters set aside for the Simbab came as quite a shock. Grady had enjoyed his comforts! The four-poster bed was carved from oak, and boasted a deep feathered mattress and plump pillows. Creamy drapes, edged with burgundy fringes, matched the damasked curtains of the bay window. The lead-light window was dazzling. It had many diamond-shaped panes, filled with sunlight and visions of the sea. In the far distance, her white sails catching the last rays of the sun, was a tiny ship. It looked like a toy. Kep's heart leapt. Could it be the *Lady Lee*? With Eldar waxing full in the sky, they expected the ship's arrival within the next few days. Molly lit a lamp, adding to the sun's golden rays.

Kep felt out of place in the ostentatious room. There was so much furniture! Far more than one person needed, including a wardrobe and a dresser to match the bed, and a writing desk with dainty legs. The richly upholstered couch was a deep mustard yellow. A pure white rug made her acutely aware of her filthy clothes and boots.

A small fire burned in the grate, the living heart of an elaborate polished mantlepiece. Hung over the centre, flanked by two huge candlesticks of polished brass, was a large portrait. Its subject looked over her shoulder at them, her hands on her hips. She had wild chestnut hair and eyes as free as the stormy seas behind her. Kep had never seen a painting like it — nor a woman, for that matter.

Stopping what she was doing, Molly smiled, joining Kep to gaze at the painting. 'That's Winifred Debreze. The original Windy.' Of course! Kep should have known. Curly had explained. Windy was the name of the innkeeper, and every innkeeper before him. It was a much-loved joke among the patrons. There would always be a Windy at Merrywinds.

The current Windy had inherited the establishment from his grandmother, a formidable woman, but not as uncompromising as *her* mother, the woman who had built all this — the woman in the portrait. The story went she'd been a pirate herself, only settling down when old bones ached for the comforts of a soft bed and family. Those eyes held Kep captive. She looked like a hard woman to refuse. 'Is it true? Was she a pirate?'

Molly's profile went still. 'It depends on what you mean by "pirate". But yes.' Her head tilted to one side. 'She was the *right* sort of pirate.' Kep frowned. *The right sort of pirate?* 'She's my great-great-grandmother.'

Kep took a breath. No *wonder* Molly walked about as if she owned the place. The innkeeper's daughter noted her dawning comprehension, and smiled slyly. 'Will you take some rum?'

Kep nodded. 'Yes. Um ... Thank you.' It seemed like something a Simbab would do. She ruined the effect by blushing, and kicked herself. If she was going to be so self-conscious, how could she hope to confront Bahjak? She couldn't stop thinking about the dirt on her boots. She decided it was best to just take them off. That would be a good start. She was Simbab, after all. She could do whatever she wanted.

Still smiling to herself, Molly picked up a crystal decanter on the sideboard. Selecting a glass, she polished it and held it up to the light. She spoke quietly as she poured. 'May I ask a question, Kep-Váli?' Kep nodded, accepting the glass. 'Is it true? Did you kill Grady?'

Kep's stomach turned. There was no point denying it. 'Yes. It's true.' She forced herself to hold Molly's gaze. The young woman's resemblance to the woman in the portrait was obvious now. Her eyes had that same light — the same strength of will. It made Kep uncomfortable, but she refused to look away.

The innkeeper's daughter gave a solemn nod. 'That was a deed well done, and *some* will thank you for it.' She turned away and opened the linen press. Selecting a pile of folded towels, she placed them on the bed and started rearranging the pillows. 'You certainly know how to set a place astir, Kep-Váli. Did you know that the coin you gave Dalkin was enough for him to buy a horse of his own?' Kep blinked. *Seriously? That funny little coin?* 'I honestly think that put more fear into him than your man threatening to cut out his liver if your horses came to harm.'

Kep winced. That sounded like Skarlon. Poor Dalkin. A horse of his own! No wonder the boy had almost fainted. Her cheeks flushed. It was just another reminder of how out of her depth she was. She was glad when a knock at the door saved her from Molly's sly scrutiny. Molly tilted her head. 'That will be Windy.'

The innkeeper was exactly as Curly had described — an affable man with broad shoulders and a shining forehead. He had the same curly hair as his daughter, which he wore tied back in a ponytail. It straggled down his back like a lamb's tail. Scars on his face and hands suggested that he had broken up brawls in the past and would cheerfully do so again. Kep suspected there was more to him than met the eye. She swallowed a sigh. Another person to be wary of. Windy made a half-bow, impeded by the small chest which he held under one arm. 'Welcome to Merrywinds.' He showed no sign of surprise that a young woman had usurped the room's former occupant. But a man who hosted pirates was probably used to surprises.

Having laid out a fresh set of clothes for Kep, Molly backed through the door. 'The guests will be hollering for more ale. But you just get your man here to call me, Kep-Váli.' Amused eyes flicked towards the stern figure of Skarlon, who stood to attention just beyond the doorframe. 'I'll bring you anything you might be needing.' She curtseyed with one hand on the door handle, as if the door was her dance partner. Then she was gone.

The innkeeper's brows quivered. 'You've made a friend of my Molly.' Kep detected surprise in his tone. 'That's good.' His eyes were thoughtful. Closing the door, he held the chest towards her with both hands, head bowed. 'This belongs to you now ... Kep-Váli. I'm sure you'll want to check that all is ... in order.' His eyes took in her stockinged feet, and he cleared his throat. 'Or perhaps a bath first? You'll find all that you need through the doors there.' He gestured at the double door, which Kep had assumed was another closet.

*A bath.* Kep's heart rejoiced. 'Thank you. I will take my bath first.'

'Very well.' Moving with ceremony, Windy placed the chest on the sideboard. 'I'll pop back shortly to call you for dinner.' He cleared his throat again, rubbing his hands on his hips in nervous circles. It seemed an odd gesture from such a large man. 'And, well, just to confirm that everything is ...'

Kep nodded. 'I trust all will be in order.' She hoped she sounded stern. Curly had explained that keeping Grady's accounts was a more dangerous job than it sounded: the innkeeper took a healthy cut, but any discrepancy was punishable by death. The poor man's life was on the line, quite literally. She couldn't imagine killing a man over a few missing coins, but Grady wouldn't have thought twice.

Kep locked the door as soon as Windy left. Skarlon would expect an update, but she just didn't have the energy — not before a bath. If the man had any sense, he'd stand down and take one himself. Nobody could get past a locked door!

It was a relief to be alone. For a moment Kep just stood there, shoulders slumped. She rubbed her hands over her grimy face, pressing fingers on her tired eyelids. All this pretence! And the audience with Bahjak was yet to come. But not yet. *A bath.* First, a bath!

Opening the double doors released a waft of steam. To Kep's delight, the little room contained a proper-sized bathtub, which was already filled with steaming-hot water. A shelf holding sponges, brushes and soap stood beside it. Somebody had scented the water, too. Lemon fragrance filled the air.

Wasting no time, Kep undressed and sank into the water's embrace.

She emerged from the bathroom sometime later, feeling rejuvenated. Molly had provided leggings and a tunic, similar in style to her own. She was tired, but at least she was clean. With a shock, she noticed a fresh log on the fire. Her newly polished boots stood next to the door, her cloak no longer dirty, but brushed and folded over the back of the chair. Someone had been here! Kep's heart gave a little skip, then calmed. *Molly.* How could she have been so naïve? Of course she'd have a spare key to the room. Her eyes shot to the chest. Still there, exactly where Windy had left it.

Breathing a sigh of relief, Kep collected the chest from the sideboard and sat down at the writing desk, Grady's legacy set in front of her. Made from cherry-coloured wood, the chest had a highly lacquered finish. The top was inlaid with fine silver-work. What she'd taken to be a star was, in fact, a compass design. Fine silver lines ran from each of its points to the edge of the lid. The key, which she'd taken from Grady's corpse, was heavy on its cord, which still hung around her neck. Kep dragged it out and, with a shiver of anticipation, pushed it into the lock. The key turned with a well-oiled click.

The chest held a velvet pouch, a cube-shaped case and a large ledger bound in red leather. The little bag made a clinking noise when Kep hefted it. Gold pieces poured into her hand. She gasped. There must have been thirty. No, fifty! A person could buy many things with that much gold. Wide-eyed, Kep replaced the coins, drew the pouch's drawstring tight and put it to one side. She picked up the ledger, feeling uneasy. She'd never been good with figures. What if she couldn't read it?

Tiny numbers filled columns on every page. Kep made out several hands. The last, she assumed, was Windy's. Thankfully, his numbers were extraordinarily neat. One column seemed to be expenses. Next to a list of dates, she saw repeated words: meals, lodging, laundry, girls. *Girls?* Kep frowned for a moment, then blushed. *Oh.* The last entry was in fresh ink: 'pig'. In the adjacent column, Windy had written *3 sl.* Three silver for a half-carcass of pig. It seemed fair. The innkeeper was certainly thorough.

Kep's eyes slid to the bottom of the column, where she saw a longer number underlined with two lines. Beside that was a single word. *Gold.* Her hand flew to her mouth. She flipped back a few pages, eyes wide. Grady was wealthy! Shamefully wealthy. No! *Kep* was wealthy.

Kep's heart raced as she closed the ledger. What might a person do with so much gold? It was ... staggering. This put the responsibility of being Simbab into a whole new light. Her heart lifted as the full significance hit her. There was enough gold to buy an entire village! Her hand flew to the back of her neck, brushing her three tiny braids. Truly, the gods were with her! However harsh Bahjak's bargain, whatever the smuggler might demand, this was *more* than enough to save her friends. Kep lifted her chin. If he demanded it all, she would give it to him — gladly.

One item remained in the chest: a battered case, chipped in one corner. Inside was a compass nestled in a bed of purple velvet. Heavy in her hand, the instrument had a bevelled face, gold bearings and a floating needle. Kep knew nothing about compasses. She had as much chance of reading it as she had of understanding the whole weird situation she now found herself in. But even she could tell that the compass was special. And, like everything else, it belonged to her. *Plunder.*

The knock at the door was far too timid for the broad-shouldered innkeeper, betraying his anxiety. So Kep put the man out of his misery, quickly complimenting him on his exceptional bookkeeping. Tension melted from him. His dealings with her predecessor had obviously been difficult. In answer to his enquiry, Kep told him she would be happy to join her companions for dinner in the main lounge. But first, another conversation.

While she waited, Kep picked up the glass of rum and gave it a sniff. It didn't smell like anything a person should drink. She took a tiny sip. It was enough! She stuck out her tongue, her face squirming in disgust. The wood polish that the slaves used on the bannisters at the Aranti Villa would have tasted better! She was setting the glass back on the sideboard and wishing for a jug of water to rinse away the taste, when a knock came at the door.

As Curly slid sideways around the frame, Kep glimpsed Jen-Jay standing guard. She sighed, but she supposed it was for the best. With so much at stake, the new Simbab needed all the protection she could get. Curly sidled into the room like a nervous puppy — eager to please, but guilty, as if some forgotten misadventure was about to be uncovered. He wore fresh clothes and had brushed out his curls. His eyes went to the portrait, and he blinked, caught by the appraising stare of the pirate queen.

'Curly.' Kep gestured at the couch. 'Sit. Please.' She stayed on her feet. 'There are things we must discuss.' Curly obliged, trapping his hands between his knees. She got straight to the point. 'If I'm successful in negotiating the release of my friends, I will be true to my word. You will become the captain of the *Lady Lee*. But, now that I understand the situation more fully, I have some conditions.'

Curly bowed his head. 'You are Simbab, Kep-Váli.'

Kep felt the portrait's eyes watching her. She put her hands on her hips. 'If you are to continue being a pirate, I want you to be the right sort of pirate.' Curly blinked, confused. 'First, you will keep to the sea.' It wasn't an imposition. The pirates had hated their time on land. 'There will be no picking on innocent villagers.' Curly shook his head, as if he wouldn't dream of doing such a thing. 'Next: you will look after the interests of every member of the crew.' Kep folded her arms. 'I don't wish to hear any more stories about card games, especially if they involve gambling with boys' lives.' Curly blinked several times. His heels bounced. He looked worried, as if wondering what other stories she had heard. Kep narrowed her eyes. 'And, most important of all, you will be *completely* honest with me.'

'Of course. Completely honest, Kep-Váli,' said Curly hurriedly, scratching at an earlobe.

Kep raised her eyebrows, took a deep breath, and sighed. 'Good. So is there anything you should have told me about? Anything you've forgotten to mention which might be important?'

Curly licked his lips. 'If there is something you wish to know, I will answer truthfully. You need only to ask, Simbab.'

Kep sighed again. This was the problem. Curly might be truthful, but he had a slave's instinct for secrecy. She'd only get answers if she knew which questions to ask. How could you manage such a man? Spike had given her a couple of threads to pull, but unravelling someone like Curly would take a lifetime. However, one glaring omission needed to be dealt with.

'Very well. You can start by telling me all about Yulia.'

16

GUARDIANS

The Merrywinds lounge had everything a tired traveller could wish for: cosy chairs and warm lamplight; two fireplaces, one at either end of the room; home brewed beer and rustic food delivered by smiling servants. Everything was homely and comfortable. It was the perfect place to relax — assuming you weren't waiting for contact with the unscrupulous smuggler who held your friends captive.

Kep and her companions occupied a nook in the corner furthest from the door. On the table between them was a platter of dried fruits and cheeses, a basket of crusty bread, and a large map of the coastline. Kep and Skarlon had been furnished with big mugs of frothy ale, Jen-Jay a tumbler of rum. The veteran warriors sat facing the room, watching the entrance and the other patrons.

Kep didn't think any of the guests looked threatening, certainly not the elderly couple who, despite having arrived in a very fancy carriage, had ordered nothing but soup. They wore sour expressions, as unhappy with each other as with their soup. A second rather rowdy group comprised four or five young men with enormous hands and gawky limbs. Their sun-tanned faces and rustic clothes confirmed Windy's information; just the sons of farmers travelling home from a trip to the markets. Their loud, honest laughter reminded Kep of Braig. She sighed. She was too tired to reflect on Braig and his untimely death. And she was supposed to be monitoring the pirates anyway.

Kep's pirates, as Jen-Jay insisted on calling them, had made themselves at home, seated at the round tables or with their feet up in front of the fire, tankards of ale in hand. At the nearest table Spike and Ratskin were playing a game involving different coloured balls and cups. The game wasn't holding Spike's full attention; he was listening to other conversations and joining in with the laughter.

Sitting at the next table over, Harden was telling stories featuring himself as the protagonist, and getting more cheery-faced by the minute. His ale consumption was steady. Kep could have sworn the man's belly had grown since they'd been at Merrywinds. Orrick smiled and nodded, with the vague air of someone pretending to listen. Creely divided his time between contradicting Harden on finer details, preening his beard, and flirting with the passing barmaids.

Rawlins made a solitary figure over at the second fireplace, his stockinged feet propped on a stool, a cloud of pipe smoke and his morose expression deterring anyone from venturing near. Greigo and Tibbs were together, of course, in a corner. Tibbs hugged his beer close to his chest with both hands, reminding Kep of a rat with an acorn. She was certain the pair was plotting mischief of some sort. At least they were in plain sight.

Realising that Curly was missing from his place at the bar, Kep frowned, her heart skipping a beat. Then she spotted him eating at a small table of his own. She breathed a sigh of relief. All accounted for and not drawing too much attention to themselves. They looked *mostly* like ordinary travellers, if a little on the colourful side.

Through a cloud of foam, Kep took her first sip of ale. Not too bad. Bitter, with a faint tang of herbs. Jen-Jay set her empty tumbler down on the table. 'So that's how he lost the ship? In a game of cards? What a ridiculous man.' She clicked her tongue. Curly had gone down yet another notch in her estimation.

Kep had relayed the story as best she could. Curly had fallen head over heels for Yulia's charms, unaware of her prior involvement with Grady. Using wit and beauty, Yulia had seduced the man, luring him first into her bed and later into a most ill-advised game of cards. The outcome of that fateful night was that Curly lost the thing most precious to him: his ship.

Curly was a terrible gambler. But Kep wondered if there was more to the story. 'Spike thinks Curly's still in love with Yulia.'

Jen-Jay harrumphed. 'And what would youngsters know about love?' Kep didn't answer. She sensed Skarlon watching her over the top of his mug. She took another sip of ale as Jen-Jay continued. 'He was made a fool of and tricked out of his ship. I suspect that's all there is to it. But this Yulia, she sounds like trouble. Did she consider herself Grady's woman?'

Kep blinked. What woman would want to be with a monster like Grady? 'I don't know. The boys didn't think so. But Ratskin and Spike are scared of her. It seems she has quite a temper.'

Skarlon growled. 'A woman with a grudge and a temper. Worst combination.' Jen-Jay shot him a glare. 'She won't take kindly to a rival, that's all I'm saying.'

'Kep is *not* her rival,' said Jen-Jay through clenched teeth. 'This ridiculous arrangement is only temporary.' Unfairly, her frown seemed as much directed at Kep as Skarlon, as if Kep had *wanted* to be Simbab!

Windy interrupted the conversation, delivering their meals himself. For Skarlon and Jen-Jay, there was pork — again. Windy smiled, placing a covered platter in front of Kep. 'The cook has rustled you up something special, Kep-Váli.' He said her name quietly, under his breath. Then he lifted the cover.

An enormous grilled fish stared up at Kep, taking up most of the platter. There were root vegetables, too, mashed into a creamy pulp and served with knobs of butter. Windy passed on the cook's apology: it was too early in the season for spring carrots, but there were bitter greens and a spicy chutney on the side. Kep felt overwhelmed as she picked up her fork. The dish looked worthy of Aranti's table!

The fish was delicious. Sweet and succulent, it fell apart in luscious chunks of white flesh. Kep ate with relish, relating the rest of her news between mouthfuls. The old warriors exchanged worried looks when she repeated what Spike had said about Bahjak. For once they agreed: under no circumstance was Kep to meet with the man alone. Kep nodded, keeping her silence. On this Curly was insistent — the Simbab *always* went alone to meet with Bahjak. None of the other pirates had even laid eyes on the smuggler.

Kep hated deceiving her companions, but she was going to bargain with the man, not fight him. She just wanted it to be over. Curly expected that the summons would come tonight, before dawn. But Bahjak had made Grady wait for days at a time. It was a horrible thought. Every day was another day of torment for her friends. Who knows how Rodine and the others were being treated? Whatever they were eating, Kep doubted it was grilled fish. Her belly stuffed to bursting, she pushed the plate away.

Things would be all right, she told herself. The gods were on their side. And Kep had gold now. Enough gold to satisfy even the greediest smuggler.

Jen-Jay's attention had returned to the map. She measured distances with her thumb, then spoke in a low voice. 'Assuming all goes well, and Curly keeps his word, we could be in Serenity by the turn of Marki.' She shook her head. 'It's cutting it fine.'

Kep stared at the island with the curious name. Serenity was the rendezvous point. Nirias and the others would already be there, wondering at the delay.

Skarlon shifted in his chair and winced, as if the movement pained him. 'And if we don't make it in time? Will Nirias move against Kara-fell without us?'

Jen-Jay scowled. 'Who knows? It's Nirias. And Kara-fell never stays in one place for long. Nirias knows that if the League doesn't strike now the opportunity will be lost.' The tension between the two warriors always intensified when Nirias's name was involved.

Kep stared at the map. How fast could a ship sail? Serenity seemed an awfully long way away. But once there, all this pretence would be over. Kep could say goodbye to the pirates because Nirias would make all of the decisions. She didn't even care if he ordered the novices back to T'al Jazure. Her heart gave a little skip at the thought of seeing Sarin and she blushed, blaming the ale.

'Kep!' Something in Jen-Jay's tone seized Kep's full attention. Her companions had stiffened. 'Don't turn around. Keep your eyes on mine.' Kep froze. Jen-Jay was smiling and nodding, as if agreeing wholeheartedly with something Skarlon had said. That was frightening in itself. Something was wrong. Very wrong. 'Stay calm. Pick up your drink and take a sip.'

Kep did as she was told, her nerves jangling. Skarlon chuckled loudly. Another false note. Tense lines had appeared around his eyes. 'What is it?' said Kep. 'What's wrong?'

Jen-Jay raised her glass, delivering the news through smiling teeth. 'Two Calkinon soldiers just walked through the door.'

## 17

**THE SHELF**

The cage dropped in a sickening rush, leaving Ash's stomach behind. A new dread replaced the temple's horrors — the gut-clenching certainty that they were about to crash to the ground. Cables whirred as the cage hurtled downwards. Ash could no longer see the guards, just the white sand floor with its curious symbols. It raced to meet them. 'Hold on!' shouted Ordelle. If only that were possible! Eyes squeezed shut, his teeth clamped in a grimace, Ash braced himself for impact. But the juddering crash didn't come. They just kept dropping, straight through the bottom level.

At first, Ash thought they were sinking into a well. Then the chimney of rock gave way. A waft of salty air hit his face. Below was the unmistakable gurgle of water. His stomach churned as he peered through the bars. The place was empty! Just rock and dark water. 'It's a cave!' Sarin sounded relieved. Ash couldn't imagine a more lifeless place. Deep beneath the temple's foundations, like an evil secret, the grotto was cold and colourless. The only light came from the cave's mouth, as grey as the sea itself.

The cage's progress slowed. With no shaft to contain it, it swung as it dropped. At last, with a gentle bump, it came to rest on a ledge of rock. Ash took a series of shallow breaths, fighting the urge to vomit. This was it, then. Their final destination. Sarin couldn't talk his way out of trouble this time. There would be no clever tricks, and no prospect of escape. That guard had spoken true; there was no hope here. Just the Shelf.

'How ingenious,' said Ordelle. Ash didn't know if she meant the cage mechanism or the manner of their death. It seemed an odd moment for her to discover sarcasm. 'Ingenious' wasn't the word that sprang to mind. He couldn't imagine a fate more cruel: trapped inside a cage, knowing that death would creep in with the tide.

Waves lapped at the edge of the Shelf already. Ordelle scowled when one ran right over the bottom of the cage to lick the edge of her boots. *'Cleansed?* Pah!' She stamped her foot, making a splash, as if the water was a pest to be scared away. 'What charlatans! To flout the terms of the Calkinon Peace. How dare they? Just wait until the Jade Bench hears of this! My father will be furious!'

Ordelle's angry reaction was out of character, which only made Ash feel more panicky. Nor could he imagine Aechon being furious.

The situation made it hard to breathe. When Tarlyn wormed her way out of his hood, he let out a cry. 'No, Tarlyn!' Too late. Her silky frame had slipped between the bars.

Tarlyn shook herself, let out an indignant mutter, either at Ash's panic or the wet ground, and slunk off to explore. Ash closed his eyes, pushing his face against the bars. His heart sank. He *wanted* Tarlyn to escape. But what if she didn't come back? What if this was goodbye?

'Neat trick, Tarlyn,' said Sarin. 'Shame we can't all do that.'

Ordelle turned on him, her eyes flashing. 'We are *not* going to die here, Sarin. I refuse to give that woman satisfaction!' Ordelle was *scary* when riled. 'Turn around. Let me see the knots,' she demanded. 'Mine are too tight to budge. We'll have to use our teeth. First we'll get free, then we can pick the lock.'

Sarin blinked, taken aback by this feisty new Ordelle. Then he nodded. 'Excellent plan.' He turned his back, pushing his forearms together. 'But hurry. Judging by those watermarks, the tide is about halfway in. This place will fill up quickly.'

Ash blew air in and out through pursed lips, trying to stay calm. He understood the wailing music of this place now. Its slow lament dragged at his heart, telling him they would die here and none of their friends would know. He stared at the cave's open mouth in dismay. How could there be so much water in the world? Wave after wave crept in, exploring the little cave and claiming it for the sea. A lump grew in his throat and his chest tightened. He closed his eyes and bowed his head. Kep would never even know that they'd tried.

The thought of his friend made Ash open his eyes again. Kep would pray to Narsis in this situation. She'd say it was all part of the gods' plan. And, most of all, she'd tell Ash to pull himself together. That was the thing about Kep — she *never* gave up hope. He let out a breath, lifted his chin and took a long, shaky breath.

Sarin stood with his feet planted, trusting Ordelle to work on his bonds. Ash understood how hard it was for Sarin to be patient and do nothing — he wasn't one to give up either. Catching Ash's eye, he grinned, despite the encroaching waves. 'Don't look so worried. You're the Grey Boy. This isn't the end. It can't be. If Rilka's right, there's *much* worse in store for you. You've got to do battle with the Melk.'

Ash rolled his eyes. He sniffed and cleared his throat. 'That's right. And Kep needs us.' A muffled grunt of agreement came from Ordelle. She was gnawing at the knots like a terrier with a bone.

'Ow!' said Sarin. 'Don't bite me, Ordelle!' Her reply was unintelligible — perhaps something about breaking his thumb. Ash couldn't help smiling. The banter was a tiny flicker of warmth in this cold-hearted place. He wriggled his shoulders and, clenching his teeth against the pain, began a concerted campaign against his bonds.

Ash thought his own thumb might break as he wrestled the prickly knots. Nobody was more astonished than he was when the bonds gave way. 'I've done it!' He held up the ropes as proof.

'How?' Ordelle stared in disbelief.

Ash hardly believed it himself. 'I don't know. Maybe my knots weren't as tight.' Had the young guard taken pity on him? It took Ash precious minutes to release Sarin, who went straight over to examine the lock.

As soon as Ordelle was free, she began rummaging in her bag. At first Ash wondered if she'd saved some food. Then she pulled out something that jingled. 'Here. Try these.' She held up a ring with curious rods of metal attached.

Sarin's mouth fell open. 'Ordelle! It's a Jiggler's Three! Have you any idea what the penalty is for carrying one of these?'

'Yes. In the tribune states, it's ten years' imprisonment. Or fifteen inside Calkinon city.' Ash blinked. Trust Ordelle to have a full set of thieves' picks *and* know the penalties. She scowled at her astonished friends. 'Hurry. The water is rising.' She had a point — it was already up to their ankles.

While Sarin worked the lock, Ordelle strung up their bags on the leftover rope and suspended them from the cage's roof, out of harm's way. With nothing to keep him occupied, Ash was left fighting off his fears of drowning. He fixed his eyes on the dry rocks at the back of the cave. If they could escape the cage, they could clamber high enough to wait out the tide. He spotted Tarlyn hunting something in the shadows. Something that scuttled. A crab? He shuddered. What other creatures lurked in the dark?

Picking a lock was harder than it looked, even with the best illegal tools. Sarin had been working at the lock for some time when larger waves inundated the cage. Ash winced, pulling the rope to hoist their bags up a little higher. Soon, the waves would soak them, too.

Sarin swore. 'I thought I had it then.' His eyes were angry as he flicked hair out of his face. He winced, flexing his fingers. 'My hands are cramping.' They were all shivering from the damp cold. As the cave mouth grew smaller with the incoming tide, the light grew gloomier. 'Ordelle, do you want to have a go?' Ordelle nodded, her expression grim. Perhaps she was thinking the same as Ash. Sarin *never* gave up.

Ordelle brought all of her energy to focus on the lock. The first thing she did was to tie a piece of rope to her belt and then secure the lock-pick to it, in case she dropped it. Ash gulped at the possibility. They should have thought of that earlier. Then she adopted a new technique. Squashing her face hard against the metal, she hooked her arm through the bars so she could jiggle at the lock from the outside. It seemed crazy to Ash. How could she see what she was doing? He bit his tongue, however, knowing better than to offer advice.

A gush of cold met with Ash's crotch, and he shuddered, dancing on his toes. Ordelle ignored the swirling water, her eyes closed in concentration. 'Warded to the west,' she muttered. 'Oh, I see!' Bringing her hand back in, she switched tools and started again. 'That means ...' Her face twitched, contorting with effort. A full minute passed. 'Got it!' The click that followed was the sweetest sound Ash had ever heard. Sarin gave a whoop of triumph. 'You *marvel*, Ordelle! Telion's light, you're clever!' Ordelle endured his hug. Then she shoved the door open.

There was no time to savour their freedom, though. Now waist-deep in the water, they retrieved their bags and splashed their way towards higher ground. As he clambered over slippery rocks, a change in the light made Ash glance over his shoulder. He let out a cry of alarm, pointing at a dark silhouette in the cave's mouth. 'There's a boat!'

Before they could work out what was happening, the craft surfed through the entrance. Knifing about, it drew right up to the edge of the rocks. Light reflected on a silver helm, as the single occupant called out to them: 'Get in! Hurry! The mouth closes.'

Sarin's reaction was swift. 'Go!'

There was no time for discussion. Ash found himself bundled into the bottom of the boat. Ordelle's elbow connected with his mouth and he tasted blood. Something else whacked him over the head as the boat lurched and wallowed — the butt of an oar, or one of their bags. All was chaos and confusion. Oars dragged at the water. Ash thrashed about, desperate to disentangle himself from Ordelle.

*Tarlyn! Where is Tarlyn?* He tried to raise his head, slipped and tried again. 'Get down!'

Ash ducked just in time, almost smashing his head against the barnacle-encrusted entrance. The boat shot from the cave like a cork from a bottle. Then, as if the sea had changed its mind, the current dragged them back. The guard let out a curse worthy of a pirate. Her boots scrabbled for purchase as she strained at the oars. The choppy sea thrashed, trying to drive them onto the rocks.

Ordelle was much better than Ash at extracting herself from the bottom of the boat. She grabbed an oar and the two women pulled side by side, grimacing and straining. For a while, the little boat went nowhere, fighting the swell. Then they made headway, each stroke taking them further from shore and into the deepening mists.

'No!' cried Ash. 'Sarin! We can't leave him!'

Their rescuer hissed at him. 'Shut up! Sound travels on water. We've not yet made the Veil.'

Ash recognised her sing-song voice. It was the guard from their cell. He smothered a whimper. *Sarin. Tarlyn.* Anguish tore at his heart. But the guard was right: they couldn't go back. Through the deepening mist, all he could see of the cave's entrance now was a foamy wash. The sea would soon swallow it. He sank back into the boat, his eyes filling with tears. Ordelle's face was a mask of concentration; her focus on the stroke of her oar, keeping the boat straight as it took them further from shore. Further from Tarlyn. Further from Sarin.

At last, they pulled free of the whirling currents, and the boat settled into a creaking rhythm. The full weight of the situation hit. They'd abandoned their friends. Ash couldn't control the gasp of grief. 'Quiet!' warned the guard. 'But feel free to do something about the rat.' She sucked the side of her thumb. 'It's got spines. What sort of rat has spines?'

Ash twisted his body around, not daring to believe. *Tarlyn!* She looked nothing like a rat — more like a soaked kitten, with flat ears and enormous eyes. He gathered the creature to his heart, wrapping his cloak around her skimpy body. He didn't care if the guard could hear his sobbing.

Their rescuer's teeth flashed in a wicked grin. 'Stop your sniffling, and pick up that paddle.' Her laughter came in a short blast, like a punch. 'And tell your mate to kick harder. It's like dragging like a dead horse.'

## 18

## PETREL

Petrel was her name. And she was no longer their guard, having dumped her silver cloak and winged helmet overboard at the first opportunity. Beneath the helm her hair was ash-blonde, cropped so short that it looked like feathers.

Ash had no idea how their guard-turned-rescuer had found the vessel in the mist. Perhaps she had counted oar strokes. Regardless, feeling somewhat stunned at their change of fortune, they were now aboard a small cutter named the *Gull*, sipping hot tea to drive away the last of their shivers.

Petrel had supplied dry clothing from one of the boat's many lockers. Ornate in their style and too large, the garments couldn't have been hers. Ash felt awkward in a pair of loose, canary-yellow trousers. He had the sneaking suspicion Petrel was mocking him, but he was grateful for the tea and the warm shawl around his shoulders.

Sarin wore a full-length robe of padded satin, deep burgundy with orange swirls embroidered across the chest. His hair was still wet — slick and very black. Ordelle accused him of looking like a prince from a faraway country with some unpronounceable name, and Petrel laughed as if it was the funniest thing she'd ever heard.

Their host moved around the cabin with a definite air of ownership, producing plates, forks and, of all things, napkins. Sarin matched Ash's raised eyebrows and shrugged. His eyes were wary, though, as he flipped his hunting knife over in his hands. It was a surprise to have their weapons returned. The prospect of food was welcome, too. From various lockers, Petrel conjured an oblong loaf of bread, smoked fish in a pot and a large wheel of blue-flecked cheese. She plonked it all down on the table and grinned at them. 'Eat.' They didn't need to be asked twice.

Ash wolfed down bread and cheese, taking in the wonders of the tiny cabin as he chewed. Clever fitting of the polished cabinetry meant there were cupboards and drawers of every size. The shelves had hooks and rails to keep things in their places. All was spick and span, the reddish timbers gleaming.

The bunks which Ash and Sarin were sitting on were well-padded, following the shape of the hull and upholstered in wine-coloured leather. On Petrel's insistence, Ordelle had claimed the large, cushioned bed which was built into the bow. She sat cross-legged, in pale green trousers with a belted tunic to match. Kettles and copper pans dangled from the panelled ceiling over the space that served as a galley. It was like a tiny cottage — except for the slight rocking motion and the gurgling sound of water lapping at the hull.

Petrel watched them all with interest, but her eyes returned most often to Ordelle. 'Is the smoked fish too salty? I love it salty, but not everyone does.' Ordelle had started on her second helping. She swallowed her mouthful, but, before she could even reply, Petrel had jumped up to forage in an overhead cupboard. 'I think there's ... Ah, here it is.' She cocked her head at the pot. 'I've forgotten what it's called. The Sisters eat it with cheese.'

After sampling the condiment on a spoon, Ordelle declared it to be chutney — relish, she explained, was more piquant. Sarin rolled his eyes, but their host laughed, delighted.

'Thank you, it's delicious,' said Ash. 'We were very hungry.'

Petrel's eyes shone. 'I'm glad. There's an elpha-stove, but it's too risky to cook. And nobody has elpha these days.'

Sarin licked his fingers. 'Thank you for the fish. And for ...', he glanced at Ash's colourful trousers, 'well, for everything else. But, forgive me for asking ... this *is* a rescue, isn't it?'

Petrel's grin was cheeky with dimples. 'Of course it's a rescue.' Her eyes flicked to Ash, and she made a small bow, bringing her hands together in prayer. 'For the food, you are welcome. As for rescue ... it's you who are rescuing me.' Here she kissed two fingers and used them to scribe a circle in the air. Her eyes slid to Ordelle, and her smile widened. '*You* have brought me hope where before there was none.'

Sarin blew out his cheeks. '*Great*. We *are* escaping then. Just thought I'd check. Because ... well, we don't seem in much of a rush. Won't the guards be searching?'

Petrel laughed. 'For you? Why? You're dead. *The sea will cleanse your memory.*' Her singsong imitation of the high priestess was scathing. 'You certainly caused a stir. Nobody's ever come *down* the river before.'

'We were lost,' said Ash.

'Right. And where were you headed?'

'Scrimpton.'

Petrel laughed. 'You *were* lost. That's on the other side of the Tella peninsula.'

'We know.' Sarin frowned, unwilling to divulge further information. He returned them to the matter at hand. 'Won't they check the Shelf? And find out we're gone?'

'Don't fret. The cage won't be inspected before noon tomorrow. Sister Revis — that's the High Priestess, to you — she'll want to gloat, and loot your poor dead bodies.' She made a face. 'Low tide is early tomorrow. Far too early for her *holiness*. Grievous Revis enjoys a long lie-in.'

Ordelle glowered. 'I'd like to embalm that woman.'

Sarin folded his arms. 'Would this be after you've killed her?'

'In her case I'd make an exception.'

Petrel hooted, clapping her hands. 'You're funny, Ordelle!'

'I am?' Ordelle looked perplexed.

'Yes! Adorably.'

Sarin frowned. 'But what about you? Won't the other guards miss you at meals?'

'No. I won't be missed.' Ash detected a tremble in the corner of Petrel's mouth. Her casual toss of her head couldn't mask the hurt in her eyes. 'That's one advantage of being Tuneless.'

In the middle of yawning, Ordelle sat up, shocked. 'No! Do not call yourself that!'

Ash blinked at her reaction. *Tuneless?* He was obliged when Ordelle explained, even if doing so made him seem ignorant. 'It's a derogatory term, Ash. Like Sarin calling himself a Farling.' Sarin lifted a brow, but Ordelle pressed on, oblivious.

To be fair, the Cryer's daughter sounded less like a lecturer than usual. 'The language of the Singing Isles is tonal, so a rising or falling inflection changes the meaning of a word. But in Ari many of the words are not words at all — they are notes. "Tuneless" is insulting and exclusionary. It refers to those born without a perfect ear for pitch. Unable to fully inhabit the language of their birth, such people are discriminated against. In extreme cases they can even be exiled.' Ordelle blinked at Petrel, perhaps wondering whether she'd gone too far. She bit her lip. 'I'm sorry. Forgive me if I misspoke. But I do not think anyone should use such a word. *Ever.*' She blinked several times. 'Especially not about themselves.'

Petrel kissed two fingers to her lips. Her eyes looked even brighter. 'You did not misspeak, Ordelle. And ... thank you.'

Ash swallowed, recalling the Zari greeting. *May your song ring true.* 'Song' was a metaphor for life in that context, making the idea of being tuneless even more dreadful. He scarcely knew Petrel, but nobody deserved such cruelty from their own people. To Ash, an outsider, her voice seemed full of music. He was still pondering that when a thought hit him. How much of an outsider was *he*? He'd got used to the idea that Wimsari blood might run in his veins. Now the idea made him shiver.

Petrel smiled at Ordelle. 'Don't be sad on my account. It is true, life in my village was difficult. But my father was a trader and he taught me Common, a barbaric language according to my people.

And he gave me a name I could pronounce. As I grew older, and started getting into trouble, he named me Storm Gull. He said I was like a bird riding the edge of a storm.' She laughed again, and Ash caught his breath. Now that he knew her story, the music of seabirds in her laughter was impossible to miss.

'Wine!' Petrel clapped her hands, shooting a mischievous glance at Sarin. 'Let's have wine and I'll tell you about Borsi Frattellik.'

Sarin frowned as Petrel dug out a bottle of wine, but Ash understood. The young woman wanted to divulge her plan in her own time. He supposed it was fair; she had rescued them, after all. And Ash suspected she enjoyed making Sarin wait for information. Perhaps she hadn't forgiven him for the dreadful whistling.

As directed, Ash reached over his head to unhook four tankards. They were silver, with elegant handles. Petrel sloshed generous portions into the gorgeous vessels from the dusty bottle. Although Sarin accepted his wine with thanks, Ash noticed how he paused, waiting for Petrel to drink first. He still didn't trust her. Petrel took a deliberate swig, her eyes merry as she watched Sarin's face. He tasted his own wine and his eyebrows shot up.

Petrel chortled, raising her tankard as if in a toast. 'If you're stealing wine, you might as well steal decent stuff.' She licked her lips. 'To the Temple's finest.'

Ash took an experimental sip. The wine was smooth, tasting of berries — it sent warmth to his belly and an immediate flush to his cheeks. Sarin savoured another mouthful, his eyes calculating. 'And the boat? Is that stolen, too?'

Petrel's mouth quirked. 'Are you judging me? Was that not your plan? To steal a boat?' She laughed. 'But no,' she gave the woodwork an affectionate pat, 'this darling is mine by right — given to me by poor Borsi Frattellik.'

'Who is Borsi Frattellik?' asked Ash dutifully.

'Borsi was an adventurer, and a pilgrim. Sadly, his journey to the Temple of Spires was his last. The poor man came seeking solace and news of his daughter.'

'The Temple is a scam,' stated Ordelle firmly.

'Oh, yes. Quite the scam. These days at least. But it wasn't always that way. The Temple is ancient — much older than the coven of witches that runs the place now. Poor Borsi was drawn to the mysteries of the Eye; he couldn't help himself. But he wasn't a stupid man. He recognised greed when he saw it. He refused to give the Sisters any more than their due — that's why he hid the *Gull* in the mists. It wasn't that he couldn't afford their exorbitant fees: Borsi was a very rich man. It was a matter of principle. This little boat was his life partner — he hated the idea of those hags getting their hands on her.' She smiled fondly. 'Stubborn old fool.'

Petrel poured herself more wine and sighed. 'Borsi was stubborn all right. He believed in the Watcher until the end, even after what happened.' She shook her head. 'Some beliefs are impossible to shake, I guess.'

'What happened?' asked Ash quietly.

Petrel's expression hardened. 'The Watcher,' she waved her hand in a flourish, 'in all her *fathomless* wisdom, told Borsi that it was too late for reconciliation. His daughter was dead. It was pure spite, I reckon. Borsi had searched for years and he was so very ill. Why break a man's heart?' Petrel stabbed a finger toward the Temple. 'Those witches tell people lies all the time, for their own profit and to benefit their sponsors.' She shook her head, and then a slow grin came over her face. 'But Borsi ... good old Borsi.' She raised her tankard. 'He got his revenge. He collapsed right there, in their stupid temple.

'Oh, how the Sisters were riled! Guests usually stay for a single night. They pay their gold, the Watcher sings and they leave. They're not supposed to hang around coughing up blood, soiling the bed linens and making a nuisance of themselves. After a few days the Sisters realised he was dying and decreed that I would be his nurse. Not because I'm well-trained or kind or anything like that, but because I speak Common. My job was to winkle the location of his boat out of him, before he shuffled off to the After.

'No doubt they thought it was punishment, for one so lowly as me. But I loved it. Because I finally had somebody to talk to. Borsi was a wonderful person. I read him books and he told me all about his adventures. Then, right at the end, he revealed the secret of finding the *Gull*.' A tear threatened, and she wiped it away with a smile. 'Silly old man. He said my name was an omen ... if he couldn't give the *Gull* to his daughter, it had to be mine.' She gestured with her glass, as if making a toast to her friend. 'Borsi died in peace, fifty-six days ago.'

'Were his organs eviscerated before cremation?'

Petrel spluttered, then laughed. 'Who knows? Knowing the priestesses, they probably chucked him into the sea for the fishes.'

Sarin frowned, clearing his throat. 'Fifty-six days? So, why are you still here?'

Petrel made a face at him. 'Are you really so dense? Because of the mists of course.'

'I've been trying to tell him,' said Ordelle.

Sarin threw up his hands, as impatient as Ash had ever seen him. 'I get it. The mists are hard to navigate. But your friend Borsi sailed here. There must be a compass, or something.'

In answer, Petrel tossed him an object, heavy and made of brass — it was lucky Sarin had quick hands. 'See for yourself. Compasses don't work in the mists. It sends them haywire.' Petrel was right. The needle circled erratically one way, then the other. She smirked when Sarin couldn't resist tapping at the glass.

Ordelle tilted her head. 'But you rescued us anyway.'

'That's true.' Petrel reached out as if to pat Ordelle's hand, then raised a finger in the air instead. 'Like I said. It's more accurate to say that you are rescuing me. Nobody can travel in the mists without a mist-singer.' Ash's heartbeat quickened. 'I can steer by the stars, under a clear sky. But I can't lift the mists.' Petrel grinned, pointing a finger. 'But he can. *He* knows the Song of Passing.'

Ash looked at his friends, flustered. 'I don't know what you mean.'

Petrel snorted. She set her tankard down for the first time. Her eyes were windows of light as she leaned forward. 'We both know *that's* not true. I was there. In the drowned city. I *heard* you singing and I saw how the mists moved. You *called* them.'

'It was you!' Ordelle sounded impressed. 'You're an excellent stalker. I only spotted you once.'

'Your eyes miss nothing, my sweet new friend.' Two fingers came to Petrel's lips in another of her soft salutes.

Ash turned his desperate gaze on Sarin. But Sarin's eyes were serious. 'She's got a point, kin. The mists move strangely when you sing. It's quite weird.'

'See?' Petrel picked up her tankard and downed the rest of her wine. 'Ordelle, could you please reach into that cupboard above your head? We can sleep later. But first, another bottle of the Temple's finest wine. And there's a jar of spiced apricots. Do you like apricots?'

Ash closed his eyes. A band of panic had been constricting his chest ever since the mention of the mist-singer. Now it tightened another notch.

## 19

## MIST-SINGER

True to her word, and apparently none the worse for drinking so much wine, Petrel woke them several hours later. Ash wondered how she'd gauged the hour. The darkness was absolute, with no sign of moons or stars, as if they'd woken in a void.

The little boat rose and fell, creaking in time with the breath of the sea. Ash still hadn't decided whether the motion was comforting or disturbing. Ordelle was busying herself with ropes, perfectly at home. Petrel bowed to Ash before taking her position at the tiller. She seemed happy to set sail into the inky darkness, trusting only in a song — in a song that Ash had no idea how to sing.

The young woman must have detected his panic. 'The mist-singers usually stand at the bow.' She shrugged. 'No idea why. Probably makes them feel important. Don't look so worried. Just bring me the stars. Ordelle and I will do the rest.'

Sarin moved to Ash's shoulder. 'I'll join you at the front, kin. It's a better view.' Ash shot him a look. *A better view?* It was pitch black!

'Good plan,' said Petrel. 'Stay out of my way. Reckon you can sort the anchor?'

'Of course.'

'Hmmm. Well, raise it as soon as the mists lift. Not before. And kill that light as soon as you're in position. No point taking chances.'

Sarin took up the lantern without comment, leaving Ash with both hands free to manoeuvre himself along the deck. Securing the lantern on a hook, Sarin settled himself with his back against the cabin housing, his feet propped on the railing. 'This'll do.'

Ash was relieved that he made no move to extinguish the lantern. The night stole the light from its halo. He doubted Petrel could see it, let alone anyone on the shore. The timber at his back felt solid, reassuring. Beside him, Sarin tilted his face to the sky. 'Do you know any constellations, Ash?'

'Um. Not many. Kep taught me to find the Crown. Do you know it? Seven stars in a curve.'

'The Crown?' Sarin laughed. 'I thought you Mildarens hated kings.'

Ash considered it for a moment. Sarin was right. And it *was* curious. 'They do now. I suppose the name is older.' He sensed Sarin's amusement.

'The Aurum call that one the Tree. It's our most beloved constellation, because the brightest star never shifts. It marks due north.' After a moment, he went on. 'The night sky is a living canopy for Aurum. We don't go in for frypans and kettles. Or crowns.' Ash knew his friend was making conversation for his sake. He appreciated the effort. 'I wonder what Petrel calls the Tree,' mused Sarin. When Ash didn't reply, he went on. 'She's a bit full of herself, but I like her. I'm pretty sure she can sail this boat. She moves like she's a part of it.' Ash nodded to himself. It was true. 'And ... maybe she's right. Maybe you do know this song of hers. You're supposed to know every song that exists. That's the deal, isn't it? So why not that song?'

Ash's throat tightened as Sarin continued. 'It seems odd, though, doesn't it? As if ... Well, as if we're exactly where we're meant to be.' Sarin clicked his tongue and chuckled softly. 'Listen to me! I sound like Kep.'

Ash snorted. 'Kep would say that Narsis had planned the whole thing.'

'True. And scold us soundly for stealing a boat.'

Ash's mouth twitched in a sad excuse for a smile. The conversation was flagging. Sarin's expectation was a third presence in the dark. Ash wet his lips, feeling his mouth dry. 'Sarin ... I don't think I can move the mists. Perhaps if I was the real Keeper of the Song. I mean, if I'd been properly trained. But I'm not in control of the Song. I never have been. It just sort of ambushes me when I'm least expecting it.' Ash hugged his knees up to his chin, staring at the bugs now circling the glowing lantern. 'I don't have the first clue how to find a particular song. I wouldn't even know where to start.'

'Well ...' Sarin shifted his legs, re-crossing his boots. 'Correct me if I'm mistaken, but I believe it's customary to start with a single note.' His eyes glinted, catching the lantern's light. 'Just give it a go, Ash.' He shrugged. 'It can't hurt. If it doesn't work, we'll just get a new plan. Who cares if you fail? I won't think any less of you, and neither will Ordelle.'

*A new plan.* The strange thing was that Ash believed him. The odds never seemed to bother Sarin. Ash relaxed his shoulders a little, swallowing some of the tension in his throat. Reaching forward, he put out the lantern. 'Sarin?'

'Yes, my pallid friend?'

'You can shut up now.'

Sarin laughed and settled back, letting the silence grow.

Except it wasn't silence. Not really. Ash sensed the rhythm of the sea, breathing in and out as it lapped at the little boat, rocking it like a cradle. The *Gull* had a creaking music of its own, too. All he had to do was listen and open his heart.

Ash laid his hands palm-up on his knees. Relaxing the tiny muscles in his jaw, he eased the frown between his brows and raised his face to the darkness. The constellations which Kep had taught him were all up there somewhere — Crown, Fish and Canoe. He just needed to find them. First, he visualised the mist as a curtain parting. Then he imagined it dissolving and sweeping away. He listened. Straining his mind, he sought a melody. Nothing. Nothing happened.

The failure didn't surprise Ash. The Song didn't work that way.

He swallowed a sigh. Since he didn't want his friends to think he hadn't tried, he cleared his throat. Best to sing a few notes and just get it over with. And that's what he did. Not thinking about anything in particular — just to prove that the whole thing was pointless — he sang four notes. The melody was half-remembered from his childhood. A charm that a frightened little boy had warbled to banish monsters. There were no words to remember. It was just a lullaby.

To Ash's surprise, the rest of the notes came easily. Unsure of the second verse, or if there even was a second verse, he sang it over. The lullaby had a gentle, rocking rhythm, very close to the song of the sea itself. He'd never noticed that as a child. How could he? He'd never experienced the sea. Now it seemed obvious. The melody lifted and fell. Hushed syllables with crooning vowels. Ash closed his eyes, caught in the lullaby's embrace.

The Song came in ribbons of bright energy, ebbing and flowing like the tides. He knew even before he opened his eyes that the mists were moving. And he understood. The goal wasn't to dispel the mists, but to embrace them. Drawing them in, he let himself drift. Sea, mist, sky and Song. All were one. *Sleep, my little one, sleep.* Her eyes were grey. Was it a memory? Or a dream? Ash didn't care. Because it didn't matter. He just knew the lullaby was his, given to him by a woman with rain-grey eyes. Safe in her arms, he sang, letting the mists draw him where they would.

Had the stars ever blazed as they did on that night? The Song rose into a wheeling sky, taking Ash with it. He sensed the boat was moving, but it was insignificant. Because here was eternity. Stories unfurled across a timeless tapestry, shot through with golden light, narrated by stars.

**20**

———————

# AN AUDIENCE WITH BAHJAK

Kep desperately wanted to turn and look at the soldiers. But not as much as she wanted to crawl under the table and hide. She ducked her head, concentrating on breaking up bread she had no intention of eating. Windy swept up to their table, his smile as broad as ever. His tray held drinks they hadn't requested. He set out glasses and poured a honey-coloured liquid, speaking in an undertone. 'They are staying. They don't wear the red collars of Calkinon, but ... everything about them smells of the lake city.'

'Kep, drop your shoulders,' said Jen-Jay, with a wolfish smile. 'You're too stiff. And pass me that loaf. You look like you're feeding ducks.' Incapable of thinking for herself, Kep appreciated the direction. She pushed her chair back and dangled an elbow over the armrest, trying to look more at ease.

Windy finished pouring. 'Good. Do nothing to draw attention to yourselves.' He murmured to Kep while collecting his tray: 'Dance with my Molly when she asks.' Before Kep could blink, he had turned to the other guests, a cheery smile on his face.

'Hurrah!' A loud shout from near the front door made Kep jump. 'Let's have some music!' A fiddler appeared from nowhere, joined by a round-faced woman with a drum to match. The young farmers began to clap and cheer. In no time they were up and dancing, whirled into the middle of the room by the barmaids. Curly needed no invitation to join in. He made extravagant flourishes with his arms as he jigged about, beaming.

Things got chaotic very quickly. Boots stomped and skirts swirled. And there was Molly! Twirling a huge red scarf as she danced. Kep stood up, clapping along and trying to look as delighted as everyone else. Even Skarlon stamped his foot to the beat. Molly's red scarf whirled closer. In a flurry of steps, the scarf changed hands — taken up by a girl who might have been Molly's younger sister. Molly caught Kep's hand, screened by the veil of cavorting fabric. 'Come with me.'

A curtain parted. A panel slid, and they were gone.

Of course, Bahjak's messenger was Molly! Kep should have guessed as much. The tunnel was clean and dry, lit by torches. It took them underground, away from the lodge, towards the coast. 'We don't bring anyone this way. Not even the Simbabs.' Molly's mouth curved in a secretive smile. 'Bahjak has made a special exception. For you, Kep-Váli.' The way the woman said her name made Kep feel uneasy. When they reached the end of the tunnel, the thrill in her stomach turned to dread.

It was a box, not much larger than a wardrobe. Attached to its top was a conglomeration of chains. Beside it, a huge crank-wheel. Molly ran an appraising glance over Kep's figure. 'We'll go together. Come!' As Molly drew her into the box, Kep took a quick look over her shoulder, back along the tunnel. *Pointless.* She had no choice but to trust this woman.

With her heart pounding, Kep squeezed herself into the tight space. Molly slipped in, too, encircling her arms around Kep's waist. 'Closer, Kep-Váli. I need to latch the door.' Kep breathed in the warm smell of Molly's skin. She closed her eyes, and the door clicked shut.

With a rattle of chains and a clanking of machinery, the box lurched into motion. In the darkness, Kep felt the floor drop beneath them. Molly's breast was warm against her arm. She felt a sudden stab of fear. Why was she trusting this woman? She could have run — taken Berry and galloped away. But in her heart, she knew that was the *worst* thing she could have done. It still didn't stop her from wishing she could go back and change her decision, though.

The box jerked to a halt, making Kep bounce on the soles of her feet. Molly continued to hold her. 'I think he will like you.' Her voice was warm and sultry in Kep's ear. 'A word of warning, Kep-Váli. Do *not* lie to him.' The door opened, letting light into the tiny chamber, and Molly brushed the side of Kep's face with her fingers. Something behind her eyes made Kep even more unsettled than their intimate proximity. 'Bahjak will ask for a gift. Be sure to offer him something he will enjoy.'

Merrywinds had two distinct personalities. The cosy inn above, and this place. The deep and secret world of smugglers. Here, wagons trundled on greased rails, quiet and sinister. Winches and hoists and other paraphernalia enabled the efficient moving of goods. Openings on either side of the tunnel afforded glimpses of stacked crates and barrels. Kep saw cages, too — with sturdy bars. *For slaves.* The cages she could see were empty, and Molly's quick pace prevented her from searching for signs of her friends.

People worked in the shadows, ignoring them as they went about their tasks. The women passed on until, at the end of the tunnel, a large door confronted them, made from pressed metal. Molly smiled as she turned the latch. Behind the door was a heavy velvet curtain, which Molly held aside as she gestured for Kep to go first. Kep swallowed her fear and stepped through into the strangest place she had ever seen.

It would be an insult to call the room a cave. It resembled a palace — a very peculiar palace, full of curious objects. The light came from lanterns of coloured glass, held aloft by statues of winged naked women, wrought in bronze. Twin orbs stood on either side of the door, sending clouds of essence into the air. The musky aroma of orange and dark spices made Kep's head spin a little. Or was it just the strangeness of the place?

Gleaming tanks stood on stands, full of vibrant fish and a blue creature with many tentacles. It glided towards Kep, fixing suckers to the glass and regarding her with intelligent, black-slitted eyes. She shuddered. A large yellow and green parrot squawked in greeting. As they approached, it raised the crest on its head, bobbing and dancing on its perch. The bird spoke, startling her. 'Cwaaaaw! Treasures!' Molly transferred the bird to her shoulder with a smile, offering it something from her pocket. The bird continued to stare at Kep from one circled eye, muttering and gloating. 'Treasures, my pretty one.'

'Yes! Oh *yes*. A treasure indeed!'

The throaty exclamation pulled Kep's attention to the centre of the room. There, atop an island of cushions, sat Bahjak, cross-legged.

The smuggler was nothing like Kep had imagined. Bahjak had a mottled complexion with a bluish gleam to his skin. His heavy-lidded eyes were green, and his mouth was very wide. When Kep made an awkward curtsy, he chortled, splitting his face from ear to ear. Mildaresh had toads that looked like this man. They had long blue tongues, and Kep half-expected to see a flash of colour when he licked his lips.

Contributing to Bahjak's bizarre appearance was his curious attire. A silk vest of deep orange left his shoulders and chest bare, except for numerous gold chains and bracelets. Crimson cloth swathed his loins. Kep could see rather more of his thighs than she would have liked, and his belly had a personality all of its own, like a large, mottled pumpkin. A huge emerald winked at her from his navel.

The smuggler chuckled, sending flesh quivering. 'A would-be Simbab! How very diverting.' A thick-fingered hand, laden with rings, waved Kep forward. 'Come, sit with me. Kep of Mildaresh. Sit.'

Against her every desire, and shooting a furtive glance at Molly, Kep settled herself on one of the huge cushions that made up part of Bahjak's strange lily-pad. Pear-shaped and squishy, the cushion moulded itself to her form. Indeed, it seemed intent on swallowing her.

Molly glided over to a small table. She picked up a small bowl, which she presented to Bahjak, then brought one over to Kep. Kep shivered. The vessel reminded her of a hollowed-out skull. It was half-filled with bright yellow liquid the consistency of thin custard, but with a slightly oily sheen. Bahjak's mouth stretched into a smile as he raised his bowl with both hands. 'We will speak of business, as we must. But first, we drink.' His mouth opened and, in one bright gloop, the liquid disappeared down his throat.

Kep's eyes darted to Molly, who stood off to one side, idly scratching the parrot's head with her fingertips. Molly nodded her head with a small frown. *Drink.* Kep lifted the bowl to her lips. The slimy liquid slid down her throat in a cool rush. Sharp yet sweet, it sent a tingle throughout her body, leaving a warm glow. Some of the tiredness washed from her bones.

Bahjak croaked a laugh. 'That's better. Now. What shall we call you, Kep of Mildaresh? Kep the Valiant, T'al Kep, Kep-Váli? Or ... Simbab? All of these names have come to my ears.'

Kep frowned. 'It's just Kep.'

Bahjak made a strange clicking noise in his throat. Kep couldn't decide whether it conveyed amusement or displeasure. 'You, sweet thing, are far from *just* anything. My Molly was right. You do amuse me. Yes. We will trade, you and I. What gift do you offer?'

Kep frowned, remembering Molly's warning. The parrot danced a few eager steps, watching everything with its flat bright eye. 'I ... I didn't know to bring a gift. But I have a chest ... It's up ... It's in my room.' She faltered. She found it hard to believe that the *room* still existed — let alone the chest.

'This chest?' Like a market magician, Bahjak whisked a coverlet aside, revealing the cherry-coloured chest. Kep shot a look at Molly, who just smiled.

'Yes.' Kep licked her lips, distracted by the drink's peculiar aftertaste. 'And I have gold. Lots of gold.'

Bahjak's displeased rumble seemed to come from his belly. He flicked a hand, dismissive. 'No! Do not bore me with offers of gold. Gold is the greedy desire of simple-minded men. Grady was just such a man. An insidious bore. Always offering Bahjak gold — as if having more of it might bring a person joy.'

'Sweetmint, my love?'

Molly offered him a tray, loaded with pale green cubes, frosted in powdered sugar, before setting it down beside him. Bahjak's scowl dissolved, and he popped two into his mouth at once. He munched with obvious relish, making his whole body wobble. 'Hurumph! Grady.' Wiping his mouth on the back of his hand, he ran his tongue around in his mouth. 'Such an unimaginative man. I'm rather delighted that you dispatched him. And I know it pleased my Molly, very much. So, I'll forgive the mistake, just this once.' He beamed. 'You are young, and new to my game. Shall we call the lesson learned?' Aware of a fleeting expression of relief on Molly's face, Kep nodded. Her heart raced a little faster. This *wasn't* going well. Everything felt like a trap — even the cushion. It sucked at her like some sort of horrible sea anemone.

'Thus,' Bahjak waved a hand, 'we have established: gold is nothing to me. Jewels, now ... *that* is another matter.' He smirked. 'But as I think you'll agree, I am quite well accommodated in that regard.' Splaying his fingertips as if he was raising an invisible ball, he invited Kep to look up. By some magic, the lanterns flared more brightly, revealing the cave's roof in all its glory.

Kep let out a gasp. Rubies, sapphires, emerald and diamonds winked down at her, set within gorgeous carvings of fantastical beasts. Kep had no idea what the creatures were — they looked like dragons.

Bahjak grunted, gratified by her astonishment. 'I *have* jewels, little Simbab. But I am always in the market for new wonders to fill my little abode. Like *you*, Kep of the gods.' His eyes turned crafty. 'Ah, now! *There's* an intriguing thought. Perhaps you are jewel enough? Shall I keep you here with me?'

Kep's heart fluttered. He was serious! But Molly shook her head. 'Don't tease, Bahjak.' She wagged a finger.

'Ho! See how my Molly's eyes flash?' Bahjak made that odd clicking noise again, deep in his throat. 'Molly does not like to share. And nor she should. For she is my most precious jewel.' To Kep's astonishment, Molly's laughter was warm. Returning the parrot to its perch, she came to join them, settling herself close to Bahjak. When she reached out to stroke his arm with her fingertips, Kep blinked. Her affection seemed genuine.

'So,' continued the smuggler, 'Kep of Mildaresh: what is your worth?'

Kep swallowed. 'What ... What do you mean ... ?'

'Come. You must be aware of the price on your head?'

Kep frowned, sensing danger. 'I know there is one.'

'Hmmm. And it rises by the day. I can tell you one thing: the man who sits beside the fire in Merrywinds Lodge would pay me *buckets* of gold were I to give you up. It is lucky, is it not, that I have so little desire for that metal?'

Kep stared at him in dismay. Her heart was galloping, her mouth dry. What did Bahjak want from her? He'd rescued her from the clutches of Calkinon, but to what end? Her exhaustion returned, weighing her down. This was impossible! What gift could satisfy a man with a jewelled ceiling?

Bahjak watched her through those strange, reptilian eyes. Kep now knew exactly how a fly felt before being swallowed. Her strange host wagged a knowing finger. 'You want to know why I whisked you away from under the noses of the soldiers? It's because I enjoy having you in play. You, my pretty falcon, are an agent of chaos. And men of my talents profit from chaos.' Flesh wobbled as he chuckled. 'I would take little joy in trading you for a bounty. What would be the fun in that? However ... snatching you away from under the nose of Ermin Rox? Delightful!'

'Ermin Rox?'

'The man who holds the leash of those guardians in the bar above. Did you not see him? Tall and alert. Rather like an oversized stoat. He was watching you with his ferrety eyes when Molly spirited you away. An interesting opponent, I grant you. Rather too good at his job, that one.'

Kep hadn't even noticed the man. 'Is he a slave hunter?'

'Not *usually*. But rumour has it that he's taken employment with the Cleric.' Bahjak seemed to expect some sort of reaction. Kep just looked confused. 'Oh, dear. It's too tragic, Molly.' He lifted an admonishing finger. 'You really *must* learn who your enemies are, my dear. The Cleric, little one, is dangerous beyond account. Nobody hates T'al Kep more than the Cleric. And he hates as only a zealot can. In the Cleric's mind, the gods exist to sponsor the prosperity and empire of Calkinon, not little slave girls from Mildaresh.'

Bahjak laughed at Kep's horrified expression. Why had she never heard of the man? 'It is all nonsense of course,' he went on. 'If the gods existed, why would they favour a regime as corrupt as Calkinon?' Helping himself to another sugared square, he extended the tray of sweetmint towards Kep with a smirk. Kep knew when she was being goaded. She gritted her teeth and kept her silence, ignoring his offer.

Bahjak made a face. 'Oh dear. I can see you are unused to the cut and thrust of bargaining.' His eyes went to Molly, who still caressed his arm. 'Oh, very well, Molly. I shall be kind. Let me make things simple. Tell me what it is that *I* have that *you* want, Kep of the gods. I may see fit to grant your wish ...' He gave her a sly look. 'Because *I* am god here.'

Kep scowled. She wanted to correct him. Gods didn't just grant wishes. But Bahjak was right. In this situation, the man might as well have been a god. Thankfully, she had practised this part with Jen-Jay. She stated her terms as simply as she could. 'I want safe passage to the *Lady Lee*.' She hesitated. 'For myself, and my crew.'

'For your crew.' Bahjak smirked. 'Very good. Anything else?'

'There were four prisoners taken by the pirates in Bixdale. Do you know of them?'

'I am acquainted with your friends. Fighters all, if I'm not mistaken.' He counted them off on his fingers. 'A feisty young woman with *delectable* skin and braids like whips; a strapping young man with straw-coloured hair and the sweetest baby mouth you ever did see; and a third, lithe and athletic, skin the colour of hazelnuts and ebony hair tied in a warrior's knot.' He stared at his fingers. 'Who have I forgotten? Oh yes. The gentle captain with thoughtful eyes. My guess is that he is the best fighter of the lot. Forty winters, give or take, yet barely a scar on his face. He *is* missing the tip of his left ear, though.' Bahjak gave Kep a crafty smile, enjoying her shock at hearing her friends described with such accuracy. Kep's stomach lurched. *How could he know so much?* 'Jaibari, Polkin, Ozu and Rodine, I believe those are their names?' Now he was showing off. 'Oh yes. I know of whom you speak.' He spread his hands. 'And I give you hope. That ship has not sailed, so to speak. It is not *entirely* too late to save them.'

'So they're here?' Kep made fists in her lap to stop her hands from trembling.

'Hmmm? Oh, I don't like to keep human merchandise for long. It gets messy. Quite literally. My guests amuse me for a while, with their secrets and news of the world, then I sell them on.' He smiled. 'Your friends proved quite profitable. A hundred pieces of gold apiece.' Kep scowled. She wanted to remind the smuggler that he didn't care for gold, but she held her tongue as Bahjak folded his hands over his vast belly. 'They *were* entertaining, too. Full of intrigue and secrets. There was a name they would not speak. I was tempted to squeeze them, I confess — I adore winkling out others' secrets.'

Kep felt a shiver of revulsion. What awful tortures had her friends endured? They wouldn't have divulged anything about the League. 'They were rather concerned about you ...' Bahjak gave her a knowing smile, 'Kep of the House of Aranti.'

Molly's expression warned Kep to stifle her anger. It was difficult — her blood felt hot in her veins. She made her voice calm. 'Where are they now?'

'They are safely aboard the *Lady Lee*. For now. But, what can I say? The agents of Kara-fell offered me a very lucrative deal.'

Kep gasped. 'You have sentenced them to death?'

'Most likely.' Bahjak nodded. 'But don't look so downcast. I'm sure they'll put up a decent fight. My money's on Rodine. That one looks as if he can handle a blade. But enough of that. What further thought have you given to my gift?'

Kep gulped. The man was insane. Cold, calculating and insane. She gazed at the treasures that surrounded her. What could she possibly offer to match such things? He was unlikely to want a bow, and Jaibari's sword wouldn't tempt him, either. Besides, it wasn't Kep's to give. She had nothing.

Her eyes fell again on the chest. 'What about the compass? The one in the chest?'

Bahjak raised his brows. 'Ah, the compass. You are right, it is extremely rare — worth a small kingdom, you know? Grady had no idea. Of course he might have, had he stopped to ask its owner before slitting her throat. A pity.' Kep felt her heart lift. *A small kingdom!* The hope died as quickly as it flared. 'But no, this offer does not amuse me. What use have I for a compass? The world travels here to me.' Bahjak yawned. 'Last chance.'

Kep knew the smuggler was tormenting her for his own amusement. Perhaps no gift would suffice. She scowled, trying to think. He valued information. She knew that much. But Kep had sworn an oath. The others hadn't parted with the secret of T'al Jazure. And nor would she. She swallowed, staring into the drinking bowl. Empty, it looked even more like a skull. She blinked as a terrible thought took shape. She lifted her chin. 'Kara-fell.' She cleared the constriction in her throat, speaking louder. 'I will bring you the head of Kara-fell.'

A curtain seemed to lift behind Bahjak's eyes. He let out a gust of laughter. 'Aha!' He croaked with glee, clutching at his jiggling belly. 'I knew it! Oh, yes! This *does* amuse me. Kep of the gods and black-hearted Kara-fell. A battle to the death!'

Almost immediately, he sobered. 'But her head? Whatever would I do with her *head*?' Kep wanted to point out that the skull of Kara-fell would be quite at home in his weird collection. 'No. It is too, too macabre. Bring me the Harp of Aedolin.' Bahjak waved a casual hand. 'Of course, that will undoubtedly involve the removal of said head.'

'A harp?'

'Yes. The instrument is wasted on that barbarian! The harp will be just the thing.'

'Very well.' Kep lifted her chin. 'I will bring you this harp.' Nirias would understand. Surely? She bit her lip, praying that the League's plans were going more smoothly than her own. If not, Kep was in serious trouble.

Bahjak wasn't just satisfied, he seemed elated. 'So! We have ourselves a bargain! And a new Simbab, Molly! With bright blue eyes and a bird on her arm. Bahjak is most pleased.' He clapped his hands to his belly. 'Now. Just in case things go awry, given the *audaciousness* of your gift, have you named a Second?' Molly leaned towards him, her lips moving near his ear. 'Ah!' Bahjak clapped his hands. 'The dancing gambler! Very good. *That* man does not lack imagination. He will do very well.' The smuggler settled into his cushions with a contended grunt. 'Molly, if you would?' He waved a hand and Molly bowed her head in assent.

Moving with languid grace, Molly rose. First, she collected the bowl from Kep's hands. Then she adjusted the incense burners and dimmed the lanterns. Her movements seemed ritualistic — except that Bahjak looked as if he was preparing to take a nap.

Kep told herself to stay alert. Which was hard, because she felt so *very* tired. The negotiations had left her with a sense of deep lethargy. Her eyelids were leaden weights. Against her will, they closed, just for a few seconds. When she opened them, Molly was beside her, stroking her hair. Kep could smell sandalwood and rose, and something else that she couldn't place. Was it Molly's perfume? She hadn't noticed it before. Something was different. *Wrong*, corrected the voice in her head. Something was *wrong*.

Kep nodded to herself, too relaxed to heed the warning. Of course it felt peculiar. Because this wasn't Molly. The woman looking into her eyes was none other than Winifred Debreze. The pirate queen took Kep's hand in her own. 'Do not be alarmed.' Kep just nodded. Her limbs felt pleasantly heavy. 'This will be ... surprising.' With an odd sense of detachment, Kep noticed how firmly the woman was holding her hand. Then she saw the snake.

It was the most gorgeous creature Kep had ever laid eyes on. Thin as a whip and iridescent blue. She watched in fascination as its tongue flickered out, tasting the air. Even when the serpent left the pirate's wrist to encircle her own, Kep did not scream. She felt perfectly calm as it wound itself around her own arm. One, two, three coils, squeezing ever more tightly around her upper arm. Kep cried out at the flash of pain, hot and searing like a branding iron. The serpent shimmered, a bright, burning blue, and became one with her flesh.

Molly released her grip and smiled. 'It is done. Sleep now, Kep-Váli.'

Bahjak cracked open an eye and let out a satisfied croak. 'Mmmm. Sleep, little Simbab. Sleep.'

Kep's head slumped, and she knew no more.

**21**

———

# BETRAYAL

According to Molly, the following things were true: it was dawn; this was a favourable tide; and the *Lady Lee* was waiting, just on the other side of Split Apple Rock. The only problem was that Kep didn't trust Molly anymore. And *nothing* seemed true in this underground labyrinth. Nothing felt *real*. It wasn't just the weird torchlight and the watery music of thc caves. The events of the previous evening had left Kep with confusing gaps in her memory. Where had she slept? When had she changed back into her own clothes? And how had she come to be standing here, at the point where Bahjak's underworld realm met the sea?

The things Kep remembered were so bizarre that she doubted her recollection: a talking parrot, Bahjak's peculiar collection of outlandish objects and the dazzling beauty of his gemstone ceiling. Not least was the chilling memory of her own trembling promise: *I'll bring you the head of Kara-fell.* Kep might have passed the whole thing off as a particularly vivid dream — had it not been for the brand on her arm.

The serpent was still there, wrapped snugly around her right upper arm, like an iridescent tattoo. When Kep touched it, she could feel the raised scales. But that wasn't the worst part. It felt alive — as if a real serpent were embedded beneath her skin. Kep shuddered, wrapping her cloak more tightly around her. What had she done?

The last of the supply boats had departed minutes ago, loaded with water and small barrels of fresh goods, leaving the two young women alone on the subterranean dock. Molly had been watching Kep out of the corner of her eye. Now she reached out to touch the younger woman's shoulder. 'I understand. It must feel strange.'

Kep pulled away. 'No! You *don't* understand. You've never worn a slave's brand, Molly. How could you *possibly* understand how I feel?'

For a moment, Molly was silent. When she spoke, her words held a note of apology. 'But this is different, Kep. Bahjak has shown you great honour. Few of the Simbabs are chosen to wear the serpent. That mark bears authority. It is Bahjak's bond.'

'So I *am* bonded.' Kep swallowed hard, fighting back tears. 'To a *smuggler.*'

'You bound *yourself*, Kep-Váli,' said Molly, a little archly. 'The moment you struck that bargain.' Then she shook her head. 'Listen. As much as you hate it, that mark could prove the difference between life and death. For yourself *and* your friends. Few pirates will challenge a Simbab who bears the serpent.' Kep ground her teeth. She understood. But she didn't have to *like* it.

A hard silence separated the two young women, broken only by the slap of water against stone. At last a vessel appeared, slipping towards them as quiet as a water beetle. Molly gave a heavy sigh. 'And so we say farewell, Kep-Váli. This boat comes for you.'

The rowboat had high sides and a deep-cut bow. It looked decidedly small to Kep. She knew little of boats, only that she disliked them. Her previous experiences had not been pleasant. As she steeled her nerves, Molly took her by the elbow. 'Wait! I cannot let you go without a gift.'

Molly reached into a cloth bag that was slung over her shoulder. 'These are yours already. My counsel is to keep them hidden.' She handed Kep the pouch of gold and the curious compass. Kep transferred them to her pockets with a sniff. 'But this ... This is from me.'

Kep scowled at the object that was pressed into her hands, and Molly laughed. 'You *can* trust me, Kep. If ever your strength fails, this elixir will help. And the tiniest sip will take away seasickness.'

Kep frowned. 'Seasickness? I don't get—'

'You will.'

The tiny phial glinted when Kep held it to the light. The liquid was a warm, golden colour — the exact shade of Sarin's eyes.

Molly gave a sudden burst of laughter. She grabbed Kep's arm, her eyes dancing with mischief. 'I see him so clearly! The young man who leaps into your thoughts. He has black hair, and ... extraordinary eyes.' Kep caught her breath. Molly's own eyes went faraway, her expression pensive. 'Yes, he is *quite* unusual.' Then she blinked, as if coming to herself. She smiled. 'I think you'll see him sooner than you think.'

Before Kep could recover from her shock, the little craft nudged against the dock. A man jumped out, looping a mooring line around the piling. He stood to careful attention, eyes averted. A second person remained in the boat, oars hovering above the water. An imperious gesture from Molly told them both to wait.

Kep blinked in confusion. 'Does that ... ? Are you saying ... you have the gift of sight?' It felt as if a piece of a puzzle had fallen into place.

Molly put a finger to her lips. She drew Kep a little further from the boat. 'Glimpses,' she confessed. 'It runs in the family.' Kep frowned, certain there was more to it. Her strange new tattoo seemed to tingle as Molly went on. 'My gift is ... complicated. You could describe it as a knack. A knack of reading people that goes a little deeper than most.' Molly dropped her voice even further. 'I have a warning for you, Kep. You mustn't trust the pirates.'

Kep folded her arms. You didn't need second sight to work that out! And it was a bit much, coming from the *descendant* of a pirate. But Molly's expression was dark. 'Be wary of the bald man. There is evil magic behind some of his tattoos.' Kep felt a quiver of dread in her stomach. *Greigo.* Molly shook her head. 'That one has darkness in his soul.'

Kep's heartbeat quickened. Was it the Melk? Is that what Molly saw? The woman went on, her eyes serious. She pressed Kep's hand between her own. 'And, Kep ... look to your friends.'

Kep felt the ground wobble beneath her feet. 'My *friends*? Do you mean Jen-Jay and Skarlon?'

'I feel nothing but loyalty from the small warrior.' Molly smiled. '*Ferocious* loyalty. But the man with the stars on his face ... ? He carries a secret.'

*Skarlon? A secret?* Kep frowned. He was the least secretive person Kep knew. 'Are you certain?'

'I sense a deep conflict in him. Almost as if he is compelled. I suspect his silence goes against his own desire.' Molly shook her head. 'I can tell you nothing more. But ... be careful, my friend.' Putting her hands on either side of Kep's face, she smiled sadly. 'I am certain of one thing only: this tide will wait no longer.' Then she pulled Kep closer and kissed her full on the mouth. 'Go, Kep-Váli! I wish you well.'

There was no time to recover from the unexpected kiss, nor wonder at Molly's strange revelations. Kep was too busy clutching at the sides of the boat as it bucked and plunged in the choppy waves. If this was a favourable swell, she hated to think what bad weather looked like. The waves broke over the bow, sending salty spray into her face. When, at last, they rounded the point of Split Apple Rock, Kep let out a gasp. There she was! The *Lady Lee*.

Curly had described the *Lady Lee* as a *small* ship. To Kep, she seemed a threatening hulk against the half-light of dawn. The ship's twin masts thrust skywards, hung with ominous spars and spiderweb rigging. A flag of uncertain insignia fluttered overhead, dark and foreboding.

The waves heaved in green-grey surges — Kep was terrified of being crushed in the gap between rowboat and ship. The attitude of the rowers was reassuring, though. They seemed almost bored as they navigated the bucking vessel close alongside the ship. Kep stood wobbling for a couple of moments, timing her leap to coincide with the lift of the waves. Then, gritting her teeth and with a silent prayer to Narsis, she jumped.

The ladder tossed like a wild thing, as if intent on shaking Kep into the ocean. Perhaps she should have taken that as a warning. Rung-over-rung, she climbed until she reached the top. Her hands gripped the solid wooden railing and, gasping with relief, she hauled herself aboard.

Something was wrong. Kep felt it in her gut, even before her feet touched the deck. Curly and her friends should have been waiting. Instead, she found herself surrounded by a pack of angry-looking pirates. They pressed in towards her, arms folded over chests, eyes hostile. Some were bloodied, as if they'd been fighting. Before Kep could gather her wits, a voice shouted: 'Seize her!' A blade flashed in the corner of her eye. She froze, sensing the prick of steel against her throat.

Not daring to move, Kep sent her gaze to the side. She recognised the sword at once. The curve of its guard was unforgettable. Skarlon's broad-sword! The man holding it giggled. *Tibbs.* His blue eyes were manic with glee as he watched Kep come to the obvious conclusion. *Mutiny!*

Kep's hand slipped to her side, fingers brushing the hilt of her sword. Just a reflex. What could she hope to achieve? She could hardly fight a ship-full of pirates on her own. Greigo's voice shouted again, 'I *said*: seize her!'

To Kep's dismay, it was Ratskin who jumped to obey. Moving more quickly than she'd thought possible, he grabbed her, pinning her arms to her sides. The shock of that embrace spurred Kep into finding her voice. 'Stop! Put me down, Ratskin! I'm your Simbab!'

'Simbab?' The crowd parted, letting Greigo through. The man was all swagger, despite the gash over one eye. He grinned, malicious and leering. 'A *slave* becoming Simbab? I don't think so.' He let out a filthy curse. Kep couldn't imagine what his poor mother could have done to deserve such revolting slander. 'She's no leader of pirates! She's just a *stupid little bitch.*' Spinning on a heel, Greigo addressed the crowd of scowling pirates. 'Oh! She killed Grady all right. When he was *helpless* and tied to a chair!' The pirates muttered, daggers in their eyes.

'That's not true!'

'A coward ain't got no right to call herself Simbab! That's what I say!'

'Liar! Grady lunged at me with a knife!' Kep's eyes searched the crew, desperately seeking allies. 'Harden! Tell them he's lying!' Harden looked away, busying himself with a rope. His ears looked very pink and his hands were trembling. Behind him, off to one side, was Rawlins. He stood with another man, arms folded, as if none of this was his concern. Kep would get no help there. She fixed on a flash of white hair. 'Orrick! You were there. Tell them! I'm your Simbab!' The words died in Kep's throat when the man shook his head. Regret filled his eyes; but whatever threats or promises Greigo had made, they were working.

Greigo chuckled, an evil grating sound. Kep glowered at him. She should have killed him when she'd had the chance. Anger rose in her chest. 'Does an oath mean nothing, then?' She raised her voice, casting her eyes over the crowd. 'I thought pirates had a *code.*' A few looked uneasy. 'Your shipmates *swore* to me. All of them. On bended knee. Even Greigo. *He swore an oath to me! As Simbab!*'

As Kep shouted the words, she felt a sudden tingling pressure around her arm. *The serpent, you idiot!* Of course! She jutted her chin. 'I *am* Simbab. And I can prove it! Bahjak gave me—'

Greigo's hand whipped out as fast as a snake strike. The backhanded cuff connected with Kep's cheek, slamming her head back. Pain came with a blinding flash. Her ears rang, and she tasted the salt of blood. Ratskin grunted, absorbing the impact. He clamped his huge hand over Kep's mouth.

Through a dazed blur, Kep noticed the crew exchanging glances. Most grinned, enjoying the spectacle. 'She's just a slave!' Greigo's laughter was loud and derisive. 'Even if we *had* sworn anything, an oath to a slave don't mean too much, I reckon!' Half of the pirates nodded, many more joined in with the laughter. Kep's head throbbed with a high-pitched singing. She closed her eyes, trying to shut out the sensation of dancing lights. It made little difference. Why had she ever believed the plan would work? And what had happened to Jen-Jay, Skarlon and Curly? All she'd done was make things worse.

Greigo spread his arms, warming to his performance. 'This one sure ain't Simbab. But I can tell you what she is! Plunder!'

'Plunder! Plunder!' Tibbs waved his hands, inviting others to join in his chant.

Several did, so Greigo shouted to make himself heard. 'Five hundred gold pieces! For one slave girl! And fifty apiece for the others, even that skinny old bitch!' Kep's heart sank even further. How could she have been such a fool? What oath could hold in the face of such riches? When she caught sight of Spike, her stomach turned. He hooted and jeered from his place in the rigging. When he saw her watching, he swung down to hang from an elbow, grinning.

'But we ain't got time for jawing,' shouted Greigo. 'There's gold to be had, boys!' The pirates cheered — even the women, who counted themselves as boys. 'Hoist the sails!' bellowed Greigo.

The order caused confusion. None of the pirates moved. They looked at each other, uncertain. Many glanced at the man standing next to Rawlins. After a moment, the pirate shrugged and shouldered his way forward. He had a deep chest and muscular arms. Although he wasn't particularly tall, there was something about him, some quality of presence. He wore his hair shaved very close to his head and dressed in pirate fashion, with a leather waistcoat and colourful breeches. An enormous ruby flashed in his left ear. Kep knew at once who he was. It could be none other than Ruby Ross.

Curly had spoken highly of the man. Ruby Ross was the best helmsman in all the seas, according to him. The man spoke in a boom, used to hollering orders above the storm. 'If *she's* not Simbab, then who is?'

'We can decide later,' said Greigo. 'If we miss the rendezvous with the *Nightingale* we lose our gold. I say we make sail!' He licked his lips. 'With Ruby at the helm!'

Ruby Ross folded his arms, directing his gaze to Kep. She sensed a steady intelligence behind his eyes. He cocked his head at Greigo. 'And the prisoner?'

Greigo's tongue ran over his lips. 'We'll keep her safe. In the captain's cabin.'

Nobody breathed as the two men locked eyes. Then Ruby Ross nodded. 'We make for Wiseman's Crook! Hoist the sails!'

Pirates scrambled to obey, running in every direction. Some swarming up the rigging, others heading to man the ropes. Chains clanked and pulleys creaked as the ship came alive.

Greigo puffed himself up, and Kep caught a flash of triumph in his eyes. 'Tibbs! Take the prisoner to the captain's cabin.'

Tibbs made a move to obey, but Ratskin seemed reluctant to give up his prize. Lifting Kep clear off her feet, he lumbered off. Spike hooted, swinging to the deck. He yelled encouragement to his friend. 'Yeah, Ratskin! Take the witch! Tie 'er up good!' Kep was startled by the intensity of the lad's glare. He made a gesture at her, two forked fingers right in her face. The other hand twitched at his side.

Ratskin shuffled down the deck, refusing to relinquish his burden. Tibbs had no choice but to scurry alongside. The horrid little man kept fumbling at Kep's waist, trying to unbuckle Jaibari's sword. She kicked out, aiming to break his knee. She missed, connecting instead with the soft flesh of his thigh. The impact threw Ratskin a little off-balance, but he kept going. Escaping his bear-like hold was impossible. Who'd have thought the boy would be so strong? Kep conserved her energy, struggling against nausea and a deep sense of panic. Where were her friends?

When a tremendous whooshing sound joined the confusion, Kep's heart thumped even more wildly. The little ship shuddered, like a bird shaking out its wings. Her sails unfurled, puffing out with air. However, the spectacle of billowing canvas was cut short as they passed through a small doorway into a cramped space reeking of tar.

Ratskin was breathing more heavily now. Ignoring a pair of hatches, he manoeuvred them towards a panelled door. As the door swung open, Kep knew that this was her last chance. Refusing to go down without a fight, she thrust out with her legs, finding leverage against the door frame. For a moment, it worked! Ratskin grunted, loosening his grip. Kep threw up her arms, wriggling down and out of his grasp. If she could just ... But Tibbs was too fast. He snapped out a fist, landing a vicious punch. Kep's head slammed into the doorframe and she fell back, slumping into Ratskin's arms. She caught the image of Ratskin's brown eyes, wide with concern. Then her own eyes rolled back. A brutal lesson had been learned. You can *never* trust a pirate.

## 22

# T'AL KEP

Kep came around slowly, struggling to make sense of the weirdly swaying room. Her stomach seemed to be sloshing around in her body of its own accord. Lifting her head from her chest, she felt saliva dribbling from the side of her mouth. But she couldn't wipe it away — her hands were bound behind her back. Coils of rope constricted her chest, making it difficult to breathe. Ratskin had done what he was told. He'd tied her up well, lashed to a huge wooden bed, the most solid thing in the captain's cabin.

Kep winced, struggling to sit a little taller. Her head throbbed, competing with the bruising ache in her left shoulder. She frowned at the bandage on her right arm. Had she injured that, too? Right now, she had worse things to worry about. For a start, her entire world had tipped on an angle.

From her place on the floor, Kep could see grey skies through the bank of window panes. The light was pale, though, making it difficult to judge the position of the sun. Now and then a grey wave humped into view, making her stomach churn. Combined with the reek of rum and wood polish, it increased her urge to vomit. Kep pulled her gaze away and, ignoring the hypnotic sway of the lanterns, concentrated on her surroundings.

Under different circumstances — and if things would just stay still — Kep might have appreciated the captain's cabin. Everything was tidy, with no space wasted. Lacking the ostentation of Grady's room at the inn, the furniture was both attractive and functional, with shelves butted up against cabinets. Decorative rails prevented items from falling, which was fortunate, because everything rattled and chinked.

Anchored in front of the slanted bank of window panes was a solid desk with deep drawers, and beside that an upholstered bench seat. Kep's cloak was on top of the seat, rolled into a bundle next to her pack. She couldn't see her bow and quiver. If she stretched out her feet, she could almost touch the curved leg of a round table. It, too, had a rail around its edge. She spied the tip of something that looked like parchment.

The most terrifying object in the room was mounted on the wall: an enormous circle of white bone studded with two sets of wicked teeth. Kep was trying to imagine the dreadful creature those jaws had belonged to when she heard voices. She dropped her head, letting it loll.

The man who entered first brought a sharp odour with him, reminiscent of weasel piss. Kep recognised his wheedling voice. Tibbs. 'See? It's like I told you, Greigo.'

The door clicked closed as his companion growled an answer. 'She's still out. How hard did you hit her? Must have been a fair crack.'

Tibbs sounded defensive. 'Like I said: 'er head hit the door. She'll pull through.' The squeak in his voice betrayed his worry.

'You better 'ope so, Tibbsy. They ain't gonna pay for a dead girl.'

Kep's senses reeled as Greigo squatted down beside her. His stench was rotten — like a festering sore. Her stomach recoiled when he breathed into her face. But she knew her only defence was to do nothing. Using the Breath as a source of strength, that's what she did.

Even when Greigo put his calloused hand against her face, she breathed smoothly, feigning oblivion. A sharp slap sent pain shearing through her skull, but she didn't so much as wince. Jen-Jay would have been proud.

Greigo grunted. 'You checked them bonds?'

'They're tight.' It was true. Kep felt them cutting into her ribs.

'And nobody saw the mark?'

'Nobody 'cepting Rats.' Tibbs giggled. 'And Rats don' count.'

'True enough. Lad's a right idiot.'

Tibbs shuffled his feet. 'Only ...' Kep sensed fear in the smaller man's voice. He cleared his throat. 'It's ... about that. The mark. Do you think ... I mean—'

'What mark? I don't see no mark, do you, Tibbs?' The threat was obvious. In the following pause, Kep guessed Tibbs had shaken his head. 'Good. We won't have no worries then, will we?'

From the direction of his voice and the clunk of things being disturbed, Greigo was clearly investigating the cabin. 'Plan's simple. Rendezvous with the *Nightingale*, trade the other prisoners and I'll be voted Simbab for my trouble. This cabin and everything in it will be mine.' Kep felt a nasty shiver go down her spine.

Tibbs sounded surprised. 'We're not trading the girl, then? I thought she was for the arena.'

'Tibbs: what did we agree 'bout you an' thinking? You nearly got it right, though. Kara-fell *would* pay a pretty price. But that's just bargaining, see?' Greigo sounded very pleased with himself. 'That Rox. *He's* the one we deal with. Reckon we can name our price once he knows we got 'er.'

'We got 'er.' Tibbs giggled. 'We got T'al Kep tied to a bed.'

'Tied to *my* bed, Tibbsy.'

To Kep's horror, Greigo crouched beside her once more, unable to resist a final gloat. He squeezed her face, squishing her mouth out of shape and parting her lips with his stinking fingers. The urge to bite him was powerful. She froze for a moment, forgetting to breathe. Fortunately, the pirate was far too pleased with himself to notice. He pinched her cheek. 'You got a new master now,' he murmured. 'And you an' me, we gonna have some fun when you wake up. *That's* an oath you can *count* on.'

Kep waited until the pirates' footsteps had faded. Then she opened her eyes, gasping for air. She gagged and spluttered, spitting on the floor, desperately trying to rid herself of the man's taste. Running her tongue over her teeth, she spat twice more. The stench lingered, a potent reminder of Greigo's threats. Any control Kep had over her breath was gone. Suppressed sobs made their way to the surface now, choked by emotion. How could she have been such a fool?

Treachery from Greigo and Tibbs was something she'd expected. It would have been a miracle had those two had stayed true. It was Ratskin and Spike's betrayal, even more than Greigo's threats, which devastated her. Hot and salty, the tears coursed down her face. She recalled the look of violence on Spike's face when he'd urged Ratskin to do Greigo's bidding. *Take the witch! Tie 'er up good!* Kep frowned, trying to make sense of it. How could she have got it so wrong?

But looking back, something about the incident seemed odd. Something about Spike's choice of words felt wrong. *The witch?* The way he'd shouted the words into her face, making that rude sign with his fingers, had seemed deliberate. As if ...

Kep's eyes flew wide open. She'd seen that gesture before! It was part of the boys' secret language. Forked fingers meant trust, she was sure of it. Her heart hammered as thoughts tumbled into place. *The witch!* If she was right, the knot would be somewhere she could reach it. She took a deep breath, jamming her shoulder blades against the bed leg for purchase. Flipping her wrists around as far as they would go, she groped with her fingertips. Her shoulder bones ached in their sockets as she stretched. The harsh rope bit into her skin. Ignoring the cramp in her neck, she strained with every ounce of her strength. And she found it. A tail! A tail of rope!

It took several minutes of strenuous wriggling to tease the rope's end from its hiding place. Grasping it as tightly as she could between her fingertips, Kep whispered a prayer to Telion and pulled. The witch's hitch didn't unravel as smoothly as Orrick's had, but it *did* unravel. The ropes fell away, releasing Kep's hands in the same movement. Her heart sang for joy. Spike and Ratskin had stayed true!

Whispering thanks to her gods, she allowed herself a moment's rest, rubbing feeling back into her aching wrists. Then, not trusting herself to stand up without being sick, she crawled over to the bench seat and dragged her cloak to the floor. She fumbled in its pockets until she found Molly's phial. She uncorked the lid and, barely hesitating, put it to her lips. If it was poison, then so be it. The amber fluid tasted faintly of cinnamon, and was fiery on her tongue. A tiny sip was all it took. The effects were nothing short of miraculous. Molly's elixir didn't just take away the nausea, it eased her throbbing head as well. The swift recovery left Kep in awe. Who *was* Molly? Was *she* some sort of witch? Kep decided she didn't care. After a deep breath, she hauled herself up to stand.

The view through the many-paned windows took Kep's breath away. There was nothing but water! Water, as far as her eyes could see. How could there *be* so much water in the world? The wake of the ship was a turbulent ribbon stretching out behind. Although Kep was no sailor, she could tell that the *Lady Lee* was making excellent headway. How long had she been unconscious? At least a couple of hours, she guessed. Maybe more. The rendezvous with the *Nightingale* loomed. She had to escape the cabin and find somewhere to hide.

Kep found her weapons displayed on the bed, like trophies. She kissed her bow and slung it over her shoulder. Next, she strapped on her knife, followed by Jaibari's sword. She spotted a plate with a hunk of bread and some cheese, and shoved the food in her pocket. To her dismay, the water jug was empty.

Sweeping her cloak around her, she cast her eyes around the room. She considered taking the small lantern but decided against it. Too dangerous. When she opened a tall cupboard, her reflection stared back at her from the mirror on the back of the door. It came as a shock. She had blood smeared on her face and arms, and several bruises in varying shades of purple. The cut over her brow looked deep, but she couldn't deal with that now. Greigo could return at any moment. Several coloured scarves hung from a rack inside the cupboard and she selected one at random, green with white stripes. She bound it around her head, tucking her warrior's tails in securely. A pathetic attempt at disguise, but better than nothing.

Now Kep turned her attention to the bandage on her arm. She tore it off, revealing the sign of the Simbab — the mark that Greigo had been so desperate to deny. It glittered peacock-blue in the dim light. She ignored the drawers of jewellery but plucked up a ring of keys. With her heart in her mouth, she staggered over to the door, fighting the motion of the ship.

The smallest key turned the lock with a click. Gathering her courage, she cracked the door open and peered out. The passage was empty. With a racing heart, she slipped out of the cabin, locking the door behind her.

As Kep stumbled down the passageway, pushing past sacks and barrels, all she could think of was making herself scarce before Greigo returned to the cabin. But where could you hide on a ship full of pirates? Panic brought her to a halt. Clearly she couldn't go up on deck, so she did the obvious: she went down, through the open hatch, taking a thin wooden ladder into the belly of the ship.

Her feet missed the bottom rungs, landing her in a cluttered space. Daylight struggled to penetrate this far. Kep peered about, trying to make sense of the darkened shapes, desperate to find somewhere to hide. Before her eyes could adjust, a beam of light dazzled her. A lantern! A figure sprang from the shadows, holding it aloft. Fear took Kep by the throat. She tried to draw her sword, but only entangled it in her cloak. The person hollered. 'C'mon, you lazy lumppet!'

Kep recognised the voice at once. Spike! He raised the lantern, grinning like some sort of manic goblin. He shouted again, more loudly this time, directing his voice through the hatch. 'Hurry up, Rats! We got water below deck!' Kep swayed on her feet, sick with relief. Putting a finger to his lips, Spike lifted a trapdoor near her feet, letting it fall back with a thump. He urged her to climb down, and she obeyed, groping her way in the darkness.

Spike's boots followed Kep down the ladder. Joining her at the bottom, he beamed and spoke over his shoulder. 'See? Didn't I tell ya, Ratskin? She ain't seasick at all!'

Beyond the glowering lamplight, his friend was bent double, mop in hand. Kep caught the flash of a smile. Then Ratskin shook his head, waggling his fingers. 'Says 'e's sorry,' translated Spike. 'For tyin' you up an' all.' Kep let out a gulp, halfway between a laugh and a sob. Spike's cheeky expression changed to one of concern. 'We're sorry we failed you, Kep-Váli.'

Kep shook her head, choking back emotion. 'You didn't fail me. I know you had no choice. You stayed true.'

Spike grinned and pushed out his chest. 'It is of the gods.'

'Yes, Spike.' Kep found it impossible not to smile. 'It is of the gods.' Her heart swelled. Of the whole sorry band, these two had stayed true.

'It was a clever trick, weren't it?'

'Very. You could be on the stage, Spike. I honestly thought you'd betrayed me. It took me ages to figure it out.'

'But you did!'

Kep nodded, enjoying the boy's delight. The motion caused her head to spin. She held a hand to her forehead, disoriented by flashes across her vision.

Spike's smile dissolved. He put out a hand to steady her. 'You can rest now, Kep-Váli. It's safe to sit for a bit. No one comes down here. Bilge water's *our* job.'

*Safe?* Nowhere was safe. Kep took a seat on one of the smaller crates. They were in the lowest part of the ship, in the smallest hold. The vessel's bare ribs dominated the space, suggesting a whale had swallowed them. She tried not to think about the vastness of water that pressed against those planks. An impossible endeavour. Everything creaked and strained, like an old woman wheezing.

To Kep's relief — despite Spike's earlier claim — there was no water below decks. The hold was snug and dry, if somewhat crowded. Every available space had been commandeered for storage. As well as large crates strapped to the floor, there were spare timbers, coils of ropes, and barrels of pitch. Several small sacks hung like fruit bats from the overhead beams. 'Jellin,' said Spike uncomfortably. 'It's the driest place for it.' Kep raised her eyebrows. So this was where the jellin from Bixdale had ended up. She shook her head, too tired to wonder at Grady's plans for the stuff.

But she was not too tired to eat. And while Kep nibbled at the cheese and bread, washed down by leathery-tasting water from Ratskin's water pouch, Spike did his best to fill her in on events. Ratskin listened in, leaning on his mop and contributing occasionally through hand gestures.

With a heavy heart, Kep learned her friends hadn't stood a chance. Somehow Greigo had sent word ahead — warning the crew that Curly had betrayed them and that strangers were trying to take over the *Lady Lee*. A mob of furious pirates, armed to the teeth, confronted Jen-Jay and Skarlon when they boarded.

Spike scowled as he recounted the scene. 'It was Greigo. He riled everyone up he did. He kept shouting "Mutiny!" And his cronies, they followed his lead. They beat Curly somepin' awful. Greigo didn't want 'im talkin' back, see?' Kep nodded. 'But they can sure fight, them old uns!' Ratskin nodded, his eyes wide. 'Took ages to take 'em down. Did some damage, too. Beatson lost half 'is nose! Ship's croaker 'ad to stitch it back on.' He grinned at Ratskin. 'He's even uglier now.'

Kep's mouth was dry from fear. 'Were Jen-Jay and Skarlon hurt?'

'They looked 'orright, last I saw. They're with your other friends, in the hold under the forecastle.' Seeing her blank look, he added, 'Near the bow. Under the foredeck.' Kep was none the wiser. And she had no idea what 'orright meant in Spike's world, but at least her friends were alive — no thanks to her. The sick feeling in her stomach grew stronger.

Ratskin plucked at Spike's sleeve. His fingers flashed and Spike nodded. 'We don't have much time, Kep-Váli.' He was right. Someone might raise the alarm at any minute. A wave of hopelessness overtook her. The pirates would search the ship. They'd find her and punish the boys, adding to her already burdened conscience.

To her surprise, both boys were grinning. Bubbling with

suppressed excitement, Spike bounced to his feet. 'What is it?' asked Kep, frowning.

'It's time for you to vanish! Just like T'al Kep!'

Kep put her head in her hands, weary with disbelief. 'I told you, Spike. I'm not T'al Kep. I can't just vanish.'

Ratskin added a strange huffing chortle to Spike's laughter. 'Course you can!'

## 23

## SERENITY

'I knew you were a singer!' The top of the sail fluttered, and Petrel pulled the tiller a little closer to her body. She grinned at the boat's swift response, and with the sail taut again turned her gaze to Ash. 'I've never seen anything like what *you* did, though. The mists move weirdly around you. Did you know that?'

The curiosity in the young woman's eyes made Ash shrink into himself. He had no response. What was mist-singing *supposed* to look like? He'd certainly found it an unsettling experience — alien, yet disturbingly familiar. Now he felt depleted, as if some part of himself had been left behind in the mists. But he had no wish to discuss the matter with Petrel. They were free of the Veil. That was all that counted. His main concern was staying upright.

Sailing boats were even more unpredictable than rowboats. Ash kept standing in the wrong place or grasping hold of moving parts. Petrel watched him for a few minutes longer and shook her head. 'Mist-singer you might be, but you're a terrible sailor!' She shot him a wicked grin. 'Sit down. We're coming about. Wouldn't want to lose you overboard.'

Ash made a clumsy lurch for the nearest bench and sat down with a bump. The little boat veered, sending the boom swinging. Sarin emerged from the cabin at the same moment and ducked to avoid his head being knocked off. Petrel's roar of laughter made Ash wonder if she'd planned it that way. Sarin swore under his breath and scrambled to a seat. Canvas flapped around them like a badly pitched tent. Then the chaos was over. The sails bellied out, and the *Gull* leaned into a fresh tack.

Ash blew out his cheeks. Was sailing always this hectic? Or did Petrel take a secret delight in making it so? She caught his eye and winked, giving the tiller an affectionate pat. 'Borsi was right,' she said. 'She sails like a dream.'

Sarin scowled at Ash, before twisting his neck around to stare at the shore. Petrel's mouth quirked. 'Peaceful, isn't it?'

'If by peaceful you mean weird and *foreboding*, then yes.'

'Ha! That's the Mistlands for you.' She laughed. 'What were you expecting?'

Ash caught his lip between his teeth and let his eyes follow the shoreline. They hadn't *expected* to be here at all. And Sarin was right: the landscape *was* foreboding. Overlapping layers of grey unfolded before them, like the scenery in a puppet show. The sharp-edged hills were forested and broody. Wisps of mist clung to their peaks like needy lovers, the morning sunlight too weak to banish them.

Stark white waterfalls provided the only counterpoint to the endless grey. Some poured down a rush, tall and straight. Others were bifurcated — seeping into the river like stealthy roots. Something about those skeletal fingers made Ash shudder. The whole place seemed under an enchantment. As if everything was asleep. Even the birds were silent. His only consolation was that the Song, too, was subdued — for now.

They sailed on without speaking until Ordelle reappeared from below, bearing dried fruit and a rolled-up chart. She passed the bag of fruit to Sarin and spread the chart out on the purpose-built console, securing two of the corners with silver clips and using the compass to weigh down a third. She frowned at the unsecured corner, but Petrel praised her for an excellent job and invited her to sit beside her.

Ash was startled when the proud young woman offered Ordelle the tiller. He was even more surprised when Ordelle accepted. The Cryer's daughter quickly demonstrated her sailing prowess. Petrel smiled, told her she was exceptional, and leaned back on an elbow. She sent Ordelle appraising glances, which went unnoticed, while Sarin pored over the map.

Ash frowned as he leaned forward, trying to make sense of the spidery marks. Scrawled notes and plotted journeys covered the yellowing parchment, presumably added by Borsi Frattellik. Many of the symbols were indecipherable — the eccentric adventurer had devised his own code. A sweeping smudge marked the position of the Veil. It covered the Bruinin peninsula and the southern parts of the Singing Isles. But it was just an estimation, according to Petrel. The Veil had mysterious rhythms and seasons of its own. Ash stared at the broken necklace of islands, trying to reconcile their shapes with the ancient map he'd seen in T'al Jazure.

Labels identified Earl, Auri and Baktah. On the map in T'al Jazure, Baktah, the largest and western-most isle, had featured a cluster of pink turrets. But the ancient home of the Wimsari had been destroyed over a thousand years ago. Borsi had scrawled the word 'uninhabited' on its face. He hadn't bothered to label the smaller islands, probably thinking them irrelevant. Except one of them was horribly relevant. Somewhere, hidden amongst the mists, was the den of Kara-fell. Ash felt a shiver of dread down his spine. Had the League already made its move? Was Kep there now? Following Nirias into danger?

Sarin lifted his head to look at Petrel, who ignored him. He narrowed his eyes, giving her another few moments. At last he sighed. 'Are you going to tell us where we are?'

Petrel grinned like a cat, as if she'd scored a point. 'Of course. We're here.' She tapped the map. 'At the very edge of the Veil. I could drop you in one of these bays, but you'll have to trek through bush-land if you want to get to Scrimpton. Can't see why you'd want to, though.'

Sarin ignored the question in her eyes. He traced his finger along the waterway. 'Can you take us here, to Serenity?'

Ordelle nodded. 'There is a refuge there.' Ash sat up a little straighter. A League refuge promised news of Nirias. And Kep. And Serenity was on their list of probable rendezvous points.

Petrel laughed. 'I've never heard Serenity called a *refuge* before. But, yes, I can take you. Can't really avoid the place. Should be a clear run. Pirates don't venture this far. *Usually.*'

Ash gulped. *Pirates?* He stared at the tiny island where Petrel's finger rested.

'We'll take on water,' she said, 'and as many stores as the *Gull* can hold. Then we keep sailing, around the top of the Singing Isles.' Her three passengers exchanged looks, and she grinned. 'Don't fret about the pirates. They'll probably ignore a vessel this small. Besides, the *Gull* is fast.' She leaned back, a proprietorial arm draped over the timber-work. Her grin widened. 'We're free to go anywhere we want!'

Petrel lifted her arms and shouted at the sky. 'Hear that, Sisters? I'm free!' She reached out to pat Ordelle's arm, and Ordelle glanced down in surprise. 'Truly, Ordelle. The world is ours. We should go south! Yes! Come south with me! It's warm there. There's sunshine and music and festivals that last for seven days straight. I've heard there are gigantic flowers ... and fruit the size of your head!'

Ash gnawed at the ragged edge of his thumbnail. It tasted of salt. He glanced over at Sarin. Somebody needed to say something. Sarin's eyes were on Ordelle. She met his gaze, and he jerked his head in Petrel's direction. Ordelle nodded and delivered the blow. 'We cannot go south. We need to find our friends.'

It was like watching the sun go behind the clouds. 'Your friends?' Petrel shook her head. 'Your friends won't be here.' She laughed. 'Unless they've turned pirate. Only pirates are stupid enough to come to these parts.' Her jest hung in the silence, making her smile waver as her eyes darted between them.

'Kep is not stupid,' said Ordelle. 'And she's not a pirate. Kep would never become a pirate.'

'Kep?' Petrel's expression melted into disbelief. 'Not ... ? No.' She shook her head. 'Tell me it's not—'

'It is,' said Sarin. 'It's *that* Kep.'

The layers of feeling in Sarin's voice caught Ash by surprise. Frustration warred with admiration, anger and deep longing.

Petrel stared at him. 'You're searching for T'al Kep? Seriously?'

Ash regretted the hurt in her eyes. They should have mentioned it before now. 'She's only T'al Kep in stories,' he said quietly. 'Kep's a normal person. She's my friend. From childhood. And she's only here because ...' He faltered. How could he even begin to explain?

Sarin came to his rescue. 'Kep's with a larger party. They're seeking news of Kara-fell.'

Petrel's laughter was a derisive gust. Then she realised Sarin was serious. When nobody elaborated, she slammed a hand on her forehead. 'Curse the fishes! You're not jesting.' A storm brewed in her eyes. 'Are you insane? One does not *seek news* of Kara-fell!' She caught Ordelle's wrist. 'Ordelle, tell me plainly! What is this madness?'

'It is true,' said Ordelle, adjusting their course. The wind kept shifting, making the sails restless. 'Our friends are planning to find Kara-fell, and destroy her.'

Petrel's mouth fell open. 'Then they truly seek death.'

Ash felt nauseous and it wasn't because of the boat's movement. He hadn't expected quite such a horrified reaction. 'We think Kep's in trouble.'

'Oh really? I wonder why?' Petrel scowled. 'It sounds to me as if you've chosen particularly foolhardy friends.' As she spoke, the sail flapped, making her words seem ominous. She reclaimed the tiller, her impatience clear as she worked to trim the sails. When she turned to Ordelle, Ash suspected she was holding back tears. 'And you are set on this course, Ordelle?'

To his amazement, Ordelle placed her hand on the tiller, covering Petrel's with her own. 'We are bound to it. By friendship, as well as by the oaths we have taken.'

Petrel closed her eyes and let out a defeated sigh before opening them again. 'I'll take you to Serenity.' She scowled at Sarin, as if it was entirely his fault. 'If it's death at the hands of cut-throats you're wanting, that's as good a place as any.' Her lip quivered, betraying a deep disappointment. Ash felt a pang of sorrow. He knew what it felt like to gain an unexpected friendship, only to have it snatched away.

Sarin thanked her with a bow of his head. 'How long will it take?'

Petrel glowered at the cheerful, billowing sails. 'With this wind we could be there by sundown.'

Ordelle nodded. She shielded her eyes, staring into the distance. Then she pointed. 'There is disturbed water ahead. On the port side.'

Petrel shook her head. 'Wild water is the least of your worries.'

'So,' said Sarin quietly, 'you're a mist-singer.'

Petrel had ordered them below deck, and she hadn't minced her words — the last thing she needed was a pair of idiots getting in her way. Idiots who *clearly* had a death wish. Only Ordelle was exempt from her scorn — at least Ordelle knew a halyard from a jib sheet.

Ash lay on the bed, flat on his back. He clasped his hands over his belly, hoping to ease his nausea. Throwing up on Petrel's bed would not go down well. Sarin seemed unaffected by the motion. He'd wedged himself against the bunk, one foot resting on a knee.

Ash avoided his question. 'Do you think Petrel is still angry with us?'

'Definitely. She also thinks she can make Ordelle change her mind. That's probably why we've been banished.' Sarin folded his arms. 'But *you* just changed the subject.'

'Sorry.'

Sarin let out a sigh. 'Ash, you have to stop doing that.'

'Doing what?'

'Apologising. Admit it, kin. What you did last night was special. In fact, it was ... *extraordinary*.'

Ash held his stomach, pressing his lips together. He wished

people would leave the matter alone. 'Yeah.' He tried to shrug. 'It's a shame I don't know what I actually did.'

Sarin gave a soft snort of dismissal. 'That's not what counts. Don't you see? None of that matters. Yes, you're grappling with the Song and the whole destiny thing. I get it. You're worried about Rilka's vision, and what it means to be the Grey Boy in her dreams. And now there's this mist-singing ...' He paused. 'But, honestly, Ash, I think you worry too much. Do *any of us* know who we truly are? Or what we're supposed to do in the world?'

Ash turned his head, surprised by his friend's intensity. If he wasn't mistaken, Sarin was talking about himself. Sarin shrugged. 'You know your problem, Ash? You look around you and assume that everyone is confident and so sure of themselves. But that's not true. What you did last night took real guts. We're here now because of you. Free of the Veil, with a chance at rescuing Kep. Because of *you*, Ash.' He paused and pulled a face. 'It's disgusting, really. If you carry on at this rate you might turn into a hero.'

Ash rolled his eyes at the ceiling. But a blush spread up his neck, sending heat to his cheeks. To his discomfort, Sarin had more to say. He leaned forward, lacing his fingers together. 'All I'm saying is, you're not a slave anymore. So ... I reckon it's time for you to stop acting like one.'

Ash blinked and met his friend's eyes. The tenderness in his expression caught him off-guard. The silence that followed felt very awkward. He was grateful when Sarin broke it with a chuckle. 'Now do what I say — and get some sleep!'

**24**

---

# THE BARNACLE

The *Gull* glided towards Serenity; her sails clipped to half-mast. Earlier they had scudded along, as if chased by wind sprites. Now the waters were gentle beneath their bow, slicing like grey silk beneath the tailor's shears.

From the distance, and softened by twilight, Serenity seemed an enchanted isle. Pinprick lights twinkled golden, promising haven and rest for weary travellers. Ash doubted they would find any such thing. Even without Petrel's grim forebodings, the smell warned them against believing the illusion. Carried on the sea breeze, wafts came to them of wood-smoke intermingled with tar, the stink of fish, and odours from the sewers. As they slipped into the harbour, the tangle of rigging and masts separated out into individual ships. To Ash, they *all* looked like pirate ships.

Five such vessels lay at anchor, their sails trussed like fat sausages. A sixth nestled against the wharf. Black-hulled, it boasted three tall masts. Putting a number on the smaller crafts was a pointless endeavour — like trying to count individual twigs in a bundle of kindling.

They dropped anchor at the far end of the harbour, near a flotilla of colourful fishing boats. According to Petrel, who knew about such things, fisherfolk were more trustworthy and less inclined to ask questions.

Petrel had not yet forgiven them, maintaining a frosty silence as she rowed them to shore, dumping the trio on a jetty that reeked of fish guts. Brushing away their gratitude, she pushed off as soon as Ordelle was safely ashore. At the last moment, she tossed a message over her shoulder: if they came to their senses by the morning tide, they knew where to find her. The catch in her voice betrayed her hurt. Ash bit his tongue as he watched the rowboat grow smaller. He already wanted to call her back.

Midway between the Singing Isles and the Tella Peninsula, Serenity owed its existence to a deep, sheltered harbour. But nothing seemed permanent about this place. The buildings looked as if they'd washed up on the tide and had somehow clung on. Perhaps the same was true of the people. Ash wondered whether the person who had named the island had ever been there. The place had an uneasy tension, as if trouble brewed just beneath the surface.

A jigsaw of floating pontoons extended the foreshore, accommodating a squabble of hawkers and traders. Ash ducked his head as he followed Sarin and Ordelle, tugging a felt cap over his ears. According to Petrel, few of the Zari lived on Serenity, and he didn't want to draw attention to himself. To his relief, the hawkers seemed more concerned with shouting abuse at each other than engaging with the newcomers. Some were just children. An urchin offered him a baked potato mounted on a stick, but he shook his head — the potato looked even grubbier than the boy. The urchin's business partner stirred a bubbling cauldron, hollering phrases that would make any sailor blush: 'Mussels! Sweet 'n' juicy! Get ya ladies' pleasure!'

The trio threaded their way through the chaos, past cages crammed with multicoloured birds. The indignant fowls contributed their screeching protests to the din, which was punctuated by the hammering of a woman who fashioned nails and hooks to order. They had almost broken free of the crowd when Ash felt something clawing at his sleeve.

Ancient and decrepit, the woman had thin grey hair which barely covered her skull. Her grip on Ash's arm, though, was monkey-tight. Black eyes glittered as she pushed her basket into his chest. Ash recoiled at the sight of withered bunches bound with twine. They looked just like severed fingers! His exclamation of horror caused Sarin to whirl. The command Sarin shouted was foreign to Ash's ears. The old woman hissed, like the sound of water hitting a hot griddle. She backed away, vanishing into the crowd.

'What ... ?' Ash spluttered, his mind trying to comprehend the objects he'd glimpsed. 'What was ... ?'

'Curses.' Sarin grabbed Ash's shoulder and propelled him ahead. Ash wasn't sure he understood. Was the woman selling curses? It made a gruesome sort of sense. Serenity was the ideal place.

They found The Barnacle where Petrel said it would be — clinging to the edge of an old stone wharf. At first they mistook the tavern for a fishmonger's. Sitting outside, beneath the fish-shaped sign, and surrounded by a fishing net, was an old man. Ash couldn't tell whether the man was trying to repair the net or escape it, but they had to step around him to reach the tavern's entrance. The man peered at them through clouded eyes, clicked his tongue, and went back to his work. Ash shot him a nervous glance. Was he trying to warn them against entering?

The inside of The Barnacle was even less welcoming than its dreary exterior. An unpleasant odour greeted them. Something was bubbling away in a cauldron at the hearth — Ash imagined fish heads and eyeballs, judging by the smell. The smoking fire had blackened the walls, adding to a general air of hopelessness. Sawdust covered the floor, to hide the grime, no doubt. The furniture comprised rough-sawn benches and mismatched tables. The few lanterns were filthy and ineffectual.

A solitary patron hunched over a mug in a shadowy corner furthest from the door. A deep hood made it impossible to make out any features. Ash shivered. Why would anyone wear a hood indoors, unless to hide some nefarious intention?

A bumping and scraping noise emanated from behind the bar.

They peered over and noticed a hatch with the top of a ladder poking up through it. Somebody was down there, but Sarin's hollering went unanswered. They waited, exchanging frowns and looking about until the thumping below gave way to the scuff of ascending steps. A barrel bumped into view, riding on the shoulders of a large man with a wild mop of blond curls. A broken nose and uneven ears suggested he'd been a brawler in his time, and he looked more than capable of wielding the cudgel that dangled at his waist. The man hefted the barrel onto its rack and turned towards them with a scowl. 'Whada ya want?'

Sarin gave him a winning smile. 'Lodging for the night, if you please. And a meal if one's going.' He rested a hand on the bar, his little finger folded under. 'Your establishment comes recommended by a friend.'

Ignoring the League's sign, the innkeeper narrowed his eyes. He glared at Ash. 'Minstrel, is it?'

Ash panicked, his eyes going wide. 'No!' He'd forgotten to cover the tattooed band on his wrist. Too late. Ordelle frowned at him.

Sarin laughed. 'Our friend's too modest.'

Ash wanted to sink through the floor. They'd rehearsed this. 'I mean ... I'm not really. I'm just an apprentice.'

The innkeeper grunted and shifted his attention to Ordelle. 'What about you? You a musician, as well?'

Ordelle looked offended. 'No, I'm an embalmer.'

The innkeeper blinked. 'Huh! S'pose it pays more. In these parts, anyhow.' His eyes flicked to the patron in the shadows and back to Ash. 'You'd best give us a song, then.'

Ash bobbed his head, trying to swallow the lump of fear in his throat. Ordelle's father had taught him several short pieces for just such an occasion. Nobody would expect much from an apprentice, the Cryer had reassured him. He hoped Aechon was right. 'Um ... I can recite "The Lay of King Efossis".'

The innkeeper grunted in disgust. 'No call for fancy poetry here, lad. Give us a proper tune.'

Ash didn't need the warning in Sarin's eyes. This was a test. He licked his lips and gathered his courage. The obvious choice would be a drinking song — they were in a tavern, after all. He took a breath, faltering before a note could pass his lips. *Not that one.*

The innkeeper folded his arms and rocked back on his heels. Ash felt his mind reach out beyond his conscious will. Searching. Something fell into place. That was it. The perfect song for this place. Lowering his defences to the Song, he let the melody come.

The song was older than the tavern. Much older. It resonated, nevertheless. As he sang, Ash caught glimpses of The Barnacle's past: a cheerful place, full of music and raucous banter. 'The Fisher's Daughter' was a saucy ditty, full of irreverent joy. It filled the dismal inn with warmth and light. Time folded into itself. Fiddlers pranced on tables as they played, sawing at their instruments to delight the crowd. The tavern overflowed with people and merriment. The patrons grinned, swinging their mugs in time with the chorus. *She'll cast out her nets and she'll feel no regrets, o' the love of the fisher's daughter.*

Brisk and jaunty, the tune was unpretentious. The verses soon tumbled to their merry conclusion, with the lovers caught in a net of their own design. The sound of loud, slow clapping hauled Ash back to the present. He blinked as the joyful vision faded. 'Well done, lad! You've been tutored well. I confess, it was a surprise to hear a local song on the lips of a stranger!' A beaming smile transformed the innkeeper. 'True, you played a bit free with the rhyme, but there's no harm in that!'

For a piece of silver, Barney, as they were now to call him, would be pleased to rent them rooms for the night. He even promised to throw in dinner, courtesy of the minstrel's talent. Ordelle nodded. 'It is a fair price.' She counted out coins. Then she laid her left hand flat on the bar, the little finger folded under.

If Barney recognised the League's sign, he still made no sign of it. 'The girl will bring water for washing.' He tugged at the rope which dangled at the end of the bar. After a second yanking, a girl appeared in the doorway. Her surly expression suggested she was unaccustomed to being summoned. 'There you are, Magden! Show our guests to their rooms.'

From behind her, they heard muffled laughter. Sarin cocked his head. 'Are there other travellers staying? We'd be glad of news and a game.'

The landlord stiffened. 'Aye, a group of traders. Down from Idira. You're welcome to join them in the back lounge.'

The girl led the way with slouched shoulders, scuffing her feet and not bothering to check whether they followed. Forced to walk in single file, they followed her down a filthy hallway, towards the sound of laughter and conversation. Reaching the end of the passage, she flung open a pair of double doors, a bored wave of her hand telling them to enter.

The source of the hilarity became obvious — a game of dice was underway in a small lounge. Three players stood around a table. A man with a patch over one eye was cheering on a skinny young woman with blonde hair. 'Go on, then! Let's see what you've got!' The girl laughed and rattled dice in a cup, readying to toss them onto the large wooden board.

Ash had barely stepped into the room when somebody grabbed him. The air in his lungs huffed out of him, and his feet left the ground. He let out a cry of alarm, flailing against the powerful arms that pinioned him. Kicking his legs, he jerked his head back, trying to connect with a nose. It achieved nothing.

Ordelle struck out with her quarterstaff, connecting with the shoulder of a second masked figure. The assailant disarmed her in one swift move and shoved her to the floor. Sarin somersaulted out of reach. His hunting knife appeared in his hand. But the dice players had blades, too — flashing as sharp as their smiles.

A voice screamed inside Ash's head. *No!* He couldn't bear to lose another friend to a knife. 'Stop!' he cried. 'We surrender!' The person holding him grunted. 'Please! We didn't come here to fight.'

'No? Well, isn't *that* lucky?'

Ash stopped struggling. He recognised that drawling voice! The man who'd disarmed Ordelle dragged off his mask, releasing a wave of long red hair. Lakmorin Spink!

The League warrior bared his teeth in a smile. 'Because we had you beat.' He snorted in derision. 'Honestly, darlings, fancy coming into a room like that. Did you *want* your skulls split?' Lakmorin pointed his long knife at Sarin. 'That was a very pretty somersault, Sarin. I'll give you that. You should join a circus.' He tossed a wave of red hair over his shoulder. 'Let them go,' he ordered, sheathing his weapon. 'They're League. *Careless idiots*, but League nonetheless.'

Ash's assailant released him with a shove, and he stumbled forward, losing his cap. Lakmorin went on. 'As to *what* they think they're doing—'

A shout of surprise cut him off. 'Ash?'

Rough hands grabbed Ash's shoulders, spinning him around. His attacker wore a dark green mask. Through woollen eyeholes, a pair of brown eyes stared back at him. They widened with sudden comprehension. 'It *is* you!' The warrior let out a whoop and swept off his mask. 'It's me! It's Braig!'

# 25

# JARLYCATS

It *was* him. Ash rubbed at the back of his head, trying to take in the miracle. Braig was *alive* ... and even bigger than he remembered. His boat-shaped grin had not changed one bit, nor his boisterousness, apparently — he capered about like an oversized puppy.

Lakmorin Spink gave three slow claps. 'Well, isn't this just peachy? Three more novices to babysit.' He made a careless flourish with a hand. 'Ash, Ordelle and Sarin, these are Shift, Bardi and Krizo. All jarlycats,' he added with a roll of his eyes.

Ash exchanged a glance with Sarin. *Jarlycats.* And Lakmorin was in charge? Where was their captain, Pharni? Lakmorin was a member of the bear jinn. His own captain had remained behind in T'al Jazure, to prepare the plans for Mildaresh. Ordelle folded her arms, making no effort to hide her dislike. Lakmorin's unrelenting sarcasm did become tiresome.

The lad called Krizo was studying them with his good eye. The patch looked like a recent addition, since he kept adjusting it. He seemed a twitchy type, shifting his weight from one foot to the other. The girl had the unlikely name of Shift. Ash guessed she was the youngest of the trio. She had freckles on her nose and her hair was very fair, almost white. The v-shaped scar on her chin stood out, satiny pink against her complexion. She'd already dismissed the newcomers and was picking up the game pieces. The thickset lad called Bardi favoured them with a terse nod. His close-clipped hair was dark and fuzzy, lying low on his brow, making his neck look even shorter. He rolled his shoulders and cracked his knuckles, obviously disappointed that there hadn't been a proper fight.

'*Apparently*,' drawled Lakmorin, making the word impossibly long, 'you know Braig already. Another bleeding jarlycat.' He averted his eyes. 'It's a veritable plague in these parts.'

Ash blinked at the news. Braig wasn't just alive. He was a League warrior!

Bemusement showed on Lakmorin's face as he looked them over, arms folded. 'I can't imagine what you three think you're doing here. Nirias will—'

'We don't answer to Nirias.' Sarin's smooth reply drew the attention of everyone in the room. Bardi growled something to Shift under his breath, and she nodded. Sarin ignored them. 'Ordelle and I have passed the trials, as you well know, Spink, but none of us have taken the Pledge. So we don't answer to Nirias ... or the captains.' Sarin let that sink in, his eyes travelling over the strangers. 'And, in case any of you are wondering about Ash's credentials ...' Ash winced, wondering what was coming. 'He's the one who opened T'al Jazure.'

Braig's eyes went wide. Ash knew that dumbfounded expression well. Questions were about to spill out of him, and not all of them sensible. He shook his head at his friend. *I'll explain. Just not here.* A flicker of understanding passed between them, and Braig gave a nod.

'Well,' continued Lakmorin, flicking his hair over his shoulder, 'you're hardly my problem. Rodine can deal with you ...' He rolled his eyes again. 'That is, if he ever decides to grace us with his presence.'

Ordelle frowned. 'Rodine?'

Lakmorin regarded her, lips pursed. Ash knew what he was thinking — what was the Cryer's daughter doing traipsing about the countryside, in such curious company? Then he shrugged. 'Rodine and Ozu took the novices to check out rumours of trouble, in a dinky little backwater called Bixdale.'

'Kep's with Rodine?' The relief in Sarin's voice was obvious. Ash took a breath. It was excellent news: Rodine was one of the League's most experienced captains.

'So *that's* why you're here, Sarin?' Lakmorin smirked. 'How sweet. Young love and all that. Yes, your girl's with Rodine.' His laughing eyes slid to Braig, whose jaw tightened. A small crease had appeared between his brows. 'Oh, I don't think you need worry about our Kep. She's been terribly busy, you know — freed the whole of the Kenting, if the latest rumours are true. And single-handedly, by all accounts.' He laughed. 'She's got a new name, too. Kep-Váli, they're calling her now.'

'Kep-Váli.' Ordelle frowned, repeating it to herself. 'Saviour of worlds?'

Lakmorin pulled a face. 'Something like that.'

Braig chuckled, and he glowed with pride as he turned to Ash. 'It's nothing new! It was exactly the same in the Elgrave.'

Ash frowned, trying to keep up. 'The Elgrave? Is that where you've been?'

'Yeah. Every village was brimming with stories about Kep. She's a legend! And not just because of,' he looked flustered for a moment, 'because of that thing she did for me. The people adore her, Ash.'

'It's true,' said Lakmorin, sighing dramatically. '*Everyone* loves our Kep.'

At that moment, the girl named Shift plonked the dice cup onto the table, hard enough to make the dice bounce out. A scowl darkened her expression. She looked up, realising everyone was looking at her. 'They're late,' she grumbled.

'Yeah. And we're bored,' moaned the youth beside her.

Lakmorin cocked his head in their direction. 'Yes, Bardi, we're all *terribly* bored. We just can't *wait* to go and get ourselves killed.' He made a lackadaisical flapping motion with his hands. 'But off we go now, children, into the back lounge.' Ash wondered if he'd had been drinking. Then again, Lakmorin always seemed drunk to him. 'As for you two ...' — he pointed a wavering finger at Braig and Ash — 'for the sake of Telion, get your stories out of the way.' His eyes rolled in exaggerated amusement. 'You're gazing at each other like a pair of lovesick sailors.'

The back lounge of The Barnacle was a complete departure from the inhospitable façade the front half presented to the world. Bright copper lanterns sat on tables polished to a honeyed gleam. A pot-bellied stove and ample sofas with squashy cushions contributed to the sense of homeliness. A jug on the bookcase overflowed with spring flowers. Ash liked the place. It felt honest.

Lakmorin had already taken himself off somewhere. On the far side of the lounge his reluctant charges were setting up their dice game, for real this time. 'We'll grab ourselves a spot in the corner,' announced Braig, a possessive arm draped around Ash's shoulders.

Ordelle pointed. 'At that table.'

Braig blinked at her and laughed. 'Why not? There's room for us all.'

Ash was pulling out a chair when Braig whacked him on his shoulder, knocking him off-balance. 'I knew it was you!' He beamed. 'As soon as I saw that grey mop! Who else could it be?' Braig's hand shot out, then he remembered and snatched it back. 'Sorry, I forgot. You don't like having your hair mussed up, do you?' His grin was wide and unapologetic. For once, Ash didn't care. He couldn't wipe the smile from his own face, either. His friend was alive, and he looked ... well, he looked incredible!

Braig had been burly before, thanks to his work as a farm slave, but he seemed different somehow. It was partly his clothes: in place of his Aranti-green tunic, he wore dark blue breeches and a leather jerkin that strained across his chest. He exuded masculine energy. There was even stubble on his chin. But there was a more subtle change, too. Ash couldn't put his finger on it until Braig leaned back in his chair to stretch out his legs. The manner in which he looked around the room, smiling across at his comrades and perfectly at ease with his situation, brought understanding in a flash. Braig had found his people. And he no longer saw himself as a slave.

Ash rubbed ruefully at his shoulder, reminding himself that *some* things hadn't changed.

'Tell me everything!' said Braig, slapping the table. 'I want to hear all about T'al Jazure. What training have you done? Wait ... What happened with Credé? And why did you—?' He stopped abruptly, open-mouthed. 'That's not ... ? It is! It's Tarlyn!'

Tarlyn had performed her usual trick of materialising when nobody was looking. Braig spluttered in disbelief as she flowed up onto Ash's shoulder and balanced there to wash a paw. 'You brought Tarlyn?'

These days Ash couldn't help thinking that Tarlyn had brought *him,* but he nodded. 'Yeah, it's a long story. And ... it's ... pretty complicated.'

'Obviously!' Braig's eyes were almost as huge as Tarlyn's. 'I mean ... Why would you bring *Tarlyn*?' Awe and disbelief warred on his face. 'She *bites.*'

The sudden crash of a chair falling over made them jerk their heads around. Jeering laughter went up from the jarlycats' end of the room. Bardi and Krizo had lost interest in their game and were wrestling on the floor. Instantly distracted, Braig joined in the laughter, yelling out a jest. Ash glanced at Sarin. His eyes were on Braig, but his expression gave nothing away. It was several moments before Braig returned his attention to Ash. He blinked at Tarlyn, who stared back at him, unimpressed. 'Tell me, Ash. I want to know everything!'

Ash blew out his cheeks. *Everything?* Braig wouldn't understand half of it. Especially the stuff about the Song — the Song had always been beyond Braig's comprehension. Ash decided to gloss over that and begin with Credé's death, but before he could get started Ordelle blurted out a question of her own. 'Why aren't you dead?' Sarin's mouth curved a fraction. 'You're supposed to be dead.'

Braig laughed. 'Well, I'm not.' His eyes flicked to Sarin. 'Sorry to disappoint.'

Sarin leaned back, lacing his hands behind his head. 'I wouldn't take it personally,' he advised. 'Ordelle prefers dead people.'

Unsure whether he was being mocked, Braig turned to Ordelle. 'Is that true?'

Ordelle lifted a shoulder. 'Sometimes.'

'Ordelle's an embalmer,' Ash explained, before things could get out of hand. But Braig didn't seem to register the information. He was frowning at Sarin, no doubt wondering whether Sarin would prefer him dead as well. What had Lakmorin told him? The tension between the two young men was unmistakable. If Braig decided Sarin was a rival, things could get uncomfortable, and quickly.

Ash cleared his throat. 'But you're *alive*, Braig.' He wanted to prod him with a finger to make sure. 'How is that even possible? I mean, there was a body. *Your* body. At the Fires of Passing.' Ash remembered it clearly: the heat of the flames and the white sun-birds wheeling. It was the worst day of his life. And there had *definitely* been a body. The priests had even argued about where the unusual sacrifice should be placed. 'We all thought you were dead.' He frowned. 'Kep *still* does.'

That caught Braig's full attention. His eyes flooded with concern. 'I know. I wish you could have found out earlier, but Gooel's message never got through. Then Skarlon was supposed to tell you ... when he got to T'al Jazure.' Braig scrunched up his face in that way he had. 'But Nirias asked him not to.' Ash caught Sarin's eye. It was true then: Skarlon had withheld the information. Braig frowned, trying to read what had passed between them. 'You don't have to look so worried — Nirias explained everything.'

'Nirias was here? When?' The sharpness of Sarin's question only caused Braig to fold his arms.

'Please, Braig, said Ash. 'It's important.'

Some of the tension went out of Braig's shoulders. 'Three days back now.'

'With others?'

'Yeah, I met the whole team.' Braig's frown dissolved into a grin. 'Tuku gave me tips. On how to hold my shield and other stuff, too.' The gigantic warrior had obviously made an impression on Braig. 'The red-haired one, Heeda, she wasn't as friendly. But the other woman,' Braig eyes were earnest as he remembered, 'she was plain scary, with those tattoos and all those bones in her hair.'

'Pretalla Chanara,' said Ordelle.

'Yeah, that's her; I met them all. But Nirias pulled me aside, so we could speak in private. Imagine that, Ash.'

'Mmmm. Imagine that,' murmured Sarin.

Braig prickled. 'Well, I reckon it was pretty thoughtful of Nirias, what with everything he has to think about, with the mission and all.'

His friend's instant loyalty to the League's leader didn't surprise Ash. It was in Braig's nature. He shook his head. 'But why? Why keep it a secret, that you were alive? It doesn't make any sense.'

'Yes, it does,' said Braig. 'It's simple: Nirias explained everything. He wanted to keep Kep safe, that's all. He said he was worried it might jeopardise the mission if she knew I was alive. I mean,' he laughed, 'it's Kep, right?' They all stared back at him. 'Do you know, Nirias actually apologised? To me.' Braig shook his head, marvelling. 'I told him I understood, because I'd see her soon. We're expecting them any day now.' He laughed. 'Didn't expect you to pop up instead, Ash. I can tell you that!'

Ordelle was frowning. 'Nirias said he wanted to keep Kep safe?'

Braig spoke slowly and a little condescendingly. 'That's right. Nirias said as soon as Kep's token was drawn he knew he had to keep her out of danger. That's why he sent her to the Kettering, with Rodine. She obviously won't be in the real fight when Nirias takes down Kara-fell. None of us novices will.' He seemed disappointed.

'How long?' asked Sarin. 'How long did Nirias and the others stay?'

Braig gave him his best scowl. 'Not saying. Mission business, and none of yours.'

'Please, Braig,' said Ash. 'This isn't about the mission.'

He considered for a long moment before relenting. 'They stayed one night. And were gone the next morning.' He frowned. 'You haven't said what you're doing here, Ash.'

'We were worried about Kep, that's all.' It was laughably weak.

'Right,' said Braig slowly. 'You came all this way because you were worried about Kep.' He looked at Ordelle and back again, scratching at his chin. 'Well, you needn't have. Like I said, there's no need. Nirias knows what he's about.'

The door opened, and everyone turned. The innkeeper backed into the room, burdened by an enormous tray. Braig sniffed the air. 'Here's your dinner! I've eaten but' — he smacked his lips — 'that sure does smell good.'

Barney transferred three large bowls to the table and, with a wink, placed a smaller portion in front of Braig, who grinned and picked up a spoon.

Unsurprisingly, the bowls were filled with fish stew. What *was* surprising was the colour — an unappetising bluish-grey. It smelt good, though, and was piping hot. Barney cleared his throat as he transferred a large basket of bread to the table. 'Sorry if I was gruff before.' He wiped his hands on his apron. 'I recognised your sign at once, and I daresay the three of you looked wholesome enough ...' He glanced at Sarin. 'Well, more wholesome than our usual patrons. But we can't be too careful. And Dom was wary.' He turned, frowning at his assistant, who had slouched up beside him. The girl rolled her eyes, plonked down mugs of ale, and stalked off in a huff. The innkeeper shook his head. 'I'll leave you to it. Braig knows where your rooms are.'

'Dom?' asked Ash as soon as the innkeeper was gone.

'He's our lookout,' explained Braig. He jabbed his spoon at Ash's bowl. 'Don't worry about the colour, that's just the inkfish.' He stuffed a large piece of bread into his mouth, making the explanation that followed somewhat muffled. 'You'd never guess it — Dom's a priest. From Mildaresh. Escaped with Pharni.' Braig's eyes watered as he swallowed. He reminded Ash of a bird gulping down a too-large fish. 'And he's a senseer. You know what that is, right?'

'We know what that is,' said Ordelle, breaking her piece of bread into smaller pieces.

Braig carried on regardless. 'Dom can detect the presence of the Melk.' He shuddered. 'Imagine that.'

Despite its off-putting colour, the fish stew was delicious, and Ash was relieved to find it entirely free of eyeballs and bones. He watched as Braig demolished his bowl, wiping it clean with a crust. It felt strange. They'd never sat down to share a meal before.

Around mouthfuls of bread, Braig told his story. 'It was Pharni who saved my life.' He shook his head, as if the fact still amazed him. 'Except she was Matapharni then. You know she's a League captain, right?' Ash nodded. 'Right, of course you do. Who'd have believed it? That Matapharni would happen on us that day. She's the reason I'm alive. They say she's the League's best healer, after Nirias. And I'm the proof!'

Braig's tale was a complete mess, full of sidetracks and irrelevant observations — he'd never been much of a storyteller. But Ash pieced things together as best he could. It seemed that Aranti's mistress had taken pity on the injured farm slave. She had lied about his death, knowing he'd be packed off to the noikos fields — there was little value in a farm slave who couldn't heft sacks and drive ploughs.

Pharni had already been in the process of smuggling a young woman out of the city — one of the herati who'd fallen pregnant and wanted to keep the child rather than be sent to the Holding. She simply included Braig in the arrangements. He remembered little of the journey to the League's refuge in the Elgrave. 'Pain,' he said with a grimace. 'There was a lot of pain. And jolting wagons ... then a boat that stank of vomit and seaweed. But it was mostly pain.'

'But there was a body,' Ash pointed out weakly.

'Just a casing, weighted with stones and wrapped in a shroud. That's Pharni for you. She's clever, all right.' Braig's delight faded when he saw Ash's expression. 'Oh. Right. I guess that must have been pretty awful for you.' He circled his thumbs. 'And for Kep, too. But it wasn't Pharni's fault. It was Maliagne Aranti's.' A flash of hatred came into his eyes as he spoke the name of his former master. 'He was so pleased with himself, coming up with the idea of sacrificing a slave's soul.' Braig's chair groaned as he leaned back on it. 'How was Pharni supposed to guess Kep would do what she did?' His brow crinkled in confusion. 'How could *anyone* guess that?'

Ash hazarded a glance at Sarin. His eyes were glinting, reflecting the light of the newly lit candles. One eyebrow rose ever so slightly. Braig was too caught up in his own troubled reasoning to notice. 'Pharni tried to put it right. She sent a message with Gooel.' He held up his hands. 'Who'd have thought that *you* of all people could outrun the most notorious tracker in Mildaresh?' Ash couldn't help feeling hurt at the dismissal. 'Still, it *is* Kep we're talking about. Don't know why I was surprised, really. And now she's a warrior. And not just any warrior: she's Kep the Valiant.'

'Kep-Váli,' corrected Ordelle.

Braig nodded. 'She's a legend now.'

The innkeeper had reappeared with a basket of firewood. He chuckled as he cleared away their plates. 'I can vouch for that! The hoariest of pirates will simmer down to listen to tales of T'al Kep. The girl holds a strange fascination for them.'

A small voice piped up. 'I seen her! I seen T'al Kep!'

Ash looked down to see a small boy sitting beneath their table. He wondered how long he'd been there, listening in to their conversation. The lad had scraped knees and was missing both front teeth. The set of his jaw and a shock of dusty curls revealed he was Barney's son. A puppy squirmed in his lap, trying to escape. 'I seen T'al Kep,' the boy announced cheerfully. 'The day she killed Mirkon Dredd. Slit 'is throat she did!'

'Perrin! What have we said about getting under customers' feet?' Barney's gentle cuff did no more harm than ruffle the boy's hair. 'And what have we said about trading fibs for glory?'

Sarin leaned down to the boy's level, a forearm on his knee. 'Who's Mirkon Dredd?'

The boy's father answered for him. 'A pirate. And a nasty one. Found dead some three days back. Washed up under the wharves. Had a lot of enemies did Mirkon Dredd. Whoever it was, did the world a favour.'

The boy nodded, his round eyes serious. 'It was T'al Kep.'

'Pay no mind to the boy.'

'It *was* her! It was T'al Kep. She said so!'

'Away with you, boy. Leave our guests be. And return that poor pup to his ma. He's too young to be away for so long.'

Barney shook his head as he wiped spills from the table, most of them caused by Braig. 'Can't blame the lad really. It's all the stories. Cruel thugs done away with ... gold coins left for the poor ... sickness healed. All the work of T'al Kep.' He clicked his tongue. 'No wonder the boy's imagination is stirred.'

The little boy stuck his lip out, his eyes filling with tears. 'It's true. I *did* seen her.'

'Hush boy. And away with you now.' The rumbled warning in his father's voice finally brought the child to his feet.

Sarin smiled. 'I bet your pup is hungry. How many in his litter?'

The boy's face cleared at once. 'Six,' he answered proudly.

'Six!' Sarin stroked the top of the puppy's head with a finger. 'No wonder he's hungry, then.' The pup mewled loudly, sensing an ally. 'Are they all as fine as this fellow?'

The child needed no further encouragement. 'Come see! They're in the boiling room.'

'I'd like that. Can I hold him?' Sarin rescued the grateful creature from the boy's stranglehold, shouldering his gear at the same time. As they left, Ash heard them discussing 'proper best' names for dogs.

Ash knew exactly what his friend was up to: he meant to find out what the boy knew. He took a large mouthful of his ale, planning to follow as soon as he could. The boiling room would also give them a private place to talk. Ordelle caught his eye, and he gave her a quick shake of his head. *Not yet.*

Braig frowned at the door. 'Can't say I like the look of your friend. Can he be trusted?'

'Mostly,' said Ordelle. 'It depends on who you are.' She blinked at Ash. 'What? Sarin is an excellent stealth. And an accomplished liar.'

Braig folded his arms, his frown deepening.

Ash winced. 'That's all true,' he admitted reluctantly. 'But I trust Sarin with my life. In fact, he's saved my life. Several times. We wouldn't have found the League without him.' It was true. It was Sarin who'd saved them from Karendon's clutches, and whose cousin had flown them out of danger at Senna. It had been Sarin's token, given to him by his grandmother that had led them through the Enigmata to find Nirias and the League. And here they were now, all because of his sister's vision. Ash frowned to himself. Sarin's grandmother Nalina had been right when she'd told them that their fates were interwoven.

Braig still didn't look convinced. Then his face cleared as he latched onto something else. 'But it was you, Ash. You were the one who opened T'al Jazure.' He scratched at his ear. 'You know, I really thought T'al Jazure was a man. It took the others ages to convince me it was a city. Was that the quest, then?'

Ash took another gulp of ale, wondering if it was impolite to leave it unfinished. 'No.'

Ordelle chose that moment to be helpful. 'Ash is the taelstaun.' Braig looked more confused. 'He's the Keeper of the Song.' Tarlyn made a low burring sound, deep in her throat. Ash couldn't decide whether it was a warning or the sound of approval.

'What? Credé's Song? You mean the same one?'

Explaining the Song to Braig was going to be impossible. And Ash wasn't sure he wanted to. It was bad enough having Kep thinking he was losing his mind. And right now, he needed to get to Sarin. His friend had taken his gear with him; it would be just like him to sneak off on his own. 'I'll tell you about the Song later, I promise. But, to be honest, I'm pretty exhausted.' Ash reached down, tugging at the strap of his bag, which had got itself caught up under the chair leg. 'I think I'll just ...'

'Give it up, Ash.' Braig gave a woeful shake of his head. 'Your friend might be an excellent stealth, but you're certainly not. I don't know what's going on, but I'll show you to the boiling room.'

There was no answer to that, so Ash just gave him a nod. When Ordelle rose as well, Ash saw a flash of the mischievous boy he'd known in Mildaresh. 'All right, all right,' Braig told her, rolling his eyes. 'You can see the puppies, too.'

# 26

# WHAT THE BOY SAW

The boiling room was an untidy space, crammed full of balled-up nets, wooden buoys and other paraphernalia. Ash put a hand on one of the enormous cauldrons, and he instantly saw the workers who had toiled here, boiling up great vats of clams and shrimps, singing as they worked. He snatched his hand away, regaining control of his defences. The steamy vision dissolved, taking their music with it. Thankfully, none of the others seemed to have noticed. He shoved his hands deep into his pockets, not wanting to repeat the mistake.

The room shared a chimney with the lounge behind it. A large basket nestled in the hearth against the brickwork was shared by the mother and her six sleepy puppies. The thin bitch lifted her head, regarded them with yellow eyes, and, deciding they weren't a threat, flopped back down with a sigh. There was no sign of the boy.

Sarin stood near the unlatched window. Turning at their arrival, he didn't seem surprised that Braig had accompanied them.

'Well?' Ordelle's impatience revealed that she was just as tired as Ash. 'What did the boy say?'

'Perrin is convinced he spoke to T'al Kep.'

Braig let out a snort. 'So what? He's just a kid.'

'He's a kid with very sharp eyes.'

'Well, it's rubbish,' scoffed Braig. 'Kep's on her way here, from the Kettering. How can she be in two places at once?'

He might have been a fly buzzing for all the attention Sarin gave him. 'Perrin's story was very detailed. I made him repeat it twice and he didn't change a thing. He says Kep spoke to him, very early in the morning, down by the wharves near the place where Mirkon Dredd was discovered. He described her perfectly, Ash.'

'Pah! Anyone who's heard the stories could do that!' Braig counted off on his fingers. 'Bright blue eyes, curly black hair—'

Sarin cut him off, his eyes still on Ash. 'Her hair was short with three tiny braids at the back, like tails. And one was tipped with feathers.' Ash caught a breath. The token! The one Sarin had made for her. 'And there's more. Perrin loves birds. He described my falcon in perfect detail, right down to the blue on her claws.'

Braig spluttered, indignant at being ignored. '*Your* falcon?'

Ash took pity on him. 'Sarin tattooed a falcon on Kep's arm. It's an Astran design, to hide her slave marks. And Ordelle cut her hair to match.'

'You gave Kep a *tattoo*?' Braig advanced on Sarin, fists clenched at his sides, his jaw working.

Ash tried to catch his old friend by the arm, but Braig shook him off. Ash understood: in Braig's mind, tattoos were a mark of slavery. 'Braig! It's all right. I've got one, too. Look!' Ash held up his wrist. 'Mine's a minstrel's band.'

Ordelle ignored the tense exchange, her mind absorbed with the matter at hand. 'You are right, Sarin. Only people who've seen Kep recently would know these things. But why would the boy claim that Kep killed Mirkon Dredd?'

Sarin held her gaze. 'Because that's what she told him.'

Ash blinked, wishing his brain was less tired. There was some underlying meaning here. Something he wasn't grasping. 'That seems a bit far-fetched.'

'A bit far-fetched? You reckon?' Braig looked fit to explode. 'Where have you people *been*? Kep's League. She can't just go around killing people, not even pirates. She's taken the Pledge. Even if she was skilled enough to beat a man like Mirkon Dredd — which she isn't — she wouldn't.'

Ash swallowed, blinking fast. He really hoped Braig was right. But Braig didn't know how much Kep had changed.

'*You* don't get it,' said Sarin. Ash winced, knowing his friend's calm tone would only antagonise Braig further. 'It doesn't matter whether Kep killed Dredd or not. The rumours will spread and it will *become* the truth.' Ash felt sharp needles of fear in his stomach.

'That's true,' said Ordelle. 'And it places Kep in greater danger.'

'Well, *I* don't believe it,' said Braig stubbornly. He looked from one to the other in the lengthy silence, then folded his arms. 'Right! That's enough. Tell me what's going on, Ash! Why are you *really* here? And why do you look like you're about to throw up?'

Ash heaved a sigh that came from the bottom of his heart. 'It's only fair, Sarin.'

Sarin shrugged, non-committal. 'If you must.'

So Ash described Rilka's vision as best he could. Braig listened in silence, his expression growing more doubtful by the minute, as if he was suspecting that he was the victim of a prank. But when it was clear the three of them were deadly serious, he was silent for a long moment. 'Well, Kep probably *was* in danger. They say she rescued children from a burning barn. And organised the village to fight off a band of thugs. You have to admit, that sounds a lot more like Kep than murdering pirates.' He scowled at Sarin. 'I'm sure she's on her way here.'

'No doubt you are right,' said Sarin coolly. 'And you should absolutely stay and wait for her.' If Sarin wasn't careful, he'd wear a punch.

'Look, I'm not stupid,' said Braig through gritted teeth. 'There's got to be a better reason why you came all this way. So out with it. Now!'

Ash held up a hand, his heart racing. 'Rilka said there was something wrong with Kep's eyes! In the vision. She said Kep wasn't herself.'

'What's that supposed to mean?' asked Braig, annoyed. Then his brain caught up. 'You mean the Melk?'

'Maybe.' It made Ash sick just thinking about it. 'She shouldn't even be in the field.' His own anger rose like a bubble in his chest. 'She should be in T'al Jazure, training. But her token was drawn and she went, believing it was the will of the gods.'

'Well, it was, wasn't it?'

Ash didn't answer, and saw Sarin gave a tiny shake of his head. He was right. They couldn't tell Braig that Nirias had lied about Kep's token being drawn. Not without incriminating Sarin. The only reason they knew was because Sarin had tampered with the sacred vessel. Nor could they tell him that Nirias was a shape-shifter — they were sworn to secrecy. Braig wouldn't believe it, anyway. He was staring at them incredulously as it was.

'And that's it? You came all this way, against orders, because of that?'

Ash couldn't help prickling at his tone. 'No,' he said miserably. 'We can't tell you everything, but when we heard about the vision we couldn't take the risk. We hated to think that Kep was locked up somewhere in a cage. And that,' he forced himself to say the words, 'that she might be in the power of the Melk.'

'A cage?' Braig's eyes widened. 'What sort of cage?'

'Rilka couldn't say. A large cage, she thought. With bars.' Ash didn't confess his fears that it might not *actually* be a cage, but a symbol for something else. Telling Braig that would just confuse him.

But Braig was staring at him with a new intensity. 'There are cages at Nokturn Isle — I saw them.'

The way Sarin pricked up his ears reminded Ash of a wolvern. 'Nokturn Isle?'

Braig licked his lips nervously. 'I'm not supposed to say, but that's where *she* is.'

Ash didn't like the look in his eyes. 'Who?'

'Kara-fell. I was there. With Skarlon. We discovered the hideout.' He hugged his arms tightly across his chest.

'And?' prompted Sarin.

'And there were cages. They're for slaves. Kara-fell pays good coin for slaves. But she wants only a certain kind. Those who can fight.' He paused. 'She forces them to do battle — to the death.'

Sarin thought for a moment. 'Is that how the League plans to infiltrate her people?'

Braig flushed, uncomfortable at having said so much. 'I don't know the plan. And even if I did, I wouldn't tell you League business. You haven't taken the Pledge.'

Sarin ignored him. 'It's what I would do. And send a team inland, with archers to create a distraction.' Braig did a poor job of hiding his dismay at Sarin's accurate guesswork. 'It's risky. But it would get them close.' Sarin looked thoughtful. 'Perrin said something else during our chat. He told me his father wouldn't have to worry about bad pirates anymore. Because he knew a secret. T'al Kep whispered it in his ear.'

Ordelle blinked. 'What secret?'

'She told him things would be better soon. Because she was going to kill Kara-fell.'

Braig looked very much the farm-boy Ash remembered as he raked his fingers through his sandy hair. 'You seriously think Kep would ...'

'What? Be reckless enough to fight Kara-fell?' Sarin's mouth twisted.

'Absolutely, she would,' Ordelle confirmed with a firm nod.

Ash felt a weight in his stomach. Braig glared at Sarin. 'Do *you* think it was Kep that the boy saw?'

'No, I don't.' Sarin lifted an eyebrow. 'You said it yourself. How can she be in two places at once?'

Sarin gave the old dog a pat on her head. 'We've paid for beds. You two should use them.'

Ash eyed the unlatched window. 'No. You're not slipping off without us, Sarin.'

Sarin gave him a sly grin. 'You're learning. But much as I'd love to leave you behind, I can't. I'll need your help with the mists.'

Ordelle folded her arms. 'And you need me, too.'

Sarin nodded. 'True. If I asked Petrel to take me to Nokturn Isle she'd tell me to go jump. But if *you* ask, Ordelle ...'

Braig threw up his hands. 'You're going to Nokturn Isle? Just going to head into danger? Even though Kep could be here any day?'

'There are no cages here. There are cages at Nokturn Isle.'

Ordelle's blunt logic was too much for Braig. He gaped, then glowered at Sarin. 'I'm coming, too.'

Sarin raised a brow. 'You're sure? Don't want to wait for Kep? If she *is* with Rodine, she could show up any day.'

Braig planted his feet. 'I'm coming. I've been to Nokturn. And you need someone who can fight.'

Sarin gave the matter consideration. As if he was choosing vegetables from a market stall. After a moment, he rolled his eyes. 'You can come. But only if you shave one half of your head.'

Ordelle's sudden scrutiny did nothing to lessen Braig's bewilderment. 'A Denchman? Yes, that might work.'

Braig stared at Ash. 'He's joking, right?'

Ash shrugged. 'I think it might be part of a plan.' As Sarin rubbed his hands together, Ash wondered whether Braig had been part of the plan all along.

'Good,' said Sarin. 'Pack up your stuff, and get some sleep.' He cast a glance at Braig. 'And work out how to leave a message for Kep — in case she *is* heading here.' With that, he opened the window and vaulted over the sill. 'I'm going fishing.'

Ordelle turned to Braig. 'He's not *actually* going fishing.'

Braig scowled as Sarin vanished into the night. 'You don't say.'

## 27

## SIMBAB

The first rays of morning broke through the clouds, striking the ornate panelling of the old capstan housing, as if bestowing a special favour. And nobody paid any attention whatsoever. Why would they? The curiously fashioned housing was just part of the old ship's character — one of her idiosyncrasies. None of the current crew had given the structure so much as a second thought, far less wondered why the elaborate side panels were pierced with tiny holes. The pirates were not an inquisitive bunch, which was just as well, otherwise they might have guessed that the woman they'd spent the night searching for was right beneath their noses.

Kep lifted her hand, letting the shafts of light play across her fingers. After the dark terrors of the night, their pale beauty was almost unbearable. A single tear ran from the corner of her eye and she prayed. *Thank you, sweet Telion. And thank you for making Curly such a devious rascal.*

Of course Curly had installed secret compartments! He was a smuggler after all. His first act after buying the old ship, even before taking on crew, had been to hire carpenters, whom he'd paid handsomely in gold to take their secret commission to their graves. But no secret can withstand the curiosity of two young boys. Spike and Ratskin had discovered the false keel by accident, and had made it their mission to find the ship's other secrets. Of the four compartments they'd found so far, only two were big enough to hide a person.

The coffin-like space in the bowels of the ship was claustrophobic. But what choice had there been? An overexcited Spike had barely garbled the plans when they'd heard shouting, signalling that the pirates had discovered Kep's escape. She would never forget the sound of those panels sliding shut. Nor the utter darkness. And the smell of her own fear as the crew searched the ship. Back and forth the pirates had run, screaming and cursing, shaking the *Lady Lee* to her bones. The timbers had shuddered against Kep's shoulder blades as they'd searched. It had seemed an eternity before the pirates had come to an obvious conclusion: Kep-Váli had thrown herself overboard.

The dark hours that followed were interminable. A nightmare of suffocating darkness. Unable to breathe. Unable to pee. Dreading that the creaking of the ship would turn to discovery at any moment. Kep didn't remember sleeping. Perhaps she'd passed out from lack of air. She'd woken to the sharp terror of a panel sliding, the stab of a lantern's light, and Spike — a goblin-like figure — urging her to follow him.

Thankfully, ships are noisy. Waves slapped at the hull, and ropes and sails had an urgent music of their own — the perfect cover for people moving about where they shouldn't. Spike hadn't risked bringing a lantern, which had left Kep going blind, bumping into struts and stumbling over crates.

At last they'd reached the end of the passageway. Using a rope and pulley, the boys had hoisted her up into the housing like a side of mutton. It had taken a fair bit of wriggling to squirm inside from below, and a similar battle to secure the ceiling panel back into place. But she'd managed it. And here she was now: hidden in plain view on the quarterdeck of a pirate ship as the sun brightened the horizon.

Kep's legs and feet were numb from lying flat on her back for so long. And she was chilled to the bone, despite her Azuran cloak. The only warmth came from the disturbing heat emanating from the snake tattoo. But after a night of suffocating darkness, she was happy to put up with the cold, and she blessed the breeze that blew through the tiny apertures to play with her hair. In the growing light, her eyes discovered the catches that secured the back panel of her hiding space. She breathed a sigh of relief — a restrained sigh, because just on the other side of that panel was the helmsman. Spike had warned her to be silent. Ruby Ross was a canny one.

Kep had been mindful of the man's presence as he'd steered the ship through the night. Now he cleared his throat, muttering as he tapped out his pipe. The ship was barely on a lean now — either the wind had dropped or they were nearing their destination. A shiver of trepidation went through her frozen body.

Through the decorative panels, Kep watched as the blue sky turned to grey. A bird wheeled into sight and disappeared. Then hills appeared. And trees! Lots of trees — so close she could identify different species. Her heart leapt, and the fragile hope she'd been nursing grew a little stronger. Spike was right: it *would* be hard to track a person in these parts.

Kep had a clear view of events on board. She watched the crew going about their tasks, searching for a friendly face. Even a glimpse of Harden would have been welcome after the lonely night. But she didn't recognise any of the pirates from Bixdale, and none of the others looked in the least bit friendly.

Ruby Ross now started hollering in earnest. The commands came thick and fast, sending the crew running. 'Hands about ship!' 'Helm's a lee!' 'Ready mainstays!' Then the cry Kep had been dreading: 'Drop anchor!' The clanking of chains made the whole vessel shake. Her heart sank as if bound to the anchor itself. This was it then. The rendezvous with the *Nightingale*.

In no time the crew had reefed the sails. As the *Lady Lee* settled into a gentle wallow, a loud yawn and the thump of boots announced that Ruby Ross was finally leaving his post at the wheel. Kep held her breath. Perhaps he'd go straight to his bunk? Surely the man needed to sleep? But that hope was in vain, as he hunkered down on the very structure in which she was hiding. She froze, heart pounding.

His boots were very close to her face — she could smell damp leather. Timbers creaked overhead as the pirate shifted his weight. When the scent of pipe smoke met Kep's nostrils, she went rigid with panic. Pipe smoke always made her sneeze! Daring to bring up her hand, she pinched her nose and breathed through her mouth.

The helmsman didn't budge. He just sat there, filling the morning with a blue haze. Kep squeezed her eyes shut, trying not to think about coughing. How long did it take to smoke a pipe? The clank of a bucket announced Spike's arrival. His cheery voice came to her ears. 'Morning, Mr Ross, sir!'

'Yes, boy. It is.'

'We've made it to Wiseman's Crook!' Kep knew the information was for her benefit.

'We have indeed, Spike. Why the bucket and rope?'

'Cap'n's windows, sir.'

'Windows?' The helmsman grunted. 'Reckon folk are thinking about windows?'

'Er ... Maybe?' Spike shuffled his feet. 'Don't want another beating, see? So ... reckon I'll just leave this 'ere. For afters.' It was part of the plan. Spike would tie the rope to the stern's railing.

Ruby Ross growled but didn't comment further, just continued puffing away on his pipe. But as the boy was about to leave, he addressed him gruffly: 'Spike, I heard something moving about in the night. Know anything about that, lad?'

Spike let out a squeak from the top of the steps. 'Mice! Could be mice, I reckon. Should I fetch the cat, Mr Ross?'

'Hmmm. You do that, boy.' The helmsman paused, lowering his voice. 'And Spike. These tales you've been spreading about the Simbab's mark. They can only lead to trouble.'

'But it's true,' muttered Spike sulkily. 'Ratskin saw it. On 'er arm!'

Ruby Ross growled. 'Nought more dangerous than truth. Button your mouth, lad. That's a warning.'

With that, Spike took himself off, promising to hunt down the ship's cat. Kep prayed he would take heed of the warning. But there was no time to fret about the trouble the lad might get himself into, as a cry went up from below.

'All hands to midship!'

Ruby Ross muttered a curse that was lost to the wind. Clambering to his feet with a groan, he spent a few moments tamping down his pipe. Kep held her breath. At last! He was leaving. Then a hand patted the timber-work right near her face. It sent a tingle of shock through her body. 'Be still, little mouse.' She caught a flash of surprisingly well-shaped legs. Then he was gone.

Kep pressed her hands to her mouth. Her breath came fast and shallow. He knew! The helmsman knew! What did it mean? Was he biding his time? She pictured Greigo's triumph at her discovery. *Unhelpful.* Taking deep breaths, she fought to calm herself. There was still a chance of escape. A slim one. The quarterdeck was empty, and the rope was in place. She just needed to slip over the side, climb down the stern and swim to shore.

Kep hated the plan. And the thought of abandoning her fellow warriors. But what was the alternative? She owed it to Jen-Jay to try. The thought of her mentor brought tears to her eyes. But she knew that Jen-Jay would growl at her and order her to escape.

Two clasps secured the top corners of the housing. Not as rusty as they looked, they budged after a few minutes' work. Kep felt a rush of panic when she couldn't find the lower clasps, then she discovered a hinge. A firm push, and it would fall open. She drew a deep breath, letting her eyes rest on the lush green forest. She would be safe there. *But alone.* She swallowed, pushing the thought away. She had to try. All she needed was a distraction.

Kep shifted onto her side, contorting her body and squashing her nose against the front panel. The uncomfortable position gave a much better view of the uneasy assembly below. The crew was an assorted bunch. Every shape, size and skin colour was represented. Some wore plaited beards, some bandanas. All wore gold. A couple had black eyes and cuts on their faces. Kep could sense the tension: it felt as if a fight could break out at any moment. She hoped so. A fight would be the perfect distraction.

Even amongst the varied throng the pirates from Bixdale were easy enough to spot. Orrick's flash of white hair stood out on the far side of the group. Next to him was Harden, and Creely in his purple hat. As before, Rawlins conversed with the helmsman, holding himself a little apart from the others. Curious. He was usually so unfriendly.

As Kep watched, a woman with flaxen hair emerged from a doorway at the opposite end of the ship. Her legs were sturdy inside red leggings, and her leather waistcoat was laced tightly across an ample bosom. Her arms and shoulders were bare, scoffing at the cool morning breeze, as she sauntered down the deck, a cutlass swinging at either hip. Kep guessed her identity at once. This had to be Yulia.

Rather than join her crewmates, the woman halted in the middle of the ship by the central mast. Kep's heart jumped when she realised that a person was bound to the mast. He lifted his bedraggled head. Curly! Had the poor man been there all night? A gag prevented him from speaking, but he locked eyes with Yulia. Kep felt the intensity of his stare. Yulia laughed and grasped him by the chin. For a moment Kep thought she might kiss him, then she slapped him hard across the face. The watching pirates roared in approval.

Even the seagulls seemed to find it hilarious. One flew down to perch on the rail of the quarterdeck, just above Kep's eye-line. It sat there squawking and bobbing, enjoying the drama. Impossibly white, the bird had a grey saddle and bright red legs. Kep wished she could shoo it away, fearing its antics might draw someone's attention and reveal her hiding place. But the gull stayed where it was, watching everything through black, beady eyes.

The door leading to the captain's quarters opened, drawing every eye. Greigo strode onto the deck with Tibbs in his wake. The bald pirate wore a green frock coat to match the tattoos on his head. The garment was too long for him; clearly purloined from the captain's wardrobe, along with the lace at his throat and the silver buckles on his boots.

When he leapt up onto the main hatch, the pirates' disgruntled muttering subsided. As they hushed, the treacherous breeze carried one voice above the others. 'I swear! It was the mark!'

Greigo snapped his head around, but before he could locate the speaker, Ruby Ross had let out a shout. 'Spike! Get to the crow's nest. Eyes peeled for a sail!'

Obeying quick-smart, Spike tore up the rigging, bare heels flashing. Greigo glared, as if he'd like nothing better than to get his hands on the lad. But Spike was safe. For now.

With an ugly sneer, Greigo turned back to the assembled crew and began his address. 'Don't think I haven't heard the filthy whispers. They're lies! I tell you, again: the girl's dead. Taken by the sea.' He raised a hand. 'And she was *never* Simbab. Never one of us!'

A ripple went through the gathering. A fellow with a bashed-in face called out. 'Hear, hear!'

To Kep's dismay, several others joined in. How many had Greigo swayed to his cause? He certainly seemed confident as he went on. 'Grady named *me* as his Second!' An outright lie. Had it been true, Windy's ledger would have recorded the fact. But the pirates didn't know that. Many nodded, as if they thought it plausible. 'There is nobody better than me to deal with the captain of the *Nightingale*. Dirkman wouldn't *dare* cross me. We've had *dealings* before. And I promise you, we'll have our gold!' Greigo waited for the cheer to subside before holding up a finger. 'And afterwards, we'll have ourselves a new Simbab!'

'So ... we'll vote?' Even as the rash interjector spoke, he read the surrounding faces and went pale, realising his mistake.

Greigo spoke through gritted teeth. 'Yes, Hogg. We vote. *After* I deal with the *Nightingale*. We'll share out all the gold' — here, he paused, giving the pirates time to absorb the idea — 'and then we'll vote.' He allowed himself a moment's gratification at the murmur of excitement that followed. Then his expression turned nasty. 'But while we wait ... we'll have ourselves some fun.' He stabbed a finger toward the central mast. 'We've got a *traitor* to deal with!'

Kep's heart beat faster, making it hard to breathe. Of course.

Greigo wanted Curly out of the way, and then he'd distribute the gold. Both would increase his chances of becoming Simbab. To her horror, the pirates roared their approval. A few cursed and spat. Yulia, who'd remained at Curly's side, pouted with amusement, a hand on her hip, one eyebrow raised.

Greigo pointed a finger at the unfortunate Curly. 'Will anyone speak for the traitor?' The silence was absolute. Kep held her breath. In the corner of her eye, she saw the gull preening its feathers, indifferent to the fate of the man below. Greigo's mouth slid into an ugly sneer. 'I thought not. What punishment, then?'

The deck erupted with helpful suggestions. 'Hang 'im!'

'String 'im up!'

'Bah! Hanging's too good for 'im. Keel haul! That's our way!'

This last bloodthirsty suggestion proved popular. Others joined in the chant. 'Keel haul! Keel haul!'

'Sell him to the *Nightingale*!'

'Yeah! Let him die in the witch's arena!'

The din grew louder. The pirates seemed united in their thirst for vengeance — even if they disagreed on the methods. Kep recognised her chance to escape. She wouldn't get a better distraction. But she couldn't tear her eyes away from the tragic figure tied to the mast. Curly wasn't an honourable man — he'd said so himself — but he didn't deserve this! Greigo raised his hands for silence, no doubt to propose some cruel torture of his own. But somebody else spoke first. 'Wait!'

Intervention came from a most unlikely quarter. Yulia's voice was clear and high-pitched. 'If it's to be death, the prisoner must speak.' She shrugged. 'That is our way.' Kep noticed that she addressed herself to her crewmates, not to Greigo.

'It is our way,' confirmed a voice. It was Orrick. Quietly spoken Orrick! Several others repeated the phrase.

Greigo glared at Yulia, hatred all too clear in his eyes. Too many were nodding agreement. 'Fine!' he snarled. 'Remove the gag.'

Yulia's dagger flashed as it emerged from its sheath. The crew laughed when she held the weapon up to Curly's throat, tracing a line. With a twist and a flick, she cut the gag. 'Speak, pretty man.' Her finger stroked his cheek and travelled along his jawline. 'What words do you have for us?'

Curly gave a strangled sort of croak. 'You stole my ship!' The woman just laughed. His voice cracked, giving way to sorrow. 'And you broke my heart.' Yulia's expression froze.

'Pah!' shouted a man, obviously hoping to win Greigo's favour. 'He's a traitor! I say cut 'im down!'

'No!' Ruby Ross folded his arms. 'He speaks. That is our way.'

Greigo was no fool. 'Of course the traitor will speak!' He spoke as if there'd never been doubt. 'Because that is our way.' He smiled. '*Then* he will die.'

Once again Kep knew that this was her chance — the perfect distraction. But she didn't dare move. The silence was absolute. Everyone was waiting for the condemned man's last words.

Beside her, the bird scratched its neck and stretched its wings. It glared at Kep, its eye dark, as if it saw into her soul.

Curly's voice rasped with emotion. ' "Our way." What *is* "our way"? Burning women and children alive? Burying innocent villagers? No! That is not our way. What happened at Bixdale was unforgivable!' A hard lump rose in Kep's throat. Her eyes pricked with tears. The pirates scratched their heads. This wasn't what they'd expected. Curly went on. 'These things are *not* what a Simbab should ask. We are pirates, not monsters! I don't regret what I did to save the village. I can't! And I don't regret my oath to Kep-Váli. Equal shares! That's what she promised. And freedom!' The mutterings grew louder. 'Harden! She saved your life! Does that mean nothing? Do our oaths as men mean nothing?'

Greigo scowled. At his gesture, one of his cronies moved to shut the man up.

But Curly gave a last impassioned plea. 'She *was* Simbab! It was in the stones!'

At this, everyone began talking at once. Over the clamour, Kep heard someone shout 'What of the mark? Ratsy saw the mark!'

Greigo let out a screech of frustration. 'There *was* no mark!'

'Yeah!' shouted an over-excited Tibbs. 'I saw it!'

Rawlins hadn't budged during the entire episode. Now he grabbed Tibbs by the front of his shirt. 'You saw it?' He shook the smaller man hard enough to rattle his teeth. 'The mark?'

Tibbs squeaked in panic. His eyes darted to Greigo and back again. 'Yes! No! I saw there weren't no mark.'

'Enough!' said Greigo swiftly. 'The traitor has confessed. For that he dies! Our lady's keel will strip the lies from his flesh!'

The ship erupted as people began throwing punches. Someone cut Curly down, ripping the shirt from his body. His skin was smooth and brown — no match for sharp-toothed barnacles. Tears of anger formed in Kep's eyes. This was *appalling!* His beloved ship would rip him to shreds! Curly had done terrible things. But this? *This* was against the gods.

The panel fell away. Nobody noticed Kep roll out onto the deck, except the bird, who, disturbed, gave a little hop. This was her moment to escape. Crawl to the rail. Shimmy down the rope and swim to shore. Kep took a deep breath. She summoned all of her courage, then hauled herself to her feet.

The bird flew up with a squawk, its wings clipping the top of Kep's head. Stumbling to the rail, she clung on tight. The movement, after so long in confinement, had made her dizzy. But the breeze was fresh on her face. It caught her cloak, whipping it out behind her. Despite her fear, Kep felt a surge of conviction. This felt right. It was the right decision. As if to confirm it, the sun chose that moment to break through the clouds. It caught the mark of Bahjak as she raised her hand. The snake dazzled, a scorching, impossible blue. 'Stop!' she commanded. 'Stop this!'

## 28

# THE NIGHTINGALE

The manner in which Ta'l Kep appeared to the pirates that morning would forever be a matter of debate. Some claimed that Argess restored her from the After itself. Others swore blind it was the bird. She'd disguised herself as a bird and transformed like magic! They all recalled a blinding light and the dazzling beauty of the mark on her arm. Their mark. The mark of the Simbab.

The astonished crew squinted into the sun, shielding their heads with their arms, expecting to be struck down for their sins. 'It's her! It's T'al Kep!' Men who hadn't said a prayer in their lives approximated the sign of the triangle.

Spike let out a whoop from above. 'Kep-Váli! Kep of the gods!'

Gripping the rail, Kep was still adjusting to the shock of being upright once more. But this wasn't the moment to show weakness, or fear — especially not of the emblem around her arm. The thing burned and writhed, making her want to claw at her flesh. Instead, she found her voice. 'I am Kep-Váli! And I *am* your Simbab!'

There was an eerie moment of paralysis. The ship seemed frozen in time. Then everything happened at once. The sun went behind a cloud and blades broke free of their scabbards.

Recovering his wits, Greigo let out a roar. 'Seize her!'

An alarming number of bodies lunged towards the quarterdeck. Kep wrestled Jaibari's sword from its scabbard and swept out her knife, whirling into a stance for two blades. She was no master of the blade, but her attackers could only come up the stairway one at a time. She would not surrender without a fight. Not this time.

Ruby Ross bounded up the steps and Kep readied herself to block. The big man grinned — and then turned his back on her! His deep voice rang out. 'Anyone wants our Simbab ... they come through me!'

The helmsman wasn't alone! Two more joined him to defend the steps — Orrick and a woman Kep didn't recognise. The little ship rocked with violence, her deck churning as people chose their side. Greigo had won over a decent proportion of the crew with his promises and lies. But not all. Some fought for the sheer joy of it. Tibbs howled like a deranged wolf, clumsy as he tried to wield Skarlon's mighty sword.

With Ruby Ross blocking her way, Kep once more became a spectator. She considered stringing her bow, but this wasn't a fight for arrows. This was chaos. Greigo danced with rage — things weren't going according to his plans. He screamed instructions from his hatch. 'Kill the traitor! Kill him!' An ugly brute with a single thick plait was attempting to beat Creely senseless and doing a reasonable job. But heeding the call, he dropped the pirate like an abandoned doll and rounded on Curly.

Curly wriggled like a caterpillar, still trying to escape his bonds. Kep felt sick as she watched; her knuckles bone-white on the rail. She whispered a prayer to Argess. *Help him! Somebody, help him!* Curly's attacker delivered a cruel kick into the ribs of his helpless victim. Then his blade went up to strike. But he paused — perhaps to deliver some insult — and that was his undoing.

Yulia was quick! Far quicker than the knife of a bully. Dancing in, she grabbed the man's braid, yanked his head back, and swept a blade across his throat. The brute fell, his expression baffled, as if Fate had dealt him a dirty trick. Yulia paid him no further heed. She laughed at Tibbs, who came swinging at her next, deflecting his blow as if batting away a fly. Then with an expression of pure contempt, she ran Tibbs through. Pivoting, she punched another man in the face before he could make up his mind whether to attack. Ratskin finished him, knocking him unconscious with the end of a gaff hook.

Kep heaved a sigh of relief as Ratskin untied Curly. The brawl seemed to be losing its intensity, but she'd lost track of Greigo. As she scanned the ship for him, a shout came from above. 'Sail ahoy! Sail to starboard!' Kep's spirits plunged. The *Nightingale!*

The pirates scarcely reacted. Then a bell started clanging, high in the crow's nest. Everyone froze, the fighting paused. Kep read the alarm on their upturned faces. Spike yelled again, shaking the bell hard enough to break it. She could barely hear him over the clamour, let alone make sense of his words. He scampered down the rigging at a pace; jumping wouldn't have been much quicker. Curly seized the boy by his shirt-front. 'Take a breath, Spike! Is it the *Nightingale*? Yes, or no?'

Spike yelped, flapping his arms. 'Yes! But she's wearing the black!'

The pirates lowered their weapons. Their faces went pale, anger giving way to fear. 'Reapers!'

The word passed as quickly as a burning coal. 'It can't be!'

'Not this far in.'

Many of the crew surged to the starboard rail. Curly cast about him. 'Orrick! Where's Orrick?'

Orrick was already in the rigging, one hand shielding his eyes. His voice floated down to them. 'It *is* the *Nightingale*. And Spike's right: there's black banners, and red on her sails.' He cursed. 'She's trailing the flume!'

Kep squinted in the direction he was pointing. Her eyesight wasn't as keen as Orrick's, but she could just make out a thin plume of black smoke issuing from the stern of the ship. Ruby Ross shouted above the panic. 'I don't know about you lot, but if we're fighting Reapers, I want the gods on my side. Kep-Váli! What is your command?' Kep read the message in his eyes. *Take control, and do it now.*

One of the crew bleated. 'But she ain't—'

Harden cut the objection short, with an uppercut to the man's jaw. He snarled at his comrades, rubbing his fist. 'Anyone *else* wanna deny Bahjak's mark?'

Yulia had watched the exchange through calculating eyes. Now she looked up at Kep. 'I acknowledge the sign of Bahjak!' The woman's decision obviously held weight. Even pirates who'd fought for Greigo found themselves nodding. Yulia didn't give them time to reconsider. 'Kep-Váli. What is your command?'

Trying not to look startled, Kep raised her voice. 'Prepare the ship for attack!' She knew nothing about what that entailed — she just hoped it would keep people busy. 'Curly! I want you with me, on the quarterdeck. Ruby Ross, you have the helm!'

Ruby Ross nodded his approval. 'You heard our Simbab! Stop gawping and move!'

Curly limped to the quarterdeck, aided by none other than Yulia. Kep wasn't comfortable with the woman's presence, but she didn't dare argue. She grasped Curly by the arm. 'You said the *Lady Lee* was swift, Curly. Can we outrun them?'

Curly frowned. 'We can try. But the *Nightingale's* a three-masted galleon. If she's rogue ...'

Yulia finished his sentence. 'She won't give up. Reapers *never* abandon their prey.'

'That is true,' said Curly. Tension remained between the pair, but they seemed to have called a truce. He frowned. 'But they'll have killed the crew, so they might not know about the rendezvous.'

Kep licked her lips. 'So they could just sail on by?' She knew that was unlikely.

Ruby Ross muttered at the wheel. 'If we're running, I'll need sail. And every scrap.'

Kep turned to him. 'What do you think, Ruby? Should we run?'

The helmsman shook his head. 'We could best them to leeward if we—'

Yulia cut him off. 'In the open sea, perhaps. Not here. We're hemmed in. If we resist the urge to run we could be overlooked.'

Kep's eyes went to the distant ship. *Like a rabbit hiding in the undergrowth.* Except there *was* no undergrowth.

Curly cleared his throat. 'We need a command, Simbab. Do we put on sail or not?'

Kep never got the chance to reply. A wild cackle drew every eye to the opposite end of the ship.

It was Greigo! He was dancing about on the forecastle, waving something in the air. It looked like a rod or a rolled-up scroll. The fever pitch of his laughter made Kep shudder. What mischief was this? As they watched, he raised his knee and cracked the object in two. Thick black smoke poured out of it.

Voices rose in panic. 'Put it out! Put it out!'

As people ran to obey, Greigo continued to crow and caper about, waving the pieces of rod above his head. Kep heard him jeering. 'No rules! One Will! No rules! One Will!' His celebration was cut short by an axe. The weapon flying across the midships, tumbling over the pirates' heads until it found a home — right between Greigo's eyes. The pirate toppled forward, his forehead cloven in two.

Kep stared at the axe's owner in stunned disbelief, joined by the rest of the crew. 'What?' said Rawlins, looking around at his surprised comrades. He jutted his chin out, scowling. 'Swore an oath, didn't I? I'm for Kep-Váli. Not that piece of scum.'

Only Ratskin had the sense of mind to remain focused on the threat. Scampering up the steps surprisingly quickly for a boy of his size, he tossed the pieces of smoking rod into the sea. Kep prayed it wasn't too late, as they all stared at the distant sail.

The bad news arrived quickly. 'She's turning!' shouted Orrick.

Curly's expression was grim. 'She's seen the signal, Kep-Váli. What is your command?'

Kep swallowed. 'There's been enough fighting today. Let's outrun them if we can. Curly, please captain the ship — you know her best.' Then she paused. 'Yulia, I hope it won't come to it, but, if it does, I want you to lead the fight.'

Yulia growled in her throat, like a cat purring. 'It'll be my pleasure, Simbab!' Before departing, she grabbed Curly and kissed him, holding his head between her hands. The passionate kiss left the pirate breathless. She grinned, patting him on the cheek. 'Stay alive, pretty man!'

'One of these days that woman's going to kill me,' said Curly, watching her back as she ran down the steps.

Ruby Ross chuckled. 'I've got money on it.' With a wink at Kep, he turned and began roaring orders. 'Give me sail, you scabby laggards!'

Curly lifted a fist to his brow and Kep heard the chink of rune-stones. She grabbed his arm. 'No, Curly! We make our own luck now.' Curly blinked. But he nodded, returning the stones to his pocket.

Moments later, Spike scampered up the steps, followed by Ratskin. The boys were beaming from ear to ear. 'We've come for our orders, Kep-Váli.'

'Good! You're just the people I need.'

Pride shone in their eyes. 'Are we fighting?' asked Spike.

Kep couldn't lie to the boy. 'Perhaps. We need to be ready.'

Spike puffed out his chest. 'Me and Ratskin *are* ready.' His face clouded. 'Only ... We ain't never fought Reapers.'

'Me neither,' said Kep. 'But I know somebody who can.'

Kep chased after Spike, with Ratskin close behind. Orders rang out. 'Haul away the mainsail!' 'Ready the topsail!' The pirates no longer looked frightened as they ran to obey. They had a shared enemy, and a single purpose — to survive. They gaped at the mark of Bahjak as Kep passed. A few muttered 'Simbab' and ducked their heads.

Leaving hammocks swinging in his wake, Spike led them through the sleeping quarters. A slender ladder took them down to the lock-up where the prisoners were being held. The sturdy door was locked and barred. Ratskin was preparing to smash it open when Kep cried out. 'Wait!' Fishing the captain's keys from her pocket, she tried them in the lock. The large black one turned easily. Ratskin lifted the bar and wrenched the door open.

A foul stench greeted them. Kep put a hand to her mouth as she peered inside. The prisoners made a fearsome sight, despite their chains. They snarled, squinting at the light, obviously anticipating some new torment. Kep's heart leapt. Her colleagues were all here. Rodine, Ozu, Jaibari and Polkin. 'It's Kep! I've come to release you!' Their angry expressions turned to ones of disbelief.

'Good,' said a voice from the gloom. 'About time.'

Tears sprang into Kep's eyes, blurring her vision. And when Jen-Jay snapped at Spike she wanted to laugh for joy. 'Don't stand gawking, boy! Do something about these chains!'

Kep and Spike began working to release the prisoners while Ratskin passed out ladles of water. The pirates hadn't underestimated their captives. A system of chains strung them together, and their wrists were bound. Rodine inclined his head towards a large padlock. 'That should release the chains.'

It took longer than Kep had hoped. The bombardment of questions didn't help as she wrestled with the padlock. Nor did Spike's over-excited interjections.

'By the gods, Kep! How did you escape?'

'She's T'al Kep, that's how!'

'We heard fighting!'

'Is it mutiny?'

Spike scoffed. 'Not anymore!'

'Shut up, boy!' This from Skarlon. 'Let your Simbab speak!'

Kep felt a wave of frustration. She'd tried the three likely keys and none of them seemed to fit. 'I can't explain everything. Not now. But we need you on deck. We need you to fight!' In desperation, she jammed the door key into the lock. When she forced it hard, the padlock burst open. Spike let out a whoop and started dragging the chains free. Kep allowed herself a breath or two. 'It's Reapers.'

'Reapers?' Polkin Dew frowned. 'Is that bad?'

'Very bad,' said Ozu. It was the first time he'd spoken.

Skarlon growled. In the low light, his face appeared misshapen. His captors had not been kind. His bonds were tight and sticky with blood. 'We first encountered them in the Elgrave. Imagine pirates, only ten times more brutal. It's part of the Melk's influence. A strong nexus creates a halo effect, drawing those in the vicinity to evil. Becoming Reapers, in this case.'

Spike couldn't contain himself. 'Greigo called them! But he's dead! An' Kep-Váli's Simbab now!'

Eyebrows shot up. Polkin Dew spluttered, unable to hide his surprise. 'So, you're *in charge*?'

'Yes. But Curly captains the ship.' Kep took shallow breaths through her mouth as she tried to unpick the slippery knots. The claustrophobic hold *stank*, making her stomach convulse. This was taking too long! Spike still hadn't freed Jen-Jay, even with *his* deft fingers.

Fighting a surge of panic, Kep drew out her knife. The green glow of its blade looked supernatural in that dim light. The feel of its hilt beneath her fingers gave her renewed confidence. 'Yulia will command the fight. And you'll answer to her.'

'Yulia?' Jen-Jay's voice was a sharp reprimand.

'Yes. She has the respect of the crew — they'll follow her orders.' The knife sent a thrill up Kep's arm as she brought it to bear on the rope. 'Hold still.'

When the bonds fell away, everyone gasped. 'That's quite the knife,' said Rodine. His look was thoughtful, but he didn't comment further.

The rest of the prisoners were soon free. As they staggered to the door, Kep had to stop herself from shoving ahead. She couldn't imagine enduring these conditions for long. She hoped her friends would be in a fit state to fight. Spike stood at the bottom of the ladder, urging them on. 'Hurry! Yulia has weapons.'

Kep mounted the ladder last. But she was forced to rest halfway up, her legs refusing to cooperate. The lack of sleep and food was catching up with her. To her surprise, she found somebody waiting at the top.

Jaibari's bearing was as proud as ever, despite her filthy appearance. She clasped Kep by the arm and Kep half-expected to be thrown to the floor. Dark eyes bored into hers. 'Thank you.' Before Kep could recover from her shock, the warrior spun away.

'Wait, Jaibari!' Kep shouted after her. 'You need this!'

Jaibari received the blade of her ancestors in profound silence. Her eyes were wells of meaning. Kep dropped her gaze, unable to bear the intensity. She felt compelled to confess. 'I ... I killed a ma— I killed a null with it.'

Jaibari paused, taken aback. Then she nodded. 'Jaibari Selenka of Manas concedes the debt.' She gave a salute, one hand pounding her chest, then sweeping open. 'Fight well, Kep-Váli.'

'You, too.'

'We die with glory!'

Kep couldn't think of a reply, and Jaibari was already gone.

## 29

## REAPERS

The *Lady Lee* came alive, like a swan lifting its wings. Her sails puffed out, harnessing the wind. Reaching the upper decks, Kep glanced at the horizon. The *Nightingale* was tearing towards them, a winged predator trailing darkness. Her bow threw up white spray as she surged through the waves. And she was huge! Much larger than Kep had imagined! Panic rose in her throat as she broke into a run.

She found Yulia on the midship deck, handing out weapons. As Kep approached, Polkin Dew let out a cry. The blonde giant had caught sight of his own axes among the stash. Ozu was less fortunate. He took his time before selecting a cutlass and a pair of knives. Shrugging in resignation, he settled down to sharpen them. Rodine accepted a sword that wasn't his without complaint. The captain of the snakes exuded calm — as if being asked to fight a ship full of raving maniacs was an everyday event. Perhaps it was for Rodine.

'What about me?' asked Spike hopefully.

'You get the most important weapon of all.' Yulia picked up a bucket and thrust it at his chest. 'Find every bucket we have and fill them with water.' The boy's face fell until she clapped him on the shoulder. 'Trust me, they *will* be flinging fire. You and Ratskin will defend the ship herself. Can you do that, Spike? Keep our *Lady* safe?'

With wide eyes, Spike swore that *nobody* could do it better and ran off to obey.

Kep couldn't help being impressed with how the woman had handled the matter. She frowned, putting images of burning sails out of her mind. 'Where do you want me?'

Yulia stuck her hands on her hips. 'Quarterdeck of course. You're Simbab, aren't you?' The woman gave her a wicked grin, plucked up a bundle of arrows and passed it over. 'Heard you're pretty good with a bow. Take out the ballistas if you can. *Nightingale* has two, one in the fighting top, the other in the bow. Other than that, keep your head down. Stick close to Curly.' A smile played on her lips. 'The man knows his way around a skirmish. But most of all, pray. Pray to your gods that we can outrun them.'

Kep found Harden lurking near the quarterdeck steps. He thrust a wrapped package into her hands, without meeting her eyes. 'It's for you, Kep-Váli.' Unwrapping the cloth, she found a dark brown square, covered in tiny seeds. 'Gives strength,' he muttered. His way of apologising.

Kep found a smile. 'Thank you, Harden. And for sticking up for me before.'

His whole head blushed pink. 'Don't you worry. Those Reapers won't take the *Lady*. We'll all die first.'

Kep's heart was heavy as she mounted the quarterdeck steps. She wished people would stop talking about dying. Eyeing the cake, she took a nibble. Stodgy and very sweet, it left an oily aftertaste. Curly eyes were wide as she joined him, still munching. 'Harden gave you tokin?'

Ruby swore behind them. 'Knew the bastard had a stash!' Curly laughed, as if it was a standing joke. Kep shot glances at her unlikely associate as she finished the rest of the cake. Curly seemed a different person. His face had come alight, whipped by salt spray, dark curls dancing in the breeze. Gone was the melancholy look. The pirate grinned, as if danger meant nothing. He was back with his ship — where he belonged. Kep couldn't help being affected by his mood; or was it the cake? Either way, she felt her spirits lift. Things had gone wrong, but her friends were free. And that was something.

They were headed towards new danger now — quite literally. Their course drove them straight at the *Nightingale*. Kep was relieved when Curly roared a string of commands. Ruby spun the wheel, hand over hand, and *Lady Lee* changed direction, like a dancer turning on her heel. Her sails bellied out, fuelling a last dash, straight to the end of the headland.

Kep clung to the railing, her hair thrashing around her face. Could a ship lean over so far without capsizing? It horrified and thrilled her. The *Lady Lee* smashed through waves, sending spray flying, hurling herself into a charge for freedom. The young woman hung on tight, praying to all her gods. *Let it be enough.*

But the *Nightingale* was fast! The rogue ship knifed towards them, sheering across the mouth of the bay. On Kep's left, the rocky headland loomed. Curly's plan was to skim past the rocks, then cut into the next bay. Having a shallower draft, they had a chance; the other ship wouldn't risk the reef. Kep wondered whether Curly understood the concept of 'skimming past'. The *Lady Lee* seemed to be heading straight for the reef!

Ruby Ross held firm at the wheel, his feet planted as if he was part of the ship. He didn't budge, ignoring the terrified gasps of the crew. 'She's holding course, Captain!'

Curly swore, hitting the railing with his fists. 'She means to ram us!'

Kep stifled a scream as warnings came from above. 'Hazard to port!' Panicked shouts vied with the alarm bell. 'Rocks to port! Rocks ahoy!'

The jagged rocks seemed to jump up at them, like sharp, gnashing teeth.

Ruby Ross hauled at the wheel. The horizon lurched as the *Lady Lee* swung about. As the vessel turned, a powerful jolt sent Kep tumbling. The deck bucked beneath her and she fell, coming down hard on her hip. Her head connected with the deck. In a blinding flash of pain, she realised they'd hit the rocks.

Sprawled on the deck, Kep watched the mast teeter against the sky. She expected the ship to start sinking around her — the crunch had been that terrible. But the *Lady Lee* was stronger than that. The heroic little ship righted herself, shaking off the blow. The crew leapt to tame her sails, like maids attending to a lady's skirts.

As Kep hauled herself to her feet, Ruby Ross delivered another blow. 'Rudder's damaged, Captain.' The helmsman's expression said everything. Their dash for freedom was over.

Curly nodded, tight-lipped. 'Go, Kep-Váli. Take a boat and head for shore. There's time before they—'

'No, Curly! I'm Simbab. And I'm staying.' The snake tightened around her arm, scorching her flesh.

Curly gave her a fierce grin. 'This is true.' A proud light came into his eyes.

Every face turned when Kep stepped up to the rail. She couldn't give them much. But she could give them hope. She raised a fist. Defiant. 'It seems the gods would have us fight! So let us win! For the *Lady Lee!*'

The answering cheer was resounding and utterly blood-curdling.

Nothing could have prepared Kep for the full horror of the *Nightingale*. The Reapers had splattered the captured vessel with red paint. Or blood. Or both. Red ribbons trailed from the sails — making the ship appear to weep blood. A black pennant streamed from the mast.

Her rigging resembled an evil spider's web, from which bodies dangled at grotesque angles. But most terrible were the nets. Packed full of globular shapes, the Reapers had strung them around the bow to display the heads of their victims. Like melons at a stall.

The first sight of the crew sent shudders down Kep's spine. The Reapers' eyes were painted black, as dark as soot. Some had daubed their limbs and faces with red and black stripes, too. These weren't humans. They were abominations — driven by one thing only, their lust for cruelty.

Their mighty drum pounded, and the Reapers began their chant. 'No rules! One Will! No rules! One Will!' The *Nightingale* dropped several smaller boats. They spread out, circling like sharks.

Kep's hands tightened on the rail. Every muscle in her body was clenched. Then a hand folded over hers, surprising her. Jen-Jay's skin was like wrinkled leather, but silky soft. 'I'm proud of you, Kep.'

The young warrior felt a warm glow, as if she'd taken a sip of Molly's elixir. Jen-Jay patted her hand. Then she sniffed. 'Just don't get cocky.'

'I wouldn't dream of it.'

Kep allowed herself a smile. She had pirates. She had League warriors. And she had Jen-Jay, the legendary Grey Wolf. The Reapers didn't have a clue what was about to hit them.

## 30

# A PROMISE KEPT

S moke. The air was thick with it. Gulls screamed from the *Nightingale's* rigging, squabbling over an easy meal of decaying flesh. Nothing could diminish their enthusiasm as they pecked at wounds and eye sockets. Not the rising smoke, not the clash of sword on sword, not the desperate shouts of the people below.

Kep clenched her teeth and nocked another arrow. Gulls were foul creatures — but not nearly as foul as the Reapers. Lifting her bow, she pulled her focus back to the dreaded ballista. Her arms trembled as they took up the tension. *Hold. Aim. Release.* She sent the arrow winging towards the target. This time, her aim was perfect. The Reaper manning the ballista toppled sideways, releasing the mechanism. A grappling hook went flying. Spiralling out of control, it splashed into the sea.

Kep sniffed, wiping her eyes on the heel of one hand. The hit gratified her, but she doubted it would make much difference. The two ships were entangled in a deadly embrace. For every rope that her crew hacked free, another flew across to snag in the riggings. The bows edged ever closer. How long before the Reapers could jump the gap? A boarding seemed inevitable. But at least Kep could stop them from flinging fire.

The gentle breeze had abandoned them to languish under a grey-orange haze. Kep found it hard to breathe as she squinted at the enemy ship. Someone had already dragged the Reaper manning the ballista away. Others swarmed to take his place. She scowled. How many Reapers could one ship hold? It was like fighting an ant nest!

The deck of the *Lady Lee* was littered with bodies now. Several Reapers had died right here on the quarterdeck — Curly and Ruby Ross had taught them not to climb up the stern. The sea was thick with their bodies. And still they came.

Kep counted her arrows. Five. Five that she could use, anyway. She didn't dare risk the blue. The Azuran arrow always found its mark, but she'd never get it back. She wished she could spare an arrow for that blasted drummer. The constant pounding hurt her brain. 'Curly! I need more arrows!'

When Curly didn't respond, Kep joined him at the rail. His expression was dark, yet full of wonder. 'Who *are* you people?' Following his gaze, she understood. The first time she'd seen the warriors in action, she'd been in awe, too. Back in Ta'l Jazure, the beauty of the Dance of Blades had entranced her. Now the blades were real, and she quailed at the sight.

On the forecastle, Polkin Dew and Ozu presided over a grim massacre. The bodies of dead Reapers choked the deck. As they watched, Polkin executed a swift chop of his axe, felling another. He tumbled the body overboard, knocking off several more who were trying to climb up. Ozu was a blur of movement, blades flashing. His unleashed braid whipped out behind him, like a thin black tail.

On the lower deck, Rodine and Jaibari fought as a team. A quick death rewarded any Reapers who scrambled up the port side. Kep's gaze fell on Skarlon, and it was like seeing the man for the first time. The way he moved! Smooth and precise, he flowed from one stance to the next. His opponents never so much as touched him. They fell before his blade, victims of a terrible beauty. Kep recognised some of his moves from their lessons together. But this was more than technique, more than perfect execution: Skarlon fought with the intuition and elegance of a master. And he didn't fight alone. He had a partner — in Jen-Jay.

The pair moved like a single piece. Their difference in height and size didn't seem to hinder them, nor that one wielded a broadsword, the other a quarterstaff. Their movements complemented each other, a flawless harmony. Kep's heart was wrenched. The veteran warriors had found unity at last. Through killing.

The pirates, on the other hand, fought like brawlers. Theirs was a righteous fury. How dare the Reapers try to take their ship! They bashed at the enemy with knives and clubs, and shoved them into the sea with poles. Ratskin had found alternative employment for his trusty gaff hook: he was using it to scoop up fireballs, hurling them back at the enemy ship. Spike dodged around him with a bucket, scurrying to put out flames.

Kep held her breath, not daring to hope. Yulia's tactics were working. While the Reapers had the numbers, the *Lady Lee* was holding them off. Half of the smaller boats were drifting. Two were on fire, thanks to Ratskin. The *Nightingale* smouldered, too. Could they survive this? Kep had barely completed the thought when a commotion on the other ship drew her attention. Something new was happening.

The awful drum had changed its beat. It thudded faster now, in a dull rolling. The Reapers chanted. *Heave! Heave! Heave!* Kep strained to see what was happening. All she could make out was a confusion of black and red. Then the end of a mighty beam began to rise. The Reapers were hoisting a gang plank! Huge metal grips were clamped to its end, like jaws. Even without Curly's curse, Kep understood. They meant to bridge the gap. 'Stay here!' yelled Curly. He was already gone, taking the steps in a leap.

The giant plank came upright. For a breath, it stayed there, poised. Then it fell. 'Move!' screamed Yulia. Pirates scrambled out of the way as the huge beam came down. A splintering crash sent a shudder through the little ship. Kep felt it in the soles of her feet. With a loud clunk, the mechanism locked into place. Reapers raced each other onto the plank. They howled with delight as they came, scenting victory. What they *didn't* expect was to be met halfway — by a little old woman.

The Reapers didn't have time to blink, let alone wipe the grins from their faces. Jen-Jay danced towards them, her quarterstaff blurring into invisibility. At first they fell one by one, like bottles being knocked off a wall. Then in groups, overbalancing even before Jen-Jay could get to them. They clutched at their comrades, dragging them into the sea. Kep heard harsh cries from the other ship: 'Kill her! Knock her off!' A voice screamed in her head. *Come back, Jen-Jay!* But Jen-Jay pushed on. Like a whirling demon, she drove the Reapers back.

She was nearly at the enemy ship when Rodine leapt up. He paused for the briefest moment, nodding to Skarlon. Some message passed between the two warriors. Then Rodine was running, chasing along the plank as if it were open ground. He reached Jen-Jay as she made a last thrust. Reapers spilled sideways and backwards. Rodine vaulted into the air and they dropped together onto the *Nightingale's* deck. Reapers fell back, howling. It was like watching twin scythes in a field of barley.

Yulia yelled, pointing with her cutlass. 'Attack!' She led the charge, with Curly close behind.

The pirates bellowed as they followed their captain across the gangplank. 'For the *Lady Lee!*'

Ozu Mako found his own way to the enemy ship: flying — with a little help from Polkin Dew. For a moment he hung in the rigging, like a hunting spider. Then he dropped. The first Reapers to die by his blades never even saw him coming.

Alone back on the *Lady Lee's* quarterdeck, Kep felt utterly helpless. A prayer ran through her head. *Let it be over. Please, Argess. Let it be over.* She spent her remaining arrows too quickly. Each found a mark, creating confusion on the *Nightingale.* Five Reapers wounded. Five fewer to attack her friends. Only the blue arrow remained.

Kep prowled the rail. Yulia and Jen-Jay had both ordered her to stay on the quarterdeck. It felt like a punishment. How could she just watch on as friends fought for their lives? She knew her duty: follow orders. But that had never been so hard! She chewed at her lip, sick with fear. Arrows! She just needed arrows!

The fighting on the *Lady Lee* had shifted to the opposite end of the ship. Ruby Ross was fighting four Reapers at once near the forecastle steps, with Harden's help. Skarlon and Jaibari still defended the midships. Spike had abandoned his bucket and was crouched next to Orrick. Propped against the mizzenmast, the older man clutched at his bloodied thigh. His face was almost as white as his hair. As Kep watched, Spike took off his shirt, struggling to tear it into strips. Emotions warred in her breast. Jen-Jay's voice in her head was the only thing stopping her from running down to help. *The League relies on discipline. Keep to your orders, Kep.* Then her heart skipped a beat. She spotted a pair of eyes ringed with black paint.

The Reaper was hauling himself over the ship's railing. A creature of corded sinew. His hair was black, hanging in long, wet hanks. He'd painted his face in diagonal stripes, black and white. Kep let out a cry, panic breaking her voice. 'Spike! Behind you!'

Now the Reaper grinned, drawing a blade from his belt. A boy and a wounded man — easy prey. Spike struggled to his feet. Kep moaned beneath her breath. 'Run, Spike. Just run!' Spike didn't run. He did something stupid — and wonderful. He picked up his bucket and threw it. The bucket connected with the Reaper's shoulder, dousing him with water. The Reaper shook his head like a dog. Spike dodged behind the mast and the Reaper cackled, as if enjoying the sport. His murderous laughter sent a rush of anger through Kep. Her fist tightened around her bow. 'That's *enough*.'

The arrow flew like a comet. An arc of blue energy, it drove deep into the base of the Reaper's skull. He dropped, narrowly missing Orrick. Kep drew a deep breath and picked up her sword. Her eyes narrowed. *Enough.* She was a League warrior. And she was *Simbab*. It was her *duty* to protect her people.

Kep had to step around several bodies to get to Orrick. He'd already fainted from a loss of blood, which soaked the surrounding deck. Spike was dabbing at the wound, terrified. 'He's bleeding. A lot!'

'Yes. But we'll look after him. Run to the captain's cabin and fetch a blanket.' Kep worked quickly, staunching the bleeding with a tourniquet. She bound the wound, wishing she could move Orrick somewhere safer. But nowhere was safe. He'd have to stay where he was. For now.

The last thing Kep wanted was to touch the Reaper's body. But she needed her precious arrow. Gritting her teeth, she placed one hand on his head. She gripped the arrow and tugged. The arrow came free in a gory rush. She wiped it off, fighting back nausea and trembling from head to foot. Arrows, she told herself. *Find arrows.*

But the thought was driven from her mind, as a Reaper seemed to drop from the sky. A chain linked one of her ears to a ring through her nose. Her garment was made of leather, like a blacksmith's apron. Black dye stained her lips and gums. She twirled a sword in her left hand, with the casual confidence of someone who knew how to use it.

Skarlon's training took over. Kep snapped into a defensive stance. The Reaper let out a warbling cry, her tongue flickering like a snake's. The first blow crashed against Kep's blade, making her stagger backwards. She felt a flash of terror. She was in trouble. Serious trouble.

The Reaper swung again. Kep ducked just in time, the blade whistling past her ear. Exhaustion was taking hold, right when she needed her strength. All she could do was block. She parried blow after blow, forced onto the back foot. She did everything wrong, but this was nothing like training. No time for deliberation. No watching for a moment to strike. Kep was outmatched.

The sword was slippery in her grasp. She blocked again, shoved almost against the starboard rail. In desperation, she aimed a swipe at her opponent's head. The Reaper smacked the blade away. Kep skidded on the slippery deck and fell to one knee, her sword ripped from her hand. The Reaper kicked the weapon aside. She snuffed at the air, nostrils flaring. Glee danced in her eyes. Changing to a two-handed grip, she raised her blade and let out a cry. 'One for the bag!'

Had the blow connected, it would have gone a long way to taking Kep's head off. But it didn't. Her saviour arrived like a wind gust, roaring with fury. His leathered amour was splattered with blood. He wore three stars on his cheek — one for each of the gods.

Skarlon barrelled into the Reaper, knocking her sideways. The bone-crunching tackle took them both down, tumbling and wrestling. The Reaper screamed, thrashing and kicking. She sank her teeth into Skarlon's arm and he roared again, struggling to get a grip around her chin. As Kep scrambled to her feet, the Reaper began to laugh. She would never forget that sound: high-pitched and triumphant, like the screech of a gull. Then the woman went limp.

Skarlon hadn't moved. He stared up at the wheeling birds, wide-eyed. Kep hurried forward, hauling the dead woman off him. As she did, the Reaper's arm flopped. A knife clattered to the deck. Its blade was bright with blood. Small. A knife you'd cut fruit with. Kep looked at Skarlon, denying the dread that crept along her spine. *Impossible.*

Skarlon's mouth was tight. One hand remained trapped beneath his armpit. 'Leave me, Kep. Get to safety.' It wasn't a command. Just a quiet plea. That frightened her more than anything.

'Lie still.' She knelt beside him. 'It's safe. Everyone here is dead.' She forced a smile. 'You killed them all.' It was true. The chaos had migrated to the *Nightingale*. At least for now.

Skarlon's wounds were many. His upper arm bled freely from punctures where the Reaper had bitten him. There was a cut on his forearm, and blood was seeping from another gash beneath his collarbone. Then she saw the real problem. The shirt beneath Skarlon's armpit was dark with blood. It welled bright between his fingers. She met his eyes. 'It might not be that deep.' Her voice wavered, betraying her fear.

Skarlon grunted. 'It's deep enough.'

Kep felt her body go cold. If anyone knew about fatal wounds, he did. Her mind rebelled. *No. The man is indestructible.* Skarlon's pain-creased eyes sought hers. 'I tried, Kep. Tell him. I tried.' His skin, where not covered in blood, was parchment grey.

'Of course.' Distracted by a sudden thought, Kep reached into her pocket. She didn't know whether Molly's concoction would help, but surely it couldn't do any harm. She unstoppered the vial. 'Open your mouth.'

Skarlon closed his eyes, trying to shake his head. Thankfully, he was too weak to argue. Kep dripped the elixir onto his tongue and his eyes opened wide. Surprise crept over his face. 'He was right about you.' His smile was more like a wince. 'Stubborn.' He tried to lift his hand, and Kep took it in hers, calloused and leathery, just like the rest of him. She studied him closely. Did his eyes seem a little brighter? 'When you see him ... tell him. I kept my promise.'

'Of course.' She leaned closer. 'Tell who? Nirias?'

Skarlon gave the faintest shake of his head. His brows came together and his mouth worked, as if it cost him an effort. Then he sighed. 'Very well.' Kep had the impression he was talking to somebody who wasn't there. It frightened her. 'I can't say, Kep. Even now.' Skarlon's gaze was distant, as if he was watching something beyond the circling gulls.

'Skarlon, no. Don't give up. Stay with me.' *Please, Argess. Save him.*

One of Kep's tears dropped onto his hand and he smiled. 'Tell him. Tell him I tried.'

'Tell who?'

But Skarlon was already gone.

Kep sat with him for a long time. Numb to everything else. Skarlon's death had stolen a part of her — the part that cared about what happened next. The battle raged on the other ship, but it seemed far away. In another world. *They will come.* Kep knew it. She tried to stir and failed. The sword lay useless in her lap.

The gulls were silent at last. They sat in groups, hunched like guilty accomplices. One ventured closer. It regarded her with a cruel eye, cocking its head. Kep growled. Deep in her throat. A dog guarding a bone. *No. You shall not have him.* She conserved her energy. *They are coming.*

Had the sky grown darker? Did the smoke seem thicker? The

drums had fallen silent, but had left an echo in Kep's chest. The dull thump of her heart. She bowed her head and waited.

Later, much later, came shouting from the *Nightingale*. Kep lifted her weary head. The gods had forsaken her. And she didn't blame them.

She sighed. Time then. Time for one last fight. Her mouth felt dry. Her eyes were bleary as she gripped her sword. She would stand. With Skarlon. They would not take him, not while she lived. She waited, eyes fixed on the end of the gangplank. Gathering strength. The cheering grew louder. More raucous. Kep tensed. *They are coming.* She closed her eyes, waiting. They chanted as they came. She frowned, hearing a name repeated. Kep-Váli. Kep-Váli.

She opened her eyes, and Jen-Jay was at her side. The warrior's grey hair hung in wisps around her face, framing a tired grin. Then her sharp eyes fell on Skarlon. 'What have you done to yourself? Silly old—' Understanding hit and joviality melted into grief. The warrior sank to her knees. Jen-Jay had never looked as ancient as she did in that moment. Grief made her haggard. She paused for a long moment. Eyes closed. Then she put her hand on Skarlon's chest. 'Be at peace, old friend.'

The words acted on Kep like a spell. Tears came in a flood. Then Jen-Jay's arms were around her.

'It's my fault,' sobbed Kep, between wracking shudders of grief. 'It's all my fault.'

**31**

---

# BEACH BURIAL

They buried him at dawn. On a grassy knoll overlooking the beach. No bird would guide Skarlon's soul to the After. His body would linger instead beneath the cold earth, weighted down by stones. Jen-Jay had explained: it was the way of his people. To Kep, it felt wrong.

The League warriors stood in a circle around the cairn, each holding a stone, ignoring the drizzling rain. Kep's stone was a weight against her heart as others shared what little they knew of the man. One thought churned in her mind, over and over. *It is all my fault.*

Ozu and Polkin went first — the young men full of admiration as they recalled how Skarlon had fought to save the ship. Jaibari followed. Formal in her gestures and words, she addressed Skarlon himself. 'Look down, oh mighty warrior!' She pointed at the three pyres, smouldering on the beach as they consumed the bodies of the Reapers. 'Look upon your work and rejoice! The gods relish the scent of your glory!' Kep's stomach squirmed at the unwelcome reminder. She'd been trying to block out the smell of burning flesh. Jaibari spoke for several minutes, hailing the man she'd known only as a warrior. But as Jaibari knelt to set her stone, Kep heard her murmur 'You stole my place, old man.'

Rodine looked over at Kep. When she shook her head, he spoke instead. Rodine knew Skarlon by reputation only, but he praised the man's steadfast loyalty to his jinn and the League. Then came Jen-Jay. The old warrior spoke as if reciting a lesson. Kep recognised few of the places she mentioned and even fewer names. The list detailed the untold victories of a man who'd spent a lifetime in the shadows, sacrificing everything to protect the world from the evil of the Melk. Unthanked. And unloved. Kep closed her eyes, clutching the stone to her heart. If anyone deserved to be legendary, it was this man, not her. At last Jen-Jay's recount brought them to Bixdale. Everyone turned to Kep.

Kep narrated the story in a tremulous voice, telling how Skarlon had whisked her away, after the jellin attack on their party. She related how the pair of them had worked with Marta and her husband, Apple, to outwit the pirate gang. The others nodded when she described how fiercely Skarlon had fought to protect the innocent villagers.

Kep wanted to tell them about their training sessions, too. About his gruff advice. About the way he'd stood guard outside her door, and all his small kindnesses. But the words dried in her mouth. All she could think about was the warm grasp of his hand. His blood soaking into the deck. *Because of me.*

Jen-Jay smiled. 'The blacksmith named his puppy Skarlon, you know.' She shook her head. 'Swore blind the blotches on its face were stars.' She nodded at the laughter. 'I warrant there will be babies, too. May the gods protect their mothers.' Her mouth twitched in dry amusement. 'He was a hard man, Skarlon. But a good one.' Jen-Jay wiped the drizzling rain from her face. And perhaps a tear as well. Then she nodded at Kep.

Kep stepped forward, half-blinded with grief. She placed her stone with trembling hands. Tears spilled as she bowed her head, watering the cold stone. *There should have been a bird.*

As the group began the solemn journey back to the boats, Jen-Jay drew Kep aside. 'You look awful.' Her own face was grey. 'You need rest, girl. Consider it an order. I don't care if you're Simbab: I'm still your captain.' Jen-Jay seemed to be expecting an argument. 'Curly will be informed that you'll be keeping to your cabin and to be ready for a ship's inspection this afternoon. That should keep the fool out of trouble.'

Kep nodded. *Poor Curly.* 'What about ... ?'

Jen-Jay held up a hand, impatient. 'Heed me in this!' Then her expression softened. She squeezed Kep's shoulder. 'Rest, Kep. Everything else can wait.'

Obeying orders had never seemed so welcome as on that terrible morning. Kep locked the cabin door and crawled back to bed, pulling the covers around her ears. The ship was alive with sound. The carpenter shouted directions to men in the water. They worked beneath the stern, trying to fix the rudder. Going by all the bumping and bashing, they were likely doing further damage.

Throughout the ship, the story was the same. A chorus of scrubbing brushes and sloshing water joined the merry rhythm of banging hammers. Laughter and lively banter filled the air. Singing erupted in bursts, well-spiced with obscenities. There was an unspoken rule, it seemed. After surviving certain death, you had to sing your lungs out — even if you *were* a tone-deaf pirate.

Kep didn't blame them. She also knew that sleep was impossible. When she closed her eyes, all she could see were visions of Reapers. She couldn't stop thinking about Skarlon's last words. *Tell him. Tell him I tried.* Tell who? If not Nirias, then who?

At last, exhaustion took her. Her dreams were fitful. She was back in the fighting. Braig was there and in danger. She had to save him. The Reapers kept coming. But she couldn't fight. She had to find a bird. She wept as she ran. Then found herself on a beach. Looking up, she saw three white gulls. They circled over Skarlon's cairn. When she lifted her arms, they dipped their wings then flew off, vanishing into the sky.

She woke to a feeling of deep peace, her pillow wet with tears.

Kep washed her face and tied back her hair. And she prayed. She gave special thanks to Telion for the dream. And to Argess, for saving her friends. She sat for a long time, practising the Breath. And she found a measure of calm. At least she was no longer shaking. She was alive. Yes, the situation was complicated. A *lot* more complicated. But the gods had brought her here. She trusted them to show her the way.

The sun was dipping towards the horizon when a knock came on the door, accompanied by muffled words. 'Are you ready, Simbab?'

Curly wore a silk shirt, bright green against his glossy black curls. His face glowed, as if he'd scrubbed it. Spike had visited earlier, bringing Kep food and gossip. Apparently, the pirate's jovial mood wasn't just because of the prospect of recovering his ship. Curly and Yulia had rediscovered their passion. 'All hot and lusty they were — enough to set the decks alight', according to the excitable cabin boy. But anyone with eyes could see it. Curly was a man in love.

Kep finished buckling on her sword belt, avoiding her reflection in the mirror. She'd rejected the fancy garments sent by Yulia. Her own clothes were sufficient. Freshly washed, they smelt of soap. Somebody had repaired the rip in her cloak with tiny blue stitches. 'I'm ready, Curly.' She wasn't. Not really. But she found the man a smile. 'Show me your ship.' Beaming from ear to ear, Curly led her out to inspect his beloved *Lady Lee*.

The pirates had assembled in the midships, jostling and preening like a flock of assorted parrots. Despite their bandages and bruises, they were even more colourful than before, with language to match. The Bixdale pirates brimmed with self-satisfaction. They were enjoying their newfound status — as 'the ones who'd sworn the oath'.

Spike had spread news of the bargain they'd struck, along with rumours that Kep-Váli might extend the arrangement to the whole crew. The idea was hard to fathom. A Simbab with no interest in plunder? Hope warred with puzzlement on the pirates' faces when they looked at her. Many of the crew trailed along, turning the inspection into a procession.

The *Lady Lee* had been scrubbed from bow to stern. Planks of fresh timber highlighted the repairs, pungent with the smell of pitch. Skipping along at Kep's side, Spike pointed out several mended sails. The patches would hold until they reached port, he said. The canvas still bore scorch marks in places. 'That's Spike's fault!' said one of the crew. 'Boy thinks buckets are for bashing Reapers!' Spike grinned at the wise-crack — the story was already a firm favourite. Given the intensity of the battle, the *Lady Lee* had fared remarkably well. Ruby Ross even reported that the rudder was now working to his satisfaction, and that they could be underway as soon as the Simbab commanded. His eyes twinkled as he apologised for the earlier noise of the repairs.

Kep felt foolish as she praised everyone for a job well done. As if she knew anything about ships! She couldn't wait for the charade to be over. The *Lady Lee* was Curly's ship now — as soon as he delivered them to the Singing Isles. The man couldn't contain his happiness. He was beaming like a proud father as the tour came to an end. Then he made her a bow. 'And now, to the *Nightingale*.'

Kep navigated the gangplank, wishing it was broader. Sharks still circled below, hopeful of another easy meal. The first thing that struck her was the *Nightingale*'s size. The ship was immense, dwarfing the *Lady Lee*. Her three masts towered overhead, black against the sky.

The vessel reeked of blood and death. Thankfully, somebody had cut down the bodies in the rigging and removed the ghastly net of trophies, but little else had been done to restore the ship's honour. Ribbons fluttered, blood-red, in the rigging. The Reapers had even defaced the ship's elaborate figurehead, cutting crude symbols into her face and breasts. Kep shuddered, a hand over her mouth, as she took in the scale of devastation. Rodine nodded at her dismay. 'She fell victim to the Reapers several days back.'

'How do you know?'

The League captain frowned. 'Not here. Come.' His slumped shoulders revealed an exhaustion that went far beyond his physical body. 'There is much to discuss.'

32
_____

# THE CAPTAIN'S CABIN

ep's feet sank into a deep green rug, so lush that her bug-eyed goats would probably have tried to eat it. The captain's cabin was twice the size of that on the *Lady Lee* and well lit. A curved array of windows framed the setting sun. Several paintings of ships decorated the walls. An ostentatious mounting must once have displayed a sword. The weapon, along with the decanters of fireshot and brandy, was missing. Apart from that, the place was unmolested. The Reapers had been otherwise engaged.

A clear-light swung overhead, caged in a large, rectangular housing. Unlit. Even pirates were short on elpha fuel these days. A branch of candles shed yellow light onto the polished oval table, around which sat four people.

A scowl darkened Jen-Jay's face, making Kep wonder what Curly had done wrong this time. It could have been the way the pirate was sitting, one boot resting on a knee as his eyes appraised the furnishings. Or perhaps the grinding of the runestones which circled in his hand? That sound never failed to infuriate the little woman. Kep frowned, unsure why Rodine had invited Curly to the meeting. Wasn't this League business?

Jen-Jay refused to meet her eye, so Kep stole glances at Rodine Gametale instead. She knew little about the captain of the snakes, just that he was a Master of the Blade. Only now did she fully understand what that meant. Rodine was one of the few League warriors who Sarin hadn't given a nickname. And that said something. On the surface, the man seemed unremarkable. He was of medium build, with mousey-grey hair and a rough-shaven face. Kep recalled gossip that he'd once been a baker, which was hard to imagine after seeing him fight.

Kep suspected Rodine didn't approve of her, and she braced herself for a reprimand. Instead, he impressed her by delivering a calm and detailed summary of their situation. In a matter of hours, he'd gathered every relevant piece of information, from the names of the pirates, including the now-deceased captain of the *Nightingale*, to the stores aboard each ship, and the damage taken.

Sometimes Rodine would direct a question at Curly. But that seemed a courtesy more than anything. The pirate frowned as he answered, shooting glances at Kep. Curly seemed to be wondering the same thing she was: What was this about? And why did it feel like a storm was brewing?

Miraculously, the *Lady Lee* had lost just six crew members, including Greigo and Tibbs. Curly bowed his head as Rodine listed them by name. After a respectful pause, Rodine continued. 'Which brings us to the survivors from the *Nightingale*.'

Kep sat up, startled. 'Survivors?'

'Yes. Four are sailors from the original crew. The Reapers spared them, to help sail the ship. I doubt the poor souls will ever recover their wits. But there are others, Kep.'

'It's part of your miracle, Kep-Váli!' Curly beamed. 'Yulia was overseeing the plunder, just as you ordered.' At this, Rodine raised his eyebrows, obviously none too impressed at the idea of a League warrior giving orders to ransack a ship. But Curly ploughed on, oblivious. 'And she found them! In the smugglers hold.'

Rodine shook his head. 'The Reapers were unaware of their human cargo — luckily for the prisoners. They are worse for wear, after days without food and water, but recovering. Several know their way around a ship. And all are clamouring to meet you, Kep.' Kep found it hard to read the meaning behind his eyes. 'It seems they want to swear an oath to their saviour.'

Jen-Jay stirred in her chair — the first movement she'd made since entering the cabin. Her gnarled hands tightened on the arms of her chair. Kep had a sudden realisation: Jen-Jay wasn't angry with Curly at all — she was furious with Rodine! But why?

Rodine sighed. 'So, that is the current state of affairs.' Kep noticed he avoided Jen-Jay's eyes. 'Now we come to the hard part.' He frowned at Kep and she gulped, preparing herself for some dire punishment. Was she about to be cast out of the League? Could Rodine do that? The possibility hadn't occurred to her. Her heart sank. Was that why Jen-Jay wouldn't meet her eye?

Rodine's bleak expression sent prickles of panic down Kep's spine. 'A novice ...' He cleared his throat. 'A novice would not usually be privy to this information, let alone ... an outsider.' He glanced at Curly and Curly shot a puzzled look at Kep. 'But we have no choice. Because the League's plans have gone awry.'

'*Awry*?' Jen-Jay pinned Rodine with her best glare. '*Obliterated*: I'd say *that* is a more fitting word.'

Rodine swallowed. 'Perhaps. But now—'

'No! Nothing has changed.' Jen-Jay thumped the table. 'An active mission against the Melk is *still* no place for novices.'

Curly looked bewildered. Kep stared from one League captain to the other. They'd obviously been arguing behind her back. Did she not have a say? After *all* that had happened? A protest burst from her mouth before she could stop it. 'Neither was Bixdale!'

Rodine blinked, taken aback. 'That's true. I'm sorry, Kep. We did our best to keep you out of harm's way. But ...' He sighed. 'It seems that the gods have other plans.'

Jen-Jay slammed the table again, making Curly sit back in alarm. '*No!* That's *not* an excuse for involving Kep in the attack on Kara-fell. I don't care—'

'What is this?' Curly's eyes flew wide open. 'You mean to attack Kara-fell? Kep-Váli, tell me! Is this true?'

Kep gulped. 'It's true.' Curly turned a paler shade than she'd thought possible for someone of his complexion.

Rodine remained calm. 'That is the League's purpose in these waters. Our *sole* purpose.' His eyes held Kep's in a level gaze. The implication stung. Did he think she'd *wanted* to become a pirate? He gestured at the map. 'After years of hunting, we know the location of Kara-fell's base.' Curly spluttered, like a kettle coming to the boil. 'Nirias and his team will be in position by now. But ... one thing was unforeseen.' Rodine sighed deeply. 'Nobody accounted for the Reapers.'

Jen-Jay ground her teeth. 'That is *not* our concern.'

Rodine rubbed a hand across his brow. 'Please, Grey Wolf, let me speak. Kep has a right to know.' Jen-Jay folded her arms, her eyes glittering, but she didn't interrupt. 'The helmsman, Ruby Ross, has managed to extract information from the two surviving Reapers — by what threat I do not know, since the man does not seem to have laid a finger on them. Both independently divulged the same information.' The furrows in his brow deepened. 'It is grim news. As we speak, Reapers are converging on Kara-fell's base,' he tapped the map, 'here at Nokturn Isle.'

Kep stared at the horseshoe-shaped island. It looked small. And insignificant.

'The cursed isle?' Curly laughed out loud, looking around the group. He raised his hands. 'It's a jest? No?'

Rodine ignored him. 'The Reapers are holding a competition, gathering as many heads as they can to present to Kara-fell. They worship her ... as a sort of god.' Kep shivered, as if a blade of ice had touched the flesh between her shoulder blades. 'The Reapers glory in the anarchy that Kara-fell represents. We have no idea how many will assemble at the island, but ... enough.'

The cabin fell silent as they all stared at the map. Rodine steepled his fingers beneath his chin, and let out a tired sigh. 'The plan relied on stealth.'

Jen-Jay snorted. 'Stealth!'

'Disguised as clammers, they planned to approach the island from this bay.' Rodine pointed to the horseshoe's curve. 'The very place where the Reapers are gathering.' Kep felt a stab of fear as she recalled those who'd set out with them from T'al Jazure. Nirias, Pretalla Chanara, Jakarmon Pyke, Tuku and Heeda — all were in danger. Not to mention Pharni and her jarlycats.

'You people are crazy,' said Curly. 'I do not think you can sneak up on Kara-fell.' Then he shrugged. As he tugged at an earring, his expression turned thoughtful. 'But many would benefit. Kara-fell makes life difficult for honest pirates.'

'Honest pirates?' Jen-Jay rolled her eyes.

Kep knew what Curly meant. She'd take pirates over the Reapers any day. *By Narsis!* What was wrong with her? Had she lost her sense of right and wrong? She took a deep breath, incriminating herself further. 'Bahjak wishes Kara-fell dead as well.'

Jen-Jay snapped her head around. 'And you claim to know the thoughts of a smuggler, do you?'

Kep blushed. 'Yes. Because that's what he told me.' She bit her lip. 'I think that's why he gave me this.' The snake writhed beneath her touch. 'So the pirates would follow me.'

Jen-Jay's gaze was icy-cold. 'And why would Bahjak want that?'

'Because ...' Kep forced herself to meet her mentor's eyes. 'He demanded a gift. And ... I offered to bring him the head of Kara-fell.'

'Flames of Telion!'

Kep's face burned like a torch. 'You weren't there, Jen-Jay.' She choked out the words. 'I had to do something.'

'So, you trade in heads now! Like a Reaper?'

'No!' Kep struggled to control her bottom lip. 'That wasn't the deal. Kara-fell has a harp. A harp that sings, with the sea, or something. I don't know. But Bahjak wants it. He collects weird things.'

Curly let out a low whistle. 'The Harp of Aedolin.' He nodded at their surprised faces. 'There are rumours that Kara-fell has this thing. She stole it from Ho-Sim, before cutting off his head. And his ears.' His head tilted. 'I wonder why his ears?' He pondered it for a moment, then shrugged. 'The harp is priceless. Yes, Bahjak would desire this thing.'

Kep wrung her hands. 'I had no choice, Jen-Jay. It's how Bahjak works.'

Curly nodded. 'This is true. The Simbabs offer gifts in exchange for the passage of goods, and sometimes their lives. Not every Simbab returns from an audience with Bahjak.'

'And you didn't think to mention this?' Jen-Jay looked as if she might murder Curly on the spot. Curly shot Kep a guilty look, looking more like a naughty puppy than ever.

Rodine frowned, as if the audacious bargain only confirmed his doubts about Kep. 'Did you tell the smuggler about the League? And our plans?'

Kep felt a surge of resentment. 'Of course not! How could I? I didn't even *know* the plans!' She felt mortified. What was she thinking? Yelling at a League captain? But her response was justified, too. Bringing her anger under control, she forced herself to take a breath. 'I didn't tell Bahjak anything. I simply made the only promise I could, to save my fellow warriors.'

Rodine blinked. 'Of course.' He bowed his head. 'I apologise, Kep. I'm sure you did what had to be done.' Behind him, the sun sank into the ocean, its molten glow slowly extinguishing. The League captain spread his hands. 'What's done is done. Let us now decide on what happens next.'

The silence grew, marked by the gentle swinging of the lamp. Jen-Jay's eyes were closed. Kep wanted to take her hand. To beg for forgiveness. To reassure the old warrior captain that her apprentice was still a good person. Except she was no longer sure that it was true.

Curly's head was bowed. The runestones ground again in his hand. Then stopped. He lifted his head. 'You want the ships,' he said softly. 'You wish to sail to Nokturn Isle. And you need Kep-Váli to command it.'

Rodine gave a slow nod. 'You *are* Simbab, Kep. You have the—'

'No.' Kep cut him short. 'The *Lady Lee* belongs to Curly. He will take us to the Singing Isles. But no more. I made a promise to the crew. The promise of freedom. Defending their ship from Reapers is one thing, but sailing into the arms of Kara-fell? No. I can't ask that of them. I *won't*.'

'But there are *two* ships. And the *Nightingale* is already expected at Nokturn Isle. All she needs is a willing crew.'

Curly's eyes opened wider. 'That is true.' Kep knew what was coming. Sure enough, the dark-eyed pirate brought the fist that held the runestones to his forehead. Then he cast the stones — straight onto the map. He read the symbols and laughed. 'Your gods, Kep-Váli: they see all, I think!' He raised a finger. 'A *choice*. *That* is what you promised! The hoard of Kara-fell is legendary. And earning the favour of Bahjak? That is no small thing. Is it not fair to give the crew this choice?'

Kep groaned. Trust Curly to think like a pirate. Ratskin and Spike would follow her. She knew it. The boys would follow her to their deaths. 'No. It's too dangerous.'

Rodine sighed. 'Then our friends are lost.'

Kep swallowed. 'Jen-Jay? What should I do?'

Jen-Jay sighed. 'They're your pirates, Kep. It's your decision to make.'

Kep got out of her chair and walked over to the window. The sky glowed red, like a warning. As she watched, the sun winked out, claimed by the dark horizon. She spoke without turning her head. 'Very well. I will ask them.'

# 33

# THE CURSED ISLE

Petrel wasn't surprised to see them back. Nobody stayed long in Serenity, not if they could help it. On discovering that their party had grown by one, the young woman let out a groan. 'Seriously? *Another* boy?' Braig stepped aboard, and she eyed the axe at his belt. 'Don't get any ideas about drinking my wine.'

Despite Petrel's swagger, Ash knew she was pleased to see them — especially Ordelle. A smile appeared in the corner of her mouth whenever she looked in Ordelle's direction. All five of them squeezed into the little cabin, making it feel cramped. Petrel had stocked up in earnest. Small sacks and fresh produce filled every available gap. Braig looked uncomfortably large, squashed between a string of onions and a leg of smoked pork.

With unceremonious flair, Petrel plonked a bag of roasted nuts on the table, scattering most of them over the charts. When Sarin produced a bottle of fireshot from nowhere she raised an eyebrow. 'It's almost as if he wants something!' She winked at Ordelle. Cracking the bottle open, despite the early hour, she poured out five measures. 'A celebration! Of getting out of Serenity alive!' Petrel knocked hers back in one, made a face and poured herself another.

Braig swallowed half his measure and went bright red, spluttering. Petrel slapped her knee, snorting with amusement. She grinned at Ordelle. 'So, you found your friend. Now what? Come south with me, Ordelle. We can pick peaches in Ebadour. Did you know they have flowers there that open under the moons? They last for one night only.'

Ordelle tilted her head in that curious way of hers. 'Moonflowers. Their fragrance is said to be intoxicating. It is a quality of the nectar. And there is a species of moth that relies on—' Sarin cleared his throat loudly. Ordelle shot him a disapproving look, but cut the lecture short. 'We can't come south. We need passage to Nokturn Isle.'

Petrel choked, spitting fireshot all over the maps. Sarin caught Ash's eye and sighed. So much for subtle persuasion! It was several moments before Petrel could speak. 'Are you people *insane*?' She wiped her streaming eyes. 'Seriously, Ordelle: if this is a joke, it's not very funny.'

'It is not a joke,' said Ordelle.

Petrel's face contorted. 'Yes, it *is*. Nobody goes to Nokturn Isle. Look!' Sweeping nuts out of the way with the side of her hand, she stabbed a finger at the map. 'Narsis marked it with a bloody great whirlpool! Could there be a more obvious warning to keep away?'

Ash stared at the spiral labelled 'Ciris'. It sat in the strait between Nokturn and the larger island of Baktah. He recalled the beautiful map he'd seen at T'al Jazure. The sundered isle had once formed part of Baktah, the ancient home of the Wimsari. His mind pieced the islands back together and added some miniature towers. He heard the brush of a melody and pushed it away, heart racing.

Petrel raved on. 'That island bears the curse of the ancients. Nobody goes there!'

'What about the clammers?' asked Sarin. 'I've heard they brave the mists.'

'Only the most foolhardy! And even they're not dumb enough to venture inland. Listen to me.' She spoke slowly, enunciating each word deliberately. 'You can't go there.'

'We have to,' said Ordelle matter-of-factly. 'Because that's where Kep has gone. To find Kara-fell.'

Petrel gawped, struck dumb. When she didn't respond, Ordelle cocked her head, as if doubting Petrel had heard her. 'Kara-fell is on Nokturn Isle.'

Expelling a breath, Petrel rolled her eyes. 'Well of course she is. Where else? Nokturn is the place of monsters. Kara-fell would fit right in.' She raised a finger. 'Another *great* reason to stay the hell away.'

Ordelle blinked. 'But we have to go. Kep is there.'

'No!' Petrel threw up her hands. 'A thousand times, no! Even if I *did* believe that you lot were T'al Kep's closest chums,' she glared at Sarin, 'which, forgive me, seems *pretty* unlikely, I can't take you. It's impossible.' Ash sensed a feeling of deep betrayal beneath her anger. Things weren't going at all the way Petrel had hoped.

Sarin shrugged. 'You're only saying that because you haven't heard the plan.'

Ash wasn't the only one to turn and stare at him.

Petrel snorted in derision. 'Of course! There's a plan!'

Braig had done remarkably well to keep silent. But now he sat up, head-butting the string of onions. 'What plan?'

'This should be good,' said Petrel with another roll of her eyes. 'Tell us! How *exactly* do you plan to navigate one of the most treacherous passages of water *and* slip past a bunch of pirates? Because Kara-fell has pirates. You knew that, right? And while you're at it, why don't you tell us your plan for the Reapers. If you think they'll ignore a small vessel like ours, you're mistaken. We're their favourite prey. They don't give a rat's hind leg about plunder — they want to cut off our heads!'

None of this had any effect on Sarin. He waited for her to finish, his fingers laced in front of him, resting on the table. Which just infuriated Petrel further. Ash's heart sank as she raised her voice. 'And if that's not enough, there's the mists! *Nobody* can plan for those.' Sarin still didn't respond. She picked up her tankard and slumped back in her chair, out of steam. 'I picked you as fools,' she muttered, swilling the liquor, 'but this is idiotic beyond belief.' Her eyes found Ordelle. 'Sorry, I won't take you to Nokturn, Ordelle. I'd sooner push you into the sea.'

Ash stared down at his hands. He didn't blame Petrel. The woman had only just gained her freedom — the last thing she needed was this sort of trouble. And she was right: it *was* insane.

Sarin nodded. 'Everything you've said is true.'

Petrel raised her tankard in a mock toast, all sarcasm. 'Thank you.'

'That's why we're not going that way.'

Sarin unlaced his fingers, and leant forward. 'We'll take the southern passage. It avoids the pirates entirely, and the Reapers, too.' Petrel took in a sharp breath.

Braig pointed at the map. 'But we can't go that way. What about the Veil?'

'Yes, we can.' Sarin smirked as he met Braig's eyes. 'Unless you're scared of mist ghouls.'

'Mist ghouls aren't real,' pointed out Ordelle, presumably for Braig's benefit.

A change had come over Petrel. She ran a hand over her mouth, blinking rapidly. Then she shook her head. 'The southern passage was swallowed hundreds of years long ago.' Her eyes fell on Ash. 'We don't have charts.' He detected a tremor in her voice.

'We don't need charts,' said Sarin. 'We have Ash.'

Ash felt a wave of queasiness that was nothing to do with the boat's insistent rocking.

'Can you do this?' asked Petrel.

'I don't know.' Ash licked his lips. It wasn't entirely true. He felt more confident now and was almost certain he could. But at what cost? He glanced at his friends. 'Um ... Yes. I think so.'

Braig opened his mouth, completely baffled, but Sarin jumped in first.

'It's a good plan, Petrel. You know it is. There won't be any guards at the edge of the Veil. Why would there be? You can drop us ashore, and wait safely in the mists until we return.'

'I'm going,' said Braig, taking the chance to assert himself. 'I've been to Nokturn before and I know the terrain.'

Ordelle nodded. 'It's true. And he does look intimidating.' Ash half-expected her to poke Braig's biceps as she made her assessment. 'Even if his fighting skills do not match his physique, he should go,' she concluded.

Sarin hid a smile. 'Ordelle wouldn't be in any danger. She'd stay aboard with you and Ash.' Ash frowned at that, but Sarin didn't meet his eye.

'And if you *don't* return?'

'You sail south, through safer waters.' Sarin smiled, spreading his hands. 'Just think. The *Gull* will be the first craft to navigate the southern passage in centuries.'

Petrel scowled at him. 'Shut up! I need time to think.'

In the heavy silence that followed, Ash contemplated the plan. Sarin was right: it could work. But did he really expect Ash to stay aboard? And sail off south if the others didn't return? Even if Sarin had suggested it in order to convince Petrel, it still hurt. It would have been nice to be consulted beforehand. That was the problem with Sarin's plans — he rarely discussed them with anyone else.

Ash listened to the water lapping against the little boat's hull. Shouting drifted over from the direction of the shore. It sounded as if a murder was being committed; it probably was.

At last, Petrel turned to Ordelle. 'Is this truly what you want, Ordelle?'

'Yes.'

Petrel blew out a breath. '*Honestly*. What is it about this Kep that makes you all so willing to die?'

Ordelle answered without hesitation. 'She is a person of faith and clear will. She follows her heart and her gods without the flaw of human indecision. Kep would die for her friends, without even thinking about it. That's why everyone loves her.'

There was something comical about Braig's frozen expression. Sarin's mouth curved in a wry smile. Ash didn't think it was the answer that Petrel wanted. Her eyes searched Ordelle's face. Then she sighed. 'Very well.' Ash felt his insides twist. 'We will brave the mists.'

They set sail just after noon, following in the wake of several small trading ships. Petrel recognised one vessel by her banner and the tilt of her sails, and pointed it out to Ash. The others were below, shaving Braig's head. It seemed Sarin hadn't been joking — it really was part of the plan.

Petrel treated Ash with a weird reverence now, but she was friendlier when there was just the two of them. With one hand on the tiller and a constant eye on the sails, she pointed out landmarks and, once, an enormous sea turtle.

The plan was to hug the coast of Auri, taking advantage of their shallow draft and keeping out of the way of larger vessels. Petrel didn't expect to encounter the mists until they rounded the southern coast of Earl. But who knew for sure? The mists followed their own devices. She estimated a two- to three-day journey. Ash tried to hide his panic and failed miserably. 'Don't look so worried!' she said. 'I get it. You haven't trained. But the mists seem to like you. It's weird.'

'Thanks,' he said morosely.

'They do. It's like something from one of the old stories.' She studied his face, then laughed. 'Still, you should get some rest while you can.'

Rest? *Impossible.* They were on a boat, after all, where nothing ever stayed still. Now that they were underway, the confined cabin made Ash feel queasy. So he opted to stay up on deck, watching the landscape and hoping not to throw up.

There was little to draw his interest, though, just the occasional fishing village. In fact, the journey was comfortingly dull.

Then Petrel pointed out another ship. A long way off, it sailed west, in open waters. It had black sails and a bright red banner. Calkinon colours! Petrel nodded. 'It's a patrol. Just be thankful for the elpha shortage. There's usually elpha-birds as well.'

Ash watched the vessel through the spyglass for several minutes. Even that far away, the sight filled him with dread. 'Argess defend us!' Petrel's outburst made him jump, nearly causing him to drop the spyglass. She was howling with laughter as Braig emerged from below. 'Look at you! All set to rape and pillage!'

The transformation was startling. The hair on one side of Braig's head resembled a bird's wing, fading to fuzz at the back of his neck. But the other side was clean-shaven. Following the curve of his ear were concentric lines of inky black symbols. Ash's mouth fell open in dismay as he stared at the geometric designs. 'Is that ... ? I mean ... Will the marks come off?'

Ordelle shrugged, having followed Braig up. 'Eventually. It's indelible ink. We've given him four years of service. That should impress anyone who can read the Dench codes.' Ash shook his head in disbelief. Trust Ordelle to know the customs of Denchmen.

Petrel whistled. 'You did this?'

'Sarin made some suggestions.'

Braig scowled. 'Apparently I've won eighteen duels and killed four men in combat.'

'Don't look so glum!' Petrel laughed wickedly. 'Where you're going, that'll be true in no time!' Her eyes narrowed. 'Where is Sarin? Plotting and planning?'

'He's reading Borsi Frattellik's journals,' said Ordelle.

'Huh. Well, at least he's out of my way.' She shot Ash and Braig a look. 'Ordelle can stay with me. You two get forward. And, Ash, get some sleep — or I'll stir your tea with a dead mouse.' Ash nodded. He didn't know whether Petrel had access to a dead mouse, but he wouldn't put it past her.

Ash didn't mind being banished to the bow anyway. They were less likely to get knocked overboard there, or shouted at by Petrel. And it would give them time to catch up.

'I don't like him.' Braig made the announcement before they'd even settled down.

Ash winced. 'It doesn't look that bad. Honestly.'

'It's not about the hair.' Braig ran a hand over his scalp. 'I know he's your friend. But ... I don't think we should trust him.'

'We can trust him. Sarin's just ... He's used to making his own plans.'

'Yeah, well he pushes everyone around. Especially you.' Ash kept his silence. 'And that Ordelle. She's plain *weird*. Do you know what she told me while she was shaving my head?'

'No.'

'The Dench stake their dead to the ground in the desert for animals to scavenge. But first they remove their eyeballs. They toss those into the fire to please Telion.' Braig's own eyes were round in disbelief. 'What sort of god would be *pleased* by an offering of burnt eyeballs?' Ash just shrugged. 'She said if I really was a Denchman, that's what she'd do. When I died. Then she interrogated me about how I *did* want to be buried — like it was happening soon and she needed to be prepared.'

'Yeah, she does that.'

'She sounded like she was looking forward to it.'

Ash couldn't help chuckling. 'She does that, too.'

Fortunately, Braig quickly moved on to other topics. As they journeyed, he related stories about his time with the jarlycats. Ash learned all about Braig's training, and far more than he needed to know about how to wield an axe. He let his friend rattle on; it was easier than trying to explain his own adventures.

Ash did try to describe T'al Jazure and its many wonders, though, but Braig quickly lost concentration. He could never pay attention for long, unless it had something to do with the League captains or Kep. He seemed most curious about Kep's warrior training, what weapons she preferred and how she'd done in the trials. Ash did his best to supply the information, but, judging by Braig's response, fell woefully short.

Braig was also interested in Sarin, more than he wished to let on.

Sarin kept to the cabin, fuelling Braig's curiosity further. Perhaps he *was* just reading Fratelli's journals and trying not to antagonise Petrel. But his behaviour had changed since Serenity, and Ash had the distinct impression that his friend was avoiding him.

Ash and Braig spent the hours dozing and chatting as the *Gull* negotiated the passage between the islands of Auri and Earl. It was late on the afternoon of the second day when Braig spoke suddenly, out of the blue. 'Lakmorin said Sarin made Kep a bow. All carved and fancy.'

Ash blinked. 'That's true. Her first bow was too long.'

Braig frowned. 'He didn't make you one, then?'

Ash laughed. 'No. I'm pretty useless with a bow.'

'Yeah, that would be a waste I suppose.' Ash tried not to look offended as Braig scratched his head. 'So what were *you* doing? While Kep was training?'

Ash had brushed over his long hours in the Knowledge Stores struggling to master the lore-stones. He sighed. 'I was trying to understand the Song.'

'Oh. Right. Sorry.' Braig hesitated, as if stuck for a response. He rubbed at the back of his head, then spoke all in a rush. 'I'm sorry. The Song was supposed to be my burden. It should have been me ... It was my quest.'

'It wasn't a quest. Credé lied.'

'I know. But remember what Tarlyn said? Back in the Malshorne's—'

'Yes. "The Song is a harsh mistress." I know, Braig. You don't have to remind me.' Braig's face fell, and Ash regretted his bitter outburst. It wasn't Braig's fault that he had never grasped the magic of the Song.

He spoke more gently. 'The Song *is* difficult. And overwhelming and downright terrifying. But it's beautiful, too.' He shook his head. 'I spent a lot of time studying in T'al Jazure and,' he frowned, realising something in that moment, 'I learned more than I thought. And I'm discovering new things every day. The Song isn't at fault. The fault is with me. I didn't do the apprenticeship.' As he spoke, a realisation struck him: Credé hadn't, either. He'd stolen the Song by impersonating the apprentice. The thought was sobering.

Haunted by the Song for a thousand years or more, Credé must have been tortured by its visions. Not to mention his own part in events. It was probably why he'd become a hermit, hiding away in his hut above Mildaresh. That, and his guilt.

When Braig cleared his throat, Ash realised that his thoughts had wandered. 'But, you'll be all right? I mean, you can handle it? The Song?'

Ash answered honestly. 'I don't know. There's a chance ... I might lose myself.' Braig winced at the idea. 'I don't know how mist-singing works, but I think it makes me vulnerable to the Song. I might not be myself for a while.' He read Braig's alarmed expression. 'Sometimes I say some strange things, that's all.'

Braig stared at him for a long moment. 'You've changed, Ash.' Ash nodded, readying himself for some sort of insult. 'I mean, you of all people. That stuff you've done. I can't believe you went back to face Credé on your own. And killed those — what were the maggot things called? Yaggits?'

'Yaggluts.'

'Yeah, them. But the Song ...' He scratched his head once more; the aftermath of the shearing clearly irritating him. 'That's the worst thing I could ever imagine.' He looked so earnest, so typically like Braig. But he spoke with a new maturity, grounded in his own experiences. 'I never would have believed you'd turn out to be so brave. I'd rather fight a dozen nulls than be Keeper of the Song.'

Ash didn't know how to react. The potent mix of admiration and heartfelt sympathy was overwhelming. He did his best to chuckle. 'Well, be careful what you wish for. That might happen, too.'

At that exact moment, the wind dropped.

**34**

---

# SONG OF MIST

Braig didn't know a boat could stop dead like that. The *Gull* settled her backside in the water like a stubborn old dog. The ribbon at the top of the mast went limp. 'Is that normal?' It sure didn't feel normal. A bright yet sullen grey, the sky felt heavy.

Ash offered no reply, just tilted his head, seeming to listen for something. He did that a lot these days. Braig heard nothing. Except swearing from the stern. *Great.* Petrel's foul mood sounded worse. He gave Ash a nudge. 'Let's find out what's happening.'

As they stepped down into the cockpit, Sarin came up from below. His golden eyes looked even more peculiar in the eerie light. 'What just happened? It feels ... strange.' Strange didn't begin to cover it. Braig's arms were prickling with goosebumps. It felt as if the boat was floating in mid-air and the shore didn't look real.

Petrel snarled. 'We're becalmed. And *yes*, it's *strange*. Just like I warned you.'

Braig shivered, despite the muggy warmth. *Becalmed?* Nothing felt calm. The air felt ... prickly, if anything. 'So, what do we do now?'

Petrel glared at him. 'What do you suggest?'

'I don't know. Can we paddle, or something?'

'Do you see any paddles?'

*Right. No paddles.* Stupid boat. When Sarin suggested they drop the anchor, Petrel was equally dismissive. 'What for? We're not going anywhere.' Scowling and yawning, she rubbed at her eyes. 'I'm going to get some sleep. Ordelle?'

Ordelle shook her head. 'One of us should stay here.' She cast a look at Braig when she said it, as if fearing he might break something.

'Suit yourself.'

Petrel disappeared below, slamming the hatch hard enough to make the timbers shudder. Sarin raised his eyebrows. 'You should rest, too, Ordelle. We'll need you when the wind picks up.' Ordelle didn't argue. With a nod, she went below. Braig rubbed the irritating stubble at the back of his head. Why did these people always do what Sarin wanted?

Claiming a corner of the cockpit, Sarin sat with his hands behind his head, one boot resting on his knee. *Casual bastard.* His eyes were on the shore, as if he hoped to spot something of interest. All Braig saw was the same monotonous view — grey trees on either side. He sighed and lowered himself to lie on one of the bench seats, arms folded across his chest. Might as well rest until the wind picked up. Ash seemed moody, lost in his thoughts, drifting about, indecisively. Then, with a sigh, he returned to the bow, with Tarlyn close behind.

Braig closed his eyes, but doubted he could sleep. He'd decided he hated sailing boats. There was nothing to do and no place to train. You couldn't fart without somebody pulling a face. And nobody appreciated his humour. Ordelle acted all high and mighty, but she wasn't even a League warrior. Not properly. He missed the jarlycats. Especially Shift. Shift always laughed at his jokes.

Braig felt guilty for sneaking off and leaving his jinn like that. Now he wished he'd stayed at Serenity. He'd thought this would be an adventure. Going after Kep had seemed heroic. Now he wondered whether Sarin had in fact made a fool of him. They only had Sarin's word about what the boy had told him at Serenity, after all. He ground his teeth. *Bloody Sarin.*

There was no point getting riled up, but who could blame him?

Braig was stuck here. On a boat. With the ugliest haircut in the world, and people who didn't respect him. His hands balled into fists. He was all set to give Sarin a piece of his mind when he heard Pharni's voice in his mind. *Choose the fights that count, Braig.*

Braig ground his teeth, toes curling in his boots. Punching Sarin in the face *would* feel fantastic. But he was a League warrior now. And that meant something. *Practise control. Turn weakness into strength.* He sighed. Telling himself that Sarin wasn't worth it, he closed his eyes and practised breathing instead.

Of everything in the League's training regime, Braig found the Breath hardest to master. These were ideal practice conditions. He forced himself to focus, counting out beats. *Deep inhale. Exhale.* Two, three, four. Hold. *Breathe.* Two, three, four. There was no stupid boat. And no Sarin. There was only the Breath. Three. Four. Only the Breath. And ... a flute?

Braig opened his eyes and sat up to listen. The melody was faint, coming from the direction of the bow. Sarin had heard it, too. His eyes glinted, and he put a finger to his lips. It wasn't a flute — it was Ash. He was singing! Braig didn't hear words, or rather none that he understood. As the melody repeated, a change came over the light, as if the flute-like song was urging it to become something new. Adding to the sense of disorientation, the space around the *Gull* began to warp. Then came the mist.

It started as frail wisps, rising off the water. But its swirling grey vapours soon engulfed their vessel. The mists flowed like an integral part of the melody. Ever-changing. Braig held tight to the gunwale. He felt light-headed, as if he'd drunk too much wine. When he staggered, someone grabbed his arm. 'Don't fall in,' said Sarin softly. That was when he realised the *Gull* was moving! He smothered a cry. The sails were limp, as before. But the boat gathered speed. Petrel and Ordelle arrived back up on deck, their faces flushed. They all watched in rapt silence as the mists swirled around them, drawn to the singer at the bow.

Braig had never felt so afraid. Not in the Malshorne's hut. Not even during his first mission, when Skarlon's team had dared the whirlpool of Ciris. As the *Gull* moved ever-faster, grey shapes formed on either side of the little boat, like some sort of ghostly escort. The misty spectres sent a shiver of horror down Braig's spine, making his guts tremble. He suppressed the urge to draw his axe. There was nothing here to fight! He planted his feet, both hands clutching the gunwale, his tongue clamped to the roof of his mouth. He could bear it. If Sarin could stand there, the picture of calm, then Braig could bear it.

Ash had warned him that things might get weird. Is this what he'd meant? Even Ordelle, the expert on everything, looked stunned, as if this phenomenon was also new to her. Petrel's eyes were shining with wonder. 'It's true!' She passed two fingers through the air, making a curious gesture. 'He's a Weaver!'

Braig forced himself to relax. *A League warrior faces many challenges, not all of them physical.* That's what Pharni always said. This was a challenge. Like any other. Ash was up there singing, facing the horrors of the Song. The least Braig could do was hold himself together. As his heart settled back into something approximating a normal beat, he started paying attention to the pictures in the mist. He was terrible at the game of finding animals in the clouds, but these images seemed to tell a story. And yet, as in a dream, as soon as he grasped at their meaning, the pictures morphed into something else.

And that music! Braig knew nothing about music. He loved whistling, but had been told many times to stick to carrying buckets, because he sure couldn't carry a tune. Yet even Braig understood: this was a song of joy. He saw clouds of butterflies transform into twirling flowers. And horses galloping free, tossing their manes. At one point, a school of fish leapt from the water and swam along in the air beside him. Their bodies gleamed blue and iridescent. Then they scattered, disturbed — by the most extraordinary person!

She rode the mists on an enormous winged lizard with a long, sinuous tail. Bright silver, her hair streamed out behind her, merging into the mist. Braig felt a deep yearning in his soul. The girl looked so joyful! So ... free! His heart rode with her, swooping and cavorting.

Then she turned her head and smiled. She'd seen him! The lizard dived. She held out a hand, laughing into his eyes. Then dissolved. Braig shook his head, like a dog with a flea in its ear. She wasn't real. Just a figment of the mist. A new story was already unravelling. It drew him on, deeper, deeper into the mist.

*Petals float on the water. Flowers twirl, like coloured cups. The oarsmen chant, setting the rhythm. Silver oars match the beating of drums. The trumpets shout. She comes! She comes! He laughs. Raises his trumpet. Glory to the bird of ages! Oh, glorious day! We bear your bride. Young Signeb rides on the wings of song. Drawn by purple-scented sails. Banners stream in anticipation. She comes! The bride of the south. She comes! Her hair is raven-dark, her skin gleams like copper. His heart lifts with pride, with joy at her majesty. His princess. A bride unparalleled in glory. Incense trails in her wake. And ahead comes the clarion call of silver horns. The fluted city sings. A song born of the sea. A wind song to welcome our princess. We lift up our hearts in joy. Come dance! Come sing! For there will be peace!*

*It is time. Time ... Aligns ... Chime ... Chime.*

A breeze was rising. *Tink. Tink, tink.* Fresh air blew into Braig's face. The bell! Calling him to pray. *Tink. Tink. Tink.* He was late!

A voice squawked, harsh like a bird. 'The anchor! Drop the anchor!'

Someone tried to push past him. Words felt cumbersome on his tongue. 'No, we're late! Mendis will be angry.'

'Braig! Wake up, you idiot! Let me through!'

He gasped when a splash of water hit his face. Before he could blink, a second serving drenched him. 'Woah!' He stuck out a hand. 'That's cold!' He squinted at his assailant, expecting a monk in pale blue robes. Instead, he saw Ordelle.

She stood over him, bucket poised. 'Wake up!'

'I *am* awake!' Braig pulled himself up. He was also sopping wet!

'Good.' Ordelle lowered the bucket and shoved a mug at him. 'Drink this. It's Sage-bright.'

Braig scowled, wiping water from his eyes. He stared at the flapping canvas, taking in the weird, patchy sky. Memory returned in a rush. The mists! They were gone!

The *Gull* had awoken, too. She strained at her anchor, stirred by the rising breeze. Nobody was paying any attention to the sails. Nor to Braig. Sarin sat next to Ash, who was wrapped in a blanket. He was rubbing a pungent-smelling ointment on Ash's temples. Braig felt a rush of concern for his friend.

Ash's skin was ghostly pale, as if he'd absorbed some quality of the mists. He seemed conscious, but his expression was far away, his eyes reflecting weirdly. As Braig watched, Sarin placed his hands on either side of Ash's face and leaned in, as if he was about to kiss him. 'Come back to us, kin.'

Braig raised his eyebrows. *Kin? Seriously?*

'You did it, Ash. The mists obeyed you. Come back to us now.' Sarin's words made no difference whatsoever. Ash kept staring into the mid-distance. Ordelle hovered, looking concerned, a second mug in her hand. She wasn't chucking water at Ash, Braig couldn't help but notice.

Petrel divided her attention between Ash and her spyglass. She scanned one shore, then the other, muttering beneath her breath. 'Where are we?' It seemed pretty pointless. Braig could only see trees. Then she startled, letting out a cry. 'Sweet Telion! Is that ... ?' She beckoned at Braig. 'You! Come here!'

Braig scowled. 'I have a name.'

'Good for you. Get over here and tell me what you can see.'

Braig snatched the scope from her hand. Initially, he saw nothing. Just a blur of grey, making him wonder whether she'd forgotten to clean the lens. Then he twiddled the wheel, and the blur sharpened into focus. He retraced the foggy shoreline and saw it. A patch of white, in the distance. He held his breath, straining his eyes. 'There's ... I don't know. Just looks like a big chunk of white rock.'

Petrel grabbed the scope and punched him on the shoulder. 'I knew it! That's Whitestone Bluff!'

'And?'

'It's on the charts!' Petrel grinned from ear to ear. It made her look different — pretty even.

Braig frowned. It sounded promising, and the shore didn't look that far away. He'd already resolved to give swimming a try — anything to get off this boat. 'So ... that's good news, right?'

Ordelle joined them at the rail. 'What does it mean, Petrel?'

Petrel laughed and took her friend by the hands. 'It means, Sweeting, that he *did* it. It's completely impossible,' she shook her head, 'but Ash did it. He brought us ... all this way.'

Sarin hadn't left Ash's side, but he looked up. 'Brought us where?'

'Nokturn Isle. We're here. That bluff marks the southern end of Heart Sink Cove.'

~

Heart Sink Cove.

Borsi's map called it Fetlock Bay. Braig thought Petrel's name was far more appropriate. The place dragged at the spirits. But they'd made it. Braig could finally *do* something — just as soon as he got his feet on solid ground. If Kep *was* here, he'd find her. And he'd fight to save her. Whatever it took.

Nobody could work out how long their journey had lasted. It should have taken at least two days, according to Petrel. But none of them remembered sleeping or eating. Braig didn't see any point in dwelling on it. He didn't know what those weird images had been about, and he didn't need to. He *did* know he was ravenous. As the others talked, he crammed cheese and smoked meat into his mouth. Food was energy. And warriors needed energy to fight.

Ash remained in the same catatonic state as before. Thankfully, his eyes were closed now. Occasionally, he groaned, as if trapped in a nightmare. Petrel couldn't take her eyes off him. She told them myths about ancient mages called Weavers who could command the mists.

Braig paid little attention: he'd had enough of magic, he just wanted to get to shore.

After a tense discussion, Petrel agreed to take them closer. She ordered Sarin to the bow to watch for obstacles and any sign of the Veil's edge. She instructed Braig to look after Ash. 'Clamp your hand over his mouth if he starts to scream,' said Sarin, 'but be gentle.' Braig scowled at him. Of *course* he'd be gentle! What did Sarin take him for?

They got underway, with half a sail set at a broken angle. Braig peered down over the railing at the water. After their earlier pace, this was painfully slow. He was about to suggest more sail when a noise made him straighten up. The muffled beat sounded again. Ordelle's eyes widened; she'd heard it too. Drums! Sarin materialised a second later. 'I think we're close enough.'

The *Gull* was already turning. 'You're telling me,' said Petrel. '*That* sounds like Reapers.'

Hand-over-hand, Sarin hauled at the rowboat's towline. 'Braig! Get ready.'

Braig *was* ready. He shouldered his gear, determined to be first aboard.

'I'm coming,' came a voice from behind, faint but distinct. They all turned to stare at Ash. 'You need me.' He looked half-asleep — or half-dead. Certainly in no fit state to go anywhere.

Petrel froze in the process of dropping a marker buoy. She met Sarin's eyes as the rowboat bumped alongside. 'I can't believe I'm saying this ... but he's right. Take him.'

Braig was stunned when Sarin nodded calmly, as if the idea wasn't crazy at all. 'Thank you. Stay safe, Petrel. Keep to the mists.'

Petrel snorted. 'Safe! Right.' Across the water, the drums rolled again. A harsh shout went up, terrifyingly close. The fear in Petrel's eyes betrayed her attempts at bravado. 'What do you say, Ordelle? Fancy a game of cat-and-mouse with the Reapers?'

Braig didn't catch Ordelle's answer, because his attention was on Ash, who was climbing into the rowboat. It tilted sharply to one side; if he wasn't careful, he'd capsize it. Braig clambered around him, commandeering the oars. As he took a seat, Sarin jumped aboard, shoving off hard.

As the rowboat shot away, Braig felt his muscles respond as he hauled at the oars. He grinned, feeling the blood course through his veins. At last! This was what he had trained for! He enjoyed the burn in his biceps and across his shoulders. With a few powerful strokes, they'd lost sight of the *Gull*. He pulled harder, forcing the water to yield. He wanted to laugh. It was insane! In a world of grey, they had no idea how far it was to shore.

They found out soon enough. The mist parted, like a creature releasing them — a creature with a vindictive sense of humour. 'Rocks!' Sarin waved his arm. 'Left! Go left!' Braig dug hard with the right oar and the boat veered. A heartbeat later, they hit.

# 35

# A GOOD SHOW

The *Nightingale* swept into Heart Sink Cove under a ridiculous amount of sail. Kep held tight to the quarterdeck rail, the wind tossing her hair. The tails of a black bandana whipped around her face and she wore red paint smeared beneath her eyes. According to Ruby Ross, these lunatics liked nothing better than a good show. Nevertheless, he refused to wear face-paint, on account of it spoiling his rugged good looks. His only concession to the charade was a blood-red headband. Nobody had argued — the man was intimidating enough, even *with* that cheeky grin.

Every crew member was on deck for the arrival at Nokturn Isle. They brandished weapons, yelling and jeering, doing their level best to look like cut-throat murderers — and of course some of them were. Most had opted for stripes of red paint, but Spike had thrown himself into the charade, covering his entire face in red. He was swinging in the rigging like a deranged monkey, yelling curses and making obscene gestures. Ratskin bashed at the huge metal drum as if his life depended on it, grinning from ear to ear. It seemed the perfect job for a boy who never spoke. Kep's skull juddered with every thump. The plan was daring, even brash, and most definitely *loud*.

Bedecked in the trappings of a gory conquest, the *Nightingale* continued her pass. They had kept the red and black streamers. And the blood-splattered sails told their own story. As did the skulls. To Kep's dismay, the ghastly trophies had been reinstated beneath the figurehead. It was sacrilege and an insult to Argess. Ordelle would have been horrified. Thank the gods she wasn't here to see it.

The *Nightingale* embodied death and destruction. And the deception was working, with the Reapers welcoming the ship's arrival with cheers and frenzied excitement. Some waved banners of black and red. Others stood with fists raised in the air, acknowledging the audacity of their conquest. The *Nightingale!* Gone rogue!

The Reapers' flotilla comprised assorted crafts, ranging from fishing boats to cutters. None was as grand as the *Nightingale*. 'I count twelve,' said Rodine. 'Not including those.' He pointed at a pair of schooners, removed from the others and closer to the shore. 'They belong to Kara-fell.' Kep swallowed. *A dozen!* She hadn't imagined so many. And every one loaded with Reapers. Rodine's brow creased with worry. 'We'll need all the luck of the gods.'

'We'll need the *Lady Lee*,' said Ruby Ross from behind them. Turning, they saw the helmsman sporting a wide grin. 'She'll be here. The runes said so.' It was a joke: Ruby had no time for superstitious nonsense. Curly did, though. But would the portent be enough to persuade the pirate captain to risk the *Lady Lee* on such a dangerous adventure? 'Don't worry, Simbab. Curly would sail through fire for you.' Ruby chuckled, adding: '*And* a share of the treasure.'

Try as she might, Kep couldn't banish her doubts, even *with* Jen-Jay overseeing the pirate's every waking breath. It was Curly, after all. She raised the scope for the twentieth time, praying for the sight of the *Lady Lee*'s sail. Nothing. But worrying was premature: things *were* going to plan. The *Nightingale* would make a show, taking up her position at the southern end of the bay, with the mists guarding her back. *The mists.* Another thing that made Kep nervous.

She shivered, staring at the bank of grey where sea and land dissolved — the place where all of the charts went blank. She hated this place already. It wasn't just the creepy curtain of mist: the sky pressed down, too, as if bearing them ill will.

'Ready?' asked Ruby.

Kep swallowed. It seemed reckless to sail into a bank of mist —
especially one that resented their presence. But she'd rather have
mist at her back than Reapers. She nodded. 'Take us in.'

Moments later, the bowsprit disappeared. As the grey murk swallowed them, Kep felt as if somebody had clamped a wet hand across
her mouth and nose. She was relieved when Ruby immediately
started spinning the wheel, bringing them hard about. As the
*Nightingale* heeled to port, the crew ran to drop the sails. She hoped
Ruby was as good a sailor as Curly said he was. She was whispering
an entreaty to Telion when Spike's disembodied voice rang out. 'Sail!
Sail, ho!'

Kep caught a momentary glimpse of the vessel. A flash of hull.
The spectral vision of a sail. She dashed to the stern rail, eyes peeled.
Nothing! Rodine was a ghostly form beside her. 'That didn't look like
a Reaper vessel.' Kep shivered. Who *else* would lurk in the mists?

With a speed that belied their short experience with the unfamiliar ship, the crew brought the sails under control and dropped
anchor. Ruby posted additional lookouts, but there was no further
sign of the phantom craft. He'd moored them in the perfect position,
right at the ragged edge of the Veil. So far, so good.

The crew above decks had a simple task: keep up the charade.
Look scary and act like Reapers. Kep had every confidence her pirates
would perform well — fighting, drinking and making a lot of noise
was what they did best. With luck, the Reapers wouldn't realise the
*Nightingale* was preparing for battle until it was too late.

Archers had already hidden themselves on the fighting tops.
Others moved to their positions in the beak, armed with heavy cross-
bows. The ballista at the bow was primed. A stash of fireballs and
spiky bolts were at the ready, along with six wrapped bundles stored
carefully in a special crate. Kep had her bow strung and ready to
hand. Yulia had insisted she wear a sword, too, in case of boarding.
'Think of it as part of the costume,' she'd said. 'And try not to cut
yourself!'

Kep found Yulia perplexing. The woman was equal parts flirtatious barmaid, crafty feline and swaggering bully. The one thing Kep *was* sure about the other woman was that she was not trustworthy, which made her a *very* dangerous second-in-command. But the crew respected her. Everyone laughed when Yulia cracked a joke, but they jumped to obey her orders, too. Kep caught herself scowling. Was she *jealous*? Of a pirate? As she watched, Yulia looked up from the midships, raised the flagon towards her, and took another swig. *Bloody woman.*

Rodine's attention was on the Reapers. He shuffled over, making room at the rail, and cocked his head. 'How are you coping?' Kep clearly wasn't putting on as good an act as she hoped.

Avoiding the question, she frowned at the enemy. The crafts swarmed with bodies, black and red. Like hornets, she thought. Only more dangerous. 'I don't understand them, Rodine. Why are they here?'

He sighed. 'I'm not sure they could tell you. They are drawn here. That is the power of the Melk.'

'But what do they want?'

'I truly don't know. To belong, I suppose. To have purpose.'

'Purpose?'

He looked her in the eye. 'To exact revenge. To hurt others as they've been hurt. The Reapers are here because they sense an ally in Kara-fell. They want recognition, for her to appreciate what they've become. Agents of destruction — like Kara-fell herself.'

The sound of footsteps made them turn. It was Yulia, smiling and threatening all at once. 'Drink!' She thrust a flagon at Kep. 'And that's an order. Drink or fight. Strip naked, even! Just don't stand about looking all deep and melancholy. Reapers have spyglasses, too!'

She was right. They hadn't been acting like pirates. Kep raised the flagon to her lips and took a cautious mouthful. It burned all the way down. Yulia grinned and slapped her on the back. 'More! And this time look like you're enjoying it!'

Kep held the bottle to her lips, pretending to take a hearty slug. As she did so, Rodine let out a cry. 'Over there!' She jumped, spilling liquor down her front. It was the little boat from before!

The vessel shot clear of the mists for a few seconds and was gone again.

'Well, *that's* a relief!' Ruby sauntered over, a thumb hooked in his belt. With a loud sniff, he reached for his pipe. Noticing Kep's frown, he elaborated. 'Trust me, Kep-Váli. Nothing makes a crew more jittery than a phantom ship. A real boat is better, even if it's your enemy.'

*An enemy?* Kep didn't like the sound of that.

Ruby scratched his chin, eyes on the point where the sail had disappeared. 'Popped out to gain a sighting. I reckon they might know these waters. Clever sailing to run the edge of the mists like that.' He grinned appreciatively. 'Ingenious.'

'I vote we sink it,' said Yulia.

Kep caught Rodine's eye. 'No,' she said steadily. 'I won't attack an unidentified vessel.' He gave her a tiny nod of approval.

Yulia snorted with derision. 'And if they attack us? Or sabotage the plan?'

'If they show *any* sign of being a threat, we'll destroy them.' Kep sensed Rodine's discomfort, but he made no further comment. Yulia subsided, looking less than pleased.

Minutes later, a cheer went up from the midships. Creely was jigging about on the hatch, waving his purple hat in the air. The prearranged signal. All was prepared.

Yulia's eyes took on a wicked glint, like a cat that's spotted a lizard. 'Ready to play, Simbab?' she said slyly.

Kep's stomach sank. This was really happening. She nodded. 'Send up the flume.'

Yulia lifted her flagon high, as if saluting Creedy's performance. Then she downed its contents in one. A loud crack came from the forecastle. On cue, the crew began to chant. 'One Will! No rules!' Harden egged them on, black smoke spewing from the rod in his hand.

Wild cheering came back from across the bay, making the chant seem to echo. 'One Will! No rules!' The dark plume rose, signalling their friends. The *Nightingale* was ready to do battle. Kep just prayed that Curly was, too.

36

GAMES IN THE MIST

'Reapers! Flaming Red Pete!'

Ordelle didn't know who Red Pete was, or why he might be on fire, but her own horror matched Petrel's. The apparition had vanished as quickly as it appeared. 'Do you think they saw us?' *Of course they had.* The awful drumming suggested they were close. Very close.

Petrel began letting out sail. 'Raise the jib, Ordelle!'

They weighed anchor, sailing blindly as Petrel worked through an impressive repertoire of curses. Her terror was justified, and the Reapers weren't their only concern. The mists had a very peculiar energy. Beneath the Veil, gusts and currents proved unpredictable. And the reef complicated matters, too.

After sailing for several tense minutes, they turned to starboard, and the canvas went slack. Ordelle admitted to being completely disoriented. She didn't know if they'd be able to locate the buoy again. It was distressing: the buoy was a reminder of their promise, and the only constant in this vapourous world.

If Ordelle didn't know better, she'd say the mists had their own personality. Possessive and jealous. But anthropomorphising a natural phenomenon was both foolish and unhelpful. She compiled a mental catalogue instead, recalling details about the Reapers' ship. Red and black ribbons; damaged railings; a defaced figurehead, as if somebody had taken to it with an axe; a clump of gory spheres dangling in a net below the beak; and the crew, wild-eyed with painted faces. She frowned.

Ordelle found it difficult to read expressions at the best of times. Yet despite their terrifying appearance, the Reapers had looked shocked to see them, afraid even. As if they hadn't expected an encounter in the mists. Was it superstition, or something else? She glanced at Petrel. 'Were those heads?'

'Trophies.' Petrel's mouth was set in a firm line as she fought to compose herself. 'I told you: the Reapers collect the heads of their victims.'

'That is abhorrent.'

'Yes.'

Petrel had a habit of wrinkling her nose when something puzzled her. It was most endearing. And it was wrinkling now.

'What's wrong?' asked Ordelle.

'Something is bothering me about that ship. Apart from the obvious. Did you see the figurehead?'

'It was defaced.' Ordelle tilted her head, recalling details. 'But female, with long, wavy hair, abundant breasts and the tail of a fish. After the manner of the Hegovan school.'

'The Hegovan ...' Petrel's voice trailed off. She shook her head. 'You're remarkable, Ordelle. Was she wearing a crown?'

'A circlet of gilded leaves.' Ordelle might have added that the leaves matched those of the tree from which the ship's timbers were hewn. Teak, in this case. But it was an irrelevant detail, she suspected.

Petrel tucked her hair behind an ear. Another curious habit, because it was far too short to stay there. 'That's what I thought.' Her frown deepened.

'What are you thinking?'

'I think it could be the *Nightingale*.' Petrel shook her head. 'But that's impossible. The Reapers couldn't defeat a ship that formidable. *Could they?*'

Right then, as they listened to the drums and the jeering chants, the Reapers seemed capable of anything. The mists deflected sound in odd ways, and fear fuelled paranoia, but it sounded to Ordelle like many more ships than just the one they'd seen. But she kept the thought to herself.

Nevertheless, Petrel's eyes were worried. 'We can't drift any longer. Earl's reef is notorious. We have to sight land, Ordelle. And I want a look at that ship.' Handing the scope over, she took a deep breath and, incredibly, managed a grin. 'Are you ready?'

Ordelle nodded. 'Ready.'

'Good. Let's find out what we're hiding from.'

A glimpse was enough to confirm their fears. The Reapers were here in numbers! They turned tail, almost capsizing when caught by an unexpected gust. Ordelle was treated to several colourful curses as they worked to calm the sails. In another time and place, she would have inquired as to the curses' origin. 'Is it the *Nightingale*?'

Petrel looked as if she'd just identified a corpse. 'It's her. I'd know her rig anywhere.'

They sat in silence, absorbing the news. The flotilla of Reaper boats wasn't even the worst part of this nightmare. The *Nightingale* was moored at the very edge of the mists, far too close to their buoy for comfort. Ordelle uncoiled a rope. Coiled it up, and repeated the action. Her hands hadn't stopped trembling. 'What should we do?'

'The only thing we can: we hide — and keep well away from whatever's happening here. But we'll need sightings. And we should be as unpredictable as possible. And ... I'm sorry, but ...'

'We can't return to the buoy.'

'No. Not unless the *Nightingale* moves away.'

Ordelle hated the thought of leaving her friends stranded. But they had to be rational: if they lost the *Gull*, none of them would escape. 'I agree.'

'Good.' Petrel tossed her head, suddenly defiant. 'Doesn't mean we can't take precautions.'

'Precautions?'

Petrel laughed, enjoying Ordelle's confusion. 'Oh yes, Sweeting. The *Gull* has some tricks you don't know about.'

The *Gull* did indeed have tricks. 'I told you!' Petrel grinned as she dragged a cloth-covered object from a locker. 'Borsi Frattellik was *disgustingly* wealthy. And he *loathed* pirates. Couldn't bear the thought of being boarded. You know how rich folk love to hang onto their riches.' She winked. 'So naturally he took precautions!'

Borsi's safeguards included more than just a stash of well-made blades. Ordelle stared at the astonishing contraption. She had never seen a ballista of this design, nor one so finely crafted. A golden crest adorned it — of the house of Frattellik, if she wasn't mistaken. The weapon looked as deadly as it was beautiful. 'What does it fire?'

Petrel hauled a second sack from behind a sliding panel. It clanked noisily as she untied the top. 'There are six of these.'

As long as Ordelle's arm, the bolts were heavy — it took two hands just to lift one. With a cruel point and three jagged flares, the missile could cause significant damage.

'Pretty impressive, eh?' Equally impressive was the swivelling mount, which slotted over a square-edged post at the stern. Ordelle had been wondering what purpose the post served.

The commotion in the bay hadn't abated. Now the smell of smoke was stronger. Petrel's expression sobered. 'Just to be clear: we're not actually going to fight.' She swallowed, fingering the hilt of the blade which hung from her belt. 'I have no idea what kind of party this is, but we *definitely* don't want an invite. We stay out of trouble, right?'

'Right.' Ordelle wasn't sure they'd have a choice, but she held her tongue.

The next foray put them further from the *Nightingale* — out of the range of missiles. An eager breeze filled their sails. What they saw dispelled any doubt: the *Nightingale* had indeed gone rogue. A plume of black smoke was issuing from her bow, accounting for the acrid stench.

Ordelle braced a shoulder against the cabin as she peered through the scope. When the Reapers' cheers redoubled, her heart jumped. For a terrible instant, she thought they were the cause. But no! She refocused the lens. *Another* ship was arriving! The little galleon sending up a plume of her own, precipitating a fresh round of drums and chanting. Petrel barked a command. 'Ready about!'

As they performed the manoeuvre, a loud clank came from the *Nightingale*. Ordelle jerked her head around just in time to see the recoil of the *Nightingale*'s mighty ballista. *Clank! Whoosh!* The projectile rose in an arc. Smacking into the mast of one of the Reapers' vessels, it blossomed into a small mustard-coloured cloud. The result was instantaneous. Reapers, who'd been whooping and celebrating seconds before, dropped to the deck. Several toppled into the water.

Petrel gasped. She shoved the tiller, sending the *Gull* into a spin. Ordelle overbalanced, lost her footing and fell, cracking her elbow on the way down. Pain speared up her arm as the mists reclaimed them.

'What by the ... ?' Petrel stared back through the murk. 'Was that ... ?' Turning her head, she gasped with dismay. 'Ordelle! Are you hurt?'

Ordelle pulled herself up, rubbing at her elbow. 'I am uninjured.' She spoke through gritted teeth, willing the pain to abate. Her mind was reeling. The *Nightingale* had just attacked the Reapers! It was a struggle to bring order to her thoughts. 'Was that a *jellin* bomb? I thought jellin was outlawed.' It was also very rare.

'It is!'

Ordelle's head throbbed. She tentatively probed her skull: a spot at the back felt tender. She must have hit it during the fall. The pain wasn't helping her think — and nor was Petrel's agitation. 'What's happening? Is it some kind of feud? Maybe they'll wipe each other out! Wait — how do you know about jellin?'

The prospect that the Reapers were turning on one another seemed optimistic, but *something* was going on. Ordelle frowned. 'The *Nightingale* seems to be our ally.'

'Our ally?' Petrel snorted. 'That's a joke. They're *pirates!*' She cocked her head. 'But if that hullabaloo is anything to go by, they're pretty keen on destroying each other right now. That's got to be good.'

They continued with their strategy: hiding in the mists for as long as they dared, then darting out to steal a sighting, never in the same spot. It was exhausting work, and Ordelle's admiration for Petrel's sailing skills increased as they battled the fickle breeze. The young woman made the *Gull* seem more dancer than boat. Her eyes danced, too, lit up with excitement, despite the peril. Sometimes she would catch Ordelle's eye and grin. Ordelle understood. There was joy in those perfect turns; in being perfectly synchronised with another woman. She might have enjoyed it, too — if they hadn't been on the edge of a pirate battle.

Ordelle remembered a carousel ride from her childhood. She'd hated how the world had lurched around her. This was similar, only with intermittent periods of blindness. Each chaotic episode left her feeling more confused. What was happening here?

The Reapers reacted to the unprovoked attack with irrational fury, throwing arrows and fire at the *Nightingale* with no thought for life or vessel, hitting their own boats as often as not. Most of the projectiles fell harmlessly into the sea — the enemy boat was out of range. The Reapers' singular lack of coordination and ineffectual tactics baffled Ordelle. They had superior numbers and more agile vessels: the *Nightingale* should have been overwhelmed.

True, the jellin bombs were effective when they hit — one unfortunate vessel smashed into the rocks under full sail, taking her unconscious crew with it. But the ballistas lacked accuracy, particularly when targeting small objects, and they took time to reload. A co-ordinated counter-attack from the Reapers should have worked: their unfocused and ineffectual response was curious.

Things became clearer when Ordelle spotted a mustard-coloured cloud on the far side of the action. It was the latecomer! She had jellin, too! The Reapers were being attacked on two sides. Ordelle's heart skipped: this would seem to be more than a scuffle between rival factions. A faint hope whispered. Could it be the League?

Ordelle focused her attention on the smaller ship after that, scanning for clues. To her dismay, fighting had erupted on board. And flames. She sensed panic in the scurrying crew — nothing is more terrifying to sailors than fire. Bringing the scope around, she saw that the *Nightingale* was faring better. A Reapers boat folded in two as she watched, but before it could sink, the *Gull* ducked back into the mists.

Petrel slumped against the woodwork, wiping her brow. 'We need to be more careful. The mists are getting patchy.'

'I agree.' Ordelle frowned. 'In principle. But ... could we get closer next time?'

'Seriously? You want to be *closer*?'

After some debate, Petrel agreed. Two ships working together posed a very different scenario. The *Nightingale* had a greater chance of victory. So they needed information. Who *were* these people? And what sort of threat did they pose?

The mists were no longer just patchy: they had retreated by a ship's length, with devastating results for the *Nightingale*. Five Reaper vessels had the ship surrounded, and Reapers were swarming up her sides. Defenders tossed many overboard. But not all.

Ordelle squinted through the scope. A longboat was harrying the bow with grapples. A smaller vessel bobbed beneath the stern, surreptitious. Ordelle frowned, catching the flash of an axe. 'The bastards!' shouted Petrel. 'They're trying to damage the rudder!' The forecastle was on fire. Amid the chaos, a blond-haired man wielded a giant quarterstaff. Ordelle glimpsed him just for a second, but long enough to see him split a Reaper's skull. Enough time to note how the body fell — and the shape of the splash. The *Gull* turned, and Ordelle lost sight of him. But she knew that young man: that was Polkin Dew!

Emotion rose in Ordelle's throat, threatening to choke her. 'It's them — my friends! They're on the *Nightingale!*'

Petrel shook her head. 'And you said they *weren't* pirates!' She laughed grimly at her own joke. It seemed an extraordinary reaction, given everything the past few days had thrown at her. Ordelle loved her for it. The young woman didn't ask questions, which was fortunate, because Ordelle had no answers. Nor did she deliberate: she just changed tack, a fierce light coming into her bright grey eyes. 'New plan, then — let's give them hell!'

Just like that, the time for hiding was over.

Momentum was everything. Thankfully, the afternoon breeze had freshened. Ordelle gripped the ballista's release lever with one hand, using the other to steady the angle, her feet firmly planted. The plan was to fly in close, cutting across the stern, to target the smaller boat of saboteurs. It would be tight. And their path would bring them in range of Reapers' longboat. The grappling hooks connecting the longboat to the larger vessel prevented it from manoeuvring, but the longboat had an archer. The greater threat was the *Nightingale* herself. Ordelle had one shot to prove they were allies. If she miscalculated, the bolt would smash into the *Nightingale*. She couldn't afford to dwell on that eventuality.

As soon as they burst from the mist, a horn blast erupted from the *Nightingale* in response. Somebody had sharp eyes! Petrel swore, ducking lower behind a shield. The *Gull* sheered through the water. Then began her pirouette. Ordelle braced herself, calculating angles. The Reapers' craft would be in her sights for only a fraction of a second. An arrow flew over her head. She held tight. *Three, two, one.* She snapped the lever back. The bolt flew, shimmying like a fish. It smashed into the centre of the saboteurs' hull, sending the occupants into disarray. Men cried out in surprise, struggling to stay on their feet. An alarm went up on the longboat. Too late! The *Gull* was gone, swallowed by the mists.

Petrel punched her fist in the air. 'That's one for Borsi!' Her grin was a wild thing. 'We're great at this, Ordelle! We could be pirates! Let's hit them again!' With aching arms, Ordelle loaded another bolt. She wound the mechanism, working as fast as she could. *Clack. Clack. Clack.* Her thoughts were ratcheting, too. One question. Repeating. Incessantly. *Where was Kep?*

The smaller boat at the *Nightingale*'s stern was already sinking. Its occupants floundering and splashing, clutching at splinters. Unleashing a second bolt at it would be wasteful. 'Target the longboat!' shouted Petrel, adjusting their course. Ordelle swivelled the weapon. The *Gull* picked up speed, leaning into the turn. Ordelle altered the angle to accommodate the longer range, and began to count. *Three, two, one. Three, two, one.*

The longboat swung into view. An immense man stood in its bow, his skin glistening, streaked with red. Muscles rippled as he whirled a grapple around and around. *Three, two—*

Ordelle gasped. Pain ripped through her arm in the instant before the bolt shot away.

A hit! Petrel's shout went up. As did the Reaper's grapple. Ordelle's eyes followed the trajectory of the mighty hurl, and locked onto its target. There! On the quarterdeck! A young woman turned her head, dark curls tousled by the breeze. A panicked shout erupted aboard the *Nightingale*. *'Kep-Váli!'* The grapple smashed against the rail. Deflected, it fell, plunging down into the sea.

'We have to go back!' Ordelle gritted her teeth. Her upper arm burned with a searing pain, but thankfully the arrow had passed straight through. 'It's Kep! She's on the *Nightingale*. She needs our help!'

'I don't care *what* Kep needs!' Petrel's eyes flashed. 'It's over, Ordelle! You can't fight with a hole in your arm!' Anger, tempered by concern, coloured her voice. 'You're bleeding all over my boat!'

Nothing Ordelle said would make Petrel change her mind. And she was right. As the rush of adrenaline subsided, Ordelle began to feel weak and light-headed. She gave in and let Petrel bathe and dress her injury. The wound was clean; it would heal, given time.

A full hour had passed before Petrel finally relented. 'Fine!' she said. 'We'll take a look. Anything to get you to rest. But we're keeping *well* out of the way.' Ordelle knew Petrel was just as curious as she was about the battle's outcome. Their ears told them that the violence had abated, but they couldn't be certain. Now and then, they caught the sound of distant drumming.

The sky had a turned murky orange, lending their sails an apricot tinge. Petrel frowned as she squinted through the scope. 'It still looks pretty chaotic.'

Ordelle wanted to see for herself, but she kept her promise and remained lying flat on the bench. 'Tell me. Even if it's bad news, I want to know.' Her arm throbbed all the way to the shoulder joint now. The lack of information only exacerbated her agony. 'What can you see?'

'The Reapers are defeated. That much is clear. But now ...'

'What?' It was a special type of torture. It took all of Ordelle's willpower not to grab the scope for herself. 'What, Petrel? What's happening?'

'The fools!' Petrel shook her head in disbelief. 'The fighting's moved to the beach. And I see people running.' She lowered the eyeglass, her expression horrified. 'They're mounting an attack! Against Kara-fell!'

Ordelle closed her eyes, pain and exhaustion overwhelming her at last. Her part in the story was over. All she could do was trust in her friends. She whispered a prayer beneath her breath. *Don't die, Kep. Please. Don't die.*

# 37

# THE ARENA OF KARA-FELL

They hit the pebbled beach with a crunch, their hull scraping along the rocks. Braig wiped the sweat from his brow, panting. No time to check for damage. Leaving Ash to stagger ashore, he hauled the boat out of the water with Sarin's help. In fact, they'd been lucky: the line of rocks would act as a screen, and the tree-line wasn't far. Just a short sprint, but over open ground they'd be plain view until they hit the scrub. Braig wanted to laugh. Where was that mist when you needed it!

He led the way, trusting the others to follow. The bank of pebbles cascaded as he ran. Panting and gasping, driving his leg muscles, eyes on the goal. He didn't look back until he reached the cover of the thick wetland rushes. Thank the gods! Ash was mere strides away, shadowed by Sarin.

Braig parted the rushes to survey the beach. What he saw filled his heart with dismay. He blew out his cheeks. They'd been right about the Reapers. Vessels filled the bay, at least a dozen, each with a banner of black. He shot a look at Sarin, whose strange eyes were narrowed. Guess *this* wasn't part of the plan.

Ash was doubled over, hands on knees, his face haggard. They should have left him behind, but it was too late now. Braig took the lead, pushing into the reeds. Once they were deep enough, he kept them parallel to the beach. Mud and midges aside, they couldn't have asked for better cover. They hadn't gone far when a shadow bounded in front of him, making his heart jump. Tarlyn! Braig looked back over his shoulder. Sure enough, Ash was lagging behind, supported by Sarin. *Great.*

Braig knew where the track lay. He'd spied it from above on his previous visit. But how much further could Ash go? He pushed ahead for a few more minutes, then, reaching a dell overgrown with vines, he waited, surrounded by buzzing insects. He'd squashed ten of the bloodsuckers before the others caught up. No wonder the Zari thought the island was cursed! It felt claustrophobic to Braig, as if the air was too heavy. He sucked from his water pouch, fighting off a sense of doom. He doubted the League was here. How could they have made it past those Reapers?

Ash stumbled into the dell and immediately collapsed. They couldn't get any sense out of him. He wouldn't drink water. He just curled into himself, like an injured bug, clutching the Taelstone to his chest. Once or twice he murmured a name. *Leynore.* Braig turned to Sarin, frustrated by the delay. 'It's the Song isn't it? He's lost in the Song.'

'Maybe. Or in Credé's memories.'

'*Wonderful.* That's *so* much better.'

'I've seen him like this before. He just needs time.'

Except they didn't have time. Braig looked around. Either the mists were drawing in or the light was fading. 'Is it getting dark?'

'I've no idea.' Sarin sniffed the air. 'Smells like noon.'

What the hell did noon smell like? Braig wiped a hand over his dumb shaven head. Sweat beaded on his scalp. A fearless Denchman? That was a joke. He just felt stupid — and vulnerable.

They sat in silence for what seemed an age. Braig had never been good at sitting still. He chewed on a piece of dried meat, just to kill time, glaring at the treetops. Where were the birds? Did they avoid the island, too? Sarin sat motionless, his eyes half-closed, settled against a tree. Braig scowled. If they didn't get going soon he was going to explode. He stuck it out as long as he could, telling himself that a warrior was wise to conserve his strength. Then he couldn't bear it any longer. 'This is stupid! We need to go.'

To his surprise, Sarin nodded. He squatted beside Ash, putting a hand on his shoulder. 'Stay here and rest, kin. We'll be back. With Kep. Ash?' No response. Sarin sighed, then he turned to Tarlyn. 'Look after him, Tarlyn.' He spoke as he would to a person, except more politely. The creature thrashed her tail, as if she'd understood. Braig shivered. He'd forgotten how unnerving Tarlyn was.

Sarin retrieved a length of rope from his bag. 'We stick to the plan.' *Great.* The plan. Braig suspected 'the plan' would get him killed. Within seconds, Sarin had secured Braig's wrists behind his back. Did the knots need to be *that* tight? 'Don't break free unless you absolutely need to.'

Braig itched to try it — just to be sure he could. And maybe he'd punch Sarin for good measure. He rolled his shoulders, controlling the urge. 'What happens if we run into a patrol?'

'I'll extemporise.'

'If that means you're going to wing it, just say so.'

'I'm going to wing it.'

Moving through undergrowth with your hands bound is far from easy, as Braig could testify when he fell over — twice. Sarin scowled over his shoulder. 'Can you make less noise?'

Braig snapped back. 'Reckon *you* can do this quietly with your hands tied?'

'Probably.'

By the time they found the path, Braig was fuming and drenched in sweat. Sarin raised an eyebrow. 'Nice scowl. You certainly look the part.' Braig opened his mouth to respond, then jerked his head around. Voices! Coming this way!

Sarin slipped a rope around Braig's neck. What? Nobody had mentioned a leash! Braig ground his teeth, but there was no time to protest. Two men came into view and strode down the path towards them, bearing unlit torches. The larger man let out an exclamation when he saw them. 'What did I tell you?'

Braig knew his part: *Keep your mouth shut and look threatening.* The second bit was easy, especially when Sarin shoved him in the back. 'Shud up and keep movin'!' A sharp crack made Braig flinch. *A whip? Where'd he get a whip?* 'I told ya! Move! Ya stinkin' Dench.' Sarin let out a few juicy swear words and shoved him again. Braig stumbled forward. He snarled, but held his tongue — just.

The strangers hurried forward. One was beefy; the other goblin-like, with a disfigured countenance, as if the side of his face had melted. Nothing marked them out as Kara-fell's men, apart from the malice in their eyes. At least they *had* eyes and weren't nulls, thanks to Argess.

The smaller one took the lead. 'What's this, then?' Braig knew his sort. Sure of himself. And nasty in a fight, despite his stature. Not to be underestimated.

Sarin jerked Braig to a halt. 'What da ya think it is? It's a bleeding fighter in'it?' The answer held the perfect amount of tough-guy bravado. Sarin was surprisingly good at this.

The men grew closer, scrutinising them through suspicious eyes. Braig put on his best glower. He snarled when Sarin tugged at the rope — it damn near choked him!

The larger man goggled at the markings on Braig's scalp. 'That's a Denchman, that is! He's got a Dench!'

'Don't care what he's got.' His companion's mouth pulled into a sneer, dragging his face with it. 'He's on the wrong path.' His hand travelled to his hip and the hilt of a jagged blade. *Nasty.*

Sarin spat on the ground. 'Nobody said nothin' about no parf.'

'There's rules, see. You can't come up 'ere. You gotta follow the rules.'

The beefy man pushed closer, letting his companion do the talking. He'd obviously never seen a Denchman up close before. Braig picked his moment, bared his teeth and lunged. To his satisfaction, the big man yelped and leapt out of harm's way.

Sarin tugged the rope taut, making a show of keeping Braig under control. 'I ain't heard a' no rules. Heard ya just need one a' these.' He held out his hand. Resting on his palm was a flat stone, engraved with a crude symbol. 'Paid good coin for this, I did.' The man with the disfigured face scowled, folding his arms.

'Speakin' of coin,' said Sarin, 'ya wanna get on this 'un. Proper nasty 'e is.' He prodded Braig in the ribs with the end of the whip, and Braig growled obligingly. 'Bashed three tuffs ta death before we took 'im down. Just with fists an' boots. An' drugged up, too!'

The man's eyes gleamed, and Braig's flesh crawled under his greedy gaze. He felt like a fattened-up bull in some sleazy market-place. The ugly fellow licked his lips, his gaze travelling over the muscles in Braig's shoulders and arms. 'Don't know what you're playing at, coming up this way, boy. But you're right about one thing: that Dench is gold. Kara-fell don't hate *nobody* more than a Denchman.'

Braig could see his brain working. 'Here's what we do: I get half, on account of me knowing the score.' He dismissed Sarin's curses, speaking over him. 'That's fair, see. For getting you set up an' all. And I'll escort you right to the front of the queue.' Braig groaned inwardly. *The front of the queue?* Maybe the plan was working *too* well.

Sarin's chuckle was wicked. 'Straight ta the front!' He jabbed Braig with the whip. ''Ear that, Dench? That's a fine deal, that is.' Braig bared his teeth. Sarin was *far* too good at this. Their new associate smiled like a shark. He ordered his companion to check on those 'snot-for-brains' Reapers, and the big man, grumbling about missing the first fights, lumbered off. Braig considered breaking free; he could handle this guy on his own. But Sarin clearly could read his thoughts and nudged him from behind. *Stick to the plan.* Fine! They'd stick to the plan — for now.

The unlikely trio climbed the path, weaving deeper into the jungle. With every step, Braig grew more anxious. What did it mean? 'The front of the queue'? Eventually, the track joined a wider path. The paved route must have been very grand once, judging by its carved edges. But its stone was cracked and green with moss now, ravaged by time. Yet a certain elegance remained. The trees had wide girths and pale, arboreal roots. Braig heard a waterfall on his right, confirming his guess: they were heading straight to the island's centre.

The gloom deepened as they grew closer to their destination. Smoking torches marked the path. The muffled thunder of the waterfall faded, replaced by the rumble of drums, which beat out a sombre, hollow rhythm, then rolled wildly. Braig heard a cheer, accompanied by the wafting scent of smoke. Their guide picked up the pace.

Sarin gave the whip a casual flick, stinging the back of Braig's calf. 'How's it all work, then?'

Their ugly companion chuckled. 'That's for me to know.' But he couldn't resist boasting. 'Don't worry. I got the sly, see?' He seemed eager to show off his superior knowledge. There was a hierarchy of fights, with every session beginning with the undefeated combatant from the previous event — to kick things off properly. The first contest of this afternoon promised to be savage. The fighter in question had beaten six already: another win, and they got to challenge a champion.

Sarin grunted. 'Got a stake?'

'Course!' The man rubbed his hands together. 'Got on early, I did. Wretch could go all the way.'

'All the way?'

'Yeah. Anyone beats the champion, they get to join our lady. For proper.' The man licked his lips. The prospect seemed to excite him. Braig frowned. This was Kara-fell's highest honour? To be at her side?

'And this one?' Sarin jerked his head in Braig's direction. 'Who'll he fight?'

'Don' worry. They'll pick sumpin' juicy for a Dench. No skinny slaves for 'im. Slaves is just fodder, see? To fill in the gaps. Lady'll want 'im done proper nasty. Might set wild beasts on 'im, an' all.'

*Beasts.* It confirmed what Braig's senses had already told him: the arena had animals. *Scared* animals. His guts twisted as they rounded a bend. They'd come to a village, if you could call a bunch of makeshift shacks cobbled together from whatever was at hand a village. A couple of men were busy dousing a campfire. Braig felt their eyes. As they straightened up, one of them sneered. 'Left it late, Ulf?'

Their companion ignored him. No camaraderie there.

The drums were closer now. Braig felt them reverberating against his ribs. He heard people, too. A crowd. They came to an ornate flight of steps curved against the hillside. Somebody had hacked away the bushes on either side. Braig hesitated. Every instinct screamed at him: *Run!* He began the climb, fear rising with every step.

Nothing could have prepared Braig for the view from the top of that stair, though. With a shock, he realised it really *was* an arena — an ancient amphitheatre, built into the natural bowl of the land. He was standing at the right-hand edge of a semi-circle of terraced seats. Like a funnel, it directed attention to the stage, seven or more tiers below. Some magic of engineering made the stage feel very close. Braig had the impression that one giant leap would land him in the middle.

For now, the stage was empty. Near the back there was a single archway; it must once have been part of some grand set design, allowing actors to come and go. Now it seemed incongruous. Huge cauldrons, serving as fire pits, flanked each side of the archway, casting flickering light over the ancient ruins. The backdrop was nightmarish. Behind the stage, a low stone building was waging a battle with the forest — and losing. The edifice was crumbling, succumbing to the stranglehold of gigantic tree roots. Its elegant doorways were decrepit, just black holes choked with rubble.

Braig shivered. It was perfectly reasonable to believe that evil spirits lived here. Not only that, Kara-fell had brought horrors of her own. The place crawled with people. Eager spectators packed the front rows while others roamed, restless. They jeered and laughed, peering into cages to inspect the occupants and placing bets.

Their guide led them down a flight of steps. Braig's heart was racing so fast it hurt. He recognised the fortifications to the right, where sentries were surveying the beach from high platforms. When he spied the scaffold, panic gripped him. Was that a woman? *Argess, have mercy!* He felt himself spinning out of control, before his thinking brain took hold. *Don't be an idiot!* It's not Kep.

The vision mentioned a cage. And here there were cages aplenty. They lined either side of the stage, each large enough to hold several grown men. Braig flinched at the smell of blood as he stepped down onto the raceway that skirted the stage. Across the arena, animals roared in fear. He wanted to join in.

Their guide led them around the raceway, in front of the crowd. Showing off the Dench. The crowd jeered and laughed, some calling out obscenities. Braig could smell their cruelty, their hunger for blood. They wanted nothing more than to see him suffer. It wasn't personal; these people hated everything, including each other.

They reached the line of cages on the left side of the stage. The guard didn't turn as they passed, but Braig glanced across at his face and gulped. He had no eyes — just vacant holes. It was his first sight of a null!

Some captives stared through the bars of the cages. Most didn't. Preserving their strength, or just too frightened to move. One cried out in a language Braig couldn't understand. He felt a flash of guilt, unable to offer the comfort of human connection. There was no humanity here.

They stopped at the last cage in the row. Set against the ancient ruins at the very edge of the jungle, it was gloomy and shrouded in mist. 'Like I promised: straight to the front!' As their escort flung the cage door open, his offsider appeared from nowhere. Braig felt the tip of a spear at his neck. Sarin caught his eye. *Play along.* Swallowing his misgivings, Braig allowed them to herd him into the cage.

'Weapons,' snapped their escort. Sarin added Braig's axe to the large pile on the stage. One of many. 'Now you. Get inside.' The jab of a spear put paid to Sarin's protests. 'Outsiders don't wander about, see?' The man smirked. 'Should charge you extra. Got the best view in the 'ouse!'

'Rules is rules. I get it.' Sarin shrugged, cool as ever. He paused before stepping through the doorway. 'Here's a starter.' He tossed the man a pouch. Braig blinked. *Where had that come from?*

The man hefted the pouch and grinned. 'Enjoy the show.' He chuckled to himself as he left. 'A Dench. A bleeding Dench.'

Braig burst free of his bonds and rounded on Sarin. If he was going to die in Kara-fell's bloody arena, he'd have the pleasure of flattening Sarin first. As he pulled back his fist, he sensed movement in the shadows at the back of the cage. 'Sarin!' said a voice. 'What are you playing at?'

Braig's heart jumped into his throat when she moved into the light. It was her! Her hair was different, but it was her! Those eyes! So blue. And *angry*. Braig wasn't the only person who wanted to smack Sarin. Kep was so angry she didn't even recognise him. *Of course, she didn't!* She thought he was dead! 'Kep — it's me! It's Braig.'

She stared. 'Braig?'

'Yes! It's me!' He stepped forward, uncertainly. Should he sweep her into his arms? Sensing something amiss, he glanced over at Sarin. Something had got into his companion: Sarin had gone stock-still.

'Braig,' she repeated. Her tone was flat — nothing like the Kep he knew. Braig frowned. This wasn't going the way he'd imagined. He'd planned out what he would say a thousand times, but seeing her like this, it wrenched his heart. 'Kep, I—'

A blare of horns cut off his words. Brash and discordant, the sound made his ears ring. The crowd roared approval over the rolling drums, as the door to their cage flew wide and Kara-fell's followers began to chant: 'Death! Death!' Braig's stomach dropped. *Front of the queue.* They'd come for him!

But it was worse. *Much* worse.

Kep shot Sarin a look of exasperation but ignored Braig entirely. Braig couldn't believe it. He was so stunned that he just stood there, frozen to the spot. 'You'd better win,' said Sarin softly.

Kep paused at the door. 'That's the plan.' Then she walked out onto that terrible stage.

Reality hit him as the cage door slammed shut. 'Kep!' Braig ran forward to shake at the bars. 'Kep!' She couldn't hear him! The din was too loud. He shook harder, rattling the cage. It achieved nothing, just earned him a whack on the knuckles from the jeering guard.

Sarin hissed. 'Settle down, idiot!' Braig swung about, ready to throttle him. 'Watch!'

The drums fell silent, signalling the crowd to hush. Kara-fell slipped out of the darkness, like a spider creeping from its lair. A long black cloak trailed behind her as she crossed the stage and stepped up onto a round platform at the front. Her cloak seemed made of black feathers or tails — Braig couldn't decide which. Her pale limbs glistened, as if made of wax. He'd expected her to be taller. A blood-red stripe ran from her forehead down to her chin, matching a head-dress of black and red feathers. Otherwise, she wore the attire of a fighter: leathers and split skirts. She raised both hands to the crowd. The drums and cheering began anew as Kara-fell took her throne.

Braig watched in dread as Kep strode to the centre of the stage. People had warned him that she'd changed. But this? What was she thinking? She was acting as if she believed her own legend! He watched his childhood sweetheart bend a knee, paying homage to their dread host. Kara-fell inclined her head, making her headdress quiver.

Grinding his teeth, Braig clutched the bars so tightly it hurt. Then a thought struck him: if Kep was here, Nirias would be, too! Was it part of the plan? Was Kep a distraction? Or the bait for a trap? No. Nirias wouldn't use her like that. Would he?

Horns brayed as the crowd began a new chant. 'Gork! Gork! Gork!' The man who strode onto the stage was massive! He carried a swing-stone, the huge spiked ball dangling almost to the ground. In his other hand he brandished a sword. If the League had a plan, they'd better act now! Braig doubted *he* could beat this monster; Kep had no chance!

Kep took up a stance, a tiny figure by comparison. Braig roared in anguish. He'd never felt so helpless. She was a novice, just a novice! He gasped in despair. It would be slaughter!

And it was.

Who would win seemed a foregone conclusion. Gork grinned, whirling the swing-stone, playing to the crowd. The spectators roared in delight. Kep ducked, dodging the hurtling lump of metal. She ducked again. Then the fight was over before it got started.

Kep moved so fast! A blizzard of flashing blades, she whirled beneath the swing-stone's arc. A blow slashed her opponent behind his knees. He roared in agony. Staggered. Kep corkscrewed, spinning back the other way. Darting in, she lunged with her sword. Then stood back.

The monster clutched at his breast, staring in wide-eyed surprise. A deathly hush descended on the crowd. His body slumped, hitting the ground with an audible thump,

Braig made croaking noises in his throat, overcome by a mix of horror and relief. 'How ... ? When did she learn to fight like that?'

Sarin fixed him with those strange golden eyes. 'She didn't.'

38

# WIMSARI

The wedding guest strolls towards the feast. Silver sandals clad his feet. A feather adorns his cap. The banners stream. Silver ribbons on fluted turrets, waggling like excited fingers, catching the people's mood. 'Welcome,' the trumpets cry. 'Welcome to the city of the sea! The Queen welcomes you, one and all. Rejoice! The bride of the southern shores has come, and we shall have peace. So stay! Dance and be merry!'

The wedding guest stays. He does not dance. And he is not merry. The people feast on juicy pheasant and peppered pork. He does not eat. The melody swirls and skips. It skips. Skips ... a beat. My. Sweet. Heart. My heart. The beat! That tune! So very merry. Bows skitter over strings. Faster. Faster. Nobody heeds the guest who simply stands and watches.

The bride's lips are soft. Her hands like silk. She twirls, stumbles. Caught in the arms of her prince. Flushed. A little too breathless. And he watches. Eyes glittering. Dance on. My liege, my lord, my ladies. The notes falter now. Dancers miss their steps. The first guest falls and Credé raises his glass. 'Here's to your peace.' The vision shatters, to the sound of a thousand screams.

.  .  .

A whisper. Hushed, like the breath of the sea, it washes a name to the shore. *Ash.*

Dark, mirrored eyes greeted Ash when his eyelids flickered open. Tarlyn! She was sitting right on his chest. Now she spun in a circle, chittering into his face. How long had she been there? Blinking and groaning, Ash eased himself up, spilling her onto the ground. The leafy dell was empty. Just Tarlyn. Nobody who might have whispered his name.

The pieces of himself came back — as if they no longer fitted. Credé's memories were vivid, an after-image that he'd never banish. His now. Bodies falling, hands clutching at throats. Ash groaned, locking his head in a cage of fingers. Those people! All those innocent people!

So *this* was the source of the Malshorne's torment — Credé's revenge for Leynore's death. Brutal and indiscriminate, he'd poisoned the Wimsari queen and all her nobles. His choice of occasion was callous: the wedding celebration of her son and his new bride. The curse which plagued these lands had a name. *Credé.* Ash sobbed, assaulted by guilt. 'I'm sorry. I'm so sorry.'

Tarlyn scolded again. Her ruff quivered, as it did when danger was near. She was right. Ash needed to pull himself together. *It was a memory, you idiot.* Something that happened long ago. Credé's guilt, not yours.

Ash drew a shuddering breath. Sweat drenched his body. Pulling himself to his feet, he braced himself against a tree, steadying his heartbeat and trying to marshal his thoughts. He looked around, confused. He remembered running up the beach. After that? Nothing. His throat felt raw. Had he been screaming or crying? Both, most likely. Somebody had hung his water bottle around his neck. *Sarin.* Ash took a few miserable gulps, drawing the obvious conclusion: Braig and Sarin had gone on without him.

Thunder rumbled in the distance. No. Drums! Memory flooded back. Reapers! The bay was full of Reapers! Ash drew a breath, forcing down panic. Petrel and Ordelle were safe. They just needed to keep to the mists. He should have stayed, too, instead of playing the hero. Too late for that now.

Ash knew the sensible thing was to wait, but he scowled as he took another sip of water. It wasn't what Sarin would do. Or Braig. And especially not Kep.

The drums rolled again. *Kep!* Was that chanting? He strained his senses. A brutal rhythm, it echoed on both sides. But that wasn't all he heard. He caught his breath at the sound of a deeper music. It spoke to him on a primal level, like the sonorous call of a conch shell. The music of the sea. And wind playing over fluted turrets. The song of his ancestors.

For a moment, Ash detected a secret chord beneath all else. He sensed a glimmer of something far beyond his understanding. Then it faded. Finding a rock, he sat down to think. Why had he come? Because Sarin believed in him. And Petrel had named him Weaver. Although he hadn't yet grasped its meaning, he now knew he could move the mists. Perhaps he could help his friends get out alive. He drank a little more water, then picked up his bag. 'Let's go find them, Tarlyn.'

Finding his friends' tracks proved easy. Sarin was a master woodsman, but Braig was nothing of the sort — a bull kattlen would have left fewer clues. Following a broken stem here, flattened leaves there, Ash made steady progress. Coming across a path, he hesitated. The weird half-light made it difficult to see far. But with Tarlyn bounding ahead, Ash set off as quickly as he dared.

Through the canopy, he caught glimpses of a smoky orange sky. The drums pounded up ahead, proclaiming their message of doom. He slowed as the track climbed higher, panting. Everything here was wet and mossy, the trees burdened with vines and trailing foliage. Mighty ferns crowded each other out, stealing the light.

Ash saw the torches before he heard the voices. Sentries! Desperate, he cast about for somewhere to hide. Tarlyn vanished. He resisted the urge to plunge after her into the undergrowth. Too noisy! Stepping off the path, he crouched in the hollow of an ancient tree and pulled his hood up over his face. *Don't see me,* he prayed. *Please don't see me.*

The men walked shoulder-to-shoulder, grumbling as they went. 'It'll be Reapers scrapping again. Dumb nulls can't tell Reapers from trouble. No eyes. No brains, I say!'

'Don't matter. Orders is orders.'

They drew closer. Ash caught a pungent waft of sweat and cheap rum. Leather straps criss-crossed their bare chests. One wore an armoured cap that resembled a hollowed-out melon. Ash felt a stab of terror when the man turned his head. He stared straight at him! 'Damn creepy mists!' The fellow scowled and rubbed his eyes, turning to his companion. 'Hurry up. That's all I'm sayin'.' Sniffing up, he spat a gob into the bushes. 'We'll miss the best fights!'

A full minute passed before Ash found the courage to move. He'd been spared! But it was nothing to do with luck, nor the man's poor eyesight. The mists had drawn around him like a cloak, as if sensing his need. Finding this both disturbing and reassuring, he gulped and got to his feet. Perhaps he *could* do this.

Tarlyn led him on, deeper into the jungle. Then she left the path, casting a look over her shoulder. Ash followed her without hesitation — he'd learned by now to trust his unusual companion. Besides, the close encounter with the sentries had left him shaken. He'd feel safer off the path.

Lacking Tarlyn's ability to slip through the tangled weave of branches, the going was slower, with Ash having to clamber over mossy trunks and roots, and tramp through the undergrowth. He eventually realised that some of the obstacles had straight edges: beneath his feet were the remains of an ancient path. He spied a stone bench standing beside the old path, overgrown with creepers. Ash put out a hand, running his fingers over the indented outline of a fish. The effect was instantaneous. The Song awoke in a cascade of shimmering bells.

People materialised, all around him. Their clothes shone, as if made of light. They all had silver hair, even the children. *Wimsari!* His ancestors. They wore blossoms in their hair and saffron garlands around their necks. Their baskets brimmed with flowers. They walked in groups, laughing and singing.

Ash stood and watched, transported by the vision and the allure of silvery music. The melody evoked water and birdsong, but something more. Excitement. Anticipation. Something wonderful was happening. He followed, drawn to the beauty of their song.

They climbed together, up through the soft ferns, to a series of sweeping terraces. The vision revealed that there had been statues once, and gigantic urns. The people paused, draping bright yellow garlands around the stone. Ash stared in wonder when a group of children, wearing masks and shimmering wings, overtook him. Squealing with delight, they flapped their arms like birds, chasing each other around the sculptures. Three young girls passed by him, holding hands and swinging their arms. The flowers in their hair smelled honeysuckle-sweet.

He mounted the broken stair, his heart swelling with anticipation. There would be dancing and poetry and pageantry. And *music*. Such music! Music sweet enough to break a person's heart. As soon as he reached the top, the dream shattered. Banished by the blare of horns. Reality hit like a punch. Ash reeled, gasping for air and clutching at a pillar for support. The Song promised a theatre of light, a joyful, life-affirming celebration. This was a theatre of death.

Ash knew he had to keep moving. Hiding behind a pillar served no purpose: he had to find Sarin and Braig. Edging around the stone, he put a hand out to steady himself. *Butter! The scent of melted butter. And pancakes flipping.* Instantaneously, he found himself at a serving hatch, on a terrace of little shops. He jerked his hand away, as if the stone was a hot griddle. He needed to be more careful: the Song was powerful here.

A dark figure pulled his gaze to the round platform at the front of the stage. The woman sat with her back to the audience, watching as a pair of fighters took the floor. Kara-fell! The source of all this darkness. As Ash watched, the crowd roared with terrible energy. This was hatred, condensed into a screaming din, then amplified. The fight was about to begin. Every eye would be on the stage. Except his. Time to move. Tarlyn brushed against his leg, and he stooped and caressed her head for reassurance. Then, with his heart in his mouth, he worked his way down the terraces, creeping unseen, along the back of the ruined shops.

The mist was both friend and enemy, making it hard to see. Ash stumbled over rubble in places, praying that he wouldn't break an ankle. As he reached the lowest level, the crowd roared again. He wanted to block out the cacophony of hatred: the foulness was all wrong — there should have been singing. And light. Resisting the temptation to escape into the trees that crowded in on the amphitheatre, he pushed on.

On circling a large clump of ferns, he discovered the first in a line of cages. The occupants crowded the front of the cage, oblivious to his shadowy presence. Every eye was on the fight. They shook at the bars, yelling encouragement. Ash crept past until, all at once, the arena fell silent. He froze. Then the crowd gasped in shock. A shout came from the cage, making him jump. 'Kep-Váli!' The captive's voice boomed with defiance. 'Kep-Váli!'

An icy fear crushed Ash's heart as the cry echoed, bouncing from cage to cage. 'Kep-Váli! Kep-Váli!' Fear became terror. *No. Please! By the gods, no.* The arena erupted. Angry shouts and boos vied with wild cheering. Ash felt the blood drain from his face, and he clutched the edge of the cage to stop himself from falling. He was struggling to breathe, not wanting to look. But he had to know. Edging sideways, he peered through the gap between the cages.

The fighter stood very straight, a sword at her side. A tousled fringe fell over one eye. The eerie twilight made her into a silhouette. Framed by fire. Ash moaned, cupping a hand to his mouth. It was Kep. It could only be Kep.

The roar of confusion reached a crescendo as Kara-fell rose to her feet. The dark queen held up her arms. Silence fell. 'Warrior!' Ash shuddered. Her voice had a peculiar quality. As if a thousand voices had spoken as one. 'You have bested seven. Great honour is within your reach. Master one of my champions and the prize is yours. Gold ... should you wish it. And boundless power at my side.'

Her followers started to chant. 'Kara-fell! Kara-fell.'

But their mistress silenced them again, raising a finger. 'By the rules of this place, you will fight to the death.' The crowd moaned in dark ecstasy. The champions formed a line on the stage, shoulders back. 'Speak, child of sorrow! Make your choice!'

Ash felt a deep and terrible despair. The sound of his friend's voice made him tremble. 'I will abide by the rules of this place.' Kep lifted her sword and used it to point. One of the champions stood a little taller when her blade seemed to single him out. But the sword moved on. The weapon didn't pause until it found Kara-fell herself.

Kep's voice rang out. 'I challenge you! Kara-fell!' She had to shout over cries of shock and outrage. 'I am Kep of Mildaresh! Slave no more. I fight for those who cannot fight alone. I fight for justice! For Narsis! And for freedom!'

A flock of bats went twittering up into the sky. A shudder went through the arena. The captives cried out as one: 'Kep-Váli!' Ash had never heard Kep speak with such arrogance. It jarred — as if someone had written her a speech. His gut twisted. Something was horribly wrong here.

Every eye was on Kara-fell. The woman looked frozen, caught by surprise. She turned her head towards the bay. An unnatural move-ment, accentuated by her feathered headdress. Darkness seemed to slither around her. Then she turned back and laughed. A throaty, wicked sound. 'Kep-Váli! I receive your challenge with gladness.' Reaching out pale arms, she called to her followers. 'Kep-Váli is a symbol of *hope*, some say.' Her laughter crackled with a weird energy. Ash felt a shiver in his bones. 'As we all know, there is no such thing! I accept the challenge. Bring me my blades!'

## 39

## DUEL

While the crowd had been a beast before, now it was truly a monster. The wave of anger and excitement rocked Ash on his feet. He watched, numb with fear, as Kep walked to the centre of the stage. She made the sign of the triangle and took up a stance. The archetype of a warrior, poised for combat. His mind rebelled — something felt amiss.

Kara-fell had removed her headdress and cloak. She was barefooted. Ash might have read significance into that detail, but the sight of her weapons distracted him. The shorter blade was like a fishbone — wicked teeth cut into both edges. The rapier gleamed with a fell light. From their cages, the captives bellowed. 'Kep-Váli!' Their voices roused Ash from his frozen state. Hope! They still had hope, he realised. They believed Kep could win.

Ash suddenly knew what he had to do. Sarin's voice spoke in his mind. *It's all about distraction.* What could be more distracting than a fight to the death? A horn signalled the beginning of the match and the whole place erupted. Ash pulled up his hood, knowing he had to hurry. Thankfully, the cages were designed for easy loading, and so had doors at the back as well as the front. He located the bolts. Shot one across, then the next. Flinging the door open, he shouted. 'For

Kep-Vali!' Faces turned, wide-eyed in shock, but he'd already moved on.

The drums pounded. Horns brayed fit to burst. Ash moved as swiftly as he could, fumbling with the bolts. He hummed beneath his breath as he worked, a talisman against fear. As he opened one door after another, the hum grew louder. Each time he shouted the words 'For Kep-Váli!', before moving on. He sensed the chaos in his wake. *Good. It was working.*

The melody grew stronger as he went. He recognised the strains of 'The Lay of Eregil and Mendolas', the ballad he'd sung at Aechon's hearth, so long ago. He incorporated threads of his own invention, too. It was a song about hope, but most of all about friendship.

Ash moved on, drawing the mists with him. The next cage was empty. Through the bars, he glimpsed a vision of Kara-fell. Blades poised ready to strike. Melody flared in his mind, in a desperate ringing chorus: *And all prevail, and none shall fail.* He forced himself to move. Now only one cage remained.

The last cage was bigger and more solidly built. A guard loitered near the front. Ash almost lost his nerve until a shout came from behind: 'The prisoners are escaping!' The guard hurried away.

Blessing his good fortune, Ash started on at the bolts. His hands were raw and bleeding, and it didn't help that someone inside was kicking at the front door, making the whole cage shudder. Taking a risk, he shouted again: 'For Kep-Vali!'

He heard a voice over the pounding. 'Stop! Stop, you idiot!' Sarin's scowling face appeared at the bars. 'Braig — stop! It's Ash!' The battering ceased. 'Ash? Where are you?'

'I'm right here,' said Ash, puffing as he wiggled at the top bolt.

Sarin frowned. 'Where? I don't see you.'

Something had bent the top bolt out of shape. It took all of Ash's strength to shift it. Braig's voice pleaded, begging him to open the door. At last it yielded and the door burst open. A wild-eyed Braig barrelled past, shouting as he went. 'Kep!'

'Braig! Stop!' Sarin cursed, but Braig was gone, crashing towards the stage. Sarin grabbed Ash by the shoulders: 'Ash! Listen to me. It's not Kep. It's not her.'

Ash blinked. 'What?' A bolt of revelation hit him. 'It's Nirias!'

Sarin nodded, his face grim. 'We need to help. Great job releasing the captives, but I'll do the other side. You're not a fighter, Ash. You don't belong here! Get away, into the trees. Stay safe!' He frowned. 'And whatever you're doing with the mist, keep doing it!' He was already gone.

Chaos spread as more of the crowd spilled onto the stage. This was no longer a spectator's sport. The captives were fighting for their lives. Every skirmish was a tiny island of hope. But a malignancy festered here, growing ever stronger. Kara-fell seemed to swallow the light. She prowled like a dark thing, circling her opponent at the arena's centre. Tentacles of fear plucked at Ash's mind. But he couldn't just slink off to hide. He felt a strange compulsion to stay and watch. Here on the brink of the abyss.

# 40

## NULLS

Braig didn't think. He just reacted. The cage door opened, and he bolted. All he saw was mist. All he smelt was blood. His ears rang. Sarin's warning registered as a squeak, like an annoying mosquito. Irrelevant. He swatted it away. Only one thing mattered: getting to Kep.

After a brief battle with the undergrowth, he burst from the mist, right at the edge of the stage. He snatched his axe from the heap of weapons, and grabbed a shield, too. Fitting it to his arm, he scanned the chaos. Kara-fell's champions surrounded her on the stage, locked in combat with the freed captives. Braig didn't blanch. He'd fight them all. Anything to get to Kep.

Within moments an opponent had collapsed beneath his axe — his first kill. His brain recoiled. *Felling a man is nothing like felling a tree.* Pushing the thought away, he charged. Blood was the price of freedom. He'd spill a river of blood to save Kep. He raised his shield barely in time. A blow glanced off his shoulder. Block. Duck. Swing. The winter's training with the jarlycats kicked in. Braig had the skills — and a slave's instinct for a dirty fight. With a mighty roar, he swung himself into the work.

Kara-fell's people were brutal but not well-drilled. Braig taught a couple of them that knives were no match for a long-handled axe. He sent a third flying with a swipe of his shield, then ducked, narrowly escaping the sweep of a broad-sword. Before he could strike, somebody else's blade plunged into its owner's neck. His saviour was dark-skinned, with unkempt hair and beard. Braig grunted. 'Thanks!'

'Pleasure.'

Nothing further was said. They worked in tandem, seeing off three more brutes. They certainly weren't short of opponents. The bloodthirsty audience had joined the frenzy. Braig caught the occasional glimpse of Kep. Miraculously, she was holding her own. He prayed to every god he could think of. *I'm coming. I'm coming, Kep!* He'd have been better off focusing on what he was doing, though, as a blow caught him on the side of the head, making his ears ring.

Braig shoved with his shield, forcing his smaller opponent to give ground. As he swung his axe, aiming for the jugular, a cry went up from the treetop platforms. 'Reapers! The Reapers are attacking!' He groaned. *Brilliant.* There was no time to dwell on it — the sound of Kara-fell's scream drove everything else from his mind. Anger personified, it shrieked with a thousand voices. Darkness swirled around her, growing ever-faster. Braig saw black shapes in the maelstrom. Flailing whips, like snakes. The Melk! It was just as Domberto had described it.

Braig's throat was raw. He bellowed regardless. 'Kep! Kep!' He swung his axe like a madman. One thought drove him — cut down *anything* that stood in his way. The melee parted before his fury. Except for one person who stood his ground.

Kara-fell's champion was a colossal figure of sinew and muscle. A single yellow braid sprouted from the top of his shaved head. He'd braided his beard and dyed it red. Studded armour and heavy weaponry signalled that he was a seasoned fighter. It didn't deter Braig. Then he noticed the man's eyes.

The fighter's eyes were blue. But as Braig watched, they flooded black — then dissolved! All that remained were pits. Black pits. People around him screamed. Braig didn't blame them. With a yelp of his own, he attacked.

The tales that Braig had heard about fighting nulls proved to be nothing compared to the real thing. This was beyond his training. As they fought, the thing took an arrow in its shoulder. It barely paused. Snapping the shaft, it carried on fighting. Braig knew that nulls this close to their nexus were fast, but this thing was *strong!* Its spiked mace bashed at his shield so hard that he thought his bones might break. He was grateful now that the bearded stranger had stuck by him, as he held his courage yet, darting in, jabbing and thrusting with his sword.

They battled on, pitting their combined strengths against the monster — strangers fighting as brothers. Parrying and thrusting, they drove the thing back, only to have it rally. Braig dealt it blow after blow. It didn't fall. He chopped deep into its shoulder. Still, it didn't die. His partner slashed at its legs and ducked. Too slow! The mace struck his head, and he stayed down. But the damage was dealt. The null buckled. Fell to one knee. Braig's axe came down. At last the thing collapsed, convulsing as it died.

Braig didn't see what hit him, but his brain passed comment as he fell, annoyingly matter-of-fact. *That felt like a quarterstaff.* His head smacked into the ground, sending a shudder through his frame. He winced as sparkles danced before his eyes. A club, not a quarterstaff, and a gnarly one. Its owner's teeth were sharpened to points.

Braig needed to roll away. *Obviously.* Except ... Something was wrong with his eyes. Ribbons of golden fire spiralled around him, forming patterns in the air. He groaned. How badly was he hurt? His opponent threw back his head, gurgling in triumph. A wicked blade swung back. Braig's mind screamed. *Roll away!*

The arrow came out of nowhere, appearing in the enemy's throat like magic. Someone stabbed him for good measure, a blade appearing in his chest, then gone again. Gurgling blood, the brute toppled over. It was a miracle. A very *heavy* miracle.

Braig knew he had to get up. And he would. He'd free himself from the dead man's body and his revolting stench. *Any moment.* But the fiery ribbons were worse now. Strange glyphs appeared before his eyes. And a bird. A bird with blazing tail-feathers. He squeezed his eyes shut. Blinked twice. He just needed to breathe. Turning his head to the side, he tried for a lungful of cleaner air. That was when he saw her.

Kep was high above him. Outlined against the sky. Firing arrows from the treetop scaffold. Braig could tell it was her, he felt it in his soul. A curious band flashed on her arm. Sapphire blue, the colour of her eyes. Strains of music came to his ears. The sweetest music he'd ever heard. He groaned. There was only one possible explanation. Braig was dying. *Again.*

## 41

# THE DARKSTONE

Ash stood in the shadows of the ancient ruins, watching in horror as the captives fought on. This was slaughter, set to the rhythm of drums. Had he released the prisoners only to watch them die? He caught glimpses of Braig swinging his axe, his face twisted in fury. And somewhere in that maelstrom of destruction was Nirias, doing battle with the person at the centre of it all: the Melk's nexus.

It was all so wrong. The arena should have been full of music. But the Melk knew only discord. Its dark intensity hammered at Ash's soul, reminding him of everything he feared. *Heroism is dead,* said the voice inside his head. *All is hatred. There can be no triumph. Only death.* Tears streamed down Ash's face. The urge to run was even stronger, but he couldn't leave his friends — and he couldn't look away. All at once, the drums faltered.

Arrows came whizzing down from above, from high in the trees! Looking up, Ash saw the lookouts topple from their treetop platform. He felt a flutter of hope. The League! Then a shout went up. 'Reapers! The Reapers are attacking!'

In the centre of the stage, Kara-fell roared. The shriek of fury made Ash tremble to the core of his being: a metallic screech, made up of a thousand angry voices. The dread queen grew taller, seeming to draw energy from the ground itself. Darkness whirled about her like a cloak. A cloak made from snakes. Kara-fell was invincible!

Nobody could prevail against such a foe. Not even Nirias. It was in that moment of deepest despondency that he saw it: Kara-fell's feet were bare! Just a tiny detail; inconsequential to anybody else. To Ash, it was a revelation. Understanding struck him like an arrow. A shaft of light in the darkness. Of course! How had he missed it? The Song had revealed the history of this place to him! The Theatre of Light was no ordinary theatre. Its stage was a darkstone!

*That* was the secret of Kara-fell's power. Just like the one in Mildaresh, the darkstone worked to amplify emotion. Right now, it intensified her rage, fuelling the Melk's power. A deep quiver went through Ash's body as a sudden conviction took him. He knew what he had to do! The whisper in his mind confirmed it. *Keeper.*

Acting against every instinct for self-preservation, Ash crept forward, towards the bloody confusion. His heart pounded in his ears as he reached the edge of the shadowy ruins. As he removed his boots, an unearthly voice rose above the din. 'Kneel, Kep-Váli! Kneel before me and take your place at my side!' The command nearly brought Ash to his knees. He froze, paralysed by fear. But he understood now: this place harboured an ancient power, one rooted in memory, and all the possibilities of human endeavour. Ash felt a tremble in his soul as the mists swept around him. Their presence lent him strength, giving him the courage to act.

Trusting in the vapours to mask his movement, Ash ran in a low crouch until he found the lip of the stage. From there he crawled, scrambling on all fours, towards the archway and the enormous urn beside it. Reaching its shadow, he curled himself into a ball, expecting a shout of alarm. Anticipating the thrust of a blade.

Seconds passed, marked out by the frantic hammering of his heart. Nothing. Nobody noticed the grey-haired youth who cowered in the shadows. They were too busy fighting. Too busy dying. Ash gave himself another moment, steeling his nerves. The terracotta urn felt rough against his face; he sensed the archway towering above him, rooted in history, oblivious to the pandemonium. Somehow, that was a comfort. Tendrils of mist flowed from Ash's shoulders, spilling onto the ground in smoky curls. That, too, was reassuring. It still took every drop of bravery to peep around the edge of the urn.

Ash drew a sharp breath. The person in front of him, just paces away, looked exactly like Kep. But it was Nirias. The leader of the League was holding his ground, refusing to bend his knee. He circled Kara-fell, watching for a weakness, waiting for his moment to strike.

It seemed futile. Kara-fell was a whirling fury of black tentacles. Ash recognised the icy touch of the Melk. It stole his courage, paralysing his body with fear. But this was the moment to take action. Kara-fell's attention wasn't on Nirias, or even on the stage. She was looking towards the bay.

*Now. Do it now.* Ash drew a deep breath. He put his hand to the ground. The stone felt rough beneath his fingers. He crouched, pressing his bare feet to its surface. The darkstone stirred. Fear sent tingles through Ash's blood. Like a diver at the top of a cliff, he readied himself for the plunge. *Start with a single note.* He found the image of the tree, just as he'd done so long ago, in the gloom of Credé's hut. That beautiful, aching tree. At the beginning and at the end. Blocking out the screams and the cruel din of battle, he began to sing.

Tendrils of light flowed from his fingertips, just as they had that first time. Sluggish at first, but quickening with every note. Veins of light became ribbons. They spread like fire. Then, all at once, everything ignited. An energy, long suppressed, found release. The Song unfurled in a burst of music. Melodies flew up like birds, borne on the wings of memory.

The Song of this place was rich and multi-layered. Somehow intrinsic to the story, the mists swirled as Ash sang, spiralling away, interwoven with fire. Pictures took shape in the air. A clasp of hands. Brothers bonded. Two swords fought as one. *And all prevail, and none shall fail.* Eregil and Mendolas. The tragic heroes, cast in golden light! Pipers piped. Horns gave their voices to the sky as he sang on.

A fierce joy resonated across several strands of music. The tale was ancient. And new. A song of camaraderie. An anthem for humanity. Ash sang for the valiant captives. And he sang of hope. But, most of all, he sang of friendship. Because this was his song, too.

The liquid beauty of the melody consumed Ash. Made him whole. Somewhere, at the edge of his consciousness, he was aware of standing. But he was far beyond his body now. The Song extended past the limits of his soul. Like a breath that never ends. He sensed the peril. The edges of his self frayed, unravelling — like a banner torn by the wind. He didn't care. He yearned to let go. To dissolve. To join with that infinite galaxy of light and sound.

Another heartbeat and it would have been too late. But he felt the tug of something calling him back. To the secret cord beneath it all. A golden tether, it returned him to himself. To one moment. One song. On a single day. The story of all that was, and all that had been. Reapers chanting. A brave little boat with a dancing sail. A woman on the deck of a pirate ship, drawing back her bow. The Song soared in a moment of recognition, taking Ash's heart with it. She was here. The *real* Kep! All part of the Song.

Ash lifted his arms in exultation and the Song rose to a crescendo. Cymbals crashed, splintering the air. Kara-fell let out a scream. A wrenching sound; it rose in fury. Then died. Cut short by the swing of a blade. *Nirias!* Ash gasped in dismay. The last notes faltered and died.

**42**

———

# PICTURES IN THE SKY

Rodine's plan had gone as well as expected. It proved easy enough to take out Kara-fell's archers, and they'd secured the treetop platforms — just. The League captain had underestimated the number of nulls, though. And they were *strong*. The two on the beach had fought with abandon, driven to their deaths by the dark will of their mistress. Now Rodine's team had lost the element of surprise. *Hold the hill. Protect your Simbab.* Those were the pirates' orders. Getting her first look at the chaos, Kep feared they could do neither.

The rickety platform was small. There was barely room for Kep, Jen-Jay and Jaibari. Jaibari was there on Rodine's orders — in keeping with her vow of protection. Jen-Jay made no bones about sticking as close to Kep as possible. *Somebody* needed to stop her from doing anything rash. Kep scowled. It was *far* too late for that.

She'd expected atrocities in Kara-fell's arena. But this? This was madness. *Everyone* was fighting — even in the stands. Who was the enemy here? Before, it had been easy. The Reapers wore face-paint. The nulls had been easy to identify, too. Something in the way they moved betrayed them — not to mention their lack of eyes. Here, Kep found it difficult to tell friends from foe. Was Nirias the cause of all this confusion? She hoped so.

The maelstrom at the centre of the stage dominated everything. Kep recognised the Melk's presence. She'd felt it before — that prickling sense of unrelenting doom. It made her want to whimper, to crawl away and hide. Her hands trembled as she reached into her quiver. Jen-Jay put a hand on her shoulder. 'Save your arrows. It's too late for that.'

Kep bit her lip. She felt like a child playing games in a world of grown-ups. How could she ever have imagined that a single arrow would destroy a nexus this powerful? At last she grasped the true power of the Melk. Kara-fell was darkness personified, a roiling mass of black tentacles. The nexus seemed to grow before Kep's eyes, pulsating as it fed on the violence. She struggled to find her voice. 'Jen-Jay? What's happening?'

'She's making more nulls.'

As they watched, several fighters disengaged from the battle. Their own will nullified, they moved at Kara-fell's command. They headed this way, moving in unison. *Great.* It was the last thing they needed. Kep feared for her already exhausted pirates. She lifted her bow. She doubted she could kill the nulls, but weakening them was better than nothing. Jen-Jay had different ideas. 'No, Kep. Aim for the champions. If the League *is* here, it might create a chance.' Her mouth twitched, betraying her lack of faith. 'And it will offer hope to those who resist.' Kep felt a cold shiver. *There is no hope.* Jen-Jay shot her a look. '*And don't* give in to despair. It only sustains our enemy.'

'We'll need more arrows,' said Jaibari. Kep blinked. Dark humour? From Jaibari? That was new.

The champions fought in a ring, defending their mistress. The challenge lay in avoiding those who attacked them. Kep's first arrow went astray. The second hit, embedding itself in the thigh of a savage-looking woman who continued fighting, ignoring the shaft sticking out of her leg. *A null.*

Kep's next target was a giant of a man, with a yellow braid. He looked impossible to miss. Two men fought him. The one wielding

an axe seemed familiar. She couldn't imagine why — he looked ferocious, his head shaven on one side. But he was fighting nulls, and *that*
made him an ally. She felt a grim stab of satisfaction when her arrow
found its mark, plunging deep into the null's shoulder.

Kep's arms trembled with fatigue, causing her to fumble. By the
time she'd fitted another arrow, the null had fallen. His opponents
had paid the price, though. Both were down. She felt a pang of
sympathy for the brave man with the axe. To take on a null was
heroic in anyone's books. A nasty brute was standing over the poor
young man, sword raised. *Oh, no you don't.* She let her arrow fly. Kep
didn't see whether the arrow found its mark because a fresh horror
stole her attention.

The mists! Haunting the trees and the ancient ruins, the vapours
contributed to the arena's creepy atmosphere. Now they took on a
strange energy, as if coming alive. Eddying near the archway on the
stage, they billowed, spiralling upwards. Kep let out a cry. Pictures
were forming in the air! She blinked her eyes. Was it exhaustion? Just
her mind playing tricks? But when Jen-Jay gasped, she knew her
mentor saw it, too.

First came the tree. It flowered, then dissolved, becoming a moun-
tainous landscape threaded with rivers. Soldiers marched from the
mists, bearing banners of grey. They bore shields with elaborate
crests. Jen-Jay muttered beneath her breath. 'Are we to fight the mists
as well?'

But that wasn't all. Now Kep saw threads of golden light. Like
ribbons, they spooled around the archway, weaving intricate patterns
across the stage. She put a hand to her mouth. *No.* Her heartbeat
quickened, hammering against her ribs. *It couldn't be!* But Kep knew it
was. Even before she heard the music.

*Ash!* Ash was down there! In the middle of that carnage. Kep
recognised his voice. She even knew the song. Aechon had
performed it for them in T'al Jazure — 'The Lay of Eregil and
Mendolas'! But Ash's voice wasn't the only one she could hear. People
were singing all around the amphitheatre. She couldn't tell whether
it was one song or several interwoven. But the meaning was the same.

*We fight together and we shall overcome.* Even the pirates were singing in joyful, albeit raucous tones. Kep felt a stirring deep in her soul. Hope!

As the music intensified, the oppressive gloom receded. And something was happening to the nulls! Their movements became broken, disjointed. With the bond between them and their nexus disrupted, they were stopping dead in their tracks. The Melk's hold was diminishing! Conquered by light and sound.

Kep watched, transfixed, as the miracle unfolded. The music took her breath away, so beautiful it hurt. This was a story of hope, transcribed in song and emblazoned across the sky. Among the visions, she saw horses charging and the clash of shields. Heroes fought, their bright swords trailing light. A ship with gold-tipped sails crested the waves, dipping and plunging. Then the seas roiled and broke, transforming. A figure emerged from the spray, cast in gold. A young woman! Trumpets called, lifting clarion voices to the sky. Kep's heart skipped a beat. Jen-Jay gave a startled cry beside her. She might have said something. Kep couldn't tear her eyes from the spectacle.

The centre of the stage was a vortex of fire and scintillating light. And that music! Soaring with the voices of a thousand singers, it climbed higher and higher until Kep thought her heart might burst. She gaped in terrified awe at the warrior in the sky — at the woman who wore her face. The hero swung her sword, two-handed. Her weapon flamed in an arc of dazzling light. The air sizzled with a bright energy. Then exploded.

The final fanfare was triumphant. Like a glacier shattering. Cascading like bells. Everything shimmered. The sky rained golden sparkles as Kara-fell met her end. A monster vanquished by song. The nulls dropped, like abandoned toys. People cheered from all around the arena, coming to their senses. Kep couldn't react. Emotion overwhelmed her. Jaibari stammered, incoherent. 'What? What just ... ?'

'The nexus has fallen.' Jen-Jay's voice was flat with shock. She gave Kep a *very* peculiar look.

Now the singing became a chant. *Kep-Váli! Kep-Váli!* It wasn't just the pirates. The words echoed around the amphitheatre. A piping voice floated down to them from above. 'Kep-Váli!' *Spike!*

Looking up, Kep spotted the lad through the branches. He was capering about on the highest platform, hooting and hollering to catch her attention. He'd fall to his death if he wasn't more careful! Ratskin was beside him, one arm hooked around a branch. Of course! Never one without the other! Ratskin made her a goofy salute, beaming all over his face. Kep laughed. They were safe. The boys were safe.

But now a new cry went up. 'Plunder! Plunder!' Kep recognised the voice of Creely. The pirate skipped towards the arena, brandishing his sword as he went, his blue frock coat flaring out behind. Time for the Simbab to intervene. Kep found Ruby Ross where she'd left him, at the bottom of the ladder. Covered in blood, he was tightening a bandage around his arm with his teeth. He straightened up and grinned, eyebrows raised. 'Nice trick, Simbab.'

Kep knew he meant the warrior in the sky. But setting him straight would have to wait. 'I want you to oversee the plunder, Ruby. And spread the word. There's to be no bloodshed. Not if it can be avoided.'

His grin grew wider. 'Aye, Simbab!' *Pirates.* Kep was fully aware he would handle her second request rather less diligently. But she had other concerns.

Some of Kara-fell's followers fought on, choosing death over surrender. Rodine was trading blows with a swarthy opponent even now. He shouted out to Kep as he sparred. 'Kep! Not yet. It's not safe!' Kep strode by, pretending she hadn't heard. That was the whole point! She needed to get to Ash.

She hadn't gone far when a hand grabbed her shoulder, swinging her about. *Jaibari.* Dark eyes met her own. 'I have your back.'

Kep nodded. 'Thanks.' It was foolish to refuse, and Jaibari would follow her anyway.

The scene at the arena was grizzly. Kep had never seen so much blood. It soaked the steps, giving the air a sweet metallic smell. She walked past a row of filthy cages. All empty. The fighting had subsided, apart from the odd scuffle. People sat around dazed, as if they'd awoken from some nightmare. Some embraced, laughing and clapping each other on the back. Most lacked the energy. Many wept, hands covering their faces.

Corpses littered the stage. Among them was the body of Kara-fell. Kep didn't care. Only one thing mattered: finding Ash. As she stepped around the bodies, somebody spoke her name. 'Kep.' A weak call, but urgent. Panic sent a hot flush through her body as she cast about. Where was he? Was he hurt? The voice croaked again. But it wasn't Ash. It was the young warrior, the one with the axe. And Kep knew him! The ground seemed to fall away beneath her — it was Braig!

Kep let out a cry. Running forward, she grabbed the belt of the brute who was pinning the young warrior down and, with Jaibari's help, tumbled the body out of the way. Kep fell to her knees. He had a short beard and the strangest tattoos on his shaven head, but it was him. It was Braig! He clasped one of her hands, and his skin's warmth confirmed it: he was *alive*. 'Braig!'

'You know me.' Tears welled in his chestnut brown eyes.

'Of *course* I know you.' Braig groaned. He tried to sit up, but she put a hand on his chest. 'Lie still, you're hurt.'

Kep's mind was reeling. First those images, and now this! People didn't come back from the After. But here Braig was. Solid. His chest rose and fell beneath her hand. *Alive!* Soaked in blood, and he had a nasty bash over one eye, but it was him. He even smelt familiar: warm and honest, like tilled soil. She stared at the symbols painted on his scalp. 'What ... ? Why ... ?' she stammered, unable to decide which question to ask first.

'I had to come. They said you were in danger. But ... I didn't believe it. Not really, not till we found out your plan. When Sarin spoke to the boy at the inn.'

Kep's stomach did a flip. *Sarin.* Her head was spinning. 'The boy ... ?'

'Yeah. He told us your plan. To fight Kara-fell.'

'My plan?' She shook her head. 'That's insane.' None of this was real.

Braig winced, as if it hurt him to smile. 'I know. I thought that, too. Then I saw you fight. And I couldn't believe my eyes.'

*What was happening here?* Kep repeated the words. 'You saw me fight?'

Braig's grin grew wider. 'Yeah. I didn't know you could, not like that. But you did it, Kep. You killed Kara-fell.'

## 43

# CLAM CHOWDER AND CUSHIONS

Ash's eyelids fluttered. He had a pressing obligation. Something urgent. Oh, yes: today was the Feast of Savina. The performance was at noon, and he needed to learn his lines. He dragged his eyes open, then frowned. Why was there a hole in the roof? His fingers brushed the tasselled fringe of a pillow — bright yellow — it only added to his sense of confusion. His nostrils flared, detecting a delicious aroma. *Hungry*, agreed his stomach. *Starving.* He blinked at the unfamiliar walls — moss-stained with deep cracks, completely at odds with his soft feather mattress. Someone had draped a cloth over the window, magenta pink, shot with gold. It gave the room a faint rosy glow. Freeing his arms from a tangle of silken covers, he pushed himself upright.

Sarin sat on a wooden crate near the window. In his hands was a bowl, and he was staring into it, a troubled look on is face. At Ash's movement he looked up, startled from his contemplation. 'About time!' Relief washed over his face. 'I was starting to think I'd lost you.' He smiled as he got to his feet. 'You've been out for two days.'

*Two days.* Memory came back in a rush. Kara-fell's last stand. The plunge of her blade. That terrible wailing scream. Ash flinched, assaulted by a tumult of emotion. '*Nirias.* I saw him fall. Is he ... ?'

'He's alive but wounded. Kara-fell's blade was poisoned. By the time I reached him he'd regained his own form, but we haven't been able to rouse him.' Sarin frowned. '*You* look terrible. Eat this — there's plenty more.' He pushed the bowl into Ash's hands. 'It's clam chowder.'

Ash picked up the ornate spoon, blinking at the fabric of his sleeve — emerald silk with silver edging. He was wearing some sort of gown, reminiscent of his dream. 'What am I wearing?' He frowned. 'And where are we?'

Sarin folded his arms. 'I'm not telling you anything until you've eaten.'

Ash took a mouthful. The chowder was creamy and packed with juicy shellfish. He could feel it sustaining him, bringing him back to life.

'Good,' said Sarin approvingly. Claiming a cushion from the enormous mound, he sat on the floor beside his friend. 'We're in one of the old clamming huts. You were unconscious, so we brought you here, out of the way.' Sarin grinned. 'You can blame Kep for the cushions. The *real* Kep.'

'She's here.' It was a statement not a question; Ash knew it already. The Song had shown him.

'Oh, yes.' Sarin rubbed at the back of his neck. 'And she's *furious*. Mostly with me. For dragging you and Ordelle into danger, and for making Braig look even more of an idiot by shaving his head. They're both alive, by the way.'

'Braig's alive?' It seemed hard to believe, after the way he'd hurled himself into the fighting.

'Yes, the moron's alive.' Sarin rolled his eyes. 'He certainly has no right to be. I'm sure he'll tell you *that* story himself.' He pointed a finger. 'Keep eating.'

Ash shovelled soup into his mouth and tried to speak around it. 'She's all right?'

Sarin raised a brow. 'Kep? Depends on what you mean. She's got her own band of pirates now. And treasure. *Lots* of treasure. She brings an armful every time she comes to check on you.' His mouth quirked as he looked around. 'I think it's her revenge: death by a thousand cushions.'

Ash couldn't tell whether Sarin was joking. While his words were light, his manner was serious. 'Pirates?'

'Yes, pirates. She's been in the Kenting. Recruiting them by the shipload.'

Ash swallowed another mouthful, trying to take it in. 'So it wasn't Kep in Rilka's vision after all — it was Nirias.'

Sarin let out a sigh. 'Makes sense after the fact, doesn't it? Rilka told us Kep wasn't herself. How were we to know that was *literally* true?'

'Does Kep know? What Nirias did?'

'Not yet.' He rubbed at his brow. 'She has no idea what really happened. She thinks people are confused, because of the singing and the images in the sky.'

Ash put down his spoon, his appetite gone.

'Nirias couldn't have planned it better himself. They're worshipping her, Ash. Everyone believes she did it. That she brought down Kara-fell, with the help of her gods. Why wouldn't they? It was there for all to see.' Sarin swept out a hand. 'Kep-Váli, hero of the ages, painted glorious across the sky.'

Ash felt a flutter of guilt. 'I didn't mean ...'

'No!' Sarin's eyes flashed. He pointed a finger. 'Don't you *dare* apologise.' He blinked, softening his tone. 'It's not your fault, kin. None of this is your fault. I have no idea what you did, or how you did it, but if you hadn't, *everyone* would have died. Kep knows that. She's angry at the moment, but she doesn't blame you. It's not your fault.'

Ash wasn't so sure. Sarin was acting strangely. His friend was hard to read at the best of times, but there was definitely something he wasn't saying. A missing piece in the narrative. Something that would make sense of the shadow behind his eyes. 'Were there many losses?' he asked.

'Some of Kara-fell's captives, but fewer than you might think. A dozen or so from the pirate ships, I think. And three of the League. That's not counting the Reapers, and Kara-fell's people.'

'The League *is* here then?'

'Yes. They mounted an attack, but nothing went to plan. They totally underestimated Kara-fell, and her strength in numbers. When they couldn't get past the Reapers, Pharni led a team inland, from a cove further north. They scaled the cliffs but were ambushed by nulls long before reaching the camp. Two of the jarlycats were killed. And Heeda.' Ash remembered Heeda from T'al Jazure. She'd been angry at Nirias, over the death of her captain. She'd stayed loyal to the League, regardless. Now she was dead, too.

Sarin reclaimed the bowl. 'You'll want to change out of that gown.' He didn't quite manage to hide a smile. 'There are normal clothes in the basket, under the wash-stand. I'd be quick if I were you — Kep's been checking in every hour.' He was already at the door.

Ash had the distinct impression Sarin was making himself scarce. 'You have to tell her, Sarin.'

Sarin's expression clouded. 'I know.' The door closed behind him with a gentle click.

Ash dressed rapidly, shedding the silken gown. Was that really what pirates wore to bed? The thought that someone had undressed him mortified him: he hoped it wasn't Kep — or Ordelle. He was still tying up his pants when he heard footsteps approaching.

Kep's face peeped around the doorframe, then the door was thrust wide open. 'Ash! You're awake!' Collecting him in a hug, she squeezed the breath from him. She muttered against his neck. 'Thank you, Argess. Thank you!' Her hair, smelling of cinnamon and oranges, was tickling his face.

After a long moment, she released him. Her eyes were bright with tears as she grabbed his hands. Ash felt a wave of relief: she didn't seem angry. 'I thought I'd lost you.' It was strange hearing an echo of Sarin's words on her lips. He stammered, uncertain how to reply.

And Kep seemed to have changed in ways he couldn't begin to understand. It wasn't the leather armour, nor the sword at her side. She just seemed *different*. Her deeply tanned skin made her eyes look impossibly blue. A snake now encircled her arm in a band of blue, glittering when she moved. Ash felt awkward, as if she was a stranger. 'That's new,' he said.

Kep scowled, and he knew he'd made a blunder. But she didn't release his hands. 'I can't believe it, Ash. That you put yourself in so much danger.' She blinked away tears. 'You *idiot*.'

Ash flinched. Of *course* it looked that way. There was too much she didn't know. 'We had to come. We ... We believed you were in trouble.'

'I know! Braig has told me all about it. But honestly, Ash: you, of all people, should have known better. You *know* about Rilka's visions. How crazy they are.'

He felt the lick of her anger. He knew it came from concern, but it still hurt. Finally she freed his hands, and he tucked them under his armpits. 'There's a bit more to it than that. Sarin hasn't told you everything.' It sounded lame, even to him.

'Of *course* there's more to it! It's Sarin! I can't believe he dragged you and Ordelle off like that.' She made it sound as though Sarin had abducted them. 'It wasn't your mission. None of you have taken the Pledge! *You're* not even trained, Ash! And poor Braig! He was nearly killed — again!'

Ash had a sudden urge to laugh. He couldn't help it: despite everything, it was funny. Laughter bubbled up, undermining the gravity of the situation. He swallowed a smile. 'How is he?'

Kep scowled. 'Confused. You know Braig. He's better now, I think. But he still swears it was me — that he saw me fight Kara-fell.' She threw up her hands. 'Like *everyone* else.' Her mouth trembled. 'It wasn't me, Ash. It was Nirias.'

'I know.' He hated to see her so distraught. 'I'm sorry. Sarin told me about the pictures in the air. It was the Song — it just took over.'

A tear ran down her cheek. 'But it's not fair, Ash. Nirias sacrificed himself. He gave everything. Just like he always does. Nobody can see that. And ...' She gulped. 'He's dying, Ash.'

Ash swallowed the lump in his own throat. 'Can you take me to see him?'

She sniffed, wiping away tears with the back of her hand. 'Are you sure you're up to it?'

He wasn't. He felt giddy, and his legs seemed to belong to someone else. 'Yes, I think so,' he lied.

Kep nodded. 'We can go there now.'

'Good. And afterwards, we'll find Sarin.' He ignored her frown. '*Together*. There are things you need to know.'

44

# NIRIAS

The curing houses were near the beach, away from the horrors of the amphitheatre. A sea breeze ruffled the front of Ash's hair as they approached. Sweet melodies came with it, like an invitation to dance. He acknowledged their presence, and they faded, as if obeying a command. He blinked in surprise. *That's new.*

Nirias had his own small tent, set apart from the makeshift structures. His bed dominated the space. Decorative chairs stood on either side of the bed. Ash guessed Kep had supplied them, along with the sumptuous velvet cushions and coverlets.

Two people were conversing at the bedside. One was Sarin. His companion turned and smiled as they entered. Ash stopped in his tracks. A pair of emerald eyes sparkled — this woman knew the effect she had on others. She was Pharni, leader of the jarlycats.

Maliagne Aranti's former mistress had lost none of her mystique, despite the bloodied apron and warrior garb she now wore. 'You must be Ash.' Her voice was low and thrilling. 'Kep has told me all about you. I am honoured to meet you properly at last. Our last encounter was somewhat brief, was it not?' Her eyes laughed, making Ash even more flustered. Then, as now, she'd caught him unawares. He'd been weeping over Braig's body. All he remembered was being called a fool and told to run. And her scent — a musky whiff of perfume. Today, she smelt of soap and healing herbs. It didn't make her any less intimidating. A blush rose from the roots of his hair as Kep shot him a look. *Pull yourself together.*

Pushing past Ash's woeful attempt at a greeting, Kep went straight to Nirias's side. She ignored Sarin, even though he stood directly opposite. 'How is he, Pharni?'

Pharni shook her head. 'There is little change. I've given him another dose of Napthine, in the hope it might slow the poison's course. I do not dare risk more.' Ash wondered how much she knew about her patient. Did she know Nirias was ... different? He tried to catch Sarin's eye, but, like everyone else, he was looking at Nirias.

The Malshorne didn't have any significant injuries — just a simple bandage on his left forearm. But something was profoundly wrong. His skin was greyish-blue, marred by purple welts, like the lashes from a whip. The tattoo that graced his cheekbone looked very black. His eyelids didn't so much as flicker — Nirias seemed to have departed his body already.

Ash couldn't help thinking about Credé's dying moments. Would Nirias undergo the same dreadful transformation? Glancing at the tent flap, he fought a wave of panic. He shouldn't have come. This was beyond his strength.

Nobody spoke to break the tension. They just continued staring at Nirias, as if he might come back to life at any moment and they didn't want to miss it.

At last Pharni sighed. 'I've done everything I can for now. Others need my attention.' She gestured at a silver ewer and washbowl. 'Continue bathing his brow, if you will.' She gave a small smile to Kep. 'It may help to bring him back — I've seen it happen before.' Ash noticed that she limped, then saw blood staining a bandage wrapped around her calf.

'Do you have everything you need?' Kep's voice sounded brittle. 'There's another lamp in my cabin: shall I bring it?'

The older woman smiled. 'No, Kep. Thank you. You've brought

more than enough already.' She put a hand on Kep's shoulder. 'Get some rest. All of you. While you can.' A cruel truth sat beneath her words. They'd defeated the nexus. But others remained, and the leader of the League was dying.

Kep swirled fresh water into the bowl as the tent flap restored itself. She rinsed out the cloth and folded it, making a soft pad. Her hands trembled as she dabbed it on Nirias's cheek, betraying her attempts at bravado. 'She's a remarkable healer, Ash. She saved Braig. If anyone can help Nirias, it's Pharni.'

'He's dying,' said Sarin.

Kep glared at him. 'Go away, Sarin. You don't need to be here.'

Sarin's answer was to draw his chair closer to Nirias's pillow. 'Yes,' he said softly, 'I do.' Kep looked like she wanted to punch him, but she could hardly throw him out. Ash took the seat next to Sarin, to give Kep more room, and because sitting down seemed less awkward than hovering. As ever, the Malshorne was a source of tension between them — even when unconscious.

Kep was gentle as she bathed Nirias's brow, as if she feared hurting him further. She seemed close to tears. Ash glanced at Sarin's profile. This seemed the ideal moment to tell her, with the three of them alone. But Sarin just sat there, one leg crossed over the other. As Kep wrung out the cloth for a third time, Ash cleared his throat, unable to bear the tension. 'Umm. You and Pharni seem to be getting along.'

Kep blinked at him. 'Yes. I suppose that seems strange.'

Ash tried a smile. 'It does a bit. I thought you wanted to kill her.'

'I know.' She shook her head. 'I couldn't have been more wrong. Did Braig tell you the story? About how she saved his life?'

'Some of it.'

'She tried to send a message, you know. With Gooel, the tracker.' Ash wished his hands would stop sweating. He glanced at Sarin. *Tell her.* 'And she sent a swift to Nirias in T'al Jazure, but it didn't get through.'

Ash remembered the bird and its cryptic message. He and Sarin had intercepted it. To his relief, Sarin stirred. 'Perhaps it *did* get through. And Nirias said nothing.'

Kep snapped at him. 'Don't be ridiculous! Why would he keep something like that a secret?'

Ash felt his heartbeat pulsing in his throat as Sarin held her gaze. This was going to be awful, but Kep had to know the truth. 'He kept it a secret because Braig was supposed to stay dead.' Sarin's mouth twitched slightly. He wasn't as calm as he looked. 'Turning up alive would have been inconvenient. Because it ruins the story. The legend of Kep the Valiant.'

Ash groaned to himself. He half-expected Kep to throw something. But the situation prevented it, so she contented herself by giving the cloth a forceful wringing. 'I've never heard anything more stupid.'

Sarin sighed. 'Nirias is many things, but he's not stupid. Think about it, Kep. Braig was supposed to be the victim. A poor dead slave, sacrificed by a cruel master. If he turns up alive, then Kep the Valiant isn't a symbol of hope, fighting for justice. She's just a lovesick girl, who caused a lot of trouble for nothing.' Ash winced at his choice of words. 'And *that's* why Nirias kept his silence.'

Kep gave an angry snort. Her eyes flashed with something very close to hatred. 'Nirias wouldn't do that. Of *course* he'd have told us. You've *never* liked him, Sarin, and the gods know you've never shown him respect. But to come out with this? Now? When he's lying here ...' Her voice cracked. 'When he's ...' She couldn't bring herself to say the words. 'It's low, Sarin. Even for you.' Her gaze went to Nirias's face. Ash knew her well enough to detect a flicker of doubt in her eyes. 'And even if it's true, it hardly matters. Not now.'

Sarin replied in a level voice. 'That's true. It doesn't matter *now*. Because the legend is secure. All thanks to the latest chapter. Kep-Váli, saving the world from the evil Kara-fell.'

Kep's eyes blazed. 'That's enough, Sarin! You *know* it wasn't me. It was Nirias. He sacrificed *everything*.'

'Yes, it was Nirias — but that's not what people saw.' Sarin sighed.

'It was a trick, a very devious trick. Have you forgotten? Nirias is a shape-shifter, Kep. He impersonated you — he *stole* your form.'

'No.' An expression of fear crossed Kep's face. 'Nirias wouldn't do that.' She turned to Ash. 'It's not true. Ash, tell him to stop.'

A flush of guilt swept over Ash. He should have stopped Kep from getting so close to the charismatic leader. Why hadn't he warned her what Nirias was capable of? 'It's true,' he said miserably. 'Nirias pretended to be you. I'm sorry.'

Now Kep's eyes were frightened. 'No. You're making it up. It's the Song. You put that story in the sky and now ... Everyone's confused. It's all mixed up and nobody knows what to believe.'

Sarin groaned. 'I'll show you, then.' He began unwrapping the bandage around Nirias's forearm.

'Leave that!' cried Kep. 'Ash, stop him! Pharni said not—-' She gasped in horror as the bandage fell away.

The wound was bizarre — more like a fissure. Fractured light spilled from Nirias's body, dazzling with the hues of a million tiny gemstones.

Kep took a step back. 'What *is* that?' she whispered.

Sarin swallowed. 'I think it's the poison. It's affecting his transformation.'

'His ... transformation.' Kep held her face between her hands. She couldn't take her eyes from the wound.

'You *have* to face the truth, Kep. Nirias impersonated you. And he planned it all along. He came here to fight Kara-fell, knowing very well that he might die.' Sarin's jaw went tight. 'That was the beauty of his plan: it worked either way. Don't you see? It doesn't matter if Nirias dies, because *you* are alive — T'al Kep lives on. *That's* the miracle. It's why he brought you on the mission. It's why he split the group, putting you with Rodine and Jen-Jay. He wanted you safe in the wings. So you'd be in the right place at the right time.'

'But Nirias didn't bring me here. The *gods* did. My token was drawn from the vessel.' Kep's mouth quivered with emotion. 'That much I *know* is true.'

Ash's heart lay like a stone in his chest. It seemed so cruel.

'Another trick.' Sarin's words were soft. Ash knew what it cost him to speak, and why he'd taken so long. 'Your token *wasn't* drawn. Nirias rigged the draw.'

'I don't believe you.' Kep's tone was dangerous. 'The ceremony is sacred! Nirias wouldn't — he just wouldn't.'

'But he did. Your token was never in the vessel, Kep.' Sarin held out his hand so that it hovered in the air, above Nirias's chest. He opened his palm. Kep startled, as if the token might bite her. 'I've had it the whole time: I swapped it with mine.' Sarin's voice broke, conveying his anguish. 'I'm sorry — I just wanted you to be safe.'

Ash couldn't imagine anyone looking more heartbroken than Kep did at that moment. Sarin hadn't just betrayed her trust; he'd betrayed the gods. His fear was justified — she might never forgive him. Her wounded silence was more terrible than words. Her eyes filled with tears as she dropped the cloth into the basin. Pushing past chairs, she pushed her way out of the tent.

Ash's first impulse was to go after her. But as he reached the end of the bed, he stopped. It would just make things worse, he told himself. Better to give her space. *Coward.*

He sat down again, opposite Sarin this time. Neither spoke as Sarin re-bandaged Nirias's arm. Sarin tucked the corner into place, then smoothed the bedcovers. 'Pass me the cloth.' Ash rinsed it out and passed it over. He felt numb. A question was circling in his mind, nagging at him. 'When did you know? That it was Nirias. That he was pretending to be Kep.'

Sarin didn't meet his eyes. 'I don't know.' He ran a hand from his brow to the back of his head. 'But I had my doubts at Serenity.'

'At Serenity?' *Why hadn't he said something?*

'Yes. But suspecting and *knowing* aren't the same thing.' Sarin shook his head, reading Ash's expression. 'I knew it couldn't have been Kep who killed Mirkon Dredd.' He gave a rueful smile. 'She's not just bound by a Pledge — she really is Kep of the *gods*. In her heart.'

'You think Nirias killed Dredd?'

'I don't know, but if you wanted to create a legend, then killing somebody as notorious as Mirkon Dredd would be just the thing. And who better than a talkative innkeeper's lad to start a rumour that T'al Kep was about to destroy Kara-fell?'

Ash frowned as he thought it over. 'Why didn't you tell me?'

Sarin's expression clouded. 'Because I wasn't *sure*. I didn't set out to get Braig killed — Kep's completely wrong about that. I tried to stop him from coming, remember?' He scowled. 'You of all people know what he's like, Ash. Stubborn as a cave hog. I planned to tell you my suspicions about Nirias on the *Gull*. But Braig was always there, not to mention Petrel and Ordelle. And then it was too late.'

Sarin's anguish seemed genuine. It would have been hard to speak in private aboard the *Gull*. But what if Sarin *had* told him? Would Ash have risked the journey to Nokturn? He doubted it. He looked at Nirias's unconscious form. The Malshorne was a death-like presence between them. It made Ash shiver to think how he'd manipulated them all. And most of all, Kep. After everything they'd been through, was Nirias just another Credé?

Sarin bathed Nirias's hands, washing each finger methodically. Ash frowned as he watched. His friend had always been so critical of Nirias. Why this concern for him now? After everything he'd done. More than ever, Ash had the feeling Sarin wasn't telling him everything. He shook his head. 'I don't get it, Sarin. I understand Nirias's death-wish. But why would you, of all people, want to come to his rescue? You don't even like him.'

Sarin looked up, his eyes sharp. 'You think he had a death-wish?'

'Maybe,' said Ash cautiously. The conversation was getting stranger by the minute. 'He's been fighting the Melk for a thousand years. It must have been lonely.' The image of Credé weeping over Leynore's body came into his mind. 'Perhaps he couldn't take any more sorrow. I think ...' He shrugged helplessly. 'I guess he thought there was nothing to live for.'

'Nothing to live for.' Sarin repeated the words, almost to himself. He was still holding one of Nirias's hands between his own.

Ash frowned. What was he missing here?

Sarin's eyes remained on Nirias as he spoke. 'Do you know what

Nalina said about secrets? She said they're like splinters. If you don't deal with them immediately, they bury themselves deeper. The longer you leave them, the more painful they become and the harder to dig out. You can pretend they're not there all you like, but they stab at you with sharp reminders. And eventually they make their own way to the surface, whether you like it or not.'

Ash smiled. 'That sounds like your grandmother.' Then he blinked. 'Nalina told you something important, didn't she? When you visited the clan.' The expression on Sarin's face told him he was right. 'She told you a secret.'

Sarin nodded. His lips pressed together. 'In the end she had no choice. Against her wishes, it had worked its way to the surface.'

Ash had never seen Sarin like this. Why was he so reluctant to speak?

'If I tell you, you can't tell Kep.'

'*Seriously?*' Another secret from Kep was *exactly* what Ash didn't need.

'Promise me, Ash. I swear I'll tell her myself. Soon.' He winced. 'Assuming she'll listen.'

Ash folded his arms. It seemed very dramatic, and most unlike Sarin. His eyes were *pleading*. 'All right.' He sighed. 'You have my promise.' He smiled, trying to lighten the mood. 'So, what is this *all-important* secret?'

Sarin nodded. 'It's me.' He licked his lips. 'I'm the secret. The baby that shouldn't have been. Nalina isn't my grandmother: she's my mother.'

Ash gaped at him, shocked. 'Nalina's your *mother*?'

'Yes. The pregnancy was unplanned and ... unexpected. She couldn't tell the clan. She thought they'd force her to abandon me. So she hid me — in plain sight. Her daughter was pregnant at the same time, so the pair concocted a plan. They told the Aurum the younger woman was bearing twins, and that travelling wouldn't be safe until after the babes were born. Nalina would winter with her daughter, in seclusion, in case of complications. And it worked. Spring came and two baby boys were welcomed into the Aurum, and nobody was the wiser.'

Ash shook his head, still confused. 'So Nalina is your mother. But why would she hide … ?' He brought his hand to his mouth. '*Nirias.*'

'Exactly,' said Sarin. 'Nirias.' They stared at the figure between them. 'Nirias is my father.' He let out a heavy sigh. 'And I have no idea what that means.'

Ash didn't protest. Strangely enough, he didn't doubt that it was true. Now that he knew, it seemed perfectly obvious.

## 45

# A PIRATE PARTY

Kep flew out of the tent, with no plan other than to escape. Someone shouted her name, and she paid them no heed. She had to get away. Away from Sarin's confession. And away from Nirias. Hurrying past the row of clamming huts, she pushed on into the jungle. On she charged, blind to danger — to anything other than the impulse to flee. At last the jungle grew too dense to penetrate further. She collapsed to the ground, her clothes soaking up water from the spongy mosses. Kep was past caring.

The grief and horror of the past few days now coalesced into an immense wave of emotion. Sobs came in wrenching contractions. A helpless anger tore at her throat. She wanted to wail, to scream at the treetops. It would only frighten the birds.

Kep cried until there were no tears left — just emptiness. After a long while, still sniffling, she pulled herself to her feet. As she did, a branch snapped nearby. She jerked her head around. Someone was standing there! Panic surged in the instant before recognition. Before she realised she knew those braids. And that proud stance. She exhaled. Of course. Jaibari.

The noise had been deliberate. Her presence thus announced, Jaibari had turned her back. Kep took a shuddering breath, bringing her emotions under control. She wiped her face, untangled a leaf from her hair and pushed back her shoulders. Jaibari had seen her crying, but so what? Since when did she care what Jaibari thought?

The young woman turned as Kep walked towards her, her gaze frank. 'It was Sarin, wasn't it? I can kill him if you like.'

Kep croaked a response. 'That would be good.' Jaibari nodded, as if happy to oblige. 'But no, I'll do it myself.'

Jaibari flashed a smile. 'I understand. He's *extremely* annoying.'

Kep couldn't trust herself to speak, so she made do with a nod. *Jaibari, you don't know the half of it.*

The other woman's dark eyes were circumspect. 'Are you returning to the beach?' She grunted approval when Kep nodded a second time. 'Good. It's not safe here. Some of Kara-fell's creatures might still be lurking.' Kep wanted to tell the warrior that she'd had *more* than enough of people trying to keep her safe, but she was too tired. And besides, Jaibari wasn't the true target of her anger.

It was a shock to see how far they'd come. They paused on regaining the path, catching their breaths. 'He's dying,' said Jaibari, blunt as ever. 'Nirias. He's dying, isn't he?'

Kep bit her lip. 'I think so.'

Jaibari scowled. 'Daska should be here. Old man'll be devastated. He loves Nirias. And they parted on an argument.'

'They did?'

She nodded. 'Daska wanted to stick with the jinns, let the captains volunteer. But Nirias said the mission was too important, that it required the blessing of the gods. That's why the vessel was used.'

Kep felt her heart sink. 'So ... that's not normal?'

'Of course not,' scoffed Jaibari. 'How would that work?' For a moment, her disdain returned, then she recovered herself. 'Daska should be here, that's all.'

'Right.' Kep felt sick. Her head pounded from too many tears.

'It is a good death,' said Jaibari with a lift of her chin. 'To defeat an enemy like Kara-fell.'

Kep blinked. 'You don't think it was me?'

The woman snorted in derision. 'Of *course* not. I was standing right next to you!'

Kep wanted to hug her. 'You have no idea how happy I am to hear you say that.'

Jaibari shrugged. *Don't get excited, we're not friends,* said her look. She quickly moved the conversation on. 'Where are you going now?'

Kep frowned. 'You don't need to guard me, Jaibari. I *can* take care of myself.'

Jaibari planted her feet. 'You returned my honour, Kep. And you saved my life. By the custom of my people, I am bound to protect you.' She scowled. 'You must allow me this service.' Jaibari's eyes were ablaze with genuine anger; it wasn't in her nature to beg.

Kep sighed. She wouldn't win. Not today. 'I'm going to find something to eat. Then I'll check on Ordelle. She's busy embalming bodies.' She hoped this might be a deterrent for Jaibari.

Jaibari just grinned. 'She's a surprise, that one.'

Kep nodded. She *certainly* was. 'After that, I'm going to a party.'

'A *pirate* party?' Jaibari flinched. The memories of being held captive were obviously raw.

'Yes. And you're not invited. But don't worry: right now I think I'm safer on the *Lady Lee* than anywhere else in T'al Agria.'

Jaibari nodded, unable to deny it. Because it was true. *For now.*

The ceremony took place at sunset. Not that there was a sunset — for that you'd need a sun. They gathered on the deck of the *Lady Lee*, just the original crew. The men and women who'd defended their ship from Reapers, who'd stormed the beach and fought the nulls. It was strange to see them gathered together like this. They seemed so few.

Curly looked dashing in a dark purple waistcoat over a mustard-yellow shirt. He'd sworn to never wear red again. The crew had scrubbed themselves as earnestly as the decks. Their faces shone, even if there was sadness in their eyes. The spoils of victory adorned their outfits; some carried it off better than others. Several had cropped their hair — a mark of respect for the dead. Ruby Ross had shaved his head even closer than usual. He wore a dark blue frock coat with a touch of lace at his cuffs. Catching Kep's eye, he sank into a curtsey. She shook her head. The man was hopelessly irreverent — even at a funeral.

The bodies were laid out to resemble the spokes of a wheel. Twelve. Twelve bodies, each wrapped in sailcloth. The ropes that secured them were still green, newly braided. Shells and mementos provided reminders of comradeship, of battles fought and voyages shared. Kep recognised one of Harden's hog tusks and knew the body must be Orrick's. Neither Spike's valour nor her own foolish actions had been enough to save him. She gulped, fighting back tears.

Curly gave her a nod. It was time. Kep recited the words: 'We give these souls to the sea, back from whence they came. Take these. They were ours, people who belonged to our ship and served her well. They stood with us as crew. As they came from water, we return them to water.' She paused, and added some words of her own. 'By Telion, by Narsis and by Argess, we release them.'

Kep made the sign of the triangle, and was surprised when so many of the crew emulated her. Then she joined her pirates in dropping to one knee. The soft music of wooden pipes drifted over them. It was Ratskin, playing from the forecastle. That boy really was full of surprises. The tune was haunting and gentle. As he played on, the pirates hoisted bodies onto their shoulders.

When it came time to put their shipmates overboard, Kep hid her dismay as best she could. Curly had prepared her. It was their custom, he said. Sailors didn't need a bird to guide their souls to the After. The currents of the sea were enough. It still felt wrong. Ratskin's piping finished, and it was done.

Kep envied the crew's ability to cast off their sadness. But they were pirates, and more accustomed than most to death. Stories and laughter would celebrate the lives of those who had passed. A rousing cheer greeted the news that Ruby Ross would captain the *Nightingale*. The big man seemed moved, but he covered it well. Further announcements could wait. People were already shuffling their feet, eager for the party to begin. Kep was about to give the command to break out the music and rum when Ruby Ross stepped up beside her. His eyes signalled for her to wait.

The pirates parted, letting Yulia pass through. She wore a white blouse with flouncy sleeves beneath her usual leathers. Jewels dripped from her ears. Rows of pearls adorned her hair. Her shipmates laughed, nudging each other in delight, obviously privy to whatever was going on. Spike gave a piercing whistle through his fingers. He and Ratskin dissolved in fits of laughter at the rude gesture Yulia gave him in response.

Curly stepped forward and bowed very low, as if asking Yulia to dance. Then he took her by both hands. Kep smiled. 'Is this what I think it is, Curly?'

Curly went bright pink, letting Yulia answer for him. 'It is, Kep-Váli. I fear I'm landed with the fool.' Her attempt at resigned indifference was a complete failure — her eyes were too full of joy. The couple beamed at each other, then turned their faces to Kep, expectant — coy almost.

Ruby Ross produced a blue ribbon from somewhere on his person. The crew hooted when he raised it high. He grinned. 'This is a sorry affair, mateys,' he shouted. 'In all my years at sea, I've never known a worse match!' The pirates roared with laughter, slapping their thighs. 'I suspect it's insanity, but they both insist it's love!' More jeers of approval.

Yulia cuffed his shoulder. 'Get on with it,' she growled. 'There's drinking to do!'

Ruby's eyes twinkled as he turned to Kep. 'They're bound to kill each other, Kep-Váli. I'm not sure it's wise, but they ask for your blessing.' The gathering drew in, better to hear their Simbab's judgment.

Kep wanted to laugh. Poor Curly looked as if his heart might break with desire. As if she could deny those puppy-dog eyes! Feeling foolish, she lifted her voice. 'Of course I give my blessing!' The pirates cheered and whistled.

The ceremony was simple. Ruby Ross wrapped the ribbon around the couple's hands. Then he whispered the words beneath his breath so Kep could repeat them. 'As your Simbab, I hereby pronounce Yulia and Curly a couple.' A cheer went up. 'Let them be happy, let them be fertile, but most of all — let them be rich.' Judging by the laughter, the last part was Ruby's own invention. 'From this day on, let two be one and none put asunder, until the sea claims her own.'

The words struck Kep as beautiful, and somehow terribly sad. As the lovers pulled each other close, she felt a twinge of longing. Tears threatened, but she banished them with a smile. She was Simbab. And she was strong. It had just been a tough day, that's all. A riotous cheer and several bawdy jests greeted Curly and Yulia's first kiss as a married pair. Neither paid any attention whatsoever.

A spirit of gaiety and celebration swept over the ship, and Kep couldn't help but smile. This was what it meant to be a crew. They were truly one now, forged through adversity. A crew of survivors brought even closer by joy. Of course it helped that the ship was nearly sinking under the weight of so much gold.

Things got rowdy quickly. As was a Simbab's duty, Kep celebrated with her pirates. She listened to the stories, sipping on rum. The *Nightingale*'s best stuff, according to Creely, who made it his business to know such things. Dark and treacly, it was served to her in a silver chalice. *Plunder*. The goblet was heavy and ostentatious, encrusted with jewels. Any other Simbab would have loved it, no doubt. Kep thought it absurd. The rum was thick on her tongue, reminding her of burnt sugar.

The music got faster, the laughter louder, and the games more boisterous. Kep felt herself withdrawing, as it became harder to paste a cheerful expression on her face. Yes, they were crew, but they weren't *her* crew. Not really. The tales grew more exaggerated as the night progressed, the adulation of Kep-Váli even more ridiculous. She wasn't their saviour. She didn't even belong here. Events on the shore tugged at Kep's thoughts. *Nirias is dying.* Her head throbbed from too much rum, and noise, and heartache.

By the time Ratskin and Spike wandered over, arm-in-arm, she'd had more than enough. 'You did it, Kep-Váli! We knew you would! You killed Kara-fell!' Spike giggled into her face. She caught the sharp tang of fireshot. A half-empty bottle was tucked under his arm. He wore a bucket on his head, like a helmet. The joke hadn't grown old yet.

'You *know* it wasn't me, Spike,' said Kep wearily. 'I was on the platform, right below you. You *saw* me.'

Spike chortled, as if that was his favourite part. 'We know!' Ratskin's fingers flashed, and he grinned at her. Spike swayed on his feet. 'It was T'al Kep a' course! But you and she ... She and her. Same!'

Kep groaned. Spike *believed* it. Even though it contradicted everything he'd seen with his own eyes, he believed it. No argument from Kep would convince him otherwise. Now he launched into a long-winded story about Rawlins and a sausage. Halfway through, Ratskin plucked at his arm and he blinked. 'Oh, yeah. Rats an' me gunna play cards now.'

Kep shook her head as they staggered off. But what could she do? Forbid it? With any luck, they'd pass out before losing too much of their newfound wealth. She sighed. *Pirates!* She drained her goblet and tucked it beneath her stool, before anyone could top it up again.

Rawlins looked the least drunk, although perhaps he was just better at hiding it. At her request he rowed Kep ashore without a word. As she disembarked, the breakers threatened to knock her over. She was concentrating on not dropping the lantern when Rawlins' rough voice startled her. 'You dragged me away.' Kep wondered at his meaning. 'From the fire.' He ducked his head, then dragged at the oars, leaving her no time to respond. His way of saying thank you. From Rawlins, it meant a lot. As she walked up the beach, Kep smiled with a fondness she would never have thought possible.

The watch-fires along the beach had burnt low. There wasn't much call for vigilance — not with a brace of pirate ships moored offshore. Kep made her way towards the red glow of the nearest fire. There she found Jen-Jay, sitting on a log and warming her hands. Setting down her lantern, Kep plonked down beside her. 'Were you waiting for me?'

'Yes. I wanted to know what's driving that dark mood of yours.'

Kep sighed. 'Nirias lied to me.'

Jen-jay snorted. 'Nirias lies to everyone. Why would you be an exception?'

'It's not just that.' Kep bit her lip, trying not to sound like a sulky child. 'Everyone thinks I killed Kara-fell. Even Spike. And he *knows* it can't be true. My whole life has been turned into a lie.' She glared at the embers. 'It's all Nirias's fault. And I can't even hate him, because he's dying.'

'Of course you can't hate him.' Jen-Jay sniffed. 'It's not your way.' Jen-Jay didn't understand. How could she? She only had half the story. The little woman clicked her tongue, disapproving. 'People will believe what they want to, Kep. And myths are far more exciting than truths.' She shook her head. 'It's too late in the evening for philosophy. Is everything set for tomorrow?'

'Yes. The *Nightingale* will leave on the tide. She'll take us to the Elgrave.'

'And Curly?'

'He'll deliver the harp to Bahjak, as promised.'

'Good. It's the *Lady Lee* they'll be looking for. Those who hunt you.'

'Yes,' said Kep.

'So,' the little woman rubbed her hands, 'we'll finally be finished with the pirates.'

'Yes.' But Kep wasn't so sure. She carried Bahjak's mark — would he let her go so easily?

'Good. It's time for the League to disappear. Ordelle is finished with her work.' The clean-up had been swift. Kara-fell's followers were already aboard one of her vessels, bound for Earl, with the surviving Reapers. The Zari could deal with them: either demanding penance or nursing them back from madness, as they saw fit. The second ship would serve as a funeral pyre for those who had given their lives to cruelty.

Jen-Jay eased herself to her feet. Kep could tell she was in pain. 'I'm glad you're back, Kep.' She didn't just mean the party. *You're a League warrior*, said her look. *Remember that.* 'Now get some sleep.'

Kep nodded and bade her goodnight. She regretted drinking the rum; her mouth felt parched now. Across the bay, a light bobbed. The *Gull*, a sensible distance from the carousing pirates, rested on its new mooring. The cabin's cosy glow reflected off the water. Ordelle's new friendship didn't bother Kep. Petrel was nice, and she seemed to adore Ordelle. It shouldn't have made Kep feel lonely and abandoned, but it did, which only made it worse. The League's campfire was just over the rise. Her bedroll awaited. But it was too early to be able to creep back unnoticed. She'd wait until everyone was asleep. Or perhaps she'd just sleep here, on the beach. She added more driftwood to the fire and settled down in the sand, her back to the log.

The fire crackled and danced, luring Kep into a trance. She blinked when a shadow appeared beside her and Tarlyn popped into existence — like some sort of dark herald. Kep sighed. Sure enough, Ash arrived moments later, his footsteps silent on the sand. He lowered himself to sit — cautiously, as if expecting Kep to object. She didn't even turn her head.

'I'm sorry.' His feet shuffled at the sand. 'I didn't know Sarin had swapped your token. Not at the time. He only told me when he came back from his visit to the Aurum, with Rilka. And then ... We really *did* think you were in danger, Kep. All of us.'

Kep sniffed. 'I know. I don't blame you, Ash. Not really.' She felt him relax a little. Until the breeze changed direction, blowing smoke at him.

He shielded his face with an elbow. 'Ow — that stings.' She wanted to tell him he deserved it, but it wasn't true. 'Were you going to sleep out here?' He rubbed at his eyes. 'It's just ... I've got an entire hut to myself.'

He paused. 'Sarin isn't there. He's with Nirias.' Ash knuckled his fringe in that awkward way he had. 'We don't need to talk about him. Or Nirias. Not unless you want to.' Kep couldn't help smiling. He could move the mists with a song and conjure weird images in the air, but he was still Ash. He gave her a small grin. 'There's plenty of cushions.'

The decrepit hut was a sanctuary. Pure and utter sanctuary. They sat on pirate cushions, eating cold clam chowder by the light of an Azuran lamp. Their stories took them far into the watches of the night. Sometimes conversation is more important than sleep.

Kep listened in rapt silence as Ash told her about their travels down the lost river. About his struggle with the Song, and the Watcher, and Ordelle's bravery. Kep filled him in on Ordelle's part in the battle with the Reapers, and they shook their heads in wonder. He told her things that were hard to fathom — about Credé's revenge and Leynore's tragic death.

She sensed gaps in his story — important gaps, if Ash's worried silences were anything to go by. It didn't matter. She didn't tell him everything either. She glossed over Grady's death and the gruesome battle with the Reapers. Nor could she bring herself to speak of her part in Skarlon's death; it was still too raw. Instead, she told him about her pirates: their ridiculous farting competitions, Harden's hog, Curly's dancing, and his obsession with runestones. Their laughter filled the hut. 'How many pirates do you have?' he asked.

'*Way* too many. But they're not mine. Not anymore.'

Kep told him things she wouldn't trust with anyone else. Like how Bahjak made her skin crawl, and the awful responsibility of being Simbab. She confessed how weird it had been to see Braig again, and together they mused on how much he had changed. They barely spoke about Sarin. Ash seemed as happy to avoid the topic as she was. And neither mentioned Nirias. Not once.

They were settling down for sleep when Ash spoke into the darkness. 'Kep, I think I've done something terrible.' She turned her head toward his voice. 'I don't think T'al Jazure was supposed to be unlocked. Credé swore an oath that he'd never go back. He made

Leynore a promise. And ... he kept it. Because he loved her. And ...
I'm worried.'

Kep closed her eyes. 'Let's worry about it later, Ash. We'll work it
out. Together. I promise. Because we're going to stay together now. No
matter what happens, we'll stick together.' She pulled the covers up
to her face. She was going to miss pirate silk. 'And one more thing.'
Her voice was muffled and very sleepy. 'Don't *ever* let anyone tell you
you're not a hero. You're the bravest person I know.'

# 46

# DAWN PARTING

Tarlyn woke Ash early the next morning — *very* early. Worried he'd disturb Kep, he pulled on a jerkin. Then he crept out, boots in hand, leaving his friend to sleep.

It was too early for anyone to be stirring, but he wasn't alone. The place held too many memories for that. The Song created a weird overlay of emotion and ghostly images. Most were just shadowy impressions, or half-formed scraps of melody. If Ash paid closer attention though, the music would sharpen, pulling him in. He tried not to, focusing instead on the birdsong and the tread of his own footfalls. He wondered for a while where Tarlyn was leading him. Then it became obvious: the arena.

The place was empty now. Ghost-grey under the morning light. Tarlyn led him directly to the saucer-shaped platform at the front of the stage. White feathers had once formed its roof, a sunshade for performers. To perform from the rotunda was the pinnacle of any career, reserved for only the greatest artists. Poets had written odes to the place.

Birds and flowers still adorned the carved balustrade. As Ash traced a petal with his fingers, a melody sprang into his mind. He smiled at the lyrics. It was a comedy — about an alchemist who fell in love with a swan. When Tarlyn jumped down the images dissolved, but the melody lingered, like a scent in the air.

Tarlyn was certainly in a frisky mood. She bounded across the stage, and, reaching the archway, began weaving around its foundations. Was she hunting for insects? Her antics usually cheered Ash up, but not this morning. His stomach was in a turmoil. He had too many things to worry about — not least the fear that he'd unlocked a city that should have stayed hidden. And still his list of fears grew longer: Kep was even more of a target now; Nirias would die without knowing his son; and they'd only defeated one nexus. During all this time, the Melk's power had increased. In Mildaresh.

But it was a much smaller concern that was troubling Ash that morning. One that nevertheless made his throat go dry. Ordelle wanted him to sing for the dead before they left the island. Who better than the Keeper of the Song? But Ash didn't have a clue where to start. Perhaps one day he would be skilled enough. But not now. Not today. Today his head was full of jumbled fragments.

A cold speck touched his face. He reached out a palm and groaned. *Wonderful.* It was raining. He should return to the hut; Tarlyn hated the rain. As the shower grew heavier, he decided to ask Kep to go with him to see Ordelle. And he'd confess that he wasn't up to the task; Rodine was a far better candidate. She'd understand that, surely?

Tarlyn was still playing at the foot of the archway when Ash started down the steps towards her. The rain had transformed the stage into a silver slate. The darkstone slumbered beneath his feet. When he reached the spot where Nirias had fallen, he paused. *Nirias.* Ordelle expected him to sing for Nirias. How could anyone do justice to *that* story? He closed his eyes. Kara-fell's story had reached its tragic conclusion here, too. Her song needed to be sung as well — perhaps hers most of all. A small voice whispered inside him: *Who will sing? If not the Keeper of the Song?*

*Remember.*

Memory brushed him; a butterfly kiss on his brow. A hum filled the air. Gazing at the archway, he glimpsed two realities. There was a figure who glowed with light, reaching out their arms as they sang. And there was Tarlyn, the darkest silhouette. Framed by the same impossible archway.

Ash stumbled forward. He let out a cry. How had he not seen it? When Tarlyn raised the ruff on her neck, he already knew what she would say. Tears sprang into his eyes as she repeated the words: *The Taelstaun must go to T'al Jazure.*

Kep didn't know what to think when Ash burst into the hut. Her nerves jangled from such a rude awakening. 'Nirias!' he shouted. 'We can save him!' His behaviour was wildly out of character, but he promised to explain everything when they got to Nirias's tent. Still half-asleep and yet again cursing the invention of rum, she chased after him, lacing the front of her shirt as she went.

They found Sarin asleep in his chair. *Actually* asleep. He'd been there all night, keeping vigil over Nirias. Snapping awake, he caught on in a blink. They transferred Nirias to a stretcher as carefully as possible. As quiet as thieves, they smuggled the leader of the League out of the tent, down the grassy slope, and into the empty arena. Kep's thoughts whirled, matching the churning of her stomach. *Could this really be happening? Could Nirias be saved?*

They laid Nirias down and stood together, staring up at the archway, glistening in the rain. Kep's head throbbed. Her tongue felt thick in her mouth as she squinted at the stonework. 'It's the same? Are you sure?'

'I'm positive,' said Ash. 'I don't know why I didn't see it before.'

Sarin raised an eyebrow. Kep knew what he was thinking — the bloodshed and mayhem probably had *something* to do with it. He smiled, and a sudden warmth swept over her. She looked away. *Stop that.*

Ash's voice had a decidedly eerie quality. Was it just the ancient amphitheatre, or something else? 'Its design is identical. Except for the colour. The one in T'al Jazure is sort of orange.'

'Orange?' Kep would have remembered that, surely? True, there were a lot of archways in T'al Jazure, each one different. But the whole thing seemed far-fetched.

Ash tilted his head. 'I should have recognised those feathers, at the top.'

Kep's frown deepened. *Feathers.* Ash seemed weirdly calm, and in that moment she realised just how much he'd changed. He seemed older now. His eyes were the same gentle grey, a perfect match for the rain clouds, but his pupils made her think of candle flames. She glanced at Sarin, wondering whether he'd noticed the change, too. But his attention had shifted to Nirias.

Crouching by the stretcher, he put two fingers to the Malshorne's neck and shook his head. 'His pulse is faint. I think he's fading.' The concern in his eyes took her by surprise. Sarin was *worried.* About *Nirias.* He got to his feet. 'Are you sure, Ash? That it leads to T'al Jazure?'

Ash smiled at him. 'Suspecting is not the same thing as *knowing*, kin.' Kep frowned as something passed between them. Some meaning she wasn't privy to. 'But, yes: I can feel the Heartstone.'

Sarin's neck looked soft when he swallowed. Vulnerable. A scratch grazed his cheekbone. Kep scowled. She shouldn't be looking at him; not like that.

Sarin nodded at Ash. 'It's worth a try. We can manage Nirias between us.'

Kep felt her heart wrench. Speaking was an effort. 'You're *both* going?' She hadn't forgiven Sarin, not for one moment. But that didn't stop the voice inside her head from pleading. *Don't leave. Not again.*

Sarin turned to her. 'Come with us, Kep.' His amber eyes were full of mystery. Impossible to read.

'No! I can't leave.' She said it firmly, as if to convince herself. Then her mouth quivered. 'I can't. I'm Simbab.' She blinked. 'I'm a League warrior.' That part should have come first — what was wrong with her? 'I've sworn oaths, to the gods, and to my captain. And besides ...' She felt a rush of panic. 'Someone has to explain. To Rodine, and to Ordelle. If ... um ...,' she grimaced at the archway, 'if it works.'

Ash licked his lips. 'I'll come back if I can. But I don't know ...'

Kep tried to smile. 'You'll work it out, Ash. You're the Keeper of the Song.'

He frowned, for a moment looking very much the timid boy she remembered. 'Tell Ordelle I'm sorry I couldn't sing. I'll bring the Cryer back ... if I can.'

'Of course. I'll tell her.'

'And Braig: tell him we'll see him soon.'

Kep blinked. In all the confusion, she'd forgotten Braig was alive. 'Of course I'll tell him.'

Ash gave her a hug. His voice was quiet beside her ear. 'Be careful.' He released her and Tarlyn claimed his shoulder. They moved away, towards the arch.

Sarin was uncharacteristically awkward. Kep sensed an apology coming, and she couldn't bear it. 'Stay. I want you to stay,' she blurted.

Sarin froze. Then he reached for her hand, drawing her closer. She breathed in his warmth. 'I want to. I really do.' *He is leaving.* She could hear it in his voice. 'I want to be with you, Kep.' He swallowed. 'Even when you hate me. But ... I have to go. I'm bound ... to Nirias.'

'To Nirias?' She stared at him, baffled. 'Why?'

'Our fates are interwoven, just like Nalina said.' He frowned. 'There are antidotes in T'al Jazure. I need to save him if I can. It's complicated. I'm sorry, Kep, I can't tell you why. Not now. But one day I will. I promise.'

Kep shook her head. He had to be the most *frustrating* person in the world. He was choosing Nirias over her after *everything* that had happened. It hurt. It really hurt. She couldn't think of anything to say, she was too bewildered. Then he kissed her.

For the sweetest moment, it was just the two of them. No stupid lies. No Nirias. And no archway. Just the sensation of his mouth on hers. It was a kiss full of longing and possibility. She knew Sarin felt it, too. She saw it in his eyes. And it changed nothing. He was leaving.

Part of Kep hoped the archway wouldn't work, that it was just a fancy lump of stonework. But something in Ash's behaviour warned her otherwise: his mind seemed elsewhere, interacting with a force she couldn't see.

The young men lifted Nirias between them, with Sarin bearing most of the weight. Kep held her breath. She expected music, or for the archway to fill with fiery patterns. There was nothing like that. Just a singing sensation in her heart. For a startling moment, she glimpsed a courtyard. And flowering trees. She gasped, her eyes dazzled by sunlight. Then the scene vanished, taking her friends with it. And Kep was alone. Again.

*In a distant world, an object changed pitch — registering the opening of a door, then resumed its low whirring. Secret. Hidden. But not forgotten.*

# ACKNOWLEDGMENTS

I'm heaving a sigh of relief as I write this, because *Darkstone* did not come easily. Life just kept getting in the way. Along with a return to teaching to pay the bills, major surgery in a different country turned out to be far more complicated than planned – if you're donating a kidney to your sister, try not to get COVID on the plane! Then, along came a beautiful new grandson and a temporary relocation to Melbourne.

But the main problem was the story itself - it just refused to play nicely. Fiercely determined that *Stones of the Azuri* should remain a trilogy, I battled on for months, trying to squish an increasingly epic tale into a single book. But Ash, Kep and Karliana had ended up in very different places at the end of book two, both geographically and psychologically – I wanted to do the story justice without taxing the reader with too many jumps in point of view. At last I succumbed and accepted the inevitable. The story needed a fourth book. The decision made, I gritted my teeth, restructured, and forged ahead to get the whole story on paper. Only when the last words of the series had been written did I return to *Darkstone* to wrestle with pirates in the mist. Honestly. Pirates and sailing ships. What was I thinking?

There are so many people to thank – but especially my family. I'm so grateful to my daughter Katie and her partner Dan for being such fantastic sounding boards on everything from character motivation to thematic concerns and plot devices. How they make sense of my half-imagined ramblings is beyond me. A fantasy writer couldn't ask for more informed alpha readers. Thanks also goes to my sister, Annette, for her thoughtful feedback on an early draft, and her unfailingly enthusiastic encouragement.

My youngest daughter Lara continues to be my greatest inspiration for this story. They're not just my consultant on all things musical, they have a deep understanding of what it means to be an indie creator. Only Lara could come up with such a complex and moving realisation of the Song when asked to 'write a snippet of audio.' To Lara's partner, Lachy, thank you for all the weird conversations about drumming and art and life. Our discussions somehow manage to be silly and profound in equal measure.

My talented daughter Nikki and her partner Nopera have performed magic once again with the stunning cover art. It is an absolute joy to see my story world captured through Nikki's vibrant designs. Nikki and Nopera have been so generous with their time in helping me build my brand – I'm incredibly lucky to have the benefit of their talents and technical expertise.

Thank you, again, to Kate Stone, my masterful editor. Kate has the uncanny ability to hunt down the phrases I've already rewritten a hundred times and fix them with a gentle tweak. I learn so much from her edits and witty responses – not to mention all things 'dinkus.' My gratitude also goes to my team of beta readers for their helpful feedback, especially Nicole Thurlow and Jenni Komarovsky. To my fellow writers in the Top of the South, thanks for being there and for 'rocking up to write.' A special thanks goes to my best friend Jessica Le Bas, for her moral support and crazy, engaging conversations about everything and nothing. I can't express the importance of our creative connection, Jessica. What would I do without you?

*Darkstone* is dedicated to another dear friend, Ross Reid, who passed away from MND in 2020. Given the choice of being a pirate or a warrior, Ross chose a pirate and thus Ruby Ross was born. I shouldn't have been surprised when the fictional Ross turned out to be just as cheeky as the real one!

To my husband Keith, thank you for proofreading, and for putting up with being ignored so often. I know it can't be easy living with somebody who spends so much time off in another world. And I mustn't forget Diva the dog, for dragging me away from the computer. Because in the real world there are beaches to be walked on and sticks to be thrown.

Which leaves a final message for my readers. Thank you for reading all the way to the end! For waiting so patiently, and for all your kind words of appreciation. The world of the Azuri is yours – a place to escape into. I get enormous pleasure from your positive responses to the story, because it lets me know that I must be doing something right.

# ABOUT THE AUTHOR

Robyn Prokop is an emerging author of new adult fantasy, writing in Nelson, New Zealand. *Darkstone* is the third book in the *Stones of the Azuri* series.

You can find more information and links to the author's social media accounts at www.robynprokop.com Be sure to sign up to the newsletter for news on upcoming books and behind the scenes insights.

If you enjoyed *Darkstone,* please consider writing a review to help other readers find this indie author. You can post your review on Amazon, Goodreads or the platform of your choice. Thank you so much!